CATASTROPHIC

DUSTIN STEVENS

Catastrophic
Copyright © 2013, Updated 2015, Dustin Stevens

Warning: All rights reserved. The unauthorized reproduction or distribution of this copyrighted work, in whole or part, in any form by any electronic, mechanical, or other means, is illegal and forbidden, without the written permission of the author.

This is a work of fiction. Characters, settings, names, and occurrences are a product of the author's imagination and bear no resemblance to any actual person, living or dead, places or settings, and/or occurrences. Any incidences of resemblance are purely coincidental.

It is good to express a thing twice right at the outset and so to give it a right foot and also a left one. Truth can surely stand on one leg, but with two it will be able to walk and get around. -Friedrich Nietzsche

CHAPTER ONE

The law firm of Webster, Banks & Cohen, like most firms of its ilk around the county, had a well-defined hierarchy. Unlike all the others though, it assigned offices in ascending order of seniority.

The first floor was comprised of the palatial offices of Martin Webster, Jack Banks, and Howard Cohen, though they were rarely, if ever, seen in them.

The second floor was subdivided into six offices, each of them filled with the first hires of the firm forty years before. Two of the men had already retired into schedules similar to the founding members, while the other four still at least pretended to be working most days.

The third floor was split into ten offices, the second-year hires, followed by eight floors with fifteen offices each. All of those offices were filled with people that had been with the firm a minimum of twenty-five years. Every one of them still showed up at least five days a week, many working the same long hours they had when they started.

Somebody had to keep their trophy ex-wives in the lifestyles they'd grown accustomed to.

Above those eleven were fifteen more floors, all belonging to the firm. Levels twelve through twenty-four consisted of attorneys ranging from those on the cusp of making partner to those just a few years removed from law school. Grouped in teams of three to five, each one had their own receptionist and paralegal, a veritable free standing entity unto themselves.

Residing at the very top, the twenty-sixth floor was reserved for the rookies. Every single attorney that had ever working for Webster, Banks & Cohen started there, a fierce testing ground for new hires.

Nicknamed the two-six, the entirety of the space was one large room with a tangle of desks strewn about. On their first day the new hires were assigned to a particular desk, but where they put it and how they chose to interact with the room was left up to them.

Corporate America's truest Rorschach test.

Some angled for the windows, taking advantage of the fact that their firm was the only one in the city that didn't bury them in the basement. Others chose the middle of the room, displaying their bravado for all to see and daring others to challenge them.

On his first day, Shane Lazlo chose the corner.

Not the one closest to the door or the one where two banks of floor-to-ceiling windows intersected, but the far corner.

As others sought out the coveted positions, shoving their heavy old desks into position while wearing expensive designer suits, Shane nudged his into the darkened corner and began unpacking his bag. By the time some of his smaller coworkers had managed to post up just where they wanted, he had already read through the employee handbook and was moving on to the standard stack of first day documentation.

Cradled by dark brown brick to his rear and left, Shane positioned his desk tight against the side wall. It afforded him a good view of the room and even a decent sightline to the windows should he so choose.

Strategically speaking, it was an excellent move.

On the social scale, it was closer to self-imposed exile.

That fact had failed to register with Shane the day he chose the seat. Not once in the months since had it done so either.

Most days Shane was the first person to arrive at the two-six, finding his spot in the corner long before anybody else bothered to come in. He wasn't much of a morning person, but his preference for the quiet solitude of dawn made up for it.

Some nights, like this one, he was the last to leave as well.

Not a single light illuminated the enormous expanse of scattered desks save the small lamp on the corner of his and the laptop screen in front of him.

New Year's Eve, a night when most people in Boston were at the North End enjoying dinner with family or at Faneuil Hall having drinks with friends, Shane sat alone in the semi-darkness. He had no family to speak of and only a few local friends, making it easy to dodge the handful of half-hearted invites tossed his way.

Not that he had much to celebrate these days anyway.

Just six months removed from law school, Shane was twenty-six years old and over a hundred thousand dollars in debt. The firm required seventy billable hours a week from him, which in actuality was more like ninety. The only person he had waiting for him at home each night was a temperamental cat.

The sadistic irony of being a twenty-six year old cat lady was not lost on him.

Ten months before, when the offer to join Banks, Webster & Cohen first came in, Shane jumped at the opportunity. The chance to practice environmental law with a renowned firm caught his interest within seconds. The chance to one day make the type of money they were telling him was possible sealed the deal.

Within weeks the new car smell of the whole thing began to wear off. By Thanksgiving, the closest he'd been to the environment or big money was wandering into the Public Gardens by mistake on his way home one evening.

With a heavy sigh, Shane tossed his pen down on the desk and rocked back in his chair. He unknotted his tie and let it hang down from either side of his neck, placing his fingertips along his temples and kneading in slow, even circles. After several long moments he dropped his hands to his sides, leaned forward and slid open the bottom drawer from his desk. He withdrew an ancient clock radio and plugged it into the wall behind him.

Brought in special for the occasion, Shane adjusted the dial through a sea of static before finding what he was looking for. Clear and even, the familiar graveled voice of Ron Rickshaw floated out from the speakers, filling the desolate two-six.

"Yes sports fans, what we saw here in the first half was a performance for the ages. Ohio Tech running back Tyler Bentley, fresh off a top five finish in this year's Heisman race, making a strong case that he should have been the one hoisting that trophy at the Yale Club three weeks ago."

Jumping in was Rickshaw's on-air sidekick, Ken Lucas. "It's a shame that the folks tuning in this evening are listening on the radio instead of watching a television, Ron. I just don't know that we can do Bentley's performance justice. Coming out of the backfield for the Crimson Knights, Bentley had rushes of 67, 45 and 38 yards, finishing the half with two hundred yards on the ground and three touchdowns. Forget the Heisman, this guy's making a strong case that this could be his last game in a college uniform."

"All week Bentley has been dodging questions about foregoing his senior season and turning pro," Rickshaw said, "stating he will not address those issues until after the Centennial Bowl. I tell you from the way he's carrying the ball right now, I can't imagine there are too many college coaches out there that wouldn't help him pack up his dorm room."

"This performance comes as no surprise to Crimson Knights fans out there though, Ron. This is what he's done pretty much all season for Coach Bob Valentine's club. Over sixteen hundred yards on the ground, another five hundred receiving, a dozen touchdowns. He's even passed for one and returned a kickoff for another. About the only things this kid hasn't done yet are tear tickets and hawk programs."

Rickshaw chuckled at the comment, his husky voice rasping out through the speakers. "Right you are, Ken. Let's take it down to the field for a moment and get the word coming out of the locker room from sideline reporter Sue Barnes. Sue?"

Shane took a long swig from a paper cup of tap water on his desk and rocked back as far as his chair would allow. He put the soles of his loafers on the corner of his desk and smirked.

"Atta boy."

Unlike his co-workers, who reminded him every single day of their Ivy League pedigree, Shane was a card carrying alum of Ohio Tech University. In total he'd spent seven years on campus there, enjoying the price breaks for local students and the life that accompanied a college town during football season.

Tailgates, student sections, road trips. Shane had done everything and regretted nothing.

"Thanks, Ron," Barnes said. "I spoke with Coach Berg of the Virginia State Falcons and he said that his team had to find a way to contain Tyler Bentley. Coming into tonight they had planned to try and take away all other options for the Crimson Knights and force Bentley to beat them. Right now their plan is quite the opposite – stop Bentley and worry about everybody else later.

"On the opposite side, Tech Coach Bob Valentine said they have no need to change up what they're doing. Remaining on the ground they've been able to control the clock and the tempo of the game while building a comfortable lead. If it's not broke...

"Back up to you guys in the booth."

"Thank you, Sue. With that we are all set to begin the second half. Darkness has fallen over Bill Irwin Stadium here in Miami and the temperature has dropped into the high-60's, a perfect night for football as Virginia State kicker Drew Lenton gets ready to kick us off.

"Lenton draws back his standard eight yards and two to the side, has the referee's whistle, and we're under way here in the second half. Ohio Tech returner Maurice Welsh settles under it just shy of the goal-line and has a bit of a crease, returning it to about the thirty-one, make it thirty-two yard line for the Crimson Knights."

"Knowing that Virginia State will be crowding the line and bringing *eight or nine guys into the box to try and contain Bentley,"* Lucas interjected, *"it'll be interesting to see if Tech tries to open it up here. Maybe catch the defense edging forward and pop a big one right off the bat."*

"First play from scrimmage Tech quarterback Nate Simmons takes the snap and drops back," Rickshaw said, "and he finds tight end Brent Hanson over the middle. Hanson breaks one tackle before being drug down by a host of Falcons. That's good for an eleven yard gain and a first down."

"If Virginia State is going to commit that heavy to stopping the run," Lucas said, *"they're going to be susceptible to that all night long. Their only hope is they can get enough pressure on Simmons to keep him off balance, otherwise this could be a very long night for the Falcons."*

Rickshaw continued with the play call, not bothering to comment on Lucas's analysis. "First and ten from the Crimson Knight's thirty-three. Simmons takes the snap and hands off to Bentley up the middle for a gain of seven. State was pressed up hard onto the line, but Bentley was still able to squeeze through to the second level."

Shane finished the water, sat the cup on the desk beside his computer and checked his watch. "One more play and then back to work. I might even make it home for the fourth quarter."

"Right now Tech has State back on its heels. The Falcons have no idea what's coming and no way of stopping it even if they did," Lucas announced.

"Here on second down Simmons takes the snap and pitches it out to Bentley, swinging hard around the right side," Rickshaw said. "Nifty spin-move to avoid the first man, crosses the line of scrimmage and—

"Oh! He just got leveled at the forty!"

An audible groan from the crowd broke like a wave through the radio.

"Oh my Ken, this does not look good," Rickshaw said, the change in his tone unmistakable. "Tyler Bentley went down hard and he is not getting up."

Shane leaned forward and rested his elbows on the desk, turning the volume up a little higher and staring at the radio.

"I'm taking a look here on the replay," Lucas said, *"as State safety Harris Burton comes flying in and..."* He let his voice trail off, offering a slight gasp as he sucked in a breath of air between his front teeth.

"Folks," Rickshaw said, *"I know you can't see this right now and be thankful for that. Burton almost put his helmet through the knee of Tyler Bentley. This does not look good."*

"Oh my, Ron," Lucas said. *"As you can see on the replay, it's a legal hit. Burton works off a block and throws himself at Bentley, whose foot is planted. Boy did he take a shot right there."*

Shane slid back in the chair and rested his chin on his chest. He closed his eyes and returned his fingertips to his temples, massaging them in even circles.

"The angle that his knee is in just after Burton connects is difficult to watch folks," Rickshaw said, a certain measure of sorrow in his voice. *"Now they are calling for the stretchers.*

"We can only hope this looks worse than it is."

CHAPTER TWO

The official population of Meeteetse, Wyoming was listed as three hundred and fifty-two people. As it stood, three hundred and fifty-one of them were packed into the local school gym.

The lone outlier was playing in the Centennial Bowl over two thousand miles away in Miami.

Situated on a stretch of dusty highway in western Wyoming, Meeteetse was the kind of place that most folks from the east coast referred to as "blink and you miss it." Just three blocks square, the town straddled State Route 120, a two-lane road that originated thirty miles north in Cody and ended fifty miles south, dead-ending into a slightly larger two-lane road running east and west.

If someone from out of town found themselves in Meeteetse, they either had family nearby or had been caught in Yellowstone after the snows came and had to go the long way back to Cody.

There was no other reason to be there.

The town featured the standard lineup of one gas station, one motel, and two bars. One was open through the day, serving breakfast and lunch to locals. The other was open at night, serving dinner and beers to ranchers and hunters. A single school sat on the edge of town, housing all seventy-seven children between the ages of six and eighteen.

Tonight, every single person in the town sat crammed tight into the drafty school gymnasium for two distinct reasons. First, it was New Year's Eve and each year the entire town came together for the evening. By all accounts it was the high point of the annual calendar, rivaled only by the 4th of July picnic and the Halloween carnival for largest attendance each year.

Second, and perhaps more important, they were there to see Tyler Bentley.

Tyler was the only child of Margie Bentley, a native daughter of Meeteetse. While in high school she dated the star of the basketball team and the two of them dreamed of running off together, maybe to the big cities of Billings or Laramie, perhaps as far as the bright lights of Denver.

In the end, the captain of the basketball team made it all the way to the east coast. Margie never even made it as far as the county line.

Armed only with a broken heart and a bulging stomach, Margie stayed with her parents until after Tyler was born. She worked long shifts as a waitress by night and learned to operate a crane at the lumber mill during the day. When she turned twenty-three, she dropped the waitressing, bought a small house on the edge of town, and together she and Tyler made a life for themselves.

Tyler had been gone three years now, but the town of Meeteetse still considered him as much their own as the flagpole that stood in the town square. They got together every fall Saturday to watch him play and would still be talking about him the next morning at Sunday school.

Margie made it out to see him play twice a year, this year attending the home opener and the Midwest Conference Championship. The roof on their house was in bad shape and she needed new snow tires on her Jeep, but she'd even managed a third trip out to New York City for the Heisman ceremony.

Most years, the main draw of the New Year's Eve celebration was a square dance caller from Jackson Hole or a country-western band from Cody. This year, the town had elected to go a different direction, for obvious reasons.

The women's chorale at the church stitched together over a dozen gleaming white sheets and hung them against one wall of the gym. A projector from the school's audio-visual department was rolled in and the game was broadcast for all to see, their very own star stretched almost twenty feet tall in front of them.

Big time college football in their little corner of Wyoming.

Clumps of spectators dotted the bleachers on either side of the gym floor, talking in low voices and enjoying the potluck spread lining the back wall. A low hum of voices hung in the air, almost drowned out by the play-by-play call from the ESPN announcers working the game.

Less than twenty feet from the wall, Margie sat in a folding chair on the gym floor. The seats on both sides of her were empty as she stared rapt at the screen, the same nervous wreck she'd been during every game she ever saw.

Margie ignored the food and gossiping going on around her, not even hearing the handful of questions lobbed her away about whether Tyler would turn pro after the game or stay in school. She barely noticed the roar of every person in the gym behind her each time Tyler broke off a big run or the thunderous applause when he scored.

Didn't hear the groans when Virginia State punched one in late in the half.

As far as anyone could tell, she didn't even hear the announcers calling the game. All she could hear was the pounding of her own heart as she clutched the edge of her seat and prayed for the safety of her son.

On the fourth play of the half Margie watched as Tyler took the pitch and swung out towards the high side of the makeshift film screen. It was the same play she'd seen him run a thousand times before and could already envision him planting his foot and making a tight spin back towards the sideline. On cue, Tyler made the move and left a defender hugging air, his body pirouetting in a tight circle.

Less than a second later he took the hit.

Margie knew the moment contact was made that Tyler was hurt. She was on her feet before he hit the ground, racing forward to the sheet and casting a long shadow across the screen. Silent tears streamed down her face as she grabbed at the material and kneaded handfuls of it between her palms. The tears grew heavier as she registered the level of concern in the announcer's voice and thicker still as the network replayed the hit again and again.

By the time an ambulance rolled onto the field she was hyperventilating, both cheeks stained red and glistening in the half-light of the gym.

Rooted in place, she watched as medics loaded Tyler onto a gurney and hoisted him into the back of the ambulance. On the field groups of players knelt in prayer as the cameras panned over the shocked faces of spectators from both sides.

The ambulance crossed the enormous logo painted at midfield and fled from the stadium as Margie stood with a hand pressed over her mouth. Every pair of eyes in the gym was locked on her, a few with tears of their own.

Nobody made any effort to go to her. Even the youngest children sensed the gravity of the moment and stood still, watching things unfold.

The sound of Margie's cell-phone rang out, just audible above the concerned voices of the ESPN crew working the game. By little more than reflex she tugged it from the pocket of her jeans and held it to her face. "Hullo?"

"Ms. Bentley," a deep baritone responded, "this is Jeromy Burbank, team doctor for the Crimson Knights. I assume you saw the play."

It was a statement, not a question.

Moisture again pooled on the underside of Margie's eyes. "Yes."

"Ms. Bentley, I'm very sorry to call like this but Tyler insisted that I do so. He wanted me to tell you that he's alright and not to worry."

Margie pushed out a breath, trying to work down the lump in her throat. "Is that the truth or is that what Tyler asked you to tell me?"

A long pause followed and Margie could hear him sigh. "All I know is we are flying Tyler back to Ohio right now to get it looked at. We're not even waiting for the game to be over. As soon as they can get his leg stabilized, they're getting him on a private plane back."

"They're taking him back to Ohio Tech? Right now?"

"I wish there was something else I could tell you, but right now that's all there is to report. Dr. Leddy is with him; he'll be doing all he can to help your son until they land."

"Thank you," Margie whispered and closed the phone. She shut her eyes as her hand fell away from her face and dropped to her side.

Without opening her eyes, she rotated to face the room. "Can someone please give me a ride to Cody? I have to go to Ohio and I don't know how long I'll be there."

Every person stood stock still for several seconds. Somebody had killed the audio on the video play and the only sound was the wheels on the projector as the game got back under way. It threw a ghostly pallor across Margie as she stood there, though nobody noticed.

After several long moments of silence, a solitary man in blue flannel and denim took a half-step forward. "You go on home and get everything you need, Margie. I'll be by in fifteen minutes to get you."

"Thank you, Burt," Margie mumbled.

With that she strode across the gym and into the night, leaving the entire town staring after her in complete silence.

CHAPTER THREE

Marcellus Sarconi wound the solid black tie around his neck and knotted it inches below his sagging chin. It was a move he had practiced almost every single day dating back over two decades, his fingers going through the motions from pure muscle memory. He pushed the knot tight up to the neck of his starched white dress shirt and flipped the collar down over it, giving himself one last check in the mirror.

As he dressed a list of things he would rather be doing on New Year's Eve ran through his mind, though he was smart enough not to voice it. This was one of the few nights a year he allowed his wife to call all the shots and though it involved a suit and forced conversation with stuffy friends, he knew better than to argue. Most of the time he was given the freedom his job demanded without hearing complaints from her or the kids, so it was a tradeoff he was willing, if not happy, to make.

The thought was still processing when Angelica, his wife of over fifteen years, swept into the bedroom. She was still dressed in a bathrobe, though her hair and makeup both looked to be pristine. This meant her inordinately long ritual was fast coming to a close, the dress always being the last thing to go on.

"Are you almost ready?" Angelica asked, sliding past him and selecting a pair of dangling pearl earrings from the vanity beside him.

"I'm ready whenever you are," Sarconi responded, forcing a smile. "Take your time, I'll be downstairs."

"I'm almost done," Angelica said, turning her head to the side and sliding in the left earring. "Just a few more minutes."

"Sounds good," Sarconi replied, his smile growing a shade larger. He pulled back out of the room and down the stairs before she could see the sullen look cross back into place and dropped himself down into his arm chair in the living room. The house was strikingly quiet without their two children running about and for a moment he sat and enjoyed the silence.

It was short lived.

A sigh of satisfaction was still rolling out when his cell-phone began to vibrate on the end table beside him. He considered letting it go to voicemail before lifting it up and checking the caller ID.

A small tangle of barbed wire formed in his stomach as he pressed the phone tight to his face. He would rather hear from his mother-in-law than receive this call out of the blue.

"Happy New Year," he answered, trying his best to sound chipper.

The caller ignored the greeting. "Are you watching this?"

A small wave of panic crept through Sarconi as he searched his brain for anything he was supposed to be watching at the moment. Nothing came to mind.

"No?"

"Turn on ESPN," the voice said. He didn't sound any angrier than usual and had not made any threats against Sarconi's person or family.

Both good signs.

On command, Sarconi turned on the television in time to see an ambulance streaking across a football field before disappearing from sight. A graphic in the corner said that Ohio Tech was beating Virginia State by a wide margin.

Sarconi wasn't against sports in general; he just preferred the traditional football played in his Italian motherland. The Americanized version was a little too crude for his taste, though he had on more than one occasion admitted it was good for business.

"I just caught the ambulance tearing away from the field. What did I miss?"

The voice scoffed, the sound a mix of exasperation and contempt. "What you just missed was the opportunity we've been looking for."

It took a moment for Sarconi to piece together what he was being told. Once it did, the image of the ambulance popped back into his mind with renewed clarity. "Seriously?"

The caller ignored the question. "Get a hold of Pink as soon as you can. You'll have to act fast."

"Yes sir, thank you sir," Sarconi said. His voice relayed a mix of relief that he hadn't done anything wrong and blind optimism at what the call could represent.

It didn't matter. The caller had already hung up without a word.

A small smile spread across Sarconi's face as he turned off the television and leaned back in his chair. It remained there as Angelica came down and retrieved him. Even stayed in place through the entirety of the evening.

This was the opportunity they'd been looking for.

CHAPTER FOUR

The only sound in the room was the rhythmic beeping of the heart rate monitor attached to Tyler's blood pressure cuff. It rallied on in a steady cadence, the previous tone falling away and allowing a moment of silence before another one followed it in an unending sequence.

Lying on the bed, Tyler's leg was wrapped from ankle to hip and held suspended in the air by a harness. His short dark hair bore thick grooves in it from a night of running his sweaty palms over his scalp. At the moment his face was clear and dry, but his puffy eyes and nostrils showed the tears weren't far gone.

The painkillers first began to ebb away just a couple of hours before, tearing him from sleep with a searing pain that stabbed at his entire body. After that, sleep was out of the question. Instead, he locked his gaze on the wall opposite him and set his jaw.

Internally, every function of his body was pounding at record pace.

Externally, his entire visage was a mask carved from granite.

On his left sat Margie, her face even more red and puffy than her son's. Just shy of forty years old, she looked at least ten years older as she stared at the floor. Her thick brown hair was mashed flat against her head and her clothes were wrinkled from over half a day spent in transit. Every so often she would reach out for her son's hand and squeeze it.

Not once did he pull back from her touch, but he made no effort to return the gesture either.

A pale half-light fell over the room, the result of the blinds drawn low over the windows. The television was off, the phone was disconnected from the wall, and the lights overhead remained dark. There was no way to tell what time of day it was or even if it was day.

They were in a timeless environment.

Neither one cared.

A light rapping sounded out against the door, snapping them both from their trance. In unison they rolled their gaze towards the sound to see two men enter, both wearing white lab coats.

The first man through was tall with receding red hair and a thin moustache. Both recognized him as Dr. Leonard Pinkering, one of the doctors seeing to Tyler since he arrived.

The second man in was shorter and somewhat plump. His black hair was greased to the side with a thin goatee encasing his mouth. He said nothing, but forced a smile that looked out of place on his features.

"Good evening," Dr. Pinkering said. "How are you feeling?"

Tyler pressed his lips together and swallowed. When he spoke, his voice was thick. "Well, I'm feeling. That's for sure."

"Which means you're in a world of pain I suspect," Dr. Pinkering finished.

"Yes, sir," Tyler mumbled, nodding.

Dr. Pinkering glanced between them and gave his best concerned look. "I'm sorry about that, but I'm afraid there's nothing we can do until after the operation. You can't go into surgery with that much narcotic in you."

Margie's mouth dropped open as if to ask a question, but she said nothing.

Dr. Pinkering picked up on the gesture. "Certain types of procedures require certain types of anesthesia. If he's already under a heavy regiment of morphine before he goes in, it could compound the effects."

Margie offered a mortified look, but again remained silent.

Dr. Pinkering held out a hand and offered his best reassuring smile. "I know it's uncomfortable right now, but we're doing it as a precautionary measure. Rarely, if ever, do we get someone in here with the unique physical dimensions of a college football player. Just to be sure everything is in order, we'd prefer to send him in with a clean system."

Silence fell in the room for a moment.

Tyler slid his gaze from his mother to Dr. Pinkering. "Be straight with me, how bad is it?"

Dr. Pinkering opened his mouth to speak, but closed it just as fast. His features fell somber and he stared at Tyler for several long seconds before nodding.

The room remained silent as Dr. Pinkering pulled a large yellow envelope from beneath the clipboard he was holding. In long strides he walked across the room to the x-ray board and flipped it on, casting a fluorescent pallor into the space as he drew out two films from the envelope.

One he kept in his hand, the other he placed on the board for everyone to see.

It was the image of a healthy knee.

Using an ink pen as a pointer, Dr. Pinkering started just below the kneecap. "This image was taken of your right leg earlier. It provides a textbook example of what a healthy joint looks like. The fibula and tibia come together from the lower leg and fit into a socket, across from which is the femur. These three bones together form a hinge and as you can see here, the knee cap covers that hinge.

"Now within the hinge there are several ligaments holding the muscles to the various bones, which are what makes the leg work. Beneath those are tendons, which hold the joint itself together."

He pulled the first film from the wall and replaced it with the second film.

"This is what your left knee looks like." He paused for a moment as Tyler exhaled and a tear slid down Margie's cheek. "As you can see, the knee cap has been shattered. The fibula and the tibia are both fractured and every ligament and tendon you've got has been torn."

For several long moments, it appeared every bit of air had been sucked from the room.

"I'm sorry," Dr. Pinkering added. "I know it's a little jarring to see laid out this way."

Tyler stared at the film for several seconds, forcing himself to look at it with borderline masochistic fervor. When every last bit of it was seared into his memory, he rolled his gaze back to the doctor.

"So what's this mean?"

"It means if you were to even have the mental image of walking right now, your leg would fold up on itself. There's no way it could support even a fraction of your bodyweight."

Margie dropped her head to her chest and sniffed.

Tyler laid his head on the pillows, processing the words. "I'm never going to play again, am I?"

"Right now, there's just no definitive way to answer that. We're going to give you a full knee replacement surgery. Beyond that, it depends on how your body responds."

Margie raised her head up from her chest. "A replacement? Can't you just repair what's there?"

Dr. Pinkering began to respond, but stopped himself short. Instead, he motioned a hand to the man beside him.

"This is Marcellus Sarconi. He represents a company called SynTronic. We have been working together for a long time now to develop something reserved for catastrophic instances such as this."

Sarconi stepped forward from behind him and dipped his head low to each of them in greeting. "Through the generosity of the good folks here at OTU and the hard work of everybody involved, we have been able to create a synthetic knee that we believe will decrease the recovery time by as much as seventy percent. So far in all our testing, the new joints have proven to be even stronger than a standard human knee."

Tyler raised his head up from the bed and glanced at his mother.

"Wait wait wait. I'm not letting you put some synthetic joint in me. I'm twenty-one years old, not seventy-five."

"Just repair the knee. That's what we're here for," Margie echoed.

Dr. Pinkering's face fell flat as he stared from Tyler to Margie and back again. "I'm very sorry, but apparently I haven't been clear. This isn't a discussion. We're not presenting you some wild alternative."

His arm jutted out to the side, pointing to the film of Tyler's shattered knee still hanging on the wall. "This is the *only* option. Not just from a football standpoint, from an ever-walking-without-a-cane standpoint."

Tyler swallowed hard, a lump traveling the length of his throat. "Why are we just now hearing this?"

"This is the first time your sedation has worn off enough to have this conversation."

"My mother's been here the past eight hours."

"You are an of-age patient. We don't discuss any medical matters until you are cognizant enough to comprehend."

Tyler's eyes slid shut. He raised a hand to his face and pinched it across the bridge of his nose, pressing his fingers down into his eyes on either side.

"Come back in an hour."

Sarconi's mouth dropped open. He swiveled to see his colleague looking just as surprised.

"Mr. Bentley," Dr. Pinkering began. "I don't think you understand."

Tyler responded without moving his hand or even turning his head. "I understand just fine. And I'm telling you to leave and come back in an hour."

"But your leg...the morphine is already starting to wear off. It's imperative we get you to surgery as soon as it does."

"Was that your plan?" Tyler asked. "Pull a bait and switch on me seconds before I was wheeled into surgery?"

There was no mistaking the venom permeating his voice. The

sound came as a surprise to all, even dropping Margie's jaw towards the floor.

Tyler removed the hand from his face and rolled his gaze towards the doctor. "Can my knee get any worse?"

"Excuse me?"

"In the next hour, could it get any worse? Is it even possible for a knee to be worse off than mine is right now?"

"Well, no, but the amount of pain you'll be in..."

"I can handle pain. Give us an hour."

There was a tone of finality in the comment that left everybody in the room knowing the conversation was over.

Margie lifted her jaw and stared at the men. Tyler rolled his head back and stared up at the ceiling, making a point of not looking at either of them.

Dr. Pinkering and Sarconi gave each other one last hopeless glance before fleeing the room as instructed.

CHAPTER FIVE

Shane Laszlo sat alone at his desk in the corner, trying in vain to hide behind the mountain of legal volumes stacked before him. Most of them had been bestowed upon him six months prior when he was studying for the bar. When he tried to return them he found out they were his and that his pay had been docked accordingly. Since he owned the things and didn't have anywhere else to put them, he had left them piled up on his desk.

Might as well put them to use.

It didn't take long to discover if people saw a clean desk they assumed he wasn't busy and were all too happy to give him something to do. If they couldn't see him behind a wall of legal jargon, then he must be earning his salary.

Every morning the first task Shane did in the silence of the two-six was rearrange the books. Never did the piles remain the same for consecutive days, his space a bastion of perpetual change.

Shane's jacket was off and his tie loosened as he worked his way through another stack of tax documentation. For just the briefest of moments he allowed himself to believe the task was the most grating thing on the planet before the all-too-familiar drum of fingers atop his computer reminded him what really was.

His boss.

Shane lowered his pen and raised his gaze to see Rex Hartman, a junior partner at the firm and his immediate supervisor. In six months, all Shane had seen him do was make Shane's life a living hell and check his hair in every reflective surface available.

"You hiding out back here, Laszlo?"

Shane faked a smile. "No sir, just going through the Martell tax forms."

Hartman nodded. "Martell, good group. One of the first clients I brought on board here. You knew that didn't you?"

"I didn't, though I guessed by your signature on the forms that they were yours."

Hartman made a small sucking noise and held his hand out to examine his cuticles. "Yeah, an old family friend. You know that's how business is often done here in New England. Ran into them at a Princeton tailgate, started schmoozing a little bit, one thing led to another."

He paused, waiting for Shane to give his story the validation he was seeking.

The first three months, he bit every time. Now, Shane made a point of waiting him out.

Hartman raised his gaze to Shane and paused a moment. "So, how were your holidays? Do anything good?"

"No, just kind of stuck around here, got caught up on some stuff. How about you?"

Shane knew the question was an affront to make him ask about Hartman's vacation, the same one he'd been talking about nonstop since Halloween.

Whether it was unrelated or as punishment to leaving him hanging a moment before, he wasn't sure.

"Took the wife and the kids down to the Bahamas for a couple of weeks, went ahead and brought her parents along, too."

Shane glanced down at his pasty own white forearms and nodded. "Get into anything exciting down there?"

"A lot of relaxing. Spent some quality time with the family, got some work done at the gym, firmed up the tan."

He paused to allow Shane to comment.

Again he was met with silence.

"Saw where your old alma mater had a pretty big win in the Centennial Bowl," Hartman said, the setup for what Shane knew was coming next.

It was the same comment that eighty percent of the firm had made to him at one point or another.

"Yeah, they did. I managed to catch a little bit of it on the radio up here, sounded like a good game. Did you watch it?"

A moment of silence passed. Shane glanced up to see Hartman looking at his reflection in the polished brass shade on his desk lamp.

"No," Hartman said, running a finger along his hairline. "I was never much of a football fan. Of course at Princeton we weren't eligible for bowl games or anything, so I didn't get into it all that much."

It took everything Shane had not to roll his eyes.

"Yeah, well, it's a pretty big deal in the Midwest. Lot of pride and tradition there."

Hartman snorted. "Pride and tradition? Over a game that involves slamming your head into others? Rhodes Scholars, multi-billion dollar endowments, now that's tradition."

Shane raised his eyebrows and nodded.

"I mean, there's a reason *A Beautiful Mind* wasn't set at Ohio Tech," Hartman added.

"Wasn't that movie about a paranoid schizophrenic that almost drowned his own child in the bath tub?"

This snapped Hartman's attention away from his own reflection. The faux camaraderie faded from his eyes, replaced by loathing.

Just as fast, the loathing passed.

The sanctimony did not.

"The reason I wandered back here was I need you to go ahead and finish things up on the Manelli and Breathable Air Foundation projects. After that nice long vacation, I'm a little behind right now."

Shane felt the blood rush to his face. Otherwise, he made no visible reaction to the statement. It wasn't the first weekend he'd spent locked away in the two-six doing Hartman's work for him.

"Yeah, sure, shouldn't be a problem."

"Great. If you could have those to me by Monday morning, I'd appreciate it."

"Sure thing, Mr. Hartman."

Hartman drummed his fingers along the top of the computer again, pondering something. Whatever it was he let it go and turned on his heel to go.

Just as fast he turned back around, still moving towards the door. "Oh, and I almost forgot. The Berkman account as well. Got Celtic tickets tonight, won't be able to get to it."

Shane didn't bother to respond. He was already back behind his stack of law books, trying his best to make sure Hartman didn't see the look of pure disgust on his face.

CHAPTER SIX

Just sixty minutes after departing, Dr. Pinkering and Sarconi walked into the room. Margie had repositioned herself at the head of the bed and together she and Tyler stared back as they entered.

Sarconi stopped just inside the door, allowing Dr. Pinkering to take the lead. He kept his hands behind his back and made his best attempt to appear pleasant.

Beside him, Dr. Pinkering swept forward a few feet and surveyed the situation. In front of him two people waited expectantly. The x-ray board on the wall had been turned off, the films put back in their envelope.

He opened his mouth to speak, but was cut off by Tyler before he ever got the chance.

"I'm sorry I snapped earlier," Tyler said. "You just have to understand some things."

Dr. Pinkering held up a hand and smiled. He started to respond, but didn't get out the first syllable before Tyler cut him off again.

"First of all, I have never missed a single practice, let alone game, in twenty years," Tyler said. "I've never had surgery. Never broken a bone. I couldn't even tell you the last time I had a cold."

Dr. Pinkering and Sarconi both stared back at him, neither daring to say a word.

"Point being, I hate lying here. I hate being at somebody else's mercy. I hate feeling like my body betrayed me."

After a moment of silence, Dr. Pinkering bowed his head. "Very understandable."

"Second," Tyler said, "I know people say this sort of thing a lot, but I am not being dramatic when I say this is my future we're talking about here. NFL contract. Signing bonus. Endorsement deals. A better life for the both of us.

"If this pitch of yours in any way runs counter to that, I don't want to hear it. I'm not concerned with the length of rehab time. I'm concerned with getting myself back to one hundred percent. That's it.

"Are we clear?"

"Absolutely," Dr. Pinkering said, turning to Sarconi for confirmation.

"Very much so," Sarconi added, the fat folds under his chin bouncing as he nodded in the affirmative.

"Okay," Tyler said. "What is this thing and why do you think I need it?"

Dr. Pinkering glanced once more to Sarconi. "I'll start on the back end and then we'll work our way forward. The reason you need it is just what we pointed out earlier. The type of injury you sustained pretty much destroyed everything at once.

"A knee can recover from a break or a tendon tear because there is enough ancillary stability to allow for a full recovery. When everything is shattered, there is no reference point, so to speak.

"We can put everything back together, but the odds of it all meshing together in perfect alignment are almost non-existent."

Sarconi stepped forward from the wall, a black three ring binder in his hand. "As for the first part of your question, that's where I come in."

He pulled a chair over to the side of the bed and positioned it just shy of Tyler's elbow, facing them both. He propped the binder up on his knee and opened the front cover, a stack of glossy printouts arranged within.

"We call it the KnightRunner, an homage to your Crimson Knights here at Ohio Tech."

On the cover page was the name KnightRunner, designed in a fancy font with bright red lettering. It was superimposed over silhouettes of football, basketball, and baseball players, all in the throes of competition.

Sarconi turned to the next page.

"In the past, almost all replacements have been made from a metal alloy. The joints are durable, but aren't without their problems. Stiffness, grinding, susceptibility to extreme weather conditions."

Another page turned.

"With the KnightRunner, we developed a product that is comprised of a synthetic with the same composite make-up of human cartilage."

"Cartilage?" Margie asked. "As in nose and ears?"

Sarconi pointed at Margie and turned another page. "Sort of. At a most basic molecular level, yes it is the same as the cartilage found in the nose and ears. The difference though is that the KnightRunner condenses the material into density that is stronger even than the original bones."

Tyler turned his head to glance at his mother, but said nothing.

Sarconi saw the gesture and pushed ahead to the next page.

"Think of it in terms of PSI, or pounds per square inch. Cartilage found in your knee or nose has a PSI of about 50. Bone, such as the femur in your thigh has a psi of about 350.

"The KnightRunner? Over 1,200."

Sarconi allowed himself the slightest hint of a smile. Behind him, Dr. Pinkering rocked back on his heels, watching the Bentley's for any outward sign of acceptance.

"If this were used, what does it mean for my playing ball?"

The small smile on Sarconi's face grew a shade larger.

Dr. Pinkering raised his left hand and snapped his wrist back to stare at his watch. "Right now it is January 1st. Most times, a surgery like this would require at least twelve months of rehab, probably closer to eighteen. After that, if everything breaks your way, you're looking at maybe returning to the form you were at last night."

"With the KnightRunner," Sarconi said, "you'll be ready to return the opening kickoff this fall."

Tyler raised his eyebrows, but said nothing.

"Dr. Pinkering, Mr. Sarconi," Margie said, her voice rough after the previous day she'd had, "I don't mean to be a fly in the ointment here, but who pays for a procedure like this? How much would it even cost?"

Dr. Pinkering was quick to reply. "This was an injury sustained during an athletic contest, meaning Tyler's scholarship will cover it."

"Yes," Margie conceded, "but I mean for this new KnightRunner thing. I'm not sure experimental procedures are covered."

"The university has catastrophic injury coverage for just this sort of thing," Dr. Pinkering said. "Everything will be taken care of."

"Besides," Sarconi said, casting a glance to Dr. Pinkering, "we were kind of hoping to make this an advantageous situation for everybody here."

"Meaning?" Tyler asked.

"Meaning we were hoping that starting this fall, when you've recovered and returned to football stardom, you could serve as a poster child of sorts for us."

"After that, it could become the first of those endorsements you mentioned," Dr. Pinkering added.

The astonishment of a moment before evaporated from both Tyler and Margie. They stared back at Dr. Pinkering and Sarconi, letting their words sink in.

"So it was a bait-and-switch," Tyler muttered.

"Who's your poster child now?" Margie asked, her voice raised to cover for her son.

"Excuse me?" Sarconi asked.

"You said you want Tyler to be your poster child. Who is it now?"

"Well, see, at the moment..." Dr. Pinkering began.

"So what you meant was guinea pig," Margie said.

"No, what he meant was, at the moment we're allowing the product to speak for itself," Sarconi said.

"But don't let that fool you," Dr. Pinkering said. "I can assure you there is quite an extensive list of patients that have achieved wonderful results with this product."

"Just none with the kind of name recognition of a Tyler Bentley," Sarconi added.

Both Margie and Dr. Pinkering began to speak, but Tyler quieted them by raising a hand. He waited a moment for the air to clear, drawing in several deep breaths.

"Again, you have to understand that this is a lot to process for us. This is my career, our future, we're talking about."

Dr. Pinkering and Sarconi both murmured their understanding.

"So two things are going to happen here. First, you're going to get one of these patients in here and let us pick his brain a little bit. If we like what we hear, we'll finish this discussion later."

Sarconi dipped his head in acknowledgement.

"And the second thing?" Dr. Pinkering asked.

"If I'm not going into surgery just yet, bring me some more morphine."

CHAPTER SEVEN

The next morning Tyler and Margie were both awoken by a heavy rapping on the door. The shades were pulled and the room still dark, making it impossible to know what time it was.

Still, it felt very early to the both of them.

Without waiting for acknowledgement, Sarconi pushed the door open and smiled. "Good morning, folks. How are you feeling this morning?"

Margie did her best to blink herself awake, a yawn distorting her features. On the bed beside her, Tyler rubbed his hands over his face and stretched his arms out above him.

"I've been better."

"Yes of course, of course," Sarconi responded. "I'm sorry if I woke either of you, it's just that I have someone here I'd like you to meet and I didn't want it to wait."

Tyler squinted and turned his head to glare at Sarconi. "Already? You were just here what, eight or nine hours ago?"

Sarconi waved a hand at the comment and said, "I make it a point to keep in touch with all of our patients. I gave Kenny a call last night and asked if he could come by. He was a little hesitant at first until I told him who was considering the replacement. After that, he couldn't get over here fast enough."

"Kenny?" Margie asked.

Sarconi pushed the door open a few more inches and motioned into the hallway. "Come on in."

Through the door a tall, slender, black man with long arms and a shaved head walked in and smiled. He was older than Tyler, though his shaved head meant he could be anywhere from late-twenties to late-thirties.

"Tyler, Ms. Bentley," Sarconi said, his voice almost a purr, "this is Kenny Walker. You might remember him from his days in the NBA."

Kenny snorted. "More like *day*. I wasn't there but a minute before I blew out my knee and that was that."

Margie glanced from her son to Kenny. "But isn't that why you're here? To tell us about this new knee and how it got you back onto the court in no time at all?"

"No, ma'am. I mean, yes I am here to tell you about the knee replacement and how effective it's been for me, but no, it didn't save my career."

Kenny smiled again and said, "You have to understand, this all happened to me fifteen years ago. Back then, medicine wasn't what it is today. They put me together the best they could, but it was never strong enough to make it back into the league."

Without thinking, Margie reached out and touched her son's shoulder.

"So what happened?" Tyler asked.

"I spent four years bouncing between surgery and try-outs. I must have worked out for every team in the NBA at one time or another. A few times they liked what they saw and would give me a couple of days in training camp. Few times they said they'd be in touch and I never heard from them. Couple of times the knee gave as I was working out for them."

"Never happened, huh?" Tyler asked.

"In the last fifteen years since my injury I've had eleven knee operations, but not a single day in the NBA."

"I'm sorry to hear that," Tyler said.

Kenny shook his head. "Don't be. I'm not a hard luck story here. I used the time I was nursing my knee to finish up my degree. Things could have been a lot worse."

A moment of silence passed, each side uncertain of how to proceed.

"So am I right to assume that at least one of those surgeries was for the KnightRunner?" Margie asked.

"Yes," Kenny said, nodding his head. "I met Marcel about a year ago at a conference here in Columbus. My knee was still giving me troubles and I was looking into every alternate treatment on the market. Acupuncture, Chinese massage, you name it and I've tried it.

"Anyway, I bumped into Marcel at the conference and we got to talking. I told him I was looking for some new therapy techniques; he told me he was looking for a market to start pitching his new product."

"So quite the chance encounter?" Tyler asked.

"No, not really," Kenny said. "At first I balked big-time. I'm in my thirties, with a long road ahead of me. I had no desire to get a full replacement, but a few months went by and my knee continued to get worse. It even got to the point I was walking with a cane.

"In the end, I called Marcel and told him I didn't care if he had to cut me open himself, I was ready to try it."

Sarconi laughed behind him. "Those were his exact words."

Kenny chuckled and nodded. "I was the third person to ever receive a KnightRunner. That was seven months ago and, well..."

In a fluid motion he crossed his ankles and turned in a sharp circle for them. He then did a series of knee raises and side to side lateral movements. Margie and Tyler watched as he jumped a few times into the air and drew his knees to his chest. To finish the impromptu routine, he stood on one leg and did a full squat.

"As you can see, I have no problems whatsoever. I can do things now I couldn't do before the injury."

Margie and Tyler both watched in rapt silence.

Another knock came at the door and Dr. Pinkering slid inside. "Pardon my tardiness; I had a few rounds to make this morning. Giving them the full display, Kenny?"

Kenny again bounced from side to side. "Just showing this young man what he has to look forward to."

Tyler glanced back to his mother. "When did you have the surgery?"

"Seven months ago," Kenny replied. "I can't believe it took me that long to have it done. The KnightRunner is better than having my own knee in there."

Silence fell once more. Tyler and Margie sat on one side of the room weighing the new information. Dr. Pinkering and Sarconi stood across from them, both watching their every move.

Between the two sides stood Kenny, who walked to the window and peered out through the blinds as the morning sun settled in over Columbus.

"What do you think, Mama?" Tyler asked.

Margie frowned. "I'm still not sold on this. Wouldn't it be safer to just repair what's there?"

Dr. Pinkering stepped forward and said, "Ms. Bentley, that is correct. The natural body parts are always preferred *whenever possible*. But as I showed you last night, that isn't the case here. The trauma was just too great.

"We are presenting the KnightRunner to you because Tyler's body doesn't have the capability to recover on its own."

"Then why do I get the impression you gentlemen are trying to sell us something?" Margie asked.

Dr. Pinkering made a face as if he'd been wounded. "Ms. Bentley, you have my word as a doctor, backed by the Hippocratic Oath, and as a man. This isn't just the best course of action for Tyler, it's the only course."

Margie fell silent and turned her attention back to her son. "Tyler, it's your decision."

Tyler shifted his focus to Kenny and nodded. "Thanks for coming by. I appreciate it."

"My pleasure. It was good to meet the star running back of the Crimson Knights."

Tyler nodded in acceptance of the compliment and shifted his gaze to Dr. Pinkering. "Give us an hour to discuss this. And just in case, you better back off on the morphine right now."

"Of course," Dr. Pinkering said.

Behind him, Kenny and Sarconi both fled the room. A moment later, the doctor joined them in the hallway. He motioned for them to follow him, and only once they were a little ways down the hall did he lean in close.

"So, what do we think?"

"I think that boy wants back on the field so bad he'll do damn near anything," Sarconi said.

"So I did alright?" Kenny asked, looking at each of them in turn.

Sarconi responded with a heavy slap on the back. "Alright? That was damn near Oscar worthy."

CHAPTER EIGHT

The anesthesia was just beginning to lift when the flash bulb went off. A small click followed by an unexpected orb of light that bathed the entire room in harsh illumination, freezing Margie in place, her eyes wide. Beside her, Tyler's eyes cracked open into thin slits, the light penetrating his narcotic-induced stupor.

"What the heck?" he mumbled, raising a hand to the side of his head, his voice thick and pained.

Margie pounced before the cameraman ever had a chance to get off a second shot. She tossed herself in front of Tyler's bed, using her prodigious girth to block her son from view.

"Get out! Now!" she yelled, shooing away the photographer that had somehow found his way to Tyler's room. "The press conference is downstairs, just like all the signs say!"

Unfazed, the photographer raised the camera again. "Adam Smarte with *Weekly Sport* magazine. Our readers want to see what Tyler looks like after all this."

"He looks like a man that just got out of surgery!" Margie yelled. "And if you or your readers ever want another word out of Tyler, you'll get out of here this instant!"

The threat froze him just long enough for Margie to burst forward and mash her oversized chest into his shoulder. Like a bulldozer pushing forward, she shoved him out into the hallway, punctuating the move with a two-handed shove that sent him stumbling backwards.

Margie stood in the hall for several long moments to make sure the man slunk away, then turned her gaze to two orderlies standing slack-jawed in the corner. "If anybody else gets near this door, I'm holding you responsible. Got it?"

Both nodded as Margie turned on a heel, stomped back inside and closed the door behind her. She pressed her back against it for several long moments, allowing the mother lion vitriol to recede, before returning to the bedside.

"How do you feel, Sweetie?"

A faint smile crossed Tyler's lips. "Like a man that just got out of surgery."

Margie's eyes were glassy but she remained free of tears.

"Have I ever mentioned I'm glad I've never had to look across the line and see you at linebacker?"

The comment forced a laugh from Margie, the sound somewhere between a gasp and a chuckle. She reached out and stroked the top of his head, her eyes avoiding his leg suspended above the bed.

Tyler sighed and raised a hand to grip his mother's. "So, how did it go?"

"Dr. Pinkering stopped by a little bit ago on his way to get ready for the press conference. Said everything went well."

"That's all he said?"

"Pretty much," Margie said and picked the remote up from the bedside table. She turned on the television and flipped through the channels until she found the local news station. Front and center was Dr. Pinkering, Sarconi and a black man they'd never seen behind him.

Margie snorted. "Apparently if we want to hear any more we need to need find out like everybody else."

"Try playing college football," Tyler replied, his voice still thick with grog. "First two years I was here the only time I ever saw Coach Valentine was on *Sportscenter*."

On the screen, the press conference got under way.

"This is a great day for Ohio Tech University athletics," Dr. Pinkering said into a bank of microphones. "Earlier today, a massive first step was taken in returning its star back to where he belongs.

"It's also a great day for Ohio Tech University medicine. Today we were able to, in a revolutionary new procedure, pair with the creative expertise of SynTronic to introduce a new product that will revamp sports injuries as we know them."

He paused for a moment and leaned back from the microphones, allowing his words to sink in.

"It is with great pride that I report the operation to repair Tyler Bentley's knee was a complete success. Performed by Dr. Manningham, orthopedic staff surgeon here at OTU, the surgery took just over seven hours and was done without any unforeseen difficulties.

"The remains of Tyler's knee were cleared away and in its place the new KnightRunner artificial joint was implanted."

"Glad they finally got around to mentioning me during their little sales pitch," Tyler mumbled.

"Who the hell is Dr. Manningham?" Margie asked. "I thought Pinkering was doing the operating?"

Tyler moved his hand to cover his eyes, his movements stiff and stilted. "I don't know. The last few days have all been a blur."

On the screen, Dr. Pinkering finished his speech and opened the floor for questions. A sea of arms sprang up in response, reporters all lobbing questions without waiting to be called.

Rising above the fray was a blonde woman in the front row, her voice an octave higher than those around her. "An artificial joint? Isn't that a bit extreme?"

Dr. Pinkering pointed to her and shook his head as the rest of the crowd quieted down. "For those of you watching the game the other night, you saw the hit Tyler Bentley took. What you didn't see was the devastation it caused his knee.

"After x-rays and evaluation, we found that the damage was so extensive that the joint was beyond repair. This wasn't just the best option, it was the only option. Next question."

The arms reappeared in front of the screen and a bald man asked, "Why go with an untested product like this? What did you call it again, the KnightRider?"

Dr. Pinkering nodded to the man and said, "That's Knight*Runner*. We in conjunction with SynTronic have been testing this product for the better part of a year now. There are no less than a dozen people already walking around with KnightRunner knee and hip replacements, all with phenomenal results."

The arms appeared again and an older gentleman asked, "So what does this do for the projected health and return to the field for Bentley?"

Dr. Pinkering shook his head in a non-committal manner, a smug smirk belying the gesture. "At this point I don't think it would be out of the question to say he'd be one hundred percent ready when camp opens this fall."

The moment the words left his lips, the hands again sprang up with renewed zest. Snippets of questions could be heard through the television, each of them wondering about Tyler's return on such a truncated time table.

Margie aimed the remote at the television and lowered the volume several decibels.

As she did, Tyler held out a hand to her. "Just turn it off."

"Heard enough huh?"

"He's not there to talk about the surgery; he's there to hawk his new toy."

Margie turned the television off and sat for a moment in the newfound quiet of the room. Beside her, Tyler slid his hand and forearm across his face, the crook of his arm shielding him from the world.

"You should try to get some rest, Mama. I bet you haven't slept in days."

Margie raised her red-rimmed eyes to her son and lifted one corner of her mouth in a smile. "Yeah? And what are you going to do?"

"I'm going back to sleep. My leg hurts."

CHAPTER NINE

Four days later, the point arrived when Margie couldn't afford to be off work any longer and was forced to return home to Worland. Her boss at the mill had given her all the time she needed to be with Tyler, but even nights spent by his bedside and meals from vending machines couldn't make up for the extra flight and lost week's wages.

True to its hype, the KnightRunner had Tyler up on crutches by the time she left. Rehab started two days later, the moment the painkillers and swelling subsided enough to allow for movement.

Phase one was a regiment of aquatic movements, the buoyancy of a controlled pool removing most impact from the joint. At first it was straight line walking, followed by jogging, followed by lateral movements.

By week three he was walking unassisted.

Phase two started a week later, the same exact regiment performed on dry land. Plenty of light strengthening exercises, quad extensions, leg presses, hamstring curls, mixed in.

By week six, he was jogging in a straight line.

Every single day for the first two months Tyler worked with his strength and conditioning coaches, the lecherous eyes of Dr. Pinkering and Sarconi never far away. For every drop of sweat he perspired, they stood before a bank of microphones and reported to the world how well their new product was working.

As spring settled in around Columbus, Tyler was certain they saw him as their personal mascot and nothing more. Day by day he bit back the animosity that welled within him, funneling it into his workouts.

By March, he began shuffling laterally. Two weeks later, he was doing it at full speed.

Every night Tyler fell asleep staring at the wall above his bed. On the left half he posted the cards and letters of support he received from coaches, fans, and friends all over the country. On the right half hung an oversized schedule for the upcoming season surrounded by detailed printouts of his progress.

Everything was going on as planned.

CHAPTER TEN

"These four a.m. workouts are killing me, Coach," Tyler joked as he and OTU strength coach Harold Curl walked through the athletic center and onto the indoor turf field. Each of them carried a large duffel bag over their shoulder filled with supplies for the morning workout.

"Four?" Curl return in mock indignation. "Look out that window there. You see that big yellow thing in the sky? Trust me, if this was four a.m., that wouldn't be there."

Tyler made no attempt to bite back a grin. "Still, this is awful early for a college kid on spring break."

"What, you think you're on MTV or something?" Curl asked, dropping the bag from his shoulder. It landed with a heavy thud against the artificial turf surface, a trio of orange cones spilling out.

A black man with very light skin and close cropped hair, Curl was an aspiring all-natural bodybuilder and thick all over. He had a quick smile and a genuine interest in the athletes, something that won him many friends throughout the school.

When Tyler first began his rehab stint, it was Curl that volunteered to come in at four a.m. to work him out. The time was less than ideal for both of them, but it was the only chance they had when another varsity sport wasn't using the facilities.

For the first time in three months, they had been able to come in at a more reasonable hour. Spring break had most of campus deserted, leaving behind just those athletes still in season.

Curl bent down and extracted the rest of the plastic cones, stacking them high atop each other. "Alright, let's get going. Two laps, you know the drill."

Tyler unloaded his bag beside Curl's and bent at the waist to slide an elastic knee brace up around his knee. He snapped it into place with a heavy slap of rubber against skin and took off at a brisk jog around the field.

Behind him, Curl unzipped the second bag and extracted a nylon harness and several thick rubber bands. He laid them out in order beside him, then took up the stack of cones and arranged them in a pattern ten yards in length.

From his own bag he removed a speed ladder, a metal sled, and a twenty-five pound weight. He attached the harness to the sled and slid the weight down onto it.

He was just positioning the speed ladder when Tyler finished his laps and sat down on the ground beside him.

"So how's life, Coach?" Tyler asked as he dropped to his bottom and spread his legs wide. Next he walked his hands forward in front of him, stretching out his hamstrings.

"Calm before the storm. Kids are about to start little league, full load of teams back in here after break, got spring tournaments coming up."

"After that things ease up again though, right? Nobody's in season. You guys divvy up the sports for the summer, get everybody ready for next year?" Tyler asked, lying flat on his back and extending his right leg into the air.

"True," Curl replied, gripping Tyler's ankle and stretching his leg back towards his head. "That's still a load though. You guys alone give me over a hundred players to keep track of."

"Yeah, we're a demanding bunch," Tyler conceded.

"Yeah, well, football money keeps the lights on for most of the other sports around here. I'd say you've earned it," Curl said, lowering the leg and shaking it out. He began to raise it again for a secondary stretch, but paused halfway up.

"You ever notice these bruises all along your calf here? Little dark spots everywhere?"

Tyler raised his head from the turf. "Oh, yeah. Damn things hurt like hell too. I keep asking the docs about it, they keep telling me it's normal. Leg getting itself back into shape, muscles adapting to the implant, all that stuff."

Curl lowered the leg and shook it out again, bringing it up for one last stretch. "I've worked with a lot of athletes and I've never seen bruising like this before, especially not from *muscles getting back into shape.*"

"I know. Everything else they said has been true though, so I guess I'll go with it."

"Alright, just keep an eye on it."

Curl finished stretching Tyler and hefted him onto his feet, moving him straight into a series of agility drills on the speed ladder. From there they shifted over onto the sled, running sprints of various lengths with the steel implement sliding along on the turf behind him.

Twenty minutes in Tyler was soaked through with sweat. He stood bent at the waist, his lungs burning for air, droplets dripping from the end of his nose.

Beside him, Curl stood with his arms folded, a half-smile on his face that resonated somewhere between self-satisfied and sadistic.

Every Ohio Tech athlete knew the look. None of them liked it.

"Looks like you've almost got your straight ahead speed back to normal," Curl said, letting the statement hang in the air.

"And?"

The smile grew broader. "Got a new one for you today."

Tyler made no effort to move as Curl lifted a trio of bands from the ground by his feet. All three were circles two feet in diameter, colored blue and constructed of rubber over an inch wide. Curl hung all three from a finger and extended them towards Tyler.

"So now we continue working on that lateral movement."

Tyler dropped his gaze to the ground for a second and shook his head, a series of mumbles escaping his lips. Just as fast, he stood to full height and snatched the bands away.

"Three bands?"

"Three bands."

"How many laps?"

"I didn't say."

Tyler carried the bands to the top of the cone formation and slid the bands around his ankles. He lowered himself into a football position, his thighs parallel to the ground and began.

Moving to his right, he extended his foot out as far as the bands would allow, planted and drug the left in behind it. Never did the two come closer than shoulder width apart. Not once did his pace increase above even and methodical.

"Come on, Superstar," Curl called as he went. "Valley game's less than six months away. You want to be ready or not?"

After just ten yards, his quads started to burn, a slow, searing ache that started at the base of his spine and wrapped clear around to his calves.

After twenty yards, his knee started to burn. Not the tingling flame of lactic acid coursing into the body, but a deep, breath-stealing blaze of pain.

Gritting his teeth, Tyler gutted out the last five yards and paused at the end of the cone formation. He put his hands on his knees and extended his legs beneath him, trying to shake away the inferno raging within them.

"Come on now," Curl called. "If you go through hell and still make it back, it doesn't count as dying, right?"

Once more Tyler dropped into a crouch and started moving, going back the way he'd just came. One by one he counted off the steps, letting his injured leg lead the way. Within five yards his progress was reduced to slow and torturous, his calves and abductors screaming as he inched along.

"That's it, that's it," Curl called. "We've got to get that thing stronger if you're going to be ready."

After ten yards the pain turned white hot beneath his skin, the agony almost unbearable. Tyler paused for a moment and drew in a deep breath, willing the leg to keep going. He raised it into the air and pushed out against the bands, the knee responding with a low cracking sound that drew Curl to his side in a flash.

"What the hell was that?"

"Nothing," Tyler muttered, his eyes closed tight and his head pointed towards the ceiling.

"No, for real, that didn't sound good. We're done here."

"Ten more yards," Tyler said, his voice just a whisper between heavy panting.

He didn't make it one more step.

Once more Tyler lifted the leg into the air and pushed to extend the bands. The moment he did, a second crack was heard, followed by a third and a fourth.

White lights danced before Tyler's eyes as he stood with his leg dangling in air, his body unable to process what was going. For several long seconds, he stood motionless, his body contorted like a macabre marionette.

By the time Curl got to him, the tension of the bands had done their job. They snapped back into shape, bringing with them Tyler's ankle and slamming into his right knee, the lower half of his leg swinging like a broken twig.

Not a single sound escaped Tyler as he went limp, his body rendering him unconscious before his brain realized the breadth of what just happened.

Curl caught him less than a foot from the ground, lowering him onto the turf and making no attempt to roll him over or even remove the bands from around his ankles.

Instead he used his cell-phone to call 911, sat down beside Tyler, and wept until the paramedics arrived.

CHAPTER ELEVEN

Margie pulled her aging Chevy truck up alongside the mailbox and rolled down her window, the engine idling as she kept her foot depressed on the brake. She lowered the lid and pulled out a small stack of envelopes, knowing in advance that most of them weren't addressed to her.

Even months later, a handful of townsfolk still insisted on sending Tyler their handwriting well-wishes on a daily basis.

With a heavy sigh, Margie tossed the stack down on the seat beside her hard hat and lunch pail, easing up alongside the house. The weariness of the last few months was evident in her movements, weighing her down in everything she did. She wrenched open the front seat of the truck and collected her things, heading for the door. As she approached, she could hear the kitchen phone ringing through the front window.

"Damnit," Margie muttered, pushing her way through and shuffling inside. She tossed the mail, hard hat, and pail down on the couch as she went, making it to the phone just in time to hear it fall silent.

"Double damnit," she said, turning back towards the living room.

She'd gone no further than a step when the phone erupted again, echoing through the silent house.

Margie snapped it up after a single ring and pressed it to her cheek. "Yeah?" she answered, agitation in her voice.

"Ms. Bentley?" a male voice she didn't recognize asked.

"Look, I just got home from work and haven't even thought about dinner yet. Whatever you're selling, I ain't interested."

"Ms. Bentley, please," the voice responded in rapid fashion. "I'm sorry to be calling like this, but I assure you I'm not trying to sell you anything. I almost wish that I was, to be honest with you."

Margie's breath caught in her chest. Her mind went blank, her body rigid. Unable to formulate a response, she waited in silence for him to continue.

"This is Dr. Manningham, the orthopedic surgeon here at OTU Hospital. We met a few months back."

"Yeah, I remember," Margie whispered.

Manningham took a long breath. "Again, I am very sorry to be calling like this, but it's about Tyler."

"Oh, God."

"Earlier today he was rushed to us from across the campus. He had been working out with one of the trainers when the knee gave way."

"No," Margie said, her eyes sliding shut. Already she could hear the impending frustration in her son's voice, the resentment on his face at the limb that kept betraying him. "Is he okay? Can I talk to him?"

Another long, drawn-out breath met her year.

"Ms. Bentley, I'm afraid the answers to those questions are no and no. Right now he's still in our post-anesthesia ward under a heavy dose of medication. He was unconscious when he arrived here and we're keeping him that way until at least tomorrow."

Margie reached out a hand for the counter, swinging it through the air until it touched Formica. She braced her palm against the cold countertop and used it to steady herself.

"Oh, Jesus."

"When Tyler came in, his entire left leg from the knee down was disjointed. They came and fetched me out of surgery when he arrived and by the time I got to him, his foot was twisted almost one hundred and eighty degrees."

Tears treaded down Margie's cheeks and dripped onto her faded tan coat, leaving water splotches across her chest.

"Dr. Manningham, were you able to fix my son's leg?"

A full moment of silence passed.

"And please don't say you're sorry again," Margie added.

"Ms. Bentley, by the time I get in there, there was nothing left to save," Manningham said, his voice low and even. "The prosthetic that was used had almost completely disintegrated. Not only was the joint itself ruined, even the synthetic compound it was made of had crumbled to almost nothing."

Margie raised her glistening face to the ceiling and attempted to draw in a deep breath. The air sucked through her teeth with the sound of an eerie sob.

"Once inside, I had to extend the incision much further than anticipated. In the end I went almost clear to his ankle looking for good tissue to try and salvage, but there just wasn't any. It appeared the joint had been crumbling for some time, tiny bits of the synthetic working themselves free and imbedding in the muscle fibers and capillaries of the lower leg."

Manningham paused there for a moment, letting the words soak in.

In the back of her mind, Margie already knew where the conversation was going. On some level she appreciated Manningham shielding her from the inevitable truth, but on another, maternal, level she had to hear it.

"Dr. Manningham, what is it you're trying to tell me right now?"

The pause lasted a full fifteen seconds.

"The damage done to both your son's muscular and vascular systems was extensive. The three bones in his leg, the femur, the tibia, and the fibula, were all severely twisted and splintered as well from the violent nature of the injury.

"Ms. Bentley, I want you to know that I did everything in my power, but in the end I had no choice but to take your son's leg."

An anguished moan slid from Marcie's throat as the phone slid from her hand, clattering against the kitchen tile. She rolled her body forward to grab the countertop with both hands before giving up and allowing her body to drop to the ground. There she remained for several long minutes, her sobs reverberating through the house.

By the time she was done, the front of her coat was soaked as her chin rested on her chest, her entire body gasping for air.

The only thing that pulled her from her trance was a small, persistent voice somewhere in the room beside her.

"Ms. Bentley? Are you there, Ms. Bentley?"

Margie's gaze searched the floor for the source of the voice before settling on the phone a few feet away. With great effort she lowered her hands to the ground and crawled to the phone, rolling her entire body flat onto the linoleum as she picked it up and pressed it to her ear.

"Dr. Manningham?"

"Yes, Ms. Bentley, I'm still here."

"You said he's still unconscious, right?"

"Yes, ma'am."

"Can you do me a favor?"

"Anything within my power, ma'am."

"Leave him there, I'm on my way."

CHAPTER TWELVE

The tears were gone. Margie had no doubt they would be back within seconds of seeing Tyler, and be there for the remainder of her trip, but for the time being they were far away. In their place was a low, even burning of vitriol that far surpassed hatred, moving closer to full-on loathing.

The no-name gypsy cab driver dropped Margie off in front of the Ohio Tech Hospital mid-afternoon, their entire interaction limited to three words. By the tone of her response, he knew better than to even attempt idle chitchat.

Margie tossed a twenty over the backseat and stomped her way through the front door of the Ohio Tech University Hospital and into the lobby. A small duffel bag was thrown over her shoulder, swinging free behind her as she walked to the reception desk, almost daring other lobby patrons to get in her way.

"Yes, ma'am, may I help you?" a pretty young blonde asked, her voice bored. On her lap was the latest issue of a celebrity gossip mag, no doubt a sorority girl carrying out work-study obligations against her will.

"Tyler Bentley's room, please." The last word was added as an afterthought, Margie forcing herself to aim her venom at those who deserved it.

The girl rolled her eyes and keyed a few strokes into the computer, pulling back when she read what it said. "I'm sorry, but Mr. Bentley isn't seeing visitors at this point." She looked up at Margie and bobbed her head in faux concern. "But we appreciate your concern and will be happy to forward along any messages you wish to leave."

Margie placed each of her palms flat on the desk in front of her and leaned in close, letting the girl see her red-rimmed eyes. "Sure, you do that. Tell him his mother is in the lobby."

The girl's eyes grew large as she stared up at Margie, her mouth framed in a circle as she grasped for words that never came to her.

"Where's my son?" Margie asked, a malevolent gaze leveled on the girl.

"Intensive care unit," she responded, her eyes the size of saucers as she stared up at Margie. "I'm very sorry. Hospital precautions."

Margie ignored the apology. "Where is the intensive care unit?"

"There's a note here from Dr. Manningham asking we page him as soon as you arrive. Would you like me to do that now?"

"If that's what the note says."

The blonde didn't wait for any further response before picking up the phone, hitting a few numbers and setting the receiver down. She fidgeted for ten seconds, avoiding Margie's gaze at all costs, before the phone rang back and she snatched it up.

"Front desk." She paused a moment, listening to the other end. "Yes Doctor, she's standing right here. I'll send her back."

The blonde rose from her chair and pointed down the hall behind her, still avoiding eye contact. "Go to the end of this hallway and turn right. About fifty feet down you'll see a small lounge. Dr. Manningham will be there in two minutes."

Margie murmured a thank you and moved down the hall, leaving the stunned receptionist in her wake. She focused on the far wall, willing herself to keep a level head, and when she reached it took a hard right. She made it only a few steps before a pair of familiar figures emerged in the hallway in front of her.

Sarconi and Dr. Pinkering stood shoulder to shoulder, Dr. Pinkering with his hands raised in front of him.

"Ms. Bentley, thank you for coming so soon. Needless to say, this is quite a shock to all—"

Margie didn't even break stride. Instead she raised her hands on either side and slammed her palms into each of their shoulders. The shot took them both by surprise, parting them just enough for her to march on without stopping.

"Don't go anywhere. I intend to talk to you assholes later."

Neither one made any attempt to chase her as she stormed down the hall and found the lounge. Manningham was already there as she arrived, dressed in a tie and white coat, pacing. He stopped as she approached and went to her, hands extended before him.

"Ms. Bentley, thank you for coming." He gripped her outstretched hand in both of his and shook it.

"Thank you for calling."

Manningham checked either direction and motioned back the way she had just came. "If you wouldn't mind, I was hoping we might be able to speak in my office for a few minutes before we do anything."

All of the venom she'd felt just a moment before drained from Margie, tears pooling beneath her eyes. For the past twelve hours she'd had a mission driving her forward, but now that she was here, the gravity of the situation was settling in on her.

"Can I see him first? Please?"

Manningham studied her for a moment and nodded. "Of course. I apologize for delaying you in the slightest."

Without another word, Manningham led her from the lounge and down the hall, hospital personnel parting to let them pass. He lingered for a moment by the elevators before pushing through a door to the stairwell and leading her up two flights.

The third floor door opened from the stairway into a single large ward. Outfitted in white with fluorescent overhead lighting, it seemed to embody the word *sterile*.

Rows of beds lined either side of the room, most sitting idle and empty. A handful of nurses moved in silence between the few that were occupied, their movements deliberate and subdued.

Manningham paused inside the door and waited for Margie to enter before closing the door behind them. He motioned to the far side of the room with his head and together they walked the ward in silence.

Not one of the nurses or their patients so much as glanced their way as they passed.

A single door sat closed along the wall. Manningham led her to it and pulled it open, motioning for her to enter. "We moved Tyler up here so he could rest easier. The media blitz around here yesterday was pretty intense. Please take your time, I'll be right outside whenever you're ready."

Margie nodded as already tears began to spill down her face. "Ready for what?"

Manningham opened his mouth as if about to speak, but instead closed it and motioned his head towards the door. Margie took the message and stepped inside the semi-darkened room, waiting until the door clicked shut behind her before stepping forward to the bed.

In front of her Tyler lay on his back sleeping, a breathing tube in his nose and over a dozen different monitors attached to various places. From what little bit of him was exposed, Margie could see his skin was ashy, his face sunken in.

To her horror, it looked like he had lost twenty pounds and aged ten years overnight.

Worse still were the two lumps descending from his waist towards the end of the bed. The right side was long and uneven, the shadow on the white blanket showing bumps where his knee and foot protruded upwards.

The left ended well above the knee, the remainder of the blanket tucked flat and smooth.

Margie choked back a sob and crept closer, gripping the corner of the crisp white bedding. She closed her eyes as a pair of teardrops slid to her chin and jerked back the blankets, her eyes opening to stare down at the stump of what was once her son's right leg.

For the second time in as many days, she fell to the floor and sobbed for several long minutes.

When she could cry no more, Margie hefted herself to her feet and replaced the blankets. She tucked them back into place and smoothed them down flat, took her son's hand in her own and stared down at him.

To the world, he was a twenty-two year old man. To her, he would always be her baby, a gift that came along when she herself was just a kid. More than once she and Tyler had talked about how they had grown up together.

If there had been even a trace of moisture left in her body, Margie would have cried it out that very instant. Instead, she just stood and stared down at her son for almost half an hour before prying herself away and returning to the door.

She cracked it open just far enough to see Manningham standing in the ward, a second man in a white coat having joined him. The two men stood with their arms folded across their chests, neither one saying anything as they stared back at her.

Margie nudged the door open and slid through, easing it closed behind her. "So what happens now?"

Her face was red and swollen and her voice held a small crack in it, but she made no effort to cover either.

Dr. Manningham drew his lips tight for a moment and stepped forward. "Ms. Bentley, this is Dr. Andrew Gibson, Head of our Anesthesia Department."

Gibson started to extend his hand, but instead retracted it and nodded to her.

"As I mentioned before, and as I'm sure you could tell, right now Tyler is under heavy sedation. He hasn't been conscious since the accident, so be forewarned that there's no way to know how he'll respond."

Margie nodded. "I understand."

"An accident like this isn't life threatening, but it is life altering.

Many times the shock of losing a limb is more debilitating than the loss itself. A large part of his recovery will be based on how he responds mentally."

Margie nodded again and forced herself to ask the words she'd been dreading for half an hour. "His leg...is there anything we can do?"

Manningham cast a glance to Gibson and nodded. "There is, though not for a while.

"Tyler will be in a wheelchair for the first month or so. He will hate it, but he needs to conserve as much strength as possible to allow his body to heal. As miserable as it will seem, being in the chair will keep him from overexerting himself.

"After that he'll transition onto crutches for a month or two, the time frame depending on his progress. He will have to strengthen what remains of his leg and get it to a position where at the end of summer we'll be able to fit him for a prosthetic."

"Prosthetic," Margie murmured, the word catching in her throat as she tried to push it out.

"Tyler's physical conditioning will put him ahead of schedule compared to most people. It will take a long time and a lot of work, but he should be able to lead a fairly normal life."

From somewhere deep within her, moisture again found its way to Margie's eyes. She shifted her gaze to Manningham and stared at him, saying nothing.

"Maybe not the normal life he's accustomed to, but normal compared to most people." Manningham paused for a moment, shifting out of physician mode. "Ms. Bentley, I know this is a difficult situation, for both of you, but it is important to remember that there are some silver linings here.

"Tyler will be able to walk. With time, he might even be able to participate in Paralympic activities. This isn't the end of the road for him."

Margie nodded, though she was unable to process what Manningham was telling her. Instead, she turned her gaze to Gibson and said, "You're here to wake Tyler up?"

Gibson nodded. "Yes, ma'am."

Margie drew in a deep breath and then another. "Okay. Let's get this over with so we can all start trying to move forward."

Manningham stared at Margie for a moment, nodded his head and extended a hand towards the door. Without prompting, Gibson made his way into the room and went straight to the head of Tyler's bed. Already in place was a stainless steel operating tray, a series of syringes waiting for him.

One by one, Dr. Gibson inserted them into the IV in Tyler's arm, checking the monitors by the bed as he went.

When he was done, he looked at each of them in turn. "It should take about three-to-five minutes for the reversal agent to wake him."

Margie nodded and took a place beside Tyler, gripping his hand and counting off the seconds in her head.

By the time she reached two hundred, his eyelids began to flutter. By three hundred, a deep and violent cough began.

On cue, Manningham disappeared from the room and returned a moment later with water, holding it to Tyler's lips and tipping it back. Not quite awake, Tyler drank the water in long gulps before laying his head back and remaining motionless.

Almost ten minutes passed before Tyler again blinked his eyes open. When he did the haze that had clouded them before was gone, his breathing even and normal.

"Mom? What are you doing here?"

Margie tried to answer, her face contorting itself into a sob before a sound escaped.

Fear and surprise flashed behind Tyler's eyes as he pushed his gaze over to Manningham. "What happened? The last thing I remember was working out."

"Tyler," Manningham began, but Margie raised a hand to stop him.

"Could you give us a minute, please?"

Manningham stared at her a moment before nodding. "Of course."

Together he and Gibson left the room without another sound.

Margie waited until the door closed behind them and stared down at her son. Tears streamed down her face as she stood above him, searching for the words.

"Mom, what happened?"

"Sweetie, you had another accident," Margie said, her voice no more than a whisper.

Tyler stared back at her, terror registering on his features.

"There...there was just too much damage. There was nothing they could do."

Tyler's eyes grew a bit larger, tears of his own beginning to leak from his eyes.

Margie tried to force herself to continue, but the words failed her. Instead she turned her gaze to the flattened stretch of bed where Tyler's leg should be, a single sob sliding from her throat.

Tyler saw his mother's gaze and raised his shoulders up from the bed. It took a moment for his mind to register what he was seeing, his face twisting itself into a mask of anguish as he dropped himself back onto the pillows, his entire body quivering.

Before he could say a word, Margie threw herself down atop her son. After a moment his arms found their way around her.

Neither one moved for a long, long time.

CHAPTER THIRTEEN

Margie stayed by Tyler's side until he cried himself into exhaustion and fell into a deep sleep. Not the peaceful sleep of a man weary after a long day, but rather the uneasy sleep of a man too exhausted to take any more.

If not for the task she was about to perform, Margie would have been in the same exact position.

As soon as Margie was certain Tyler would be asleep for some time, she stole from the room and down the stairs to the main level. Her face was red and puffy, clothes disheveled, hair a tangled mess, but none of it even registered with her.

All that did was the tiny, persistent flame burning within.

Margie burst through the stairwell door onto the main level and out into the hallway, peering into open doors and meeting areas as she passed. Several people cast her wary glances as she went by and a few even attempted to ask her if she needed help, but she blew past them and continued with her search as if they didn't exist.

She spotted Sarconi filling a tall Styrofoam cup with coffee at the end of the hallway and went straight for him. He spotted her from the corner of his eye a moment too late and tried to turn a shoulder to her, a move that only heightened her animosity.

She was on him before he had a chance to move, gripping his elbow. "Where's Pinkering? We need to talk."

Sarconi glanced from her face to his elbow and back again. "I'm sorry. I'm afraid I don't know where *Dr.* Pinkering is right now."

Through gritted teeth Margie seethed, "Then call him, you sanctimonious bastard."

Sarconi again glanced at her grip on his arm. "He's a doctor for crying out loud, he has responsibilities. I'm sure wherever he is right now is where he needs to be. Now, is there something I can help you with?"

"You can help me by finding Pinkering and the two of you explaining why the hell my son lost his leg today!" Margie raised her voice several levels, both out of frustration and to let Sarconi know he wasn't the one in charge at the moment. The tone also brought along the side benefit of causing several curious onlookers to begin peering down the hall at them.

"Ms. Bentley, please. Maybe it would be best to give you a day or so to calm down, perhaps reconvene tomorrow when cooler heads have had a chance to prevail."

"Do not patronize me and do not talk down to me," Margie grunted, her voice lower but just as venomous. "Get his ass here now or I will make the biggest scene this hospital's ever known."

Sarconi stared for a moment at the fire burning in Margie's eyes, then pulled a phone from his hip and dialed a number. "Herb? Yeah, meet me down here by the coffee pot. Ms. Bentley has asked to see us."

Margie released the grip on Sarconi's arm and stood back with arms crossed. A full minute of silence passed between them before Dr. Pinkering swept into the room. He wore the practiced expression of a man used to delivering bad news and extended his arms as if to give Margie a hug.

"Don't you dare touch me," Margie warned, her demeanor stone. "Now, should we do this in private or right out here in the open?"

"Please, Ms. Bentley..." Dr. Pinkering began.

"Private or here?" Margie repeated, her voice rising.

Dr. Pinkering drew himself up a little higher and extended an arm down the hall. "There's an empty conference room just this way."

Margie went first, giving him a contemptuous stare as she passed. Sarconi followed behind her, flicking his gaze towards Margie before rolling his eyes. Dr. Pinkering smirked before circling back in front and leading them into the conference room.

The room was little more than a basic meeting area, with an elongated table dominating the space and a series of high-backed chairs around it. Sarconi went straight to the nearest one and took a seat as Dr. Pinkering closed the door and joined him.

Margie chose to remain standing, pacing back and forth as her hatred-filled stare never left them.

"Why the hell is my son now lying upstairs without his leg?" The words were clipped and measured, the tone clear.

Dr. Pinkering raised a hand and said, "Ms. Bentley, we'd just like to start by saying how sorry—"

"Do not give me that!" Margie screamed, her hands balled into fists by her side. "Why *the hell* is my son missing a leg?!"

The two men sat in stunned silence for a moment. Margie stopped pacing and stared down at them, hell bent not to let either one off the hook.

"Ms. Bentley," Sarconi said, "you can't think this is through some fault of ours, do you? This was a freak accident, nothing more."

"Nothing more? How many people have joints replaced *every day* in this country? How many of them are now lying around without a limb?"

"Ms. Bentley, please you must be reasonable," Dr. Pinkering said.

"Reasonable? *Reasonable*?! My son just had his life ruined and you want me to be reasonable?"

"Ms. Bentley," Dr. Pinkering said, "we are very sorry for the loss of Tyler's leg. We know what that future could have meant to your family, however—"

"Is that what you think?! I'm pissed because our family lost out on some money?!" Margie leaned forward and slapped her palms flat on the desk. "Fuck you, you sick sonsabitches. You make me sick."

"Again," Sarconi persisted, "there is nothing here that says this is our fault. I can appreciate you being upset, but coming after us like this isn't the answer."

"And what is? Letting you guys stick another of your cockamamie contraptions in my son? Somebody else's son?"

"There is no reason to believe the KnightRunner had anything to do with this," Sarconi said, defensiveness evident in his tone. From his seat he matched Margie's stance, leaning forward and staring back at her.

"So Dr. Manningham was lying when he said he split Tyler's leg clear to the ankle looking for something he could save? And that all he found was a bunch of shit broken off from your little gizmo?"

"We still have Tyler's leg here and with your permission we would like to do a complete dissection of it," Dr. Pinkering said.

Margie's lip curled into a snarl as she swung her head from side to side. "If I find out either one of you has been near that leg, I'm coming back here with my chainsaw in hand and taking one of yours."

For the first time, Dr. Pinkering and Sarconi were both wise enough not to question her. Margie remained fixed in place staring down at them for several long moments before pushing herself upright and heading for the door.

"I've already spoken to Dr. Manningham. The minute Tyler is safe to travel, we're heading back to Wyoming before you two fool around and take both his legs from him."

CHAPTER FOURTEEN

Shane hadn't slept a full night since accepting the position with Banks, Webster & Cohen. Six solid months of checking the clock every twenty minutes, of waking up at four-thirty and being unable to go back to sleep.

He hated it, thoroughly despised it in fact, but had long since resigned himself to that being his new reality. It was what it was.

The problem wasn't so much a deep-rooted fear of being late, but rather a complete inability to turn off his mind. The moment his eyes flickered open and coherent thought wormed its way into his brain he was off and racing, his mind running through all the things that needed to get done that day.

Six months of it had turned him into a full blown insomniac. Every morning he was the first to meet a Russian-born immigrant named Victor at his coffee cart on the corner of State Street, the sun still considering whether to make an appearance for the day or not.

Victor was the only person Shane knew that worked as many hours as he did, and was one of just a couple people that he saw outside the office with any regularity. He also knew Victor was supporting a wife and daughter, was grateful for the business, and had grown up in St. Petersburg under Stalin's regime.

That was more than he knew about any of the other friends in his life at the moment.

From there, Shane made the six block trek to work under the watchful eyes of the downtown Boston streetlights each morning. The cleaning crew in his building always finished their rounds just shy of six-thirty, giving him at least a full half hour to drink his coffee and read the paper in the atrium on the first floor.

Aside from the occasional low rumble of a janitor pushing a trash bin or mop bucket past, the building was all his.

At three minutes after six Shane took up his customary chair in the corner and unloaded the bag from his shoulder. He popped the top on his coffee and flipped open the paper, bypassing the Entertainment and Arts sections. He gave a perfunctory glance over the headline news, laughed as he set aside the Money section, and finished up with Sports.

The front page was consumed by early Red Sox action, the hometown boys fresh off a sweep of the Yankees in their first clash of the season. A local resident for less than a year, Shane read the article with bemused detachment. More than once he'd been needled by Bostonians about the Midwest and their love of college football, never once realizing they were every bit as bad when it came to the Sox.

The second page was focused on the latest NBA action, the playoffs now less than a month away. The article held even less appeal to him than the sport itself and he flipped it over, lifting his cup for another pull of coffee. The cup made it half way to his lips before being lowered back to the table, his gaze fixed on a headline tucked away in the bottom corner of the fourth page.

Ohio Tech Star's Career Cut Short

Shane set the coffee down and leaned forward, the elbows of his suit coat resting on the table. He lifted the corners of the paper up so the article was just a few inches away from his face and read.

CATASTROPHIC

Ohio Tech running back Tyler Bentley's career was cut short yesterday when doctors at OTU University Hospital were forced to amputate his right leg several inches above the knee. The University has not issued a statement yet, but it is believed that the amputation is connected to the horrific injury Bentley received to that same leg during the Centennial Bowl.

"This is a tragic day for Tyler Bentley, for Ohio Tech University and for the entirety of college football," OTU Coach Bob Valentine stated last night from his home. "Tyler is an outstanding individual, the kind of individual you hate to see have something like this happen to. Our thoughts and prayers are with him."

Bentley, coming off a season in which he accounted for over 1,700 all purpose-yards and fourteen touchdowns, was expected to be the favorite in this year's Heisman race. He was a top five finisher last season.

    Shane dropped the paper onto the table and leaned back in his chair, his index fingers finding his temples and massaging them in even circles.
    "Really a shame, isn't it?" a voice said, jolting Shane upright. He looked up to see Arthur Webster standing over him, his own coffee in hand and paper folded under his arm.
    Shane swept the paper closed and pushed it off to the side, rising from his chair. "I'm sorry sir, I didn't realize you were standing there."
    Webster smiled and waved a hand at him. "Nonsense, I startled you, I should be the one apologizing. May I join you?"
    Shane extended a hand across the table. "By all means."
    Webster took a seat as Shane lowered himself back into his chair, a slight flush of heat rising to his cheeks. One of the namesake partners of the firm, the man was a veritable icon in New England, someone so far above Shane in the pecking order they had met only once six months before.

"I assume you were reading the article about the kid from Ohio Tech. Quite a shame."

Shane glanced down at the paper in front of him. "Yeah, it is. Tyler's a heck of a good guy, hate to see something like that happen to him."

Webster furrowed his brow and gave Shane a quizzical twist of the head, but said nothing.

"I attended Ohio Tech for undergrad and law school. Last year I had Tyler as a student in a course I was teaching."

Webster's eyebrows rose a bit and he nodded. "Ah, that makes sense. I knew you were an OTU man, just wasn't sure how you and Mr. Bentley knew each other."

Shane drew his lips tight and nodded his head, forcing himself to keep an even tone. "Yes, sir."

The gesture was not lost on Webster, who raised a hand to calm him and chuckled. "Easy now, no need to get offended. I'm not Rex Hartman, I don't much care where people went to school as long they can do the work." He paused and took a swig of his own coffee, his eyes locked on the upside down sports page between them. "I find it rather admirable that you made your own path."

Shane furrowed his brow and raised his gaze to Webster's, this time offering the same quizzical look.

"Your mother was one of the greats, a gentlewoman to deal with and a bulldog in the courtroom. It would have been easy for you to follow in her footsteps to Harvard, go into corporate law, ride her coattails to dizzying heights, but you didn't. You became your own man and I appreciate that about you."

The words hit Shane out of nowhere, as much the subject matter as the praise itself. He could feel his face grow warm and a trickle of sweat form along the small of his back. "Thank you, sir."

"How is your mother these days?"

Just as fast, the blood drained from Shane's face.

"The same, sir."

Webster looked at Shane for several moments with doleful eyes before reaching out and picking up his coffee. "I should be heading in. Only here one day a month, have to make it count. Have a good day, Shane."

"Thank you Mr. Webster, you too."

Shane checked his watch and found it approaching six-thirty, but decided to wait a few extra minutes to let Webster be on his way. The man was nice enough, but if any further awkward conversation could be avoided it would be for the best.

Older people and employers both had a way of doing that. Webster had the extreme misfortune of being both.

Shane watched as the last of the cleaning crew filed out before taking the elevator up to the two-six. It was a few minutes later than usual, but the place was still deserted. Faint sunlight drifted in through the windows and the scent of cleaning product hung in the air.

His mind in several places at once, Shane avoided the latest project that was stacked on the corner of his desk and instead went straight to his laptop. While he waited for it to boot up, he shrugged off his jacket and wrapped it around the back of his chair, gave a quick rearranging of the books piled high in front him.

When his desktop was loaded and ready, Shane went onto the internet and opened the same personal Yahoo Mail account he'd used since he was thirteen years old. He ignored a handful of messages advertising new home interest loans and telling him big beautiful women were looking for him, opting instead to compose a new message.

For several minutes he stared at the cursor blinking in even rhythm back at him before taking a deep breath and beginning to type.

Dear Tyler,

I'm sure you're getting a number of letters of support from your many well-earned fans, but I wanted to pass along a message as well to express my condolences. I was saddened to hear about the loss of your leg and wish you the very best in your recovery process.

I know many people try to say they know what you're going through when in fact they have no idea. I won't fall victim to doing the same thing myself, but I will encourage you to know you are not alone in this and there are many people out there willing to do whatever they can to help along the way.

Best Wishes,
Shane Laszlo

Shane entered the e-mail address saved into his contacts from teaching Tyler a year before and hit send.

Less than a second later, a response landed in his inbox.

Your last message was not received – account no longer valid.

CHAPTER FIFTEEN

Tyler snatched the pitch midair and swung out around the right end, his feet running the play from pure muscle memory. It was the same play he'd been running since he first put on cleats fourteen years ago, his favorite play for almost the same length of time.

Whenever the coaches asked him what play to run, whether it was the state championship in high school or the first day of spring practice his freshman year at Ohio Tech, the answer was always the same.

Pitch right. Just give me the ball and some space.

He hit the corner at full stride and swung around the end, juked past the first defender and cut hard up field. The cornerback flew in off the edge, his momentum wild and out of control. Tyler gave him an easy shoulder fake and left him hugging air, spinning past him like he wasn't even there.

His eyes looked ahead and he saw the linebacker closing and the end swinging free, both converging hard. He never saw the safety. Didn't even know he was there until he felt a blow slam into his left knee, pirouetting him into the air.

There, in that exact moment, is where he always woke up. Never before, never after. Just a second after the hit, long enough to remember, to feel, the pain again as it rippled through his body.

Tyler lay in bed in the darkness of his childhood bedroom and stared at the ceiling, waiting for his heart beat to slow down. He mopped a handful of sweat from his brow and flung heavy droplets to the floor, exhaled and sat up.

The damned wheelchair he'd grown to despise was parked beside the bed, always waiting for him. With no small amount of disgust he pulled it parallel to his mattress, dropped his left leg onto the bare wooden floor and hopped down into it.

His body landed with a thud and he paused a moment to catch his breath before wheeling himself out into the hallway.

Morning number three, in the books.

The clock on the stove said it was not yet seven, but his mother was already gone. He hadn't heard her leave, but it was no secret what a burden he'd become to her. She would never say a word about it, but between unexpected flights to Ohio and having another person around the house, he knew he was putting her in a real crunch.

Tyler wheeled himself to the sink and stood up, using both hands to balance himself on the counter. He took down a glass from the cupboard and filled it with water, then broke a banana off a bunch and settled back into his chair.

Rolling across the kitchen, he shoved a desk chair aside and positioned himself in front of their ancient computer. Several years before the Worland Public Library had upgraded their systems and given the remainders to a half dozen people throughout the community.

The Bentleys had been one of the lucky recipients.

The old Acer whirred and clanked as he finished the banana and water, willing itself to life. Tyler opened a web browser and entered the site for the OTU email access and waited for it to open. Once it did he entered his school issued username and password and waited for it to access his account.

Instead of the traditional interface of his email, a warning popped onto the screen in red letters telling him the combination was incorrect.

Tyler entered the information a second time, a little slower, careful to input every character perfectly. The result was the same, nothing but a stone wall accentuated by red lettering.

"Son of a bitch," Tyler muttered, leaning forward and pecking out the information one letter at a time, using only his two index fingers.

A third warning showed itself.

Tyler took a deep breath and exhaled through his nose, doing his best to remain patient. After only three days in a wheelchair, it was a task that was proving much harder than anticipated.

He glanced again at the clock, the green digits reporting that it was a quarter past seven. "It's after nine in Ohio already."

Tyler closed the webpage and opened a second one, this time navigating to the OTU IT department. As it loaded he wheeled himself to the sink and dropped off his glass, then on to his room to fetch his cell phone. He arrived back in front of the computer just in time to find the IT page ready and waiting.

He thumbed in the number he was looking for and held the phone to his ear. It was answered on the third ring.

"Hello, IT help desk, how may I help you?" a thin and nasal female voice asked.

"Hi, I'm trying to log into my OTU e-mail and keep getting booted for having an invalid username/password combo."

"Alright, your name please."

"Tyler Bentley."

"Just one second," she said, a cacophony of keys echoing in the background. "Our records here show your e-mail was disabled yesterday as the registrar's office informed us you had withdrawn from the university."

Tyler's eyes snapped open wide, his pulse picking up a tick. "Wait, it says that I withdrew for the remainder of the semester, or that I withdrew from the university?"

"Let's see," the girl said, her voice trailing off a bit. "Yeah, here it is. The records show you have withdrawn permanently from the university. All accounts invalid, all outstanding bills turned over to collections."

Tyler's tongue felt like it swelled several times too large for his mouth, one breath after another pushed out through his nose. "You wouldn't happen to have the registrar's number there would you?"

"Certainly," the girl responded and rattled off a string of digits. Tyler jotted them down and thanked her for her time, doing his best to keep his voice even. She didn't have a chance to respond before he thumbed his phone off and back on again and input the new number.

"Good morning, registrar's office, how may I help you?" an older woman asked.

"Yes, ma'am, I was speaking to the IT department earlier about a problem with my e-mail account when I was informed that I have been listed as withdrawn from the university. Is there anybody I can speak to about this?"

"Um, one moment please," the receptionist said and put Tyler on hold.

A full five minutes of bad elevator music passed before a man with a thick voice said, "Brent Sargus here."

"Mr. Sargus, my name is Tyler Bentley—"

"*The* Tyler Bentley?" Sargus asked, astonishment in his voice.

"Feels more like the former Tyler Bentley these days." The words were out of him before he even had a chance to think about what he was saying.

"I was awful sorry to hear about your leg son, you were a damn fine ball player," Sargus said.

Despite the fact that the statement sounded genuine, Tyler couldn't get past his use of the past tense.

He opted to ignore it anyway.

"That's why I'm calling. As you know, I lost my leg a few days ago and withdrew for the remainder of the semester to recover and rehab it at home here in Wyoming. I was told when I left I would still be considered a member of the university and would have full e-mail access, etc. in the meantime."

"Right."

"Well, as of this morning, that's all been stripped away on orders of your office. I've been listed as permanently withdrawn, all accounts inactive immediately."

Tyler could hear papers shuffling on the other end of the line.

"Yes," Sargus said, "that's also true. So what can I do for you?"

"Um, can you start by telling me why?" Tyler asked, the ability to hide his annoyance fading.

"I'm sorry son, but e-mail privileges, loan deferments, things like that are reserved for university students."

"Which I am. I'm just taking a semester off due to injury."

"No son, you withdrew. There's a difference."

The situation itself was starting to wear thin on Tyler's nerves. Sargus's insistence on referring to him as *son* was not helping things any.

"I did not withdraw. I informed Coach Valentine that I was going home for the summer to recover and would be back in the fall to finish my degree and be around the team as much as possible. He said that was fine and he'd take care of everything."

By the time he was done, Tyler realized his voice had risen to a decibel just below yelling. At the moment, he was unable to even pretend to feel bad about it.

The other side of the line went silent for several long seconds before Sargus sighed long and loud. "Son, I think you need to have a talk with your coach."

"I think I do. He'll straighten this out."

Again Sargus paused. "That's not what I meant."

Tyler started to respond, but stopped short. "Meaning?"

"Son, I think you better give your coach a call. If after you talk to him you still need to talk to me, I'll tell Helen at the front desk to patch you straight through. Just give her your name, alright?"

"Um, okay?" Tyler said and signed off the call without another word, a dozen different thoughts running through his mind. Frustrated and confused, he scrolled through his call log, found the athletics office and pressed 'Send.'

A familiar voice answered after two rings. "Good morning, OTU Athletics Office."

"Hey Mindy, is Coach Valentine in?"

"Tyler!" Mindy gushed, her mother hen tendencies pulsating through the word. "How are you feeling?"

Mindy was in her 37th year as receptionist for the athletics office and served as surrogate mother for at least half of the players that came through. She loved doing it and the players loved her for it.

"I'm...I'm getting there," Tyler responded, hoping to stem a flood of questions from her. "It's going to take a while, but I'll get there. Is Coach V around?"

The answer was far more confident than Tyler felt, but he wasn't about to say it.

Mindy seemed to sense it, but let it pass without comment. "Alright hon, well, know I'm thinking about you and praying for you. You come in and see me the second you get back alright?"

"Yes ma'am, I will."

"Alright then, I'll put you through to Coach V."

"Thank you," Tyler said and waited as the line clicked over and rang twice.

"Valentine," a gruff and harried voice responded. It always made Tyler smirk as it couldn't have been more out of place on Valentine. Medium height, painfully skinny and without a single hair on his head, he was anything but gruff and harried.

"Coach, it's Tyler."

Valentine paused a split second before saying, "Hey Ty, how's the leg?"

"Leg's fine, Coach," Tyler said, his tone relaying that their lack of communication had been noticed, "but that's not why I'm calling. I talked to a guy named Sargus over at the registrar's office today and he told me to give you a call."

Valentine let out a long sigh, his voice lowering a bit. "I was going to call you this morning Tyler, I swear I was. I was just waiting for it to be a reasonable hour out there in Wyoming."

"Well, I'm up and here now, so what's going on?"

Valentine paused again. "There's no easy way to say this and I wouldn't begin to sugarcoat it for you even if I wanted to...And I want you to know I did everything in my power to fight this..."

"Just tell me what's going on," Tyler snapped, exasperation in his voice.

"Tyler, the board has decided that due to the nature and severity of your injury, they are rescinding your scholarship."

Every bit of the wind sucked out of the room. Sweat again beaded on Tyler's forehead as he tried to suck in a deep breath of air. "They *what?*"

"The overseers felt that since there's no way you'll ever play football again, those funds should be kept with the team, used to bring in another freshman with this year's class."

Tyler continued gulping in deep breaths. "Coach, you know my family's situation. Without that scholarship, there's no chance in hell I can finish my degree."

"I know Tyler, and I'm very sorry about that, but there's nothing I can do. It was out of my hands."

Hot tears formed along the underside of Tyler's eyes as he continued trying to catch his breath. After several minutes Coach Valentine asked, "Tyler? You alright?"

"I gotta go," Tyler whispered. He signed off the call and flung the phone across the room, the small projectile skittering along the kitchen floor.

Bitter tears leaked down onto his cheeks, but Tyler ignored them as he rose from the wheelchair and hopped out through the backdoor and onto the patio. His bare foot registered the cold concrete beneath him as he moved across it to the old stump in the back yard they used as a chopping block.

An ax handle protruded straight up from the stump, the head buried deep into the ash wood. Tyler dug the head free with his right hand and hefted the ax high above his head, smashing it back down into the stump. Using the handle for balance, he hopped several times to keep himself upright before jerking the ax free and swinging it overhead again.

And again.

Each time the blade hit the wood he screamed, his voice carrying out through the crisp morning air. On the fourth swing he mustered every bit of strength he had and drove the ax head clear to the hilt, the momentum throwing him off balance. For a moment he hung suspended in the air before crashing flat onto his back, the air driven from his lungs.

Upon landing, Tyler made no attempt to get up. Not even an attempt to move. Instead he just laid there, bitter tears spilling sideways down his face, silently cursing everyone and everything he could think of.

CHAPTER SIXTEEN

Most days, Margie worked through her lunch hour without thinking twice. She'd eat a sandwich one bite at a time while running the forklift, using the downtime to make sure the next few loads were ready and waiting when the crew got back on. If she already had the conveyors stacked high, she'd jump on the Bobcat and scoop sawdust or maybe even grab a broom.

It was a lumber yard, Lord knew there was always something to be done.

For whatever reason, when lunch rolled around she had the feeling she should go home and check on Tyler. All morning she'd been trying to shake an empty feeling deep within her stomach, a persistent dread that had started to churn within her.

Something was not right, even if she had no idea what.

The moment the lunchtime whistle sounded, she scurried to her truck and made the short drive home, white-knuckling the steering wheel the entire way. She pulled up to the house at half-past eleven to find all the windows dark, not a sign of life anywhere. Leaving the truck parked at a diagonal on the lawn, she burst through the front door and tossed her gaze from side to side.

"Tyler?" she called a handful of times, each one going unanswered. She pushed through the living room and into the kitchen, coming to a complete stop as she saw the wheelchair sitting empty by the door, Tyler's cell-phone on the floor beside it.

"Oh sweet Jesus, no," she whispered, a band of sweat creasing her brow. She stood rooted in place, unable to move, for several long moments before taking off with renewed vigor, searching every room.

Starting in the bathroom and moving to the bedrooms, she moved through the small house in record time, throwing open doors and calling for her son as she went. When there was no sign of him, she went to the kitchen and grabbed up the phone, her finger poised to dial the local sheriff.

Before it got to the number pad of the phone, Margie stared out the window above the sink. She lowered the phone back to the counter and leaned forward, praying her eyes were deceiving her.

Sitting on the ground leaning back against the splitting stump sat Tyler, his arms by his side and his chin resting on his chest.

Behind him, the thick handle of the ax emerged, only the bottom foot of it visible

"Oh no, oh God, no," she whispered and pushed herself away from the sink and through the back door. She jerked it open and spilled out onto the back porch, the sound causing Tyler to raise his head to stare at her.

"Oh, thank God," Margie whispered, tears spilling down her face as she drew in a deep breath and put her hands to her chest.

Tyler remained where he sat, staring at her, saying nothing.

"Tyler, what are you doing out here? In just a t-shirt and shorts?" she asked, edging towards him. She could see sweat glistening on his forehead, his dark hair wet. "What's going on? How long have you been out here?"

Tyler gazed up at her with red rimmed eyes and shook his head. "Awhile."

"Come on, I'll help you inside."

Tyler shook his head again. "I'd rather stay here for a bit. I like the cool air."

"Cool? Tyler, it's forty-five degrees outside. You're going to catch pneumonia."

Tyler let out a soft smirk. "Kind of be the least of my problems right now, wouldn't it?"

A single tear slid down Margie's face. "Tyler, you can't talk like that. I know you lost your leg, but we're going to get through this."

Tyler raised his head to stare off into the distance, his eyes focusing on nothing as his voice took on a far-off tone. "I talked to Coach Valentine today. Since I can't play ball anymore, my scholarship's been rescinded."

Margie's eyes slid shut as the breath caught in her chest. She made no attempt to respond. The words just weren't there.

"Best part was, I found out because my email account was turned off. Bastards couldn't even extend me the common courtesy of a phone call."

Margie remained motionless, willing herself not break down again in front of Tyler.

"I've gave them three years, three thousand yards and my left leg and they couldn't even give me a year's education. Hell, they couldn't even give me a phone call."

Silence followed, the bitter tone of Tyler's last words hanging in the air. After several long minutes Tyler raised his backside up onto the stump and pulled the ax free. He gripped the head of it and used it as a makeshift cane, hobbling towards the house.

He paused beside Margie just long enough to give her a hug with his other arm before walking on towards the back door.

Margie remained where she was until she heard the back door close behind her. Finally her eyes opened and she followed Tyler inside, standing in the kitchen as he retook his seat in the wheelchair.

"I'm sorry Honey, but I have to get back to work."

"I know, you go on ahead."

"You going to be alright?"

Tyler answered without looking at her. "Yeah, I'll be alright."

Margie nodded and walked to the front door. She paused with her hand on the doorknob and turned to look at Tyler, still seated with his gaze focused out the window above the sink. "What are you going to do?"

The question seemed to pull Tyler from his thoughts. He snapped his focus away from the window and wheeled himself back towards the computer.

"I don't know yet, but I've got a few ideas."

CHAPTER SEVENTEEN

A late spring rain washed over Boston for most of the afternoon, departing just in time to leave the sidewalks wet and glistening as Shane left for the night. The storm clouds had brought with them dark grey overcast and the only light was the fluorescent hue of the street lamps above.

Despite the moisture, the air was warm and Shane decided to walk home. It seemed as good a way as any to spend a Friday evening with no particular plans in sight.

On his way, Shane wandered by a corner pizzeria and got two slices of New York style pie and ate them at a window stool. He sat a few extra minutes to watch handfuls of college students filter past from nearby Emerson and Northeastern before taking up his bag and heading for home.

His mind wandered to the events of the week, and everything still left to do this weekend, as his hands found their way deep into his pockets. Gaze averted, he let himself recede deep into thought before being pulled back by a single vibrating pulse from his cell phone against the back of his hand. Without breaking stride he fished his original 2005 model phone out and flipped it open.

FOUR MISSED CALLS.

Effectively four more than he received the rest of the week combined.

Raising a glance just long enough to make sure he wasn't in anybody's way, Shane scrolled through his phone log to see the same phone number listed four times, all from the 307 area code. For a moment he tried to place who the number might belong to, another to determine if he even knew where the 307 area code was.

Nowhere in Ohio or Boston. Anything beyond that would be pure speculation.

Shane thumbed in the number for his voicemail account and held the phone to his ear, waiting as a digitized voice told him he had four unheard messages. In quick succession they played, the first two nothing more than hang-ups, the third a pair of heavy sighs before signing off.

On the fourth, he hit pay dirt.

"Hey, Shane. This is Tyler Bentley...from Ohio Tech...I don't know if you remember me, but you taught a class I was in last year...."

Shane stopped walking and pressed the phone harder to his ear, his eyebrows raised in surprise.

"Listen, I'm real sorry to call like this but I was kind of hoping to talk to you about something. If you could, please give me a call back at 307-555-4836. It's very important.

"Thanks a lot, hope you are well."

The message ended and Shane pulled the phone away and stared at it in a bit of a shocked stupor. Just that morning he'd tried emailing Tyler, and to his knowledge it hadn't even gone through. The fact that he was now getting a personal phone call from him was surprising to say the least.

A young couple excused themselves around him on the sidewalk, forcing Shane back into the present. He apologized to them and nodded, his feet finding their way home without any active participation from his mind. He waited until he was about to ascend the steps to his building before thumbing on the phone and listening to the message again.

Shane bypassed the elevator and trudged up the stairs to his fourth floor apartment, the message weighing on his mind. There was only one, maybe two, reasons in the world that Tyler would be calling him, neither of which seemed plausible.

Shane walked into his apartment and let his suit jacket slide off his shoulders, tossing it on a chair back. He filled the empty stainless steel bowl on the counter with Friskees for his cat Molly and grabbed a bottle of water from the fridge. Moving slowly he changed out of his suit and into a pair of gym shorts and a hooded sweatshirt, settling down onto his couch at half past ten.

He stared down at his phone for several more minutes before opening it, scrolling through the saved call list and hitting send. The call rang only once before it was snatched up, a brusque voice answering on the other end.

"Hello?"

"Um, yeah, this is Shane Laszlo calling for—"

"Hey Shane, it's me. Thanks for calling me back." Already the tone was lighter.

"No, of course. I'm sorry it took me a while, I got out of work late again with the month end approaching and everything."

"Please don't apologize. Again, I'm just glad you called me back."

Shane leaned back on the couch and propped his feet on the coffee table in front of him. Already the apprehension of calling was fading away, even if the confusion wasn't.

"It's kind of ironic that you called. Just this morning I tried sending you an e-mail, but it bounced back to me. I read about what happened man, just wanted to say I was real sorry to hear about it."

A few seconds of silence passed before Tyler answered, his voice low. "Thank you, I appreciate that."

Shane made a face and cursed himself for saying anything. He should have known Tyler was going through a hard time right now without everyone mentioning it all the time.

"So, uh, what can I do for you Tyler?"

"It starts with that email bouncing back to you this morning, oddly enough. That was about the same time that I found out my email was shut down and my access denied, too."

A banging sound rang out from the kitchen and Shane turned to see Molly up on the counter, already face deep in her food dish. He watched her for just a moment before turning his attention back to the phone.

"I called the IT department and asked if that was standard, and they told me it was for students the registrar's office lists as having withdrawn."

"Withdrawn? As in, permanent?"

"Apparently," Tyler answered, agitation evident in his voice. "And let me tell you, it was news to me as well. I called the registrar's office and asked what the deal was and they routed me to Coach Valentine. Took a whole bunch of hemming and hawing before he'd just level with me."

"Nobody wants to be the bad guy."

"Nope. Took almost an hour on the phone for someone to tell me the athletic department decided to rescind my scholarship the minute I couldn't play anymore."

Shane's jaw dropped open and before he could think to stop himself, he heard his voice say, "You've got be shitting me."

"I wish I were. Three years and just like that, out I went."

A few seconds passed as Shane tried to wrap his head around the news. No less than twenty questions sprang to mind, but he forced them aside. Instead, all he said was, "Damn, I'm sorry to hear that."

Almost a full minute of silence passed, long enough to make Shane fidget. He was about to ask if Tyler was still there when he spoke again.

"Listen Shane, I know we don't know each other all that well, and of everybody I knew at OUT, you don't owe me a thing, but I could really use your help."

Shane made no attempt to hide his surprise. "Well sure, I mean, I'd like to help in any way I can. Fact of it is though, I'm not a doctor or a therapist or anything like that. I don't know if you remember, but I'm a lawyer. I'm not sure how much help I can be."

"That's just it, I don't need somebody in the medical field right now. That damage has already been done. What I need now is a lawyer to help me get what's coming to me."

Shane blew out a puff of air and ran a hand back through his hair. "Tyler, I don't mean be obtuse here, but I'm not sure what you mean."

"They took my damn leg, Shane," Tyler said, his tone non-negotiable. "I did everything they asked me to, and that still wasn't enough."

"Tyler, don't take this the wrong way because I'm on your side here, but you can't go after the athletic department to get your scholarship back. It wouldn't be worth the time or money you have invested, even if you win."

"I'm not worried about the scholarship right now. To be honest, I don't know that I'd go back there even if they begged me to."

Shane remained silent a moment, his mind racing. "If you're thinking of going after the university for civil damages..." He let his voice trail off, trying to figure out how that would play out, almost certain it wouldn't be good.

"I'm not thinking of going after the university for civil damages," Tyler said, his tone even, resolute. "When I hurt my knee I was convinced by my doctors that it was beyond saving, that the only chance I ever had at walking, of playing, ever again was to try this joint implant of theirs. My doctors, the medical reps, everybody told me this new KnightRunner was my golden ticket. I'd be back on the field by this fall, be ready for the draft next spring.

"Not even four months later and I'm sitting here talking to you from a wheelchair."

Shane could hear the bitterness in Tyler's tone, almost see the expression that must be worn on the other side of the line.

"So you want to do what? Go after the company that made the device?"

"Yes," Tyler answered without even a pause to consider his answer.

"Hmm," Shane said, mulling the proposition. "Plusses and minuses there for sure. Public opinion would be on your side, and they'd have deep, deep pockets should you win. Of course, the flip side of that is they'll be able to bring in teams of lawyers, experts, customer testimony."

"But you're telling me it can be done?"

"I'm doing nothing of the sort. I'm just giving you my very preliminary, very off-the-record impression. That's all."

Tyler sighed on the other end. "Look, Shane, I appreciate that, but I'm not calling you off-the-record. I'm calling to see if you'll take my case."

Shane leaned forward on the couch, his elbows resting on his knees. "Your case? Tyler, all I even know about this situation is a one-paragraph article I read in the paper and now a three-minute phone call with you. There's no way I can tell if you have a case here."

Tyler pushed ahead as if he hadn't heard a word Shane said. "The only other lawyer I know is here in Worland, handles wills and bankruptcies. Great guy, older than dirt, pretty sure he doesn't even know what Viagra is, let alone a KnightRunner."

"That still doesn't necessarily make me any better," Shane said, his voicing rising. He almost continued, but stopped himself short and took a deep breath. When he began again, his voice was lower, more even.

"Look, Tyler, I appreciate the gesture and am even quite flattered, but I'm not what you're looking for either. I'm an environmental lawyer fresh out of law school. I'm not even licensed in Ohio and I have no idea what their reciprocity rules are. There has to be hundreds of guys better qualified out there for this than me."

Tyler paused just a moment before pushing on, undeterred. "Shane, I had all day to think about this. I called you for two reasons. One, I know you and trust you. You were always very fair to me and never treated me like a football star. I appreciated that.

"Two, I called you because you're young and fresh out of law school. I can't afford anybody else."

Shane rubbed the temples on either side of his forehead in small circles. What Tyler was saying wasn't wrong, but that didn't mean it was what he wanted to hear either. "Yeah, I get what you're saying."

"I can't pay you for the trial, but if we win, I promise to make it worth your while."

Shane continued on his temples as Molly joined him on the couch, her pink tongue darting out to clean around her mouth. She ventured a dark grey paw out as if she might crawl up onto his lap, but thought better of it and retreated.

"Believe me when I tell you, the money isn't what I'm worried about. It's just, in addition to every reason I just told you, there are issues that make this a bad idea for me personally.

"I'm a junior man in a very coveted position at a firm here in Boston. It was not easy to get into and I doubt they'd be too keen on letting me leave for several months to try a civil case."

This time Tyler took several moments to respond, and when he did his voice was soft and low. "Shane, I understand that, I do. And Lord knows nobody hates asking for help more than me, but I am asking for your help. This isn't about greed, this is about protecting my mother. About giving her the life my leg won't let me anymore."

Shane stared out the window at the city lights dancing off the water of the Charles River. Every impulse in his body told him to apologize and hang up the phone, but something in Tyler's words wouldn't let him.

"Who's this medical company you're thinking about going after anyway?"

There was paper shuffling on the other end of the line and Tyler said, "Guy's name was Sarconi, works for a company named SynTronic."

Shane's eyes hardened as he stared at a single orange light visible on the opposite bank of the river. His breath caught in his chest as he locked in on it, the temperature in the room rising several degrees. "SynTronic?"

"Yeah, you ever heard of them?"

Shane nodded his head. "You could say that."

CHAPTER EIGHTEEN

All told, Tyler and Shane spent two hours on the phone Friday night. Shane was back in the office by seven the next morning, using company resources to perform research that had nothing to do with the environment. He stopped just after four in the afternoon and returned home with a ream of printouts in hand, a list of questions as long as his arm in his briefcase.

That afternoon they talked for four more hours, this time being joined on the call by Margie. One by one Shane went through his list of questions, scrupulously taking down every note he could, and recording the conversation to be sure he didn't miss anything. More than once a question led him down a path he'd never even considered, the time disappearing before his eyes.

After a Sunday spent the same exact way, two things were brutally clear to Shane. He was in way over his head, and there was no way he could hope to do Tyler justice and remain in his current state of employment with Banks, Webster & Cohen.

Monday morning, Shane arrived at the office even earlier than usual. He spent a couple of hours taking a stab at some of the paperwork Hartman had left for him, but after the events of the weekend he just wasn't interested in it. His mind couldn't turn off the case at hand, his thoughts drifting back to dwell on some unanswered question, to reconsider an as-yet-untouched angle.

By noon, he shoved the paperwork to the side and opened a blank email box. For someone that had spent the previous six months being as invisible as possible, sending such an email was one of the very last things on earth Shane wanted to do. He'd been trying to send it since Saturday morning, when he first realized this was a conversation that had to happen, and fast, but he couldn't bring himself to type it. Same thing all day on Sunday.

Now here it was midday on Monday, precious time dripping away, and he was still trying to find the words.

Shane slid his eyes closed and took a deep breath, pushing aside the din of office noise around him. He thought back to the previous few days, to the unwavering conviction in Tyler, to the quiet desperation in Margie, and swallowed the lump in his throat.

He typed the email and hit send without once even raising his eyelids.

Mr. Hartman,

I need to speak with you this afternoon in private. It's important.

Shane

The rest of the afternoon was spent alternating glances between the clock and his email account, hoping for a response that never came. As the afternoon withered away and other associates began to head for the door, Shane had the feeling he was being blown off.

At a quarter after six Hartman surprised him by showing up, already shrugging on his jacket and carrying a briefcase in hand. His face worse a mask of indifference, everything about him letting Shane know that he didn't appreciate being summoned.

"Hey, you needed to see me?"

Shane felt his stomach tighten, the visit coming as a surprise. Already he'd resigned himself to at least one more day waiting to talk to him, his guard down. Still, he wasn't about to let an opportunity pass. "Yeah, you have a few minutes?"

Hartman made a show of checking his watch and sighing. "I have to have the kids at little league practice in an hour, but I can spare a couple. What's up?"

Shane glanced around the two-six to see a large handful of associates still around, a few even casting sideways glance their way. "Can we step down into the conference room for a moment?"

Hartman checked his watch again, gave a look that bordered on a glare to Shane, and sighed again. "Alright, but the clock's running, make it quick."

Shane was already on his feet and past him, opting against the elevator and leading them down a flight of stairs to the twenty-fifth floor. He paused outside the conference room door and let Hartman enter before closing the door behind them.

Hartman slapped his briefcase down on the table and fell into a seat, watching Shane as he stood pacing just inside the door. "Look, Shane, I don't know what this is all about, but I really should be going."

Shane nodded and decided to come right out with it. "I've been asked to handle a civil matter back in Ohio. It has the potential to be an enormous case with far reaching implications."

Hartman's eyebrows rose a bit and he smirked. "Regarding what, might I ask?"

"Medical malpractice."

Another smirk. "You do realize you work for an environmental firm in Massachusetts? And that there are plenty of lawyers in Ohio that are much better suited for that kind of thing, right?"

"I realize both of those things, but this is different. I know this guy, and it's a pretty outrageous set of circumstances."

Hartman cocked his head to the side and studied Shane for a moment, condescension evident in his gaze. "Please tell me this isn't actually what you wanted to speak to me about, that you're not seriously considering this?"

"Well..."

"Because if you are, you're a bigger idiot than I thought."

The statement evaporated any sort of a response from Shane's mind, instead filling it with white-hot anger. He closed his mouth and leveled a stare on Hartman, his dark eyes flashing.

"Do you have any idea how many people lined up for your job? How many we passed over to hire you? People with much better credentials, but maybe not quite as much *name recognition*?"

Shane felt his face grow two shades hotter, venom rising into the back of his throat. Still, he tried to swallow it. He was here to ask for a special circumstance, not quit his job.

"I realize all of that, but just the same I was hoping I might be able to take a sabbatical for a while, just until this case is wrapped."

"Sabbatical? Wrapped?" Hartman asked with a contorted face. "What do you think this is? Undergrad at Pissant College in Ohio, where you can just take a semester off to go find yourself? This is one of the preeminent environmental law firms in the country, the kind of opportunity first year law students go to bed and jerk off thinking about."

"I realize that, but—"

Hartman slammed his feet on the floor and stood, snatching his briefcase up from the table. "But nothing, Laszlo. Believe me when I tell you your ass better be here tomorrow, and every day after that, or I'll find someone that will!"

Red faced and angry, Hartman stomped out, purposely slamming his shoulder against Shane's on the way past. The blow twisted Shane a half turn at the waist, his gaze following his boss out into the hall. He stood rooted in place a moment, listening to Hartman mutter as he stomped away, before following him out into the hall.

"Hey, Rex," Shane called, his voice oozing with insubordination, loud enough that several heads turned to stare at him. "Go ahead and start looking for that someone. I'm doing this withf or without your approval.

"I quit."

CHAPTER NINETEEN

Monday night Shane slept seven uninterrupted hours, the shades drawn low and Molly curled up against his hip. By the time he finally rousted himself awake and stood before his bedroom window, he was amazed how much better he felt.

Even more amazed to see the sun rise from somewhere other than his desk.

Living a Spartan existence since moving to Boston, the entire process of preparing himself for relocation took no more than a couple of hours. A single phone call to the furniture rental company took care of the bed, dresser, and sofa that furnished his apartment. The place was little more than an above average sized room and there wasn't space for any more than that.

A second call went to the landlord, who agreed to let Shane out of his lease provided she could keep the deposit and Shane could be out by the next day.

Shane agreed to both terms readily.

After that went calls to the electric company and his internet provider to discontinue services, his every connection to the Boston community cut off just that fast.

Shane enjoyed a slow morning around the apartment with Molly while waiting for the morning traffic to abate before loading everything he owned into his faded blue Honda. A couple of bags of clothes, a George Foreman grill, a few picture frames, and a box already overflowing with information for the case at hand.

Shane made one last stop in the North End for some cannoli from Mike's Pastry before jumping on the Mass Pike and heading east. Just shy of noon, he was headed home, pastry in hand, famous Citgo sign in the rearview mirror.

Molly made it just barely out of Massachusetts and into Rhode Island before finding a sunny spot in the passenger seat and curling into a tight ball. By the time they crossed over into Connecticut a half hour later, she was asleep and purring, her thick charcoal fur warm to the touch.

Shane left the radio off as he set the cruise control and steered them through the clear spring day, his mind chewing on a dozen different questions. One by one he tried to work through them, the various strings of thought eventually all melding into one in his mind.

A sign welcomed them to New York as he shook himself from his thoughts and lifted his cell-phone from the dash. He thumbed four-one-one in and waited as an automated voice asked him what listing he desired.

"Ohio Tech University Law School, please."

"One moment," the digitized female voice responded, and a second later the line began to ring. It was answered after the third ring by a real life woman that sounded only faintly less automated and infinitely more bored.

"Good afternoon, OTU Law, this is Sandra. How may I help you?"

"Professor Jon Prescott, please."

"May I ask whose calling?"

"Shane Laszlo."

"Please hold," Sandra said and flipped him over to an elevator music cover of Eric Clapton's *Layla*.

Shane put the phone on speaker and dropped it into his lap,

humming along as he changed lanes through the light traffic. He strummed his thumbs against the steering for several bars as the song played on, Molly opening a condemning eye to stare at him from the passenger seat.

She was saved by a warm voice filling the line.

"Jon Prescott."

Shane snapped the phone up from his lap and turned off the speakerphone, pressing it against his face.

"Professor Prescott, Shane Laszlo. How are you, sir?"

Shane could picture Prescott's face as a heavy chuckle boomed through the phone. "Shane! My boy, so good to hear from you! I am very well indeed, and how are you?"

Over the years Prescott had gotten quite adept at masking his English accent while lecturing, but in the company of friends it came across much thicker. Shane couldn't help but smile at the last words that came out 'how aww you?'

"I am also very well."

"So to what do I owe the pleasant surprise of hearing from one of my favorite students out of the blue?"

"You mean former students, right?" Shane corrected.

"Nonsense dear boy, my students will always be my students. They may go far and do great things, but they are always my students."

Shane smiled, knowing full well this was what made Prescott such a favorite at the school. He genuinely cared about them and how they fared.

It was also why, of everybody, Shane made the first call to him.

"Well," Shane said, taking a deep breath, "I'm calling with a bit of an unusual request. I know the end of term is coming up, but I was wondering if you might know of any students in need of a summer internship-type position."

"Internship-type position?" Prescott asked, feeling the words out even as he spoke them. "Banks, Webster & Cohen opening up the doors a little bit this summer are they?"

"Not quite. This wouldn't be a firm gig, it would be working with me directly."

"For you? Has something happened?"

Shane decided to change directions. "Let me start over. I know to you football will always be Manchester United, but have you managed to watch any of the American game in your time at OTU?"

"Well I should say I have," Prescott responded, his voice full of pride at the admission. "Every year the faculties gather and watch the Michigan A&M game at the end of the season. Quite a good show I might add. Not as much fun as a penalty kick shootout, but a right good time just the same."

Shane smiled and shook his head. "Then you might have noticed a player for OTU by the name of Tyler Bentley."

"Oh yes, of course. Extraordinary player as I remember it, I'm told he should be quite the professional player."

"Well, not anymore," Shane said, deciding to cut directly to the heart of the matter. There would be plenty of time for tiptoeing around the gravity of the situation at a later date.

"In the last game of the season Tyler hurt his knee. The University hospital partnered with a company called SynTronic and developed some sort of new prosthetic implant and convinced Tyler to try it.

"Long story short, it didn't work and now he only has one leg."

Prescott's breath caught in his throat, a low rumbling sound that sounded like a smoker first waking in the morning. "My heavens! That's horrible. What's he going to do?"

"He went back home to Wyoming to recover from his injuries with the intention of returning in the fall to finish his degree, but to his surprise the minute he left they rescinded his scholarship."

"Oh my," Prescott said, a low shrill whistle sounding through the line. "So he's turning to the law?"

"Believe me when I say, he doesn't want to, but he's kind of backed into a corner here. It's just he and his mom and they come from very limited means."

"I see, I see," Prescott said in rapid-fire fashion, his voice faraway.

Shane could picture him staring off into space, scratching his beard, rolling the situation around in his mind.

When he spoke, his voice was serious. "You know what you're going to be up against here don't you?"

Shane raised his eyebrows and nodded his head. "That's why I'm calling to see if there are any students that might be able to help me.

"We want to move fast on this, while his name is still fresh in people's minds and so he can finish his studies and get on with his life. I know most students have already secured positions for the summer, but if there is anybody that you might know of…"

Shane let his voice drift off, the question hanging in the air. Prescott didn't grab the bait for several long moments.

When he did, his tone was hurried, almost fervent. "Where are you right now? When will you want to start?"

"I'm on the road to Ohio now, should be arriving sometime late tonight."

"Can you be in my office by ten o'clock tomorrow morning?"

Again Shane's eyes bulged a bit with surprise. "Does that mean you know someone?"

"I look forward to seeing you tomorrow at ten o'clock Shane," Prescott repeated, avoiding Shane's question. "Good day, sir."

"You too, Professor. Good day," Shane responded and hung up the phone. He couldn't be sure what Prescott had in mind, but he knew he had enough other things to figure out between now and then to let it go until tomorrow.

CHAPTER TWENTY

The fact that Shane was from Ohio didn't necessarily mean it was home. Most of his friends from law school had scattered to the winds for work, just as he did. Very few from undergrad did he keep up with. The ones he followed from his childhood were almost all married, with children, or both.

He had even less family, which was to say virtually none, to call on.

Shane and Molly rolled into Columbus a little after midnight, pulling into a Comfort Inn on the edge of town. The plan wasn't to drive the whole way in one day, but after Prescott asked him to be on hand the following morning, he didn't have a choice.

Not that it much mattered to Shane. He'd gotten enough sleep the night before and had enough on his mind to drive for days. When the white sign with blue lettering passed overhead welcoming to him to The Buckeye State, it just vaguely registered. Little more than a few hours later when the signs started naming off suburbs he'd played ball in as a kid.

Besides, Prescott was going out of his way to help him. The least he could do was show up when asked to.

The room was small and smelled bad, the dregs of the place being all that was available for somebody that shuffled in as late as he did with a pet. For the second night in a row he slept well, though his body jerked awake after just five hours, still not used to the amount of blissful sleep it was receiving.

The next morning he rose, showered and shaved, loaded Molly and his overnight bag back into the car and drove the remaining few miles to the OTU campus. Almost a full year had passed since he'd stepped foot on the place, thought it still held a familiarity that felt like he'd only been gone a couple of weeks.

Conscious not to let his mind fall into a state of nostalgia, he maneuvered his Honda from memory and parked in one of a handful of visitor's spots in front of the law school. He emerged from the car and took a deep breath, looking out at the place that for three years had been his home.

The OTU Law School consisted of a tight cluster of buildings on the northern end of campus, not far from the Columbus outer belt. All of them were done in a matching colonial style, outfitted in dark red brick that easily set them apart from the rest of campus.

A handful of students walked back and forth between the buildings and two young girls sat outside on the steps reading, though none so much as glanced his way. Molly opened but one eye as Shane pulled his briefcase from the backseat, making no effort to move as he slammed the door shut.

Now in their fourth year together, the two had covered much of the country in the Honda. Shane knew she would be just fine for up to fourteen hours so long as she had a sunbeam to stretch out in.

Dressed in tan slacks and a burgundy button down, Shane stepped into the Anderson Hewlett Law Building at ten minutes to ten and headed for Prescott's office. There waiting on him was a note taped to the door telling him to meet in the conference room.

Without a second glance, Shane reversed his course and headed to the third floor.

The heavy oak double doors at the top of stairwell were propped open and Shane stuck his head inside to see a long dark wood table taking up much of the space. The heavy buzz of conversation filled the air as throngs of students stood around the table, many lost in conversation. Along the far wall Shane recognized Prescott, his white hair and omnipresent cup of tea unmistakable amongst the young crowd.

Shane turned his shoulders and slid inside without pushing open the door, walking towards the far end. Again, nobody even looked his way as he lowered his briefcase onto the table and strode towards Prescott.

His old friend greeted him the way he always did, with arms wide and a hearty embrace, just one of many ways that he didn't quite fit the mannerisms of his native England. "Shane Laszlo, quite good to see you, sir!"

Prescott practically beamed as he apprised Shane, his voice just a decibel or two below shouting.

"Good to see you as well," Shane returned. "And again, thank you so much for doing this."

"Nonsense," Prescott said with a wave of the hand. "It was nothing, no need for thanks."

Shane smiled and nodded. Almost a year had passed, but Prescott was the same as he had been the last time they spoke. He had a thick shock of wavy white hair he was in a perpetual battle to keep tamed and a ruddy face with a bulbous nose and watery blue eyes. His style trended towards plaid ties and cardigan sweaters, both stretched taut over a well fed midsection.

Sprinkled liberally with a British accent and booming personality, he was almost a walking caricature unto himself.

"Wow, this is, uh, quite a showing," Shane said, waving a hand around the room. "All these people are interested to help out with the case?"

Prescott gave a non-committal turn of his head. "Well, not quite. On such short notice the best I could do was put out the word that a prized former pupil was looking for help on a case this summer and in need of interns. I went to bed last night hoping somebody would show and came back this morning to see a throng of people waiting for me to open the doors."

"Lot of first-years still looking for summer work?" Shane asked, his gaze sweeping over the crowd, most of which trended quite young.

Prescott offered a wan smile. "That obvious?"

"Hey, I'll take it," Shane said, patting his friend on the arm, glancing at the clock on the wall above them. "It's now five minutes past. Shall we get started?"

Prescott extended a hand towards the table. "It's your room Counselor, by all means proceed."

Shane smirked at the choice of words and walked back to retrieve his briefcase. He became aware of several pairs of eyes following him as he walked to the head of the table and set the case down again, leaving it unopened in front of him.

"If you could all please find a seat, I'd like to get started."

It took a moment for the instruction to pass through the crowd, the noise dying away as students lowered themselves into seats or turned to face him. Shane did a quick scan as they settled into place and found he didn't recognize a single face.

The OTU Law School graduated just over one hundred people each year, meaning the student body got to know each other quite well. The fact that Shane was only a year removed and didn't recognize anybody meant every last person before him was a first year.

Despite what he'd said to Prescott just a moment before, he felt a small tug in the pit of his stomach. It wasn't the best way to start things off.

Shane turned over his shoulder and whispered to Prescott, "So these students have no idea why they're here right now?"

"Just that you might have a summer job for them."

Shane nodded and turned back to the silent and waiting cluster of people before him. "First of all, thank you all for coming. Professor Prescott and I both appreciate it, especially on such short notice.

"I apologize in advance if I seem harsh or curt, but the fact is I don't have a lot of time and I know at this point in the semester most of you don't either. For that reason, and to protect the confidentiality of my client, I'll be brief. If selected, you'll be brought up to speed very, very quickly.

"My name is Shane Laszlo and the reason I contacted Professor Prescott, and he by extension contacted you, is I am looking for a team of interns to assist me in a case that I will be working this summer.

"Part medical malpractice, part contract fraud, and at least a few parts something I haven't yet discovered. I was hired on a couple of days ago and have only just begun to research everything that will be involved."

"Who's the client?" a young man with blonde hair asked.

"Again, due to confidentiality purposes, I cannot disclose that until I have hired my team. I will go as far as to say though, most if not all of you have heard of them before."

"Alright, so who's the defendant?" the same man asked.

Shane glanced over at the young man, knowing the type all too well from his time in school. Some called people like him gunners, others called them sharks.

Shane preferred to say they were pricks, occasionally bastards, once in a great while assholes.

It didn't bode well for this guy already.

"Like I said, all the moving parts are still being parsed out. On the med-mal portion we're looking at a company called SynTronic out of New Jersey. Big place with a lot of money, experts on staff, and no doubt a top flight legal team.

"On the contract portion, we're looking at none other than Ohio Tech University."

The last statement was meant to be a grenade, and it landed with exact precision. Within seconds the air seemed to suck out of the room, many faces averting their gaze to avoid eye contact. One young woman even went as far as to push a low shrill whistle out between her teeth.

Shane scanned the faces once more. "I'm fully aware that this might be more than some of you bargained for, and believe me, I understand. For that reason, we'll now take a quick five minute break.

Anybody that wants to leave may do so, no questions asked, no hard feelings.

"Thank you all for coming."

With that, Shane shifted his focus to his briefcase, removing a legal pad, a pen, and over two inches of research he'd already printed out. Around him he could hear chairs sliding and people moving about, but he made a concerted effort not look up.

Despite appearing immersed in the papers before him, Shane did little more than count off seconds in his head as the time ticked by. At the conclusion of five minutes he raised his gaze to assess who would be in the trenches with him for the next several months, helping him navigate what could well be a landmark case.

His hope was to pull as much as twenty percent from the crowd that had gathered, enough to have a half dozen gophers running after everything he needed.

What he got were two people, both looking terrified.

The deserted room, just a moment before filled, jarred Shane and for a moment he stared, his lips parting in an involuntary expression of surprise. Both stared back at him before lowering their gaze, one fidgeting in place while the other looked down at a blank legal pad.

Shane blinked hard twice, drew in a deep breath and moved to shut the heavy oak door. "Alright, if you would both please come down here to the end of the table, we'll get started."

This was his first time leading a legal team of any kind before, but he'd seen Hartman do it enough over the preceding six months to know how and how not to interact with people. Besides, one of the few upsides to working with first years was it would be a lot like his teaching experience the year before.

Shane returned to his chair as the two of them rose and slid their belongings to the end of the table. He waited for them to get seated before turning over his shoulder to say, "Professor Prescott, I can't thank you enough for your help and I realize I have already taken up a great deal of your time. If it's alright we work in here, I won't bother you any longer."

Prescott stirred his tea once more, tapped the spoon against the rim of the cup and placed it on the table behind him. "If you don't mind, I would like to stick around. You said you are in need of help and I intend to give it."

Shane's mouth fell open, his second round of shock in as many minutes.

"Do bear in mind," Prescott cautioned, "I am an academic and have been for many years, I'm not even bar certified in Ohio. I won't be of much aid in the courtroom, but anything else please do not hesitate to ask."

"Thank you very much," Shane said and stood up from his chair, extending a hand towards it. "Please."

"Nonsense," Prescott said, taking back up his tea. "Like I said before, this is your room Counselor."

Shane lowered himself back into the seat and regarded the two new recruits in front of him. "As I said before, my name is Shane Laszlo, undergrad and JD both from OTU. I've spent my time since working for Webster, Banks & Cohen in Boston." He left the year of his graduation and the length of his tenure with the firm both vague on purpose. "And you are?"

They both sat in silence a moment as Shane kept his head pointed forward, his gaze flicking from one to the other. The young man to his right spoke first, nodding his head to each person in the room.

"Heath Wilson, grew up on a farm in southern Ohio. Studied mechanical engineering in undergraduate here, ended up in law school after all the fuss over genetically modified products almost bankrupted the farming industry."

Shane nodded his head and studied Heath for a moment. He was of average size with close cropped hair and a skin tone that made him look very tan. His voice held a bit of both a drawl and a reserved nature.

"Welcome," Shane said, shifting his attention to a young lady to his left. She was several inches shorter than Shane and had a slight build, her sandy brown hair rail straight. It fell just past her shoulders and framed simple features, free from any sort of cosmetic enhancement.

"Hi," she said with a partial smile, "Abby Hill, from Coshocton. I graduated from Kent State last year with a degree in early childhood education and decided to come here after my grandfather passed. He was a longtime lawyer in our community."

Shane waited a moment to see if she would continue, but just as fast she retreated back into silence.

As far as first impressions go, Shane was at least glad he wouldn't have any gunners to deal with. On the flip side, it appeared that he would be doing all the talking in every meeting they ever had, internal or external.

Shane nodded. "Thank you both for being here, and for having the courage to stick around. I know this is all very last second and a pretty daunting task, so I appreciate the help.

"First and foremost, I was being a little dramatic earlier. We have no intention of going after Ohio Tech for contract fraud. Given the circumstances, it wouldn't be a very good use of our time or limited resources.

"I only said that because I didn't have the time to conduct a formal interview process for over two dozen people. Instead, I thinned the crowd by dropping one little hint of adversity and seeing who ran away."

He paused, cracking a half smile. "Wasn't expecting it to work quite that well, but here we are."

Heath kept his gaze locked on Shane, while Abby offered a half smile in response.

"Make no mistake though, I wasn't kidding when I mentioned SynTronic and their endless resources. There's a chance this could get quite ugly before it's all over."

Shane glanced back at Prescott, who nodded. He was off to a good start.

"Alright, let's get started," Shane said, clapping his hands in front of him and rising. Heath and Abby both sat back in surprise as he stood and walked to a bank of controls on the wall, turning on the overhead projector. A blue square appeared on command from it, illuminating the far wall across from them.

Shane returned to the table and pulled his laptop from his bag, booting it to life and running a long cord from it into a wall jack below the bank of switches he was just using. His computer desktop sprang up on the wall, the three others watching in surprise as Shane connected to the internet and opened a video chat program.

Less than a minute later, the face of Tyler Bentley filled the wall.

The image caused Shane to take pause for just a moment. It had been not quite a year since he'd last seen him in person, significantly less since he'd seen him on television, but already he looked like a different person. His eyes were sunken back into his face, his cheeks hollow. A few days of growth was spread across his jawline.

Shane blinked himself back into the moment and turned to the others in the room. "Lo-tech video conferencing," he said with a smile, dimming the lights so Tyler's face was more visible.

"Can you hear me alright?" Shane asked, raising his voice just a bit for effect.

"Sure can," Tyler responded, a thumb-up appearing in the corner of the screen below it.

"Tyler, I am here with Professor Prescott from the law school and Heath Wilson and Abby Hill, both students here. I apologize that you can't see us but my web cam is still in a box somewhere. I promise you'll have video before next time.

"Everyone, meet Tyler Bentley."

Tyler waved a hand in front of the screen. "That's alright, I'm just sorry you all have to look at me right now. My mother always said I have a face for radio."

Everyone at the table chuckled.

"No, but seriously, I appreciate you doing this and I'm glad to know all of you."

"Okay," Shane said, "we're all here, legal pads out and ready, recorder on the laptop running. I know you've already gone through this once in the last few days for me, but would you mind doing it again?"

"From the top?" Tyler asked.

Shane paused and considered the question. "Tell you what, why don't you cut to the punch line here at first, then go back and start at the beginning. Might as well get the shock factor out of the way and let everybody know what they're working with."

Tyler nodded his head and pushed himself back from the computer. As he did, his voice grew further away, the sound of movement masking some of his words.

"I don't know if any of you folks are football fans, but up until recently I played for Tech. I don't know how true it is, but I've been told I was pretty good."

Heath snorted and whispered, "You could say that."

Shane nodded and watched as Tyler rose from his wheelchair and pulled back the leg of his gym shorts to reveal the stump of his left leg. The skin of his thigh was pale white, ending in a twist of scar tissue several inches above the knee.

"Of course, that was before the Centennial Bowl. Since then, with more than a little help from the folks at OTU Hospital, this is what I've been working with."

Tyler remained balanced on one leg, wagging the stub at the camera so everybody got a good look at it. Shane was past the point of being surprised, but he could tell his two new cohorts weren't there yet. To his right, Heath stared at his legal pad, glancing up every few seconds as if seeing something he shouldn't be. Across from him, Abby sat in muted silence, her face so pale it was almost translucent.

Behind them Prescott took in a sharp breath of air, but said nothing.

Once everybody had gotten a good look, Tyler lowered himself back into the wheelchair. Shane reached out, muted the microphone on the computer and asked, "Does anybody have anywhere they need to be today?"

Heath and Abby both shook their heads from side to side.

Shane turned the volume back on as Tyler repositioned himself in front of the camera. "Alright, now start at the beginning. Everything you say here is confidential, so take all the time you need and spare no details."

It took almost two solid hours for Tyler to relay back everything that happened, starting with the hit on New Year's Eve and ending with his conversation with Coach Valentine a couple days before. On a few occasions Shane or Prescott interjected clarifying questions, but for the most part everyone listened in silence, taking notes.

Despite already having a complete copy, Shane again transcribed every word that was said. If there was additional information the second time through, he wanted to be sure to have it. If there was any discrepancy between the stories, he needed to be sure to clarify that as well.

Several times throughout the call Tyler's voice broke and once he even had to look away for a moment, but he managed to hold himself together. When he was done, he looked exhausted, dotted with perspiration.

Shane thanked him for his time and told him they had more than enough to begin with before letting him go.

Just after noon, Prescott excused himself to prepare for a class. Heath and Abby broke for lunch before returning to find Shane in the law library, the results of his weekend efforts spread across the table. They both settled in across from him in silence, waiting as he typed on his laptop.

"So here's the plan, for the time being," Shane said, never taking his gaze from the screen. "Keep track of every hour you spend working on this case. You don't have to be as scrupulous as writing down every minute you're even thinking on it, that can wait until you start firm life in a couple of years, but keep as accurate a running count as possible.

"You'll be paid $20 an hour and I'd prefer to keep it under-the-table if that's alright. Save you both a lot in taxes and me a ton in paperwork."

He paused and flicked his gaze to each of them, both nodding in response.

"Good. Heath, you have an engineering background, so I'd like you to start digging on the KnightRunner and other similar implements. Composite makeup, manufacturing design, whatever you think we can use. I'm more concerned with content than aesthetics here, so package it anyway you feel best conveys the information. Don't worry about drafting a memo, none of that IRAC stuff, you got me?"

For the first time, Heath smiled. "Got it."

Shane slid a piece of paper across the table with a name and pass code scribbled onto it to Abby.

"This is the LexusNexus login for my former law firm. Trust me, they hand this thing out like Halloween candy, so it's not a big deal.

"Start with SynTronic. Pull everything you can find on them. Cases they were a plaintiff or a defendant in, cases where they acted as an expert witness, cases where they settled out of court, cases where they got their milk money stolen from them on the playground. I don't care, if it had their name on it, print it out."

Shane continued pecking away on the computer in front of him, his fingers flying across the keyboard in a vain attempt to keep up with his mind. "Right now I am drafting our initial complaint, listing Tyler as the plaintiff and SynTronic as the defendant. I know it's a little bit premature, but the idea is to get us on the court docket and get the clock moving. The faster we can strike on this the better."

Without waiting for a response, he slid a pair of business cards across the table to them. "About the only things that are still valid on these are my name and phone number, but that's all you'll need for now. Anything comes up, day or night, don't hesitate to call."

They both nodded in understanding and rose to go, pausing to make sure they were being released.

"Oh, one more thing," Shane said, drawing them both back to the table. "Thank you both in advance for doing this. If at any point this summer things are moving too fast, I'm not making any sense, or if I just flat become a dick, please tell me. This is my first time handling something this enormous, so I can pretty much promise in advance there are going to be sticky moments."

Abby smiled, her teeth somehow even whiter than her complexion. Beside her, Heath did the same before both departed.

Shane didn't see either one of them for the next four hours. In fact, he didn't see much of anything. His focus was locked in on the screen before him, his fingers drafting and redrafting the complaint that could well direct how the next few months, and the rest of Tyler's life, played out.

At fifteen minutes past four he made the last revisions and printed it out, returning from the printer to find Abby sitting across the table from his laptop. She offered a half smile as he approached, a stack of research in front of her.

Shane dropped the pleading down on the table and slid into his chair. She pulled the document over and thumbed through it, scanning the pages.

"Is this the complaint?" she asked.

"We can amend it later if we need to," Shane said, "but for the time being that's what we're going with."

Abby read through a few sections of it, more than once casting a glance up to Shane as she went. Whether or not that was out of respect to or in question of his work, Shane wasn't sure. When she was done, she closed it up and pushed it back over to him.

"Looks good."

Shane checked the clock hanging above the library reference desk and said, "I now have forty-three minutes to get that over to the clerk's office and filed."

"Where's that at?"

"Just down the street, shouldn't be a big deal."

"Ah," Abby said, nodding. "I just stopped by to let you know I was going to get out of here. I have a few things to do this afternoon but I'll start in on this pile later tonight."

Shane smiled and waved a hand at her. "Abby, this is a job, not indentured servitude. You don't have to check in with me. Just so long as everything gets done, we're good."

Abby nodded and began to rise, but lowered herself back into her seat. She cast a glance in either direction and chewed on her bottom lip, clearly wanting to ask something.

Shane beat her to it.

"You found the case."

Abby exhaled, relief on her face. "How did you...?"

"It was to be expected."

"And was it...?"

"Yes."

There was just enough finality in Shane's voice to let her know he wasn't angry, but he wasn't open to discussing the topic further. She sat for another minute before bobbing her head and rising. "Well, see you tomorrow."

"See you tomorrow," Shane said, giving a half wave as he leaned back in his chair and watched her depart. Once she was gone he packed up his things and took them out to his car before walking the complaint down to the courthouse and filing it.

On the walk back he let the warm late day sun splash across his face, walking slowly as afternoon traffic trudged by on the freeway just a few blocks away. For a moment he considered joining the throngs of people eager to get home, but decided there was nothing waiting for him at the Comfort Inn that necessitated rushing back to.

The thought of returning to the library and continuing to work also entered his mind, but he opted against that as well. Now that the complaint was filed, Syntronic had two weeks to respond, another few weeks beyond that for discovery, assuming the court pushed the case through fast. Otherwise, the entire process could lag on for months.

That last thought stuck with Shane for a moment. There was only one thing for him to do.

It was time to call Christine.

CHAPTER TWENTY-ONE

"Get somewhere you can talk. Now."

The voice was unmistakable, the tone without question. Marc Sarconi slid the phone down and tugged a pasta spattered napkin from his neck. He kept the phone in his right hand and extended the index finger on his left towards his wife, dropping the napkin on his chair as he departed.

She had seen this scenario play out enough times to know not to question whenever he was pulled away from dinner. At this point, she was past even rolling her eyes.

Sarconi stepped into his study and closed the door, pausing behind it just long enough to make sure his wife hadn't followed him.

"Alright, what's up?"

"When I said get somewhere you can talk, I didn't mean take your sweet ass time doing it."

Sarconi closed his eyes and exhaled through his nose, careful not to let a sound escape. He hated this guy with every last fiber of his being, but that didn't change the fact that he was also scared shitless of him.

Of every person he'd ever encountered, they all had a breaking point, some shred of conscience that kept them from going too far, except for this guy. He preferred to identify where the boundary lines were before waving as he pissed all over them for the world to see.

Sarconi had no doubt that in his particular case, that meant his family. For all the pain in the ass they could be, he couldn't bear the thought of this sadistic son of a bitch going anywhere near them.

For that reason, and that reason alone, he deferred to him at all costs.

"Sorry, you caught me during dinner. What's going on?"

"Marc Sarconi stuffing his face, why aren't I surprised?"

Again Sarconi closed his eyes and breathed out through his nose, but said nothing. He'd already asked twice what was going on, he wouldn't give him the satisfaction of a third.

The man waited a full minute before breaking the silence. "You already know why I'm calling, when are the only two times I ever call?"

Sarconi paused, rolling the question through his head. He'd never thought of it in those terms before, just that he always hated hearing from the guy, regardless of the occasion.

"I guess whenever there's an opportunity..."

"Or whenever shit hits the fan," the man finished for him.

"And it's hitting the fan now," Sarconi said, his mind trying to piece together what he was being told.

"Hey, somebody hand the fat man a cigar," the voice said in a tone that was faux jovial.

Sarconi swallowed hard, the jowls in his neck bunching and jiggling from the effort. "How bad?"

"Bentley went out and got himself a lawyer."

Sarconi waited for him to continue, but no further explanation came.

"A lawyer? For what?"

A loud scoff was his reply. "You took a leg out from under a Heisman Trophy finalist and you have to ask me *for what?*"

Heat burned just beneath Sarconi's face, but he let it pass. In the back of his mind he'd been thinking for a while this moment was coming, he just didn't think it would arrive so fast. Still, he couldn't let this guy know he was worried in the slightest.

"Big damn deal. You know how many two-bit lawyers we've come across in this line of work? Call me when you've got something real for me."

The other end of the line hung silent for several seconds before the man spoke again, his voice no more than a hiss. "You gonna let me finish or not?"

"I'm sorry, please continue," Sarconi said. The words came out without even thinking about them, a conditioned response over years of interaction. Very seldom did he apologize to anyone, but rare was the person that demanded respect the way this guy did.

"He hired *Shane Laszlo* as his attorney."

Sarconi's eyes squinted, focusing on nothing as he tried to place the name. "Shane Laszlo...Shane Laszlo...Laszlo."

Once it clicked in his mind, his jaw dropped slack and his eyebrows rose in unison.

"As in...?"

"Very same."

"Holy shit, there's a curveball for you."

"Leave it to Marc Sarconi to understate the obvious."

Sarconi ignored the insult, working his tongue around the inside of his mouth in an attempt to generate some moisture. It felt like sandpaper scraping against his teeth, his entire body parched.

"What are you going to do?"

"Orders are to do nothing at the moment, just monitor. The kid's already filed a complaint, so it would be a little too suspicious if something happened to him now."

Sarconi nodded to nobody. "What do you need from me?"

Again a scoff came back to him, this one louder than the one before. "You think you could do a damn thing to help me? I'm calling to tell you I'll be in your backyard for a while, so stay the hell out of my way."

The line fell silent as Sarconi stared out the window into the night. "I can do that. Thank you for the heads up."

There was no reply, the man on the other end had already hung up. Sarconi looked down at the display on his phone a moment longer and shook his head. He hoped he never saw that number come up on his caller ID again, but had a feeling he would be seeing it many more times before everything was done.

"Shane Laszlo," Sarconi muttered, his voice far away, borderline stunned. On stilted legs he walked back down the hall and into the dining room, taking his napkin up from the chair and resuming his meal.

Nobody else at the table even noticed he'd been gone.

CHAPTER TWENTY-TWO

Molly stretched the entire length of the pillows lining the top of the bed, somehow extending her feline frame to almost twice its normal length. She held the pose for several seconds before recoiling and staring at Shane with an expression that made it clear what she was thinking.

He was being ridiculous.

Shane ignored her gaze as he buzzed about the rented extended stay room that would be his home for the remainder of the case. Equipped with a bed, a desk, an arm chair, a television, and a small kitchenette, it wasn't how he would have chosen to spend the summer, but in truth it wasn't that far removed from the place he'd just left behind in Boston.

At least this place had HBO and the NFL Network.

The only thing Shane had unpacked was his clothes, at least half of which were sprawled across the bed and armchair. It took him over twenty minutes to decide on the right outfit, another ten wrestling with the cheap hotel iron to get into something halfway presentable.

Close friends or not, he knew better than to show up in front of Christine wearing rumpled pajamas.

Shane first met Christine in the spring of his freshman year. The two were neighbors in a co-ed dorm and despite living within twenty feet of one another didn't say a word beyond the occasional perfunctory hello.

Their silence wasn't born of animosity or even indifference, they just weren't the type of people whose circles crossed.

The first conversation they ever had occurred on New Year's Eve. Shane, having nowhere to go and no plans for the night, had already returned to school, the only one in the entire hall. While most of Columbus was out in drunken revelry, he was seated alone in the common room. His feet were propped up beside a half-eaten pizza and unfinished six pack, the latest James Patterson novel in his hands.

"Ah, spending your New Year's filling your mind and your body with self-indulgent, overrated crap I see?" a voice said from the doorway, jerking Shane away from his novel with a start. His heart pounding, his face red with embarrassment, he spun around to see Christine standing in the doorway, all dolled up for a night on the town.

"Hey, I didn't hear you come in, thought I was alone," Shane said, leaning forward to close the pizza box and place it off to the side. "And I'm sorry, but did you just quote *Bull Durham?*"

Christine stood in the doorway for several long moments, a half-smile on her face, sizing Shane up. After deciding he passed whatever mental test she was subjecting him to, she entered and took a spot on the couch beside him.

"Mind if I join you?"

The question was rhetorical and she didn't wait for a response, instead flipping the box back open and going right in for a slice.

"By all means," Shane said, watching with mild astonishment. "Would you like a beer to wash that down?"

"No thanks, more of a wine girl," Christine said, pretending not to notice the sarcasm in his voice. "Big plans for New Year's I see?"

"Hey, you're here too, and I promise you I'm more comfortable at the moment," Shane replied, motioning to the sweat pants and t-shirt he was wearing.

Christine paused mid-bite and looked over at him, a curious smile on her face. "I don't scare you, do I?"

"Why the hell would you scare me?"

A full moment passed, she wearing a look of bemusement, he one of genuine misunderstanding.

"I'm Christine."

"I know, we live across the hall from each other."

A chuckle rolled out. "I don't know why, but I like you, *Shane*."

Just like that, a friendship that was equal parts respect and agitation, challenge and affection, was born.

The two became good friends through college and had worked hard to maintain it in the time since. Never more than a week passed without some form of correspondence, even if it was just the occasional funny email forward. Christmas cards were mandatory, birthday gifts a must.

On paper a more unlikely duo never existed. Shane was a local kid that grew up without a father and could care less about the label on his clothes or the car he drove. Christine was from a blue-blood family on the Lake Michigan shores of Chicago. She could trace her lineage back hundreds of years to encompass everything from pioneering businessmen to Civil War heroes.

Rarely, if ever, was she seen looking anything but pristine.

In some ways, they were good for each other. In others, it was a train wreck that somehow never came to pass.

For whatever reason, the two of them just worked.

Shane arrived to their agreed-upon restaurant three minutes ahead of schedule, half-jogging to the door, knowing already that he was late. The hostess gave him a bemused smile as he approached, expecting him. "Ms. Beldon is waiting for you. Shall I show you to her table?"

Shane slowed to a stop in front of her, making no effort to keep the smile from his face. His head dropped towards the floor and he shook it from side to side. "No thank you, it'll only give her more ammo. Just point me in the right direction."

The hostess smirked again and extended a bony digit towards the glass embankment lining the far left well. Through the window was the skyline of downtown Columbus, buildings rising against the night sky, a thousand yellow lights shining bright. In the foreground the Olentangy River flowed by, reflecting the scene in a menagerie of color.

Seated at a table for two, wine glass in her hand, pretending to study the view, sat Christine.

Shane knew full well she was staring at the reflection in anticipation of his arrival, but he decided to play the part anyway. He walked straight up to her, put on his most dashing faux smile and approached the table with all the aplomb he could muster. "Excuse me Miss, but it is far too early in the evening for such a pretty lady to be drinking alone."

Moving in slow motion, Christine shifted her shoulders to look at him, her face impassive. "I'm aware. I was supposed to meet a young stud here for dinner, but since it doesn't look like he's going to show, I guess you'll have to do."

Shane did his best to hide a smile as several patrons seated nearby turned to stare. "That might have been meant as an insult, but I'm taking it as an invitation just the same."

Without waiting for a response, he slid into the chair across from her. He lowered his head a bit and whispered, "I can see two gaping jaws and an old biddy still staring."

"Three and two by my count," Christine responded. "You're getting better at this game, but you're not quite there yet."

"Good to see you learned something of value out at mighty Stanford Business School. Thanks for waiting for me, by the way."

Christine smiled and waved a hand at him, taking another sip of wine for effect. "You know the rules. Early is on time and on time is late."

"Thanks, Sarge. And don't give me that, I was three minutes early and you're already halfway through the glass. How long you been here?"

She fixed her gaze on him for a moment, a look that would have left most of the men in the place a puddle on the floor. After eight years of their back-and-forth, Shane was almost impervious.

Almost.

"Alright, fine, you caught me. My meeting finished ahead of schedule, so I came on over. I keep forgetting I can't slide things past a lawyer the way I can businessmen."

Shane stared at her for a moment and admitted she probably could get away with most anything she wanted. Her thick dark hair was swept back from her face and just enough makeup had been applied to enhance without distracting. A sleeveless black dress adorned her body, contrasted against smooth olive skin.

For the entirety of dinner, conversation was corralled to catching up, filling in the blanks from the past six months. Over stuffed mushrooms and calamari, Shane told her about life in Boston and the trials and tribulations of firm life. Through pasta primavera and veal parmesan, Christine told him about her new position and the adjustment to being back in Columbus, a town she never dreamed she'd return to. They both joked about the sham that was their respective love lives while sharing an enormous chunk of tiramisu.

More than once their tales were interrupted by stories from the past, enjoying the inhibition that old friends and good wine tended to bring about.

Not until the last of the dishes were cleared away did Christine fix her stare on him and ask, "So when are you going to tell me about it?"

Shane matched the look for several long moments, opting to feign a bit of ignorance. "*It* being?"

A heavy eye roll responded to his question. Christine shifted her gaze back out the window, any trace of natural light now gone from the sky.

"Come on, who do you think you're dealing with here? Don't get me wrong, I'm thrilled to see you, but why am I looking at you instead of talking to you on the phone from Boston?"

Shane shook his head, shifting his attention to the view outside as well. "Nothing gets by you, I'll give you that," he mumbled. "Alright, here goes. I'm no longer with the firm. Or to be more apt, I quit my job and told my boss to stick it up his ass on the way out."

The revelation spun Christine's head back around to face him. "Wow. Seriously?"

"More or less."

A look that bordered on admiration spread across her face. "Damn, and here I thought I was the impulsive one."

"I was asked to take a civil case here in Columbus. The firm wasn't willing to let me take leave long enough to do it, so I just left."

Christine pursed her lips and twisted her head to the side, considering the information. She weighed it for several long moments, her brow furrowed. "What's the angle?"

The question surprised Shane, causing him to lean back in his chair, his eyebrows raised. "The angle?"

"We both know you didn't leave your dream job in environmental law in Boston to try a civil case here without a damn good reason. So...out with it."

A reflexive smile adorned Shane's face, the kind that sprang from knowing he was in the company of the only person in the world who could both see through and call him out on his bullshit.

"There's a lot of moving parts. The plaintiff is someone I used to know. The case is chock full of fraud, deceit, abuse of system..."

Christine's left eyebrow shot up a fraction of an inch. "Go ahead and drop the punch line any time now."

"Medical malpractice."

Her face went blank for just a moment, her lips moving just enough to repeat the words back to herself. Once she did, a moment of clear realization passed over her features. "Am I to presume?"

Shane kept his gaze angled outside for a moment before shifting his focus back to her. He kept his mouth pressed tight together and nodded once, a short, unmistakable movement.

The confirmation hung in the air, the sounds of the restaurant seeming to fade away around them.

"I will be damned," Christine whispered.

Another small nod in agreement. "Any suggestions? Advice?"

In a rare gesture, Christine slid her hand across the table and grasped his. She kept it there for several moments, the warmth of her palm passing through to him. "I have to assume this is as much about making yourself whole as it is about helping your client."

Shane stared back at her unblinking face. "Maybe. Probably."

"And the only way you come out a winner in this is if you're on your game. I mean *really* on your game."

Shane shifted his gaze away from hers. "And maybe not even then."

The grip on his hand grew tighter. "And the only way that happens is if you know everything is coming out in the end. It'll just be a distraction, the oversized, multi-colored elephant in the room, otherwise."

Shane rolled the words around in his mind. On some level he'd been thinking the same thing since the moment Tyler mentioned SynTronic, but he hadn't allowed the notion to coalesce. He could feel Christine's eyes on him as he thought it out before meeting her gaze and offering a quick smile in response.

That was all he had to give for the time being.

"How's she doing?" Christine asked, her voice much lower, softer. She didn't have to elaborate any further.

Shane stared at her a moment before again diverting his attention to the world outside. He shook his head from side-to-side, fighting to push back a well of emotions he knew resided just beneath the surface.

"I just got back last night."

"You haven't been out there yet?" Christine asked, her eyes a touch wider.

"She still can't even talk to me. Like you said, I didn't want it to become the enormous elephant in the room."

CHAPTER TWENTY-THREE

Shane checked his watch for the fourth time, confirming that he'd been seated in the waiting room for over an hour. He sighed and shifted his focus downward, back to the rolled up copy of *Sports Illustrated* bunched in his hands. He read a quick preseason report from Peter King about the Patriots, glanced over the Faces in the Crowd section, even made it halfway through the cover article about blood doping in cycling before giving up and tossing the magazine onto the table beside him.

Another check of the watch revealed it to be ten past nine. The goal had been to be the first one in the door when the Office of Attorney Affairs for the Ohio Supreme Court opened at eight, to get his *pro hac vice* forms signed and authorized, and be back in the law library by nine. The first half of that plan had come to fruition, Shane arriving so early he even beat the receptionist into the office.

The second half of it was still a work in progress.

Beside him a middle-aged woman sat with her eyes closed, head reclined back against the wall behind her. A cloth satchel overflowing with notebooks and knitting utensils rested at her feet.

Otherwise, the reception area was empty.

What was taking so long Shane couldn't quite figure out, a fact that continued to gnaw at him as time slipped away. By now SynTronic had been notified of the filing. He had to get back and get as far ahead of them as he could while he still had the advantage.

At half past nine, an older man with a short sleeve dress shirt that gapped at the neck and an argyle tie stepped out from around the reception desk. He paused just in front of the counter and stared down at the clipboard in his hand, trying to make out the words in front of him.

"Shane..."

"Laszlo," Shane said, standing and walking forward.

"Laszlo," the man repeated, looking up to assess Shane. He started at his feet and lifted his gaze, taking in the pressed blue suit with white shirt and yellow tie. When he reached the top he nodded, as if satisfied that Shane had passed some sort of preliminary eyeball test. "Right this way, please."

The old man turned and shuffled back the way he had come, Shane slowing to keep from running up on him from behind. Together they traversed a narrow hallway, made a right, and went down a second short corridor. Around them most of the offices stood empty with their lights off, the place almost silent.

Whether that was from everybody being out of the office this morning, or from the offices being vacant, Shane wasn't sure. Given that the morning was fast getting away from him, he didn't much care to ask.

The old man hooked a right into the rear office in the hallway, his slow meander at last finding its way back behind his desk. He motioned for Shane to have a seat across from him before setting the clipboard down and lowering himself into his chair.

Shane waited for him to sit before doing the same, his bottom coming to rest on a hard wooden straight back. He cast a quick glance around the room, taking in the faded Winslow Homer lithographs with gold plated frames and the potted cactus in the corner. A brass nameplate announcing the man to be George Carmichael sat on the desk, no doubt an attempt at a forced retirement gift that the man had misunderstood.

The faint smell of Old Spice and body odor hung in the air, though Shane still held out hope that he would make his escape before either one clung to him.

"So, Mr. Laszlo, what brings you in today?" George began, his fingers laced on the desk in front of him.

"Well, sir, as you can see from my paperwork there, I'm here to file to practice *pro hac vice*."

George stared at him for several long moments, past the point of waiting to see if Shane had more to say, long enough that Shane began to wonder if he was still breathing.

"I see, and for what reason are you filing?" George asked, each word drawn out.

"I have been retained as counsel in a civil trial," Shane replied. "The plaintiff is a student at Ohio Tech, and the arising incident took place here in Columbus, giving Ohio controlling jurisdiction."

"Mhmm," George responded, the sound more of a grunt than an acknowledgement of Shane's answer. "And the defendant?"

"A corporation headquartered in New Jersey, but doing business in Ohio."

Another heavy nod from George. "And are you licensed to practice law in any state?"

"Massachusetts, admitted last year, in good standing."

For the first time, George glanced down at the sheet in front of him. He lowered his face just inches away from it to read, the liver spots atop his head peeking out through thin hair. "Will this be the only case you intend to try here in Ohio?"

"Yes."

"And who is your sponsoring attorney for this request?"

Shane paused a moment, a flush of heat rising to his face. He felt a thin sheen of sweat hit his forehead, but kept his voice even. "Alexandra Laszlo."

Shane held his breath and waited for some form of response, but there was none. Instead George kept his head lowered down over the forms, staring at them. A few more moments passed before he raised his head to gaze back at Shane.

The two sat locked in a stare before George pushed himself to his feet and extended a withered hand across his desk. "Welcome back to Ohio, Mr. Laszlo. Best of luck in your case."

The action took Shane by surprise, for a moment his only response to look from the hand to George and back again. At last the words registered in his mind and he stood, returning the handshake. "That's it? We're good here?"

For the first time all morning, George smiled. "That's it. You can pick up your authorization form from the receptionist on the way out."

"Thank you," Shane said, pumping the old man's hand harder than necessary.

"Do you need me to show you the way out?"

"No, I think I've got it," Shane said, releasing the shake and snatching his briefcase up from the ground beside his chair. He exited the room without waiting for further response and almost sprinted as he headed for the front desk.

The same receptionist he'd walked in with an hour and a half before was waiting for him as he got back to the waiting room, a disdainful look on her face and an authorization form in her hand. Shane thanked her for the form and apologized again for being so early before exiting the building and going straight for the parking lot in hopes of making it back to the library before ten.

Halfway there his cell-phone chirped to life, the theme song from *The Good, The Bad and The Ugly* erupting from his hip. Shane pulled it out without breaking stride and stared down at the display, an unknown number from an Ohio area code staring back at him. Still moving fast, he accepted the call and pressed it to his ear.

"Shane Laszlo."

"Hey, Shane, Heath Wilson here."

It took a moment for Shane to place the name as he slid in behind the wheel of his Honda. "Hey Heath, what's going on?"

"Are you busy right now?"

Shane glanced down at the clock on the dash before checking his rearview mirror and easing out into morning traffic. "Kind of, what's going on?"

"I sent a couple of emails last night to some of my old professors in the engineering department, asked if any of them have ever done anything with medical devices before."

A wince came to Shane's face as he listened, hoping his newfound help wasn't already doing more harm than good. Still, this wasn't the time for a lecture on confidentiality. That would come later, in person.

"Yeah, and?"

"One of them got back to me and said he'd worked on implants before getting into teaching. Said he's available this morning if I'd like to stop by and talk to him."

Shane's eyebrows shot up in surprise. "Nice, for sure do that. Do you want me to come with you?"

"Would you mind? I'm afraid I still don't know the case well enough to ask everything I should."

Shane glanced at the clock once more, but dismissed the thought. This was important, maybe even an insightful break. There was nothing the library presented that could be more helpful than that.

"I'll meet you at the library in twenty minutes."

CHAPTER TWENTY-FOUR

The pages fed out from the fax machine, the decrepit old device whining in protest every step of the way. One by one they emerged into the catch tray, the ink a little too thick, the clarity fuzzy at best.

Beside it stood Lauren Egan, her arms folded across her silk blouse, the toe of her Manolo Bhlanik heels tapping out a steady cadence against the floor. At the completion of each page she checked to see if the transmission was done before dropping the entire stack back into the tray and resuming her stance.

After the better part of ten minutes the machine came to a halt, emitting one last wail that Lauren swore sounded like the dying gasps of a hyena. She pulled the plug from the wall behind the machine to stop it mid-sound and snatched the pages free, turning on a heel and stomping away. Over her shoulder she commanded an intern to do something with that machine, whether it be put it away or throw it in a dumpster, she couldn't care less.

Blonde hair streaming behind her, Lauren stomped towards the end of the hall, her heels beating out a steady pace beneath her. What was just a moment before a busy hallway fell empty as she strode through, a few wayward glances peeking out from offices as she went.

Her destination was the single door at the end of the hall, the one standing open that entered into an office spanning the entire width of the building. Without so much as once glancing down at the document in her hand Lauren strode through the door, pausing just long enough to offer a faint knock with the back of her hand as she went.

The sound of her heels clicking against tile fell away, the points on her three inch pumps digging into soft carpeting. The change of surface did nothing to slow her pace as she spotted who she was looking for and moved for them, swinging the door shut in her wake.

On the right side of the office, facing out into the room, was an enormous oak desk. It was situated congruent to the corners of the room, floor to wall windows framing either side of it. Behind the desk sat Connor Reed, Senior Counsel for SynTronic Corporation. Across from him was William Ramirez, longtime partner and the only person Reed ever allowed to sit second chair in the courtroom.

A bemused expression was splashed across Reed's face as Lauren entered, his head reclined against his high-backed chair. It was still well before noon, though a tumbler of Johnnie Walker Blue already sat on the desk in front of him.

The Breakfast of Champions, as those around the office called it.

"I was just telling Willie that the Dragon Lady must be on the move. It got very quiet around here all of a sudden."

Lauren ignored the comment and slapped the pages down on the desk. The pile splayed out in an arc as they landed, the top sheet flipping over from the force of the landing. "Have you seen this yet?"

Reed arched an eyebrow and looked at Lauren before lowering his gaze to the stack. He shifted his attention up to Ramirez sitting across from him and shook his head twice before raising his head from the chair.

"Sometimes I think we forget who works for whom around here."

Lauren again crossed her arms in front of her, swallowing hard. "Sorry sir, but I have a feeling you're about to be just as angry as I am. Besides, you know dealing with that guy creeps me out."

Reed's hand stopped halfway to the pages and his focus again found its way to Lauren. "So this came from *him*?"

"Do you know anybody else that still uses a freaking fax machine?" Lauren said, motioning towards the stack in front of him.

Reed ignored the question, straightening the pages back into a pile and sliding them over in front of himself. Across the desk, Ramirez leaned in, though refrained from reaching for them.

Silence settled over the office for a full five minutes as Reed flipped through. Twice he offered grunts at what he read, once he reached out to ignore an incoming call on his cell-phone. Otherwise he made no visible indication of anything until he was done, at which point he lifted the tumbler and drained it in one gulp.

"That bad, huh?" Ramirez asked, the question rhetorical. He'd been with Reed long enough to know the only time he ever disrespected good whiskey was after receiving unsettling news.

Reed shoved the pages towards Ramirez and rose from behind his desk. He walked to the mini bar along the wall and grabbed two more tumblers, along with the almost full decanter. While Ramirez read, he put a glass in front of him and Lauren both, pouring them each a healthy shot before doing the same in his own glass.

By the time he'd returned to his seat, Ramirez had finished and was staring back at him.

"Good call, Dragon Lady," Ramirez said with a sigh, breaking his own workplace rule and lifting the tumbler in front of him. He raised it to each of them in salute before downing it in one gulp.

Reed reached out and pulled the document back over in front of him. He stared down at the title page, the words *United States District Court – Southern District of Ohio* printed across the top. Below that in bold faced block letters, *Tyler Bentley, Plaintiff, vs. SynTronic Corporation, Defendant*.

"When did this come in?"

The question seemed to snap Lauren awake, her face blank as she stared down at nothing. "*He* called about a half hour ago. Said he'd gotten his hands on something we needed to see."

"Hmm," Reed said, his gaze still fixed on the pages in front of him. He flicked his attention over to Ramirez. "Something tells me we don't want to know how he managed that."

"I asked," Lauren inserted. "All he said was don't ask questions I don't want to know the answer to."

A small snort slid from Reed. "I don't doubt that."

Ramirez leaned back in his armchair and crossed his legs in front of him. He readjusted his tie across an ever growing paunch and fixed his gaze on Reed. "Initial reaction?"

Reed's eyebrows shot up a fraction of an inch and his right hand rose from the armrest of his chair. Using his thumb as a counter, he started at the tip of his index finger and worked his way across.

"To begin with, the complaint itself doesn't concern me in the slightest. Lord knows we've seen more of these faulty product claims than we know what to do with. Negligence, fraud, failure to obtain informed consent. Pretty standard stuff."

Lauren fidgeted a bit as she listened, taking up her tumbler from the table and sinking into the chair beside Ramirez.

"Second," Reed said, not even registering her movement as his thumb slid to his middle finger, "it was filed in District Court. That means we're either dealing with someone wanting a big chunk of change or someone insistent on taking this in front of a jury."

"Most likely both," Ramirez proffered.

"Most likely," Reed echoed. "Third, the timing of this issue. I've never heard of Tyler Bentley, but based on what is written here, he was a football star. Planning this thing so it hits the court in the summertime, when people are thinking about football but before it starts and becomes a distraction, is pretty smart. Will make it easier to gain a sympathetic jury."

"And a mountain load of media exposure," Ramirez added.

Reed nodded in agreement, his thumb moving on to his pinkie. "Fourth, the amount prayed for is blank. Tells me they either haven't done their homework yet, or they're swinging for the fences."

Ramirez raised a finger and pointed it across at Reed. "The writing seems solid, but not overdone. We're either dealing with a teetotaler or someone straight out of law school."

"I got that impression too," Reed said, nodding his head. "Which means he'll be hung up on issues like principals and doing the right thing."

Ramirez winced, the words sounding horrible in his ear. "Drives the price up in a hurry."

"Mhmm," Reed said, nodding his head. Silence again fell over the room as he stared down at the complaint before shifting his gaze to Lauren. She hadn't said a single word since handing it over, retreating so far back into herself she was almost catatonic. Her slight frame seemed to be shrinking before them as she hugged herself tight, her gaze never rising to meet his.

"Lauren, why don't you take the rest of the day off? Go for a run or something, we'll manage here just fine."

The words jerked Lauren's face up to his, her eyes wide. After several long moments she nodded and stood, her legs trembling beneath her.

"But first, please for the love of all things Holy do not leave that whiskey sitting there," Reed said. "After it's been poured, it needs to be drunk."

Lauren looked uneasy, staring from him to the glass. She took two steps forward and downed it, spun on her heel and left without a word.

Reed and Ramirez both watched from where they sat, neither saying a thing until she was gone, the door closed behind her.

Ramirez remained turned in his chair for several moments after she was gone, staring at the door. "What the hell was that all about?"

"She needed a drink," Reed said, "whether she realized it or not."

Shifting back in his chair, Ramirez gave a slight twist of his head. "That's for damn sure. Poor girl needs the whole bottle. I meant, have you ever seen her go from Dragon Lady to scared kitten that fast?"

The question lingered with Reed for a moment, his brow furrowed in thought. "No, but I can't say that I'd be much happier getting a call from that guy either."

"True, but again, with the transformation..."

"My guess? Whatever he said pissed her off at first, the more she thought about it though, the more it scared her."

A puff of breath slid out over Ramirez's teeth. "Damn, that is one sick bastard."

Reed didn't bother agreeing with the obvious, opting to swivel in his chair to stare out the window instead. Below him the Passaic River flowed by, brown and dirty, a perpetual stench rising from the pollutant cocktail that fed into it every day. A mile upstream the Newark Bay expanded out towards the Atlantic, a handful of commercial trawlers visible in the midday sun.

Despite what his stretched tight skin and thick head of salt-and-pepper hair would indicate, he was fast approaching his sixty-fifth year. His patience with his employer and his profession were both starting to wear thin, a fact made apparent every day when he found himself wishing he was on his yacht headed out to sea instead of sitting behind his desk, staring at another nasty court case.

"So what are you really thinking?" Ramirez asked, his gaze shifting between Reed and the river below.

The question drew a smirk from Reed. "I must be getting predictable."

"Not to anybody but me. Fifteen years of working with someone highlights peccadilloes in a way that few other interactions do."

Reed paused, considering the words. Maybe he was feeling reflective today, maybe his dalliances with hanging it up were starting to wear on him, but they seemed to find their mark and settle there.

"Two things are bothering me. First, the fact that after serving as counsel of record for SynTronic for almost a decade now, never once did the question of whether or not they did it enter my mind. Over the years we've spent more than our share of time with the scourge of society, but these guys might top the list. At least when thugs or gangsters kill or maim to turn a profit, they hold it out for the world to see.

"These guys do it, then pay you off to keep you silent so they can do it again to the next guy."

"So you don't want to settle?"

Reed kept his eyes focused outside. "Of course we're going to try and settle. Like I said, there's no doubt SynTronic is guilty. We know what they're willing to pay to keep that out of the papers, we just have to hope it's enough to make this one go away."

"You don't sound certain."

Reed spun himself around and looked down at the complaint on his desk. He checked the name listed as the plaintiff and asked, "You ever heard of this kid, Tyler Bentley?"

Ramirez shook his head from side to side, his jowls jiggling beneath a thin-trimmed beard. "Naw, but I'm not much of a sports guy."

"Me neither, not since the days of Broadway Joe and the boys. From what this complaint says though, the kid was good, NFL good."

"Meaning our usual dollar amount won't be enough to make this one go away."

"Probably not," Reed agreed.

"Huh," Ramirez replied, chewing at the inside of his cheek as he bobbed his head up and down, deep in thought. "Still, we've got to try."

A heavy sigh slid from Reed. "And we will, but I'm just saying, I have a feeling they're going to tell us to go to hell."

"Suits at corporate won't be happy."

"Nothing we can do about that."

Ramirez raised his eyebrows in agreement, conceding the point. "Might even set *him* loose to try and help them see things our way."

A wizened hand reached out and tapped the top of the pages stacked in the middle of the desk. "I think the fact that these are here now, ahead of the official court-served copy, means that's already happened."

A small nod was the only response. Both sat in silence for several long seconds before Ramirez raised his eyes, focusing on Reed. "So we're going to trial."

The left corner of Reed's mouth played up into a smile as he stood, returning to the bar and grabbing up the decanter. "And we know what that means."

A mischievous grin spread across Ramirez's fleshy features. "We sit here and kill this bottle..."

"We call a cab to take us down to Fernandes for a steak..." Reed continued, filling each of their tumblers with four fingers of whiskey.

"And come back here tomorrow, ready to tear these guys a new asshole," Ramirez said, lifting his drink.

Across from him, Reed set the decanter down and did the same. It was a ritual they'd been practicing for over ten years now. When a case came in, they'd stuff themselves full of alcohol and red meat, a proverbial last meal before a two month dredge through the judicial process.

Once the night was over, they wouldn't touch either again until the final verdict was rendered.

"One last time," Reed said, looking at his glass, studying the amber liquid inside it.

"Ride off into the sunset?" Ramirez asked, a questioning look on his face.

Reed's response was a smile as they clinked glasses, draining them in one elongated swallow. When they were done, both dropped them back to the desktop, Reed already moving to refill.

"What was the other thing?" Ramirez asked, his hand still on the glass, his gaze fixed down on it as the smooth Scottish rye filled it again.

"Hmm?"

"A few minutes ago, you said there were two things you didn't mention when Lauren was here. What was the other one?"

Reed's movements slowed as he put the crystal stopper back in the decanter and lowered it to the desk. He picked up his glass once more and looked at it, the previous drink tasting a bit sour in his throat.

"Did you happen to notice who the counsel of record was for the plaintiff?"

"Yeah, Shane Laszlo," Ramirez said. "Never heard of him."

"Not him," Reed said. "The other one."

Ramirez narrowed his eyes for a moment, trying to recall the name on the forms, before giving up and reaching for the complaint. He spun it around and pulled it over in front of himself, his gaze scanning the title page until it found what Reed was alluding to.

Reed watched as his face registered alarm, followed by confusion.

"Wait, what? How is that even possible?"

"I don't know," Reed said, "but there it is."

Ramirez pushed himself to full height, ignoring the glass in front of him. "That has to be a scare tactic, right? Some boogeyman stuff to force our hand?"

Reed shrugged, already raising his glass. "I guess we'll find out."

CHAPTER TWENTY-FIVE

Heath was sitting on the front steps of the library as Shane approached, elbows propped up on his knees, staring down at his cell-phone. His focus was filled by the device in his hand, his face contorted as he stabbed at the screen like a gorilla trying to work a remote control.

"New phone?" Shane asked as a way of greeting, not bothering to ascend the stairs.

Heath's head shot up at the sound of Shane's voice, a small smile in place. "Birthday gift from the parents. I kept telling them my old flip phone was fine, but they wouldn't hear of it."

Shane pulled a flip phone from his pocket and wagged it at him. "I feel you. Sometimes it's nice not to be so damn accessible all the time."

"I miss it already," Heath said, pushing himself to a standing position. He looked Shane up and down once before motioning to the faded jeans, scuffed boots, and t-shirt he was wearing. "I know I'm new to the whole process, but I didn't think a tie was necessary for this kind of meeting."

A laugh snapped out of Shane, accompanied by a wave of his hand. He'd left his suit coat in the car and rolled up his sleeves, but for the rest of the day he was stuck in slacks and a tie. "It's not. I had to be over at the Supreme Court to file some paperwork this morning. Trust me, tomorrow I'll look just like you do."

Heath fell in beside Shane and together they walked across campus, the midday sun bathing them in warmth as they crossed the quad and headed for the engineering department. The conversation remained light the entire way, each feeling the other out as they went. Using the case as a common starting point, they talked about college football and the upcoming season before drifting over to the NFL. Halfway to their destination they were derailed by a gaggle of co-eds out for a morning run, finishing the journey with a spirited debate about blondes versus brunettes.

There was no clear winner.

Shane let Heath take the lead as they entered the engineering building, one of the newer additions that hadn't existed when he enrolled eight years before. Unlike most of the buildings on campus its façade didn't make use of a single brick, opting instead for just enough steel to keep the glass house upright. Inside, the foyer was open and airy, tons of natural light filtering in.

"Not bad, huh?" Heath asked as they walked across the white tile floors, casting a sideways glance to Shane.

"Not at all," Shane agreed. "I guess if you're going to build a new engineering building, it had better live up to the title."

Heath nodded his head in agreement as they hopped into the elevator, taking it up to the fifth floor. Together they stepped out in a wide hallway, the ground and walls varying shades of white. A handful of people that Shane guessed to be graduate students by their advanced ages drifted down the hall towards them in ones and twos, no doubt the flow of a class just released.

"Looks like we're right on time," Heath said, stepping aside from a doorway as two men with beards passed by. He leaned in and took a quick glance around before knocking on the doorframe with the back of his knuckles.

A man in his late forties stood at the front of the room as Heath and Shane walked in, loading various objects into a cloth shoulder bag. He was dressed in jeans, hiking boots, and a plaid shirt tucked in tight, a trimmed beard on his face making up for the hair that was fast receding from his head.

"Come in," he answered without looking up.

"Professor Lomax," Heath said, leading Shane towards the front of the room.

The words drew Lomax's gaze up from his bag, a smile spreading across his face. He stepped out from behind the table and walked towards them, hand outstretched. "Heath Wilson, good to see you."

"Good to see you as well," Heath replied. "Thank you for responding to the email. This is Shane Laszlo, the attorney I mentioned earlier."

"Yes," Lomax said, releasing Heath's grip and extending his hand to Shane. "Heath tells me you're working on a case and had some questions about prosthetics."

"That's right," Shane said, returning the handshake. "Thank you so much for meeting with us."

"No problem," Lomax said, moving back behind his desk and putting the last of a stack of papers into his bag. "I don't know how much help I can be to you, but I'll tell you what I know."

"Anything at all would be appreciated," Shane said.

"Alright," Lomax said, "Just know that I'm a scientist, not a doctor, so anything I tell you is coming from that side, and that side changes pretty fast. Some of what I say might be a touch outdated already."

"Forewarned is forearmed. Like I said, we appreciate anything you can give us. Is there somewhere we should go to talk?"

Lomax extended a hand towards the row of desks stretched out in front of him. "You're welcome to come back to my office with me, but to be honest we'd have more space in here. I have a design review coming up and the place is stacked high with blueprints and models at the moment."

Shane looked over at Heath and shrugged. "I'm good, let's do it."

Heath nodded in agreement, both of them pulling up a chair as Lomax perched himself atop the table, feet swinging free beneath him.

"Do you mind if I record this?" Shane asked. "I'm new to this side of things, want to be sure I don't miss any of it."

"Go right ahead," Lomax said.

Shane pulled out a legal pad, turned his recorder on, and asked, "Alright, what we're most interested in here today are knee replacements. What can you tell us about those?"

A long, heavy breath slid out from beneath Lomax's beard as he leaned back and shook his head. "Nasty, nasty business right there. Pray you never have to have one."

"Why's that?" Shane asked.

"Because of the nature of the joint," Lomax said. "Take for example a shoulder or a hip, simple ball and socket joints. Everything is made out of titanium alloy, there's never any friction, no corrosion, just a nice smooth surface to let everything rotate on.

"Not the case with a knee. You've got three bones feeding into a joint that acts like a hinge, the whole thing held together by a knee cap and a bunch of tendons and ligaments. You can use stainless steel for the cap, but the rest of it has to be from plastics. It's an inexact science to say the least."

"And when you say plastics..." Shane prompted without looking from his pad as he scribbled notes.

"Polyethylene," Lomax replied. "High end stuff for sure, but still a far cry from steel."

"What do you mean?" Heath asked, speaking up for the first time since introductions.

"Again, steel is more durable. Check that, *a lot* more durable. The average knee replacement lasts about twenty years before the components start to break down and the whole thing has to be done again. That would never be an issue with steel."

"So then why don't companies just make them using steel?" Shane asked.

"Simple physiology. Yeah, steel is a lot more durable, but it also lacks the necessary give that a hinge joint requires. Think about every time you extend your knee, if there was no cushion in there, nothing but two solid pieces of metal slamming together, it would snap all the bones in your leg. They just wouldn't be able to take the pressure."

From the corner of his eye Shane could see Heath extend his leg beside him, wincing at the thought. The right corner of his mouth played up into a smile as he continued writing, his mind formulating the next question.

"Walk me through the design process. How does a replacement go from theoretical to experimental to operational?"

"You chose the right word for it," Lomax said, pointing a finger at him, "*process*, because that's just what it is. You have it wrong though in thinking it's linear, from Point A to Point B to Point C. It's a cycle, A to B to C and back to A again."

Shane traced out the pattern at the bottom of his page and flipped to the next one as Lomax continued.

"Step one is the research. At this point, most companies have their products in enough people that they can study how they work in actual transplant patients. How their bodies respond to the implants, what kind of range of motion they have, what their recovery time was, everything.

"From there they look at the previous model and determine what they can work with. Is there a way to make the prosthetic fit better? Is there a material out now that a body might receive easier? Has a more durable polymer been developed?

"They take all that information and move it into Step Two, which is where I was. Once a year or so a whole bunch of eggheads would come and present all their new findings to us. They'd tell us what they'd like to see done, then set us loose to figure it out."

"Just like that?" Shane asked.

Lomax scrunched one side of his face and wagged a hand at the question. "Well, I'm simplifying of course. There was heavy scrutiny from the Feds every step of the way to make sure we were properly testing our developments, that our designs had the correct documentation, etc. I'm just giving you the basic in-house process."

"Got it," Shane said. "Sorry to interrupt."

"Naw, it was a good question," Lomax said, the professor in him rising to the surface. "Once we had a new design in hand, we put it through every test imaginable. I mean, we beat the hell out of those things. Stress tests, endurance tests, you name it, we did it. It's a wonder we didn't all die from taking prosthetic shrapnel inside the lab."

He paused for a moment and chuckled, his deep voice rolling out through the near-empty classroom. "After that, we'd conduct initial human testing. Again, whole bunch of red tape with finding and vetting participants, obtaining informed consent, that kind of thing.

"Once we had a group ready to go, the transplants would be made and the entire process would start again."

Lomax fell silent as Shane continued scribbling, his hand racing to keep up. "And how long would this entire process last, on average?"

"Well, there wasn't what I would call a quote-unquote average, but on the whole I would say the process took a year minimum, but in reality closer to two."

"Mhmm," Shane mumbled, jotting down the information and pulling out the legal pad with the transcript from Tyler written on it. His gaze danced over the pages, looking for anything that might jump out at him.

"Tell me, Professor, in all your time designing and testing prosthetics, did you ever have any disintegrate on you?"

Heath stopped writing beside him and stared at Lomax, who pressed his lips together and raised his eyes to the ceiling. He remained that way for a moment and said, "Disintegrate? No, never. Like I said, we had them snap, break, even explode at times, but never disintegrate."

Shane cast a quick glance over to Heath. "Tell me, what would cause something like that?"

Lomax raised his eyebrows and said, "Truth? Only two things come to mind. They were either using a faulty polymer or a really cheap one."

A thin smile tugged at the corners of Shane's lips. "Professor Lomax, thank you very, very much for your time."

CHAPTER TWENTY-SIX

The smell of curlers filled the air, fluffy fried goodness coated with a thin layer of cinnamon infused glaze. It swirled like an aromatic hurricane, Marcellus Sarconi standing in the eye of it as he made his way down the hall.

The clock on the wall above reception said it was just a couple of minutes past six, but Sarconi had already been up for hours. Truth was he'd been awake for almost two days solid, ever since he'd gotten the phone call informing him that things could be getting ugly fast.

The call had turned out to be an understatement.

The very next day a formal complaint was filed, something his informant felt the need to deliver in person. The mere presence of the guy was enough to make anybody nervous, but the fact that he had shown up just before dinner and made a point of introducing himself to Sarconi's wife and children made it that much worse. Standing rigid in the living room, he had been forced to watch as the guy put on a smile and introduced himself under a fake name, shaking hands and over-laughing at everything they said.

Whether his appearance was a directive of corporate or just the sick bastard's idea of having some fun, Sarconi didn't know and didn't much care. However it originated, the intent had found its mark. He, and his family, was accessible at any time.

If things got bad for SynTronic, they would get bad for the Sarconis as well.

The minute the guy left, Sarconi excused himself to his office and had an anxiety attack that lasted ten minutes. By the time he was able to breathe again his face was pale and his shirt was plastered to his skin, any hope of eating dinner or facing his wife the rest of the night obliterated.

Instead, he called Pinkering and told him they needed to meet first thing in the morning before excusing himself to bed under the guise of feeling ill. As it turned out, the ruse did little more than make a night of staring at the ceiling that much longer for him.

Eight minutes after six Sarconi walked into the same conference room they had met with Margie Bentley in just a week before. Seated across the table from him was Pinkering, his white lab coat draped over a chair back, a tie atop it. He yawned as Sarconi entered, still rubbing sleep from his eyes.

"This had better be important, you know I was on until after midnight last night."

Sarconi stepped forward and slid the box of donuts across the table. "Here, eat one of these you skinny bastard. The sugar will wake you up in no time."

Halfway through his eye rub Pinkering stopped and stared at Sarconi, his hand frozen by his temple. Sarconi ignored the look, going straight back to the door and checking the hallway before closing it behind him. The sound of the deadbolt turning rang out, cold and metallic, in the room.

"What the hell's going on here?" Pinkering asked, ignoring the pastries.

Sarconi dropped into a chair across from him and leaned forward, his elbows resting on the table. Dark circles hung in concentric rings under his eyes, his hair oiled down even heavier than usual. When he spoke, his voice was somewhere between a hiss and a whisper.

"Tyler Bentley filed a lawsuit against us yesterday."

Three long wrinkles creased Pinkering's forehead, his eyebrows rising almost to his scalp. A knot in his throat worked itself up and down as he tried to swallow. "Us as in you and I?"

"Us as in SynTronic," Sarconi replied, his eyes flashing dark. "Though I don't think that matters now, do you?"

A sheen of sweat appeared on Pinkering's forehead as he leaned forward in his chair, matching Sarconi's pose, elbows braced against the table.

"What are they claiming?"

"The usual stuff. Gross negligence, fraud, misrepresentation. Just civil charges right now, but they could go for maiming if anybody tried to press criminal charges."

The response was met by another heavy swallow from Pinkering, followed by a small twist of the head. "How do you know this? Did he contact you?"

Sarconi leaned back just an inch or two, trying to decide how to best answer that one. There was no way he wanted Pinkering knowing about his contact, especially if things started happening to people connected to the case in the very near future. For the time being, it was best to be as vague as possible.

"Our lawyers received notice yesterday that a complaint had been filed against us. They called me last night, I called you."

A terse bob of the head relayed that Pinkering bought the story.

"What's he asking for?"

"We don't know yet. That part was left blank, though my guys say that's not uncommon in a jury trial. They'll just pray for damages, pain and suffering, lost wages, let the system figure out what all that's worth."

Pinkering fell silent for a moment, mulling the information. "My God, Tyler Bentley was set to become a top-five draft pick. That could end up being millions."

"Yeah, no shit," Sarconi muttered. He raised a hand to his forehead and kneaded it with his hand, pushing the soft tissue back and forth with his thumb and forefinger.

"What are your guys saying?" Pinkering asked.

Sarconi stopped rubbing and sighed, leaning back in his chair until the stopper on it kept him from going any further. "This isn't the first time one of our devices has failed. Our attorneys will reach out to Bentley and offer a settlement. After that, we'll see what happens."

Pinkering nodded several times in rapid succession, his mind chewing through the new information. After a moment he stopped, his gaze focused on Sarconi.

"*We'll see what happens?* Is that supposed to be some sort of joke? This thing could sink us, both of us. If this goes to trial...we took the leg from a Heisman Trophy finalist for crying out loud!"

As Pinkering spoke, his voice raised several decibels, the initial fear of the situation subsiding into anger. The words echoed through the small room, drowning out all other sounds, even overtaking the smell of the crullers between them.

In response Sarconi just sat and stared, his face impassive.

"You think I don't know that? You think SynTronic doesn't know that? You think the fact that we produced a complete piece of shit and then stuck it in one of the most visible athletes on the planet is lost on any of us?"

Several tense moments passed as Pinkering stared back at him, both men panting.

Pinkering was the first to blink, leaning back and shaking his head in disbelief.

"Sorry," he mumbled. "This just isn't what I expected this morning."

Sarconi waved off the apology, saying nothing.

"Alright, so what do we do now? Rally the troops?"

"Right now, I think we are the troops," Sarconi said, his face even more dour than usual. "The only other person to have any actual contact with the Bentley's was Manningham, and he didn't come in until after they'd agreed to the procedure."

"Yeah, and he's got a reputation as a real company man around here anyway," Pinkering added. "No way he goes to bat for us."

"After that, who else is there?" Sarconi asked. "The hospital director? The University president? Those guys are in the business of saving their asses, nothing more."

"And that's what we need to do."

The Adam's apple again bobbed up and down as Pinkering nodded in agreement. "Alright, I'm with you. How's this going to go?"

"According to my guys, the first step is still to look for a settlement. Maybe this won't be anything after all. If not though, we need to get our story straight, and fast."

More enthusiastic nodding from Pinkering. "You lie and I'll swear to it."

"Good," Sarconi said, rising from the table. He shoved the box of donuts over in front of Pinkering and turned towards the door. "Have a curler, it'll help calm your nerves. Don't mention a word of this to anybody until we hear back from our guys."

"Got it," Pinkering said, reaching out for the box in front of him.

Sarconi went straight for the door, unlocking it and cracking it open. He started to pass through into the hallway, but stopped to look back at his colleague.

"Oh, and Leo? Put your tie on for Christ's sake. You look like shit."

CHAPTER TWENTY-SEVEN

A tiny circle of sweat droplets formed on the concrete floor beneath Tyler, each one starting high up on his scalp, running down his forehead, and ending on the tip of his nose. It would hang there, swaying back and forth for several long seconds before falling to the floor, a new one appearing with each pushup he pressed out.

"Ninety-seven," came the cadence, shouted out in the same ingratiating nasal voice that was fast starting to haunt Tyler's dreams.

Another push-up, another droplet of sweat to the misshapen amoeba on the floor beneath him.

"Ninety-eight."

Chest screaming, shoulders burning, breath coming in ragged gasps, Tyler paused at the top before lowering himself towards the floor.

"Nine-nine. Come on now, one more. You mean to tell me Mr. All-American can't do one more pushup?"

A small flame ignited deep inside of Tyler, a rage that started somewhere in his stomach and permeated his limbs. With it came a complete dulling of the senses, a total dissonance from the fatigue gripping him. In its place was fury, a tidal wave of pain and anger.

"Seventeen...eighteen...nineteen..." the voice kept calling out, that same stilted accent that refused to ever relent.

Tyler made it to one hundred and twenty seven, a small puddle on the floor beneath him, before no amount of fury could overcome the lactic acid coursing through his body. One moment he was pumping out pushups, the next he was face down on the ground, his lungs clawing for air, heartbeat pounding in his ears.

There was no effort to move from the floor, the cool concrete soothing his aching body. Tyler lay there for almost two full minutes, a misshapen star fish with his head turned to the side, cheek pressed flat to the ground. He stayed that way until a gym towel smelling of fabric softener landed on his head, blocking all light from view.

A deep, guttural groan slid from Tyler's lips as he pulled the towel away from his head and rolled over onto his back. He didn't give a single thought to the fact that he was lying on the concrete floor, could care less that he was wallowing in his own sweat.

Above him, a middle-aged woman with a tight halo of orange and silver curls peered down, a quizzical look on her face. She was dressed in a black track suit with a hot pink t-shirt beneath it, a whistle hanging from around her neck.

"Damn boy, I'm dying to know where those last thirty came from," she said, a bemused expression serving as the front for her annoying voice.

Disgusted, Tyler wiped his face with the towel and sat up, his right leg pawing at the floor for traction while his left remained inert. He leaned forward and rested his forearms around his knee, staring up at her with a look that bordered on contemptuous. "Do me a favor, don't ever call me All-American, superstar, football hero, anything like that again."

The words surprised the woman, blowing her back a bit, eyebrows raised.

Tyler stared at her a moment longer before shaking his head, his face softening. "Listen, Trudy, I appreciate everything you're doing here for me, I do. Just...let's leave that stuff at the door, alright?"

Trudy stared back at him, considering the words, before nodding and extending a hand down towards him. Tyler accepted it and pulled himself to his foot, hopping over to the leg extension machine.

"Apology accepted," Trudy said, "though unnecessary."

"Still," Tyler said, sliding himself onto the seat of the machine and selecting a weight, his ankle fitting in behind the pad. "I didn't mean to snap like that."

A snort lifted Trudy's head towards the ceiling, followed by a deep guffaw that started in her diaphragm and rolled out in a slow wave. "You call that snapping? I'm a physical therapist, I see people at their weakest, their most vulnerable, their most angry. I've been called every name you can imagine and had my mama called worse. That, my boy, was not snapping."

Tyler smirked at the comment, his lips cracking into the faintest bit of a smile. "Sounds a lot like freshman football camp."

"Yeah, except I get paid to be here. So let's stop talking and get back to work. Fifty reps and you're done for the day."

Tyler's eyes bulged at the command, but he said nothing, knowing better than to argue. It would only up the total to sixty. Instead he set his jaw and started into the set, his right quad burning, Trudy's voice keeping count.

When at long last the set, and the misery of the workout, was done, Tyler thanked Trudy for her time and retired to the locker room of the Worland Community Hospital. Armed with the only fitness facilities in town not at the high school, it would have been far too Spartan for him to try and train for an upcoming season, but given his current state it was enough to make him flat miserable.

A pair of young orderlies was finishing changing after their shift as Tyler entered, both of them pausing by the door to give him a second glance as they passed. He pretended not to notice as he wheeled himself in and dropped down onto the floor, letting the cool relief of the tile seep into his skin. The towel went back over his face as he laid there, lactic burn retreating from his muscles, when his phone chirped to life beside him.

Tyler pushed an exhausted sigh out and rolled onto his side, reaching into a side pocket of his wheelchair and fishing for the phone. He had no doubt who the call was from before even answering it, his mother having done so after every workout he'd been to so far.

Every *anything* he'd been to for that matter.

The towel still affixed across his face, Tyler thumbed the phone on and pressed it to his face, a heavy sigh preceding his voice. "Hey, Ma."

A full moment of silence met his ears.

"Um, I'm sorry, I must have the wrong number," responded a male voice, familiar but not quite recognizable.

Tyler snapped the towel away from his face and pulled the phone back, staring down at the screen before pressing it back to his ear.

"Damn Shane, I'm sorry. I wasn't expecting it to be you."

A quick chuckle returned to his ear. "Don't sweat it, just the first time I've been called Ma before."

A smile cracked Tyler's face as he raised the towel to wipe away another trickle of sweat. "Yeah, ever since I got back she's been kind of hovering. Makes sure I'm eating, calls and checks on me every time I go to the bathroom, everything."

There was a small but noticeable pause.

"Must be nice," Shane said, a different tone in his voice. He paused once more, before saying, "So listen, the reason I'm calling is to give you an update and to ask you a question."

"Shoot."

"I heard back from SynTronic's counsel this morning, guy named Connor Reed. Used to be a big-time litigator back in the day, was brought on in-house almost fifteen years ago."

Tyler closed his eyes, swallowing hard. "So that's bad?"

"It ain't good, but it doesn't have to be bad either. Sometimes guys that have been around the block know when they've got a losing hand. This guy seems like one of them."

"What makes you say that?"

"He called this morning and wants to set up a meeting to talk about a settlement."

Tyler's eyes flew open, bulging a bit at the words. "Already?"

"Yeah, though don't let that fool you, could be nothing more than an attempt to keep the thing out of the paper. Even if he thinks they have the upper hand, they could be willing to pay just to make it disappear."

"Alright," Tyler said, working his jaw and nodding his head. "So what did you tell him?"

"Well, that leads me to my question. I told him I'd set it up for just as soon as I could talk to you."

Tyler pulled the phone away again and checked the time. He ran the towel back over his face before pressing the phone back to his ear. "Can you give me three hours? I'd like for mom to be in the room when we talk about this, if you don't mind."

There was the sound of movement through the phone, as if Shane was checking the time himself. "That's perfect. I'm on my way over to the athletic department this afternoon to do a little research, I'll give you a call then."

"Sounds good."

"Alright Tyler, I'll talk to you later tonight then," Shane said, finality in his voice.

Tyler nodded, his gaze far away, before snapping his focus back to the phone. "Hey, Shane?"

"Yeah?"

"Do you think I should be there for the settlement meeting?"

A long pause met his ears, long enough that Tyler had to check to make sure the connection wasn't interrupted.

"No. If this thing goes to trial, I want that to be the first time anybody sees you."

Tyler made a face, no idea what Shane was alluding to.

"Just, trust me," Shane said, sensing the uncertainty through the silence. "If it gets that far, I'll explain it all to you, I promise."

CHAPTER TWENTY-EIGHT

An enormous emblem of the OTU Crimson Knight mascot was stamped into the floor of the athletic complex as Shane stepped through the front doors. It was the same traditional logo that had been in place for decades, a galloping knight with helmet visor pulled down, lance at the ready. Beneath the knight was his trusty steed, eyes wide, nostrils snorting steam.

Whatever this tandem of terror is headed at is in for a world of hurt, make no mistake of that.

Without a second thought to the impending doom that the duo might bring him, Shane strode across it and through the circular rotunda to the single desk on the far side of the room. A handful of student-athletes shuffled out as he entered, none giving him even a passing glance.

A young black man with close cropped hair sat behind the desk, a dog-eared paperback in his hands. In front of him was a half-full sign-in log, a computer off to the side. He seemed to sense Shane as he approached, setting the book off to the side and folding his hands atop the desk in front of him.

"Good afternoon," the young man said, his voice much deeper than expected.

"Um, hi," Shane said, his own coming out a decibel lower as if by a subconscious attempt to keep up. "Shane Laszlo here to see Marty Graham, please."

"Okay, please sign in," the young man said, motioning towards the page in front of him while lifting the receiver on the phone. He spoke into it for a moment, mumbling only a few words, before placing it back in its cradle. "Be down in just a moment."

Shane thanked the young man and retreated away from the desk, circling to his left around the room. The entire rotunda was lined with floor-to-ceiling trophy cases, all of them bursting with team memorabilia.

Each of the cases represented a different sport, at least one for all twenty-seven OTU competed in at the Division-I level. The first in the order was synchronized swimming, the centerpiece a trophy three feet in height. Surrounding it were team photos and newspaper articles, all of them touting national dominance.

The next in line was golf, followed by softball.

Fourth in line, located right in the middle of the wall, was football. Formed by several sections with the partitions removed, it was far and away the largest compartment in the room. Even at that, it could have filled three or four more with ease.

Conference and Centennial Bowl championship trophies served as the focal points of the display, everything else spiraling out away from them. It included an oversized photo of Coach Valentine, his body bent forward as a shower of lemon-lime Gatorade was poured on him after a win. To the sides, stretched out ten feet in either direction, were footballs, photos, articles, and trophies of every kind.

Front and center in every one of them was Tyler Bentley.

Shane moved to the far side of the display and stared at a life-sized cutout of Tyler for several seconds. The team was on the road somewhere that still used natural grass, his white jersey streaked with mud and field paint. His eyes were aimed downfield, veins bulging in his arm as it cradled the ball against his body. Beneath him his legs pointed straight ahead, no doubt in search of a distant goal line.

The picture held Shane's gaze for several moments before he stepped back and pulled his phone out. He held it at arm's length in front of him, taking a quick picture of the entire display, followed by a close-up of Tyler.

The phone wasn't even back in his bag when a voice behind him said, "Shane Laszlo?"

Shane whirled to see a woman no more than thirty-five standing before him. She was wearing a pant suit and heels, short black hair spiked on top and combed back on the side. She seemed to sense both his guilt at being caught and his surprise at seeing her standing there.

"Marty Graham?" Shane asked, walking forward and extending a hand.

"Short for Martina," she replied, returning the handshake. She pumped it twice and released her grip, waving a hand towards the case. "They're something aren't they?"

"Yeah, they are. First time I've ever been in here."

Falling in beside him, Marty began walking, directing without having to tell him where to go. They walked in silence until they were past the front desk before she leaned in and whispered, "Don't worry, I took pictures my first time too."

A flash of color rose to Shane's cheeks as they walked on. "I assure you, that wasn't what you think it was."

"Mhmm," Marty replied, her voice belying obvious disbelief. She came to a stop outside a glass door with her name on it, the title of External Relations Consultant on the frosted pane, and waved him inside. "After you."

With a nod of thanks, Shane stepped in and slid his bag from his shoulder. Marty circled around her desk as he took up the chair opposite her, his eyes doing a quick pass around the room.

Two things jumped straight out at him. There was not a thing out of place, and there was not a single shred of Ohio Tech merchandise anywhere.

"So, Mr. Laszlo, what can I do for you?" Marty asked, leaning back and leveling her gaze on him.

"Please, just Shane."

He pulled his gaze away from the room and removed a legal pad from his bag. He slid out the tape recorder and held it up, an inaudible question, to which Marty replied with nod and a wave.

Once the tape was rolling, he began.

"So, Ms. Graham-"

"Please, just Marty," she interjected, smiling.

Shane matched the smile. "Okay, Marty, I'm not sure what your assistant told you when she set this meeting up, but I am the counsel of record for Tyler Bentley."

The mirth faded from Marty's face at the mere mention of the name. "That's why you were taking pictures."

"Yes," Shane said, nodding. "But let me be clear, Ohio Tech is not a named party in this case, nor does my client have any intention of going after the university."

The same even stare looked back at him.

"Also, as his lawyer, it would be very bad form for me to bring up something with you in here that might be construed as a conflict of interest and get the entire case thrown out."

Her face softened a bit, though still not back to the original level.

"I assure you, my reason for asking to speak with you is as a subject matter expert."

The ice completely dropped away at that, a curious smile taking its place. "And what subject might that be?"

Shane pointed a thumb over his shoulder at the door behind him. "I'm told most of your job as External Relations Consultant is dealing with players that go pro. Is that true?"

A small noise somewhere between a chuckle and a scoff slid out of Marty, followed by a small eye roll. "Yes, I suppose you could say that, in the same way you could say most of a lawyer's job is writing briefs."

"Point taken," Shane said, smiling in concession. "Please, tell me what you do."

"First of all, you must disregard the title on the door. That was just something fancy they came up with as a way to explain my position and salary. If they were interested in accuracy, it would say Martina Graham, Brand Manager."

"The brand being...?"

"Yes," Marty said, the corner of her mouth playing upward to let him know she was joking. "The university, individual players, specific teams, you name it."

"Okay," Shane said, head down, scribbling notes. "So walk me through it."

"Alright, let's go with, oh, say, Tyler Bentley," Marty said, extending a hand towards him.

"Perfect."

"First thing every summer all twenty-seven teams send me a list of those players we should be pushing this year. Sometimes it's an established starter, sometimes a senior that has worked his way up, sometimes, as was the case last summer with Tyler, it's a player poised to break out in a big way.

"I have three people that work beneath me. Once I get those lists, I dole them out among my staff and we get to work. Low man on the totem gets fencing, lacrosse. Next guy up scores wrestling, track and field. My second in charge receives baseball, softball. The big ones, football, basketball, women's volleyball, I work on."

"And then you build a promotional campaign around them?" Shane asked, still taking down notes.

"Yes, but not like you think. My role here isn't to showcase the university, there's an entire marketing wing for that. All those trophy cases outside, commercials you see on TV, posters, t-shirts? That's their thing.

"What we do is manage the sports themselves and our athletes within them. We track how they're being presented on social media, in the press, in paraphernalia. We determine how they stack up in terms of other players in the nation, formulate draft strategies, design ways to better present our players, both for helping them get to the next level and for recruiting their replacements."

Shane's head shot up, his eyes a bit wider. "Damn, I did come to the right place."

Marty raised her eyebrows in agreement, but remained silent.

"Alright, so walk me through Tyler Bentley."

A faint, sad smile grew on Marty's face as she tilted her head back and rested it against her chair. "Ah, Tyler, easiest case I ever had."

"How's that?"

Marty shifted her head forward and turned to face Shane, her elbows resting on the table. "The kid damn near managed himself. No Facebook, no Twitter, no MySpace, no social media gaffes of any kind to ever control, no user feedback to monitor. Clean academic and criminal records. Never said a wrong word to the media, never said much of anything to them to be honest. No kids, no crazy girlfriends.

"On the field, his numbers spoke for themselves. Guy went from a solid contributor as a sophomore to a world beater as a junior. The university didn't have to run much of a Heisman campaign for him, he was too good to ignore."

She stopped there, swiveling back to her previous position, legs crossed, head leaning back. "Shame we're not going to see what he could have been capable of as a senior."

Shane looked up from his notes, his face drawn, and nodded. "You also mentioned that you help with getting athletes to the next level?"

"That we do. Put them in contact with top trainers, nutritionists, bring in agents and set up meetings for them after the season, everything. None of that applied to Tyler, but it would have this winter for sure."

"Hmm," Shane said. "And what about the draft itself?"

"We were always monitoring where our players would be taken, how they stacked up compared to others on the Big Board, what they should expect to earn coming out."

"All of that?" Shane asked, his eyes wide.

"Like I said, it is as much to help the current players as to lure in the next batch."

"Ahh," Shane said, a hint of bitter in his tone.

"Welcome to college athletics," Marty said, spreading her hands wide. "Everyone, even myself, is expendable."

A low whistle slid out from between Shane's lips, a look of surprise on his face.

"Don't give me the shocked routine, it's not like your firm would keep you on staff if you weren't producing. It's business for all of us."

Shane opened his mouth to respond, paused, and closed it just as fast. Nothing she'd said was wrong, he'd just never quite framed it that way in his mind. Something told him he should start, for the next few months anyway.

"Just a couple more questions and I'll get out of your hair, I promise."

Marty gestured for him to continue without responding.

"How good was Tyler Bentley?"

Marty met his eye and responded without the smallest hint of a hesitation. "He was the best running back we've had come through here in twenty-five years. A surefire first round pick, in my opinion a definite top ten, maybe even top five."

The declaration gave Shane pause, his pen poised just above his legal pad. "And what kind of remuneration are we talking for that level of talent?"

Turning towards her computer, Marty made a few clicks and brought up a spreadsheet. She turned the screen so Shane could see it, using her finger as a pointer.

"These are the salaries from last year's draft, the only one you can rely on because of the new collective bargaining agreement and rookie salary cap that just took effect. You can see here, the very last player in the first round took home almost seven million in guaranteed money."

Shane smirked and shook his head, trying to fathom the figure.

"The tenth player selected pocketed just over twelve million,"

Marty said, scrolling up a little further. "And last year the top overall running back walked off with a cool twenty-one-point-five and change."

The number sent Shane back in his chair, Marty smiling as she spun the monitor back around to face her. She sat with a bemused expression on her face for several seconds, an elbow propped on the desk as she chewed at her pinkie nail.

"Pretty incredible, huh?"

"Wow," Shane said, shaking his head from side to side. He sat in complete silence for several long moments, trying to comprehend the enormity of what Tyler had before him, of what now lay on his shoulders to try and secure. Through the tangle of thoughts, one in particular jumped out to him.

"Tell me," he began, the words met with an upraised chin from Marty, "what were top players going for before the new system was put in place?"

A knowing smile crept across Marty's face, her eyes leveled on his. "Well, there isn't a usual amount per say, but two years ago the top player drafted was a quarterback. He signed for just shy of eighty million dollars."

CHAPTER TWENTY-NINE

Shane came within an eyelash of bringing Heath and Abby with him, but in the end decided against it. Despite whatever perceived leverage he might lose from being outmanned on his side of the table, he couldn't take the risk of having either one show up underdressed or even worse revealing themselves as first year law students. As invaluable as their research and input had been thus far, they were nowhere near ready to go into a room with Connor Reed and whatever contingent he brought along.

Even after a year working with the Rex Hartman's of the world, Shane wasn't sure he was either.

The thought of asking Professor Prescott to join him also entered his mind, but he decided against it as well, choosing to walk in alone. If this didn't go well and a trial loomed right around the corner, he wanted to save as many surprises as he could for the courtroom. That included the jolting appearance of Tyler on one leg, of Margie's raw emotion, and a front row loaded with co-counsel.

At seven minutes before ten, Shane entered the lobby of the Omni Waterfront Hotel, just five blocks off campus and three from the federal courthouse. It was far and away the nicest hotel in the city, the kind of place visiting professional sports teams and foreign dignitaries stayed at while in town. There was no doubt this is where Reed and his crew were staying right now, and would be for as long as the matter took to resolve.

Shane walked right through the front desk and across the main foyer, past an open air fountain and a row of boutique shops selling coffees, clothing, and organic soaps. He followed the signs to the executive conference room, arriving there four minutes before the agreed-to time.

To his surprise, there were two men in the room, both already seated at the table, no conversation between them. They both rose as he entered, the man on the right motioning towards the door.

"You can go ahead and close that behind you, nobody else will be joining us." He was an older man, somewhere between fifty-five and sixty-five, with thick hair combed back and an impeccable pinstriped suit draped across narrow shoulders. He extended his hand as Shane approached. "Connor Reed."

"Shane Laszlo." He gripped Reed's hand for a moment before shifting to the other man, a fleshy Hispanic with dark hair buzzed short, a close-cut beard and wire-rimmed glasses.

"William Ramirez."

"Good to meet you both," Shane said, sliding his briefcase to the opposite side of the table and taking a seat. Neither of the men could be construed as warm or friendly, though they didn't seem hostile either. The fact that just the two of them had come was a good sign.

Shane thought for a moment about unpacking his bag, but noticed the blank table before each of the men and opted against it. "Gentlemen, you asked for this meeting, so why don't I let you take the lead?"

Without even a glance between them, Reed began. "Well Mr. Laszlo, it goes without saying we're here because of the complaint you filed earlier this week."

"Mhmm," Shane said, leaning forward so his forearms rested on the table, his fingers laced before him. "Is your concern with something found in the complaint, or with the fact that it was filed at all?"

Reed studied Shane for several moments with a wary gaze, as if trying to size him up. Shane met the gaze, staring back without giving an inch, forcing himself to not so much as even blink. The air seemed to withdraw from the room as the two peered at one another, neither giving the other the satisfaction of looking away first.

Age and experience on one side of the table, trying to assert his will on a situation. Youth and conviction on the other side, refusing to be pushed around.

Ramirez might as well have not even been in the room.

After several long moments, Reed lowered a hand to his side, his eyes never wavering. He lifted up a document almost a quarter inch thick and set it on the table beside him, placing his hand atop it.

"You know why we're here, so we might as well just get down to it. This is our formal response to your complaint. At the conclusion of this meeting, one of two things will happen. Either you will accept our settlement offer and your client will become a wealthy man, you take what should amount to a very nice salary for the year, and we all part as friends."

Reed paused there for several moments, as if willing that option onto Shane, trying to force him to realize it was the only acceptable choice.

Shane would have none of it.

"Or?"

"Or we walk out of here, go straight over to the courthouse and file this response, and we all prepare to go to trial in a few weeks. The choice is yours."

After the conversation he'd had with Tyler and Margie the night before, Shane knew it would take an exorbitant offer for him to even consider settling. Still, he kept his face drawn, his emotions in check, as he stared back at them.

"Understood," Shane said. "Let's hear what SynTronic has to say."

Reed stared a moment longer before shifting his gaze over to Ramirez and nodding. On cue, Ramirez reached down to his side and produced a single piece of paper folded down the middle. He placed the paper on the desk and tapped his index finger on it three times before sliding it over to Shane.

The room was silent as Shane looked from Ramirez to Reed and back again, waiting until Ramirez removed his hand before reaching out. He snagged the paper with the pad of his index finger and pulled it towards him, never once lowering his gaze to look at it. Once it was in front of him, he lifted the top half of the paper, studied it a moment, and lowered it back into place.

No outward reaction of any kind passed Shane's face, though inside him a coil of barbed wire tried to fight its way up through his stomach. He and the Bentley's had decided on a number that would be optimal, a number they would like to see, and a bottom line number they could live with if it came down to it.

This one was significantly south of all three.

Shane had known when he walked in that the odds of SynTronic meeting his price were long, but he hadn't expected the opening volley to be quite so low. This wasn't just an exercise in negotiation, it was a full-on slap in the face, an attempt to sweep things under the rug for pennies on the dollar.

Still, if this stoic round of window dressing was what they wanted, he would give it to them.

Shane slid the paper back into the middle of the table and studied both of the men before him. He withdrew his hand and again laced his fingers in front of him, his face a mask.

"I assume that's an opening offer."

The sentence came out as a statement of fact, the intent clear. The amount was insulting and if the meeting was going to continue, a real figure had better be mentioned and fast.

"No, that *is* the offer," Reed said, his voice a bit deeper.

Beside him Ramirez added, "This is the standard settlement amount for negligence claims arising against our client."

Shane looked between each of the men a long moment before nodding his head. "Tell me though, how many of those claims were filed by college athletes that lost a limb due to one of SynTronic's products?"

With that one sentence, the atmosphere in the room went from indifferent to icy. Reed pressed his lips together so tight a vein in his neck began to bulge. Beside him, Ramirez's eyes seem to grow two sizes larger in an attempt to impose his will.

On the opposite side of the table, a strong desire to laugh out loud at the men welled within Shane, fighting with the extreme insult he felt from their lowball offer for the predominant emotion within him. There was not a bullying tactic on the planet that he hadn't witnessed firsthand dating back long before he ever enrolled in law school. If these two thought for a second they were going to force him into an offer so laughable, they were very much mistaken.

"Are you sure that's how you want to handle this?" Reed asked, as if giving Shane one last chance to do the right thing. "That may not be the figure you walked in here wanting, but it does ensure your client goes home with something."

Using the same move both of the men in front of him had just employed, Shane reached for his briefcase without looking down at it and stood. He ran a hand down his tie to make sure it was flat against his torso and stared at each of them, neither making any attempt to rise.

"You'll want to take a left out of here."

Confusion clouded both faces, though neither looked to one another, both still focused on him.

"Courthouse is down the street on the right, the big building with a lot of steps. You can't miss it. Clerk's office is on the second floor, closes at five."

Shane departed without looking back, striding right out the way he'd came, his briefcase by his side, his face impassive. He didn't so much as look from side to side as he left, even keeping his phone stowed away in his bag until reaching the car. Once there, he dialed a single number and held it to his ear before pulling away from the curb.

It was answered after only a single ring.

"Well, what did they say?"

"Can you be back in Columbus within the next two weeks? We're going to trial."

CHAPTER THIRTY

Six hours after meeting with Shane, Reed and Ramirez hosted a second meeting in the executive conference room of the Omni. The set-up, the mood, the participants, everything, was different from the encounter they had that morning.

Reed and Ramirez remained in their respective rooms until one minute after four o'clock, a conscious decision to make sure everybody was present and seated before they arrived. They met in the hallway at the agreed-to time and took the back stairwell down to the first floor, emerging just ten feet away from the conference room and walking into it. Neither one spoke as they made the trip, never even so much as glancing around to see who was nearby.

This was a move they had practiced many times in the past, a vital part of the act that reinforced their belief that practicing law was equal parts showmanship and intellectual acumen.

The two men, despite being several feet wide, managed to enter the door at the same time, complete silence falling as they did so. Reed walked right to the head of the table, a white board and pull-down projector screen behind him. Ramirez stopped just long enough to close the door behind them before taking a place off to the side. Both men made sure to be in direct eye line of everybody at all times, and to always, always be standing.

The crowd in the room had swelled, most of them arriving less than an hour before on the private Cessna Citation Mustang SynTronic kept on standby for just such purposes. The left side of the table was lined with a pair of associate attorneys, both men in their late 30's with matching haircuts and glasses. The only distinguishable difference between them was one wore a blue suit and the other one grey. Over the years, Reed and Ramirez had even taken to referring to them behind closed as doors as The Twins.

Past them were two paralegals, one male and one female, that looked to be in their early thirties. Both wore white dress shirts and slacks, no ties or jackets. A legal pad and pen was positioned before both, their task outlined for them on the way in.

Write down everything, get anything the attorneys ask for, speak only when asking clarifying questions.

On the right side of the table sat Marcellus Sarconi and Dr. Leonard Pinkering, two men that Reed had spoken to just once before, two days prior via video conference. The men appeared before him as they had on the screen, the idiosyncrasies of their appearances, Sarconi's weight, Pinkering's hair color, a touch more pronounced in person.

Behind them sat the Dragon Lady, her usual disapproving scowl in place. Her primary role for the next few months would be to serve as project manager and task master for the team, both positions she relished with a fervor that bordered on zeal.

Reed surveyed the room from left to right and back again, glanced over to Ramirez, and folded his arms across his chest. "Three days ago a complaint was lodged against the SynTronic Corporation by Shane Laszlo on behalf of his client, Tyler Bentley. Two days ago, we had a brief meeting with Mr. Sarconi and Dr. Pinkering here to ferret out the legitimacy of the claim. Finding it to be rather credible, Mr. Ramirez and I caught a plane for this hellhole of a city and set a meeting for this morning with Mr. Laszlo."

Reed rattled the facts off one after another, reducing the entirety of the case chronology into just a few simple sentences. When they were done he looked to Ramirez and gave a single nod, sliding himself off to the side without ever removing his arms from across his torso.

"As should be obvious by the fact that we're all here," Ramirez began, "that meeting did not go well. We extended the standard SynTronic settlement amount to Mr. Laszlo, which was refused. Once the meeting was over we went to the courthouse and filed our response. A trial date has been set for three weeks from Monday."

The left side of the table took the information with practiced indifference, the only movement of any kind being from the paralegals as they took notes. Across from them, Sarconi and Pinkering both looked to be sick.

"Are there any questions before we get started?"

Blue twin looked at Ramirez and asked, "How strong is their case?"

Ramirez flicked his gaze over to Sarconi and Pinkering. He let it linger just long enough so everyone in the room knew what he was alluding to before looking back. "The claims are valid, the case well thought out. There is little doubt of what happened, even less that SynTronic was the cause of it."

"Our job on this case will be to establish four things," Reed said, walking back to stand beside Ramirez, arms still frozen in place, a deep frown on his face. "First, that the Bentley's were fully apprised of their options and in their haste to get Tyler back on the field, made an unwise decision."

"Did they?" Grey twin asked.

This time, both Reed and Ramirez fixed an accusatory stare on Sarconi and Pinkering.

"No," Ramirez said. "Not even a little bit. Like I said, there is no doubt that SynTronic was the cause of this situation."

Pinkering's face went through three shades of red as he sat staring back, his fingers tapping out an inaudible beat on the table in front of him. Sarconi went in the opposite direction, every bit of blood draining from his face, leaving his visage chalky white. He seemed to retract himself back as far into his seat as he could, like a turtle trying to retreat into its shell.

All he managed to do was increase the number of skin folds around his neck.

"Second," Reed said, shifting his attention back to the room at large, "is to make clear the mutilation that rendered the leg unsalvageable was done by poor surgical work and not by any fault of the product itself, that the leg should have survived product failure just the way it survived the original injury."

Pinkering's jaw dropped open at this statement, the revelation that he would be attacking a friend and colleague in the courtroom hitting him square in the face. His jaw worked up and down a few times in silence, trying to find the words. By the time they came to him, Reed was charging ahead, intent on keeping the discussion to a minimum.

"Three, we will assert that no small part of the product's demise was due to the wanton disregard for the limitations placed upon it by Tyler Bentley himself."

The paralegals continued to scribble in the back of the room as he spoke, everyone else listening in motionless silence.

"And last, we will do everything in our power to drive down the amount of damages that could be awarded to the family."

The words hung with a heavy connotation over the room. Despite the previous three points, the fact that a stated goal of the defense was to minimize damages meant that even the attorneys before them knew they were fighting a losing battle.

"Did you get a sense from Mr. Laszlo what they will be asking in damages?" Grey Twin asked. If he was at all surprised by the previous revelation, he gave no indication.

"There was no stated amount in the complaint," Ramirez said, "but as you all know that's not uncommon in civil cases. Plaintiffs prefer not to have a ceiling in place, to put forth a case and hope a sympathetic jury takes pity and awards them the moon, especially against large, faceless corporation like SynTronic."

The Twins both nodded in unison, the paralegals continuing to take notes beside them. In the corner, Lauren watched the entire proceeding with a sense of icy detachment, watching the people around the table more than the two men in front of it.

Pinkering and Sarconi both looked like they might vomit. Pinkering's face was such a deep hue of crimson it appeared his head might explode at any time while Sarconi was so pale that passing out appeared to be a real possibility. Both stared straight down at the table before them, looking at no one, saying nothing.

"Based on the actions of Mr. Laszlo this morning though," Reed said, "I would venture to guess that it's no small amount they are seeking."

There was a pause from the room, waiting for him to continue. When he did not, Blue Twin prompted him.

"What makes you say that?"

Reed glanced over at Ramirez, giving him the go ahead to answer without saying a word.

"The kid looked at our settlement offer, looked at us, pushed it back across the table, and told us to go to hell," Ramirez said.

Even the paralegals stopped writing at that revelation, every face in the room turned to Ramirez.

"Not in those words by any stretch of the imagination," Ramirez said. "He was very polite, very professional, but it was clear from the moment he walked in that they weren't accepting a lowball offer."

"Did we expect them to?" Grey Twin asked.

"No," Reed replied, "the offer was more to feel them out than anything. The young man in question was a star athlete that is now facing a lifetime of prosthetics, therapy, everything that comes with the loss of a limb. That's no small matter."

"Still, the manner with which our offer was denied showed that they are swinging for the fences," Ramirez added.

The Twins nodded in unison, as if the information was what they'd expected to hear all along.

"What do you make of Laszlo?" Grey Twin asked. "What did you call him, The Kid?"

"Not *The* Kid, a kid," Reed said. "He seems sharp, but he's just a year out of law school, been practicing environmental law since then in Boston."

Blue Twin made a reflexive face, confusion splayed across his nondescript features. "So what's he doing here?"

Reed and Ramirez exchanged a long, doleful glance that lasted almost a full minute, drawing the attention of everyone at the table. The two focused in hard on one another the entire time, each wondering how much to divulge just yet, not knowing how relevant it might be.

"We'll get to that," Reed said at last, his words traced with a bit of uncertainty.

Before anybody could question the directive, Ramirez clasped his hands in front of him. "Alright, any more questions, or should we get started?"

"What about me?" a man in the back of the room asked, snapping half the heads at the table towards the unknown voice.

The other half recognized it right off.

On the end of the table, Lauren went rigid, her lips parting in horror. She sat frozen in place, making no attempt to turn to the man she knew was seated within easy reach of her. Two seats over, Sarconi tried to pull himself even further into his turtle shell, his jowls trembling as a heavy swallow passed down his throat. The pasty complexion of his bloodless face remained, now shiny with sweat. At the head of the table Reed and Ramirez both stood unmoving, each of them making sure to avoid eye contact.

Silence hung for almost a full minute.

Pinkering, along with the entire left side of the table, stared at the man sprawled in a chair in the far corner of the room with a mix of surprise and curiosity. He was not there when they had entered and Ramirez had shut the door behind him fifteen minutes before. Nobody had come or gone from the room, nobody had seen the door open, yet somehow the man sat here now as if he hadn't a care in the world.

"It's not very nice to ignore someone when they ask you a question," the man said, his voice somewhere between a leer and a smirk.

From where he was seated, the man did not appear especially tall or large, though he was well put together. He wore faded jeans with rips at the knees and scuffed black boots, a grey Henley thermal with the sleeves pushed up, and a long gold chain around his neck. A tangle of short brown hair seemed to sprout out in every direction above a two-day beard and humorless eyes.

"Everybody, this is Ute Carbone, Special Consultant to SynTronic," Reed said, his voice heavy with resignation. "You will all be seeing him around here from time to time in the coming months, though his role is more of a behind-the-scenes one."

The remark drew a wide grin from Carbone, followed by a smirk. "Special Consultant...behind the scenes..." he muttered, just loud enough for everybody in the room to hear. The implication that the title and the description were both complete fabrications was very clear.

"And to answer your question," Reed said, his voice rising just enough to try and stem any further comments Carbone might say, "no. Right now, we won't be needing your services."

The smile faded from Carbone's face, a look of genuine disappointment replacing it.

Reed gave a glance to Ramirez, his face heavy with guilt. "But if you wouldn't mind sticking around town for a while, we might very well yet."

The smile returned just as fast as it had faded, Carbone's features twisting with sadistic pleasure. He raised two fingers to his brow and saluted in understanding, rising and leaving before another word was said.

CHAPTER THIRTY-ONE

The mid-May sun was strong, the kind of weather that made school children long for summer vacation and working adults yearn for the weekend. Spring had been a little slower than usual in arriving this year, but when it finally showed up it did so in spectacular fashion.

Overnight, days of gray and low hanging clouds dousing the world in a fine mist capitulated, leaving lustrous color in their wake. The dead grasses and barren tree limbs of a Midwestern winter yielded, replaced by rolling fields and leaves of varying shades of green. Flowers sprouted from every available orifice of the earth, pushing their way towards the sky in exultation of a season forever in coming.

Despite the cornucopia of color going on around him, Shane was in a dour mood as he steered his car east of Columbus, Molly on the seat beside him. The trial was just nine days from starting, his nights of sleeping until morning now a distant memory. Most of his waking hours were spent in the law library at OTU, the only people he spoke to with any regularity being Heath, Abby, Prescott, and the occasional phone call to Tyler.

Otherwise, it was just him, a stack of legal precedent, and a desk lamp. At least at Webster, Banks & Cohen he'd been afforded a view.

Over a year had passed since he'd last made this drive, though not one thing along the route had changed. As he exited the freeway and steered south through farmland, rows of winter wheat now standing a foot tall in the fields, a feeling of déjà vu crept through him. He'd gone on this journey no less than two dozen times in the past, each one a little harder than the time before. Even this time, despite the months that had passed, would be difficult.

The same old feeling had been waiting for him when he awoke that morning, sitting right behind his eyes, a tiny lead weight pressing on his thoughts. As he rose, showered, dressed, ate, it managed to work its way south, resting like a heavy lump in his throat he spent all morning trying to swallow.

All he managed to do was force it down into his stomach, where it now sat like a brick, jolting his insides with every move he made.

On the seat beside him Molly seemed to be having none of the same concerns, her body twisted into a tight ball, somehow maximizing every last bit of a small square of sunshine. For some reason Shane couldn't quite pinpoint, he shook his head in irritation as he made a left onto a tiny gravel lane.

The road was marked by a row of shrubbery on either side, a pair of flowering dogwoods in full bloom behind them. On the left side a low slung simple sign of white with peach lettering welcomed them to Shady Lanes.

No other words, no further description of where they were.

True to its moniker, a thicket of towering elm trees blocked out the midday sun as Shane drove, the brushed gravel drive passing beneath his tires. His heart began to have slight palpitations as a large home appeared at the end of the drive, a bit of sweat hitting his forehead, his breath becoming audible in his ears.

With each second the home grew closer, materializing to resemble a plantation estate from somewhere in the Deep South, everything painted white with enormous columns lining the front. Flowerbeds extended out around the house like a halo, the yard well groomed.

About the only thing that seemed out of place at all was a shiny black Audi parked off to the side.

Seeing the car silent and waiting for him brought a smile to Shane's face as he angled his Honda alongside it and stepped out. Beside him, the driver's side door of the Audi opened and Christine emerged, a pink and white sundress offset by her dark complexion.

"Bout time you got here," she said, reaching down into her car and extracting a pair of sunglasses, opening them and placing them over her eyes with only one hand.

Shane ignored the comment, fighting back the urge to rush over and envelope her in a hug. "Thank you for coming." He reached back into the car and slid his hand beneath Molly's warm belly, the cat protesting just a bit as he lifted her out and tucked her close against his hip. "Even if I didn't ask you to."

Christine circled the back of her car and came up alongside them, sliding a hand through the crook of Shane's left arm. "Have you ever had to?"

The comment elicited a smirk from Shane, who shook his head, unable to argue with it. "No, I guess I haven't."

Arm in arm they walked across the gravel, their feet crunching beneath them, towards the house. A pair of elderly men sat in rocking chairs playing checkers as they approached, neither one so much as looking their way. An orderly dressed in all white stood watch nearby, nodding to Shane, his eyes lingering a bit longer on Christine, as they passed.

Both returned the gesture and headed inside, a set of wide double doors opening into a deceptively large space, the spacious old home having been refitted into a functioning convalescent home.

Just stepping into the place brought back a flood of memories, all of which Shane could do without. The roiling in his stomach grew stronger with each step, a sharp intake of breath passing through his nose. He could feel Christine's grip on his arm grow stronger as they walked, her other hand reaching up to remove the sunglasses, a quick look of reassurance aimed his direction.

As best he could Shane blocked it out, aiming his focus on the diminutive woman sitting behind the desk.

She was short and thin, her hair more like wisps of silver, a white cardigan draped over her narrow shoulders. Her face was pinched in deep concentration as they approached, only looking up at the sound of their footfalls against the wooden floor. Once she did a look of recognition flooded her features and she was on her feet in no time, arms outstretched before her.

"Oh, Shane!"

Despite her tiny stature, she held a strength Shane didn't know possible as she pulled him into a hug. He released Christine's hand and returned it with one arm, Molly extended from his side in the other.

As fast as she had overtaken him she pulled back, her hands finding Molly's head and scratching her ears.

"Oh, it's so good to see you, she's going to be so happy. And you even brought this old rascal for her to too."

"Good to see you as well, Kay. How have you been?"

Kay pulled back from Molly and rested her fists on her hips, shoulders rising and falling in an exaggerated sigh. "Good, busy. Same old thing."

"Which isn't always a bad thing," Shane said. "Kay, do you remember my friend Christine? She came out here with me once before."

"Of course, of course," Kay said, arms shooting out from her side to engulf Christine in a squeeze as well. "How could I forget?"

"Nice to see you again," Christine said, her voice a touch strained from the force of the hug laid upon her.

Kay held the pose for several seconds before pulling back, again resting her fists on her hips. She pressed her lips tight together and shook her head, a touch of moisture glistening from the corners of her eyes.

"I'm just so glad you all came out here today. We don't get enough surprise visits from family, and it just does them a world of good. A *world* of good."

Shane stood and smiled, letting the statement pass. "How is she?"

"She's..." Kay said, searching for the right words, "the same too."

Shane gave her a knowing nod, all-too-familiar with what she meant.

"Is she in the same room? Can we head back there?"

A bony wrist shot up in front of Kay, her other hand rising to push back the sleeve of her sweater to check a wristwatch. "Let's see here. Yes, you most certainly can. The nurses have already made their rounds, lunchtime isn't for another couple of hours. You know where it is, right?"

"Yes, thank you," Shane said, reaching for Christine's hand and pulling her towards the hallway. "Nice to see you again."

"Nice to see you!" Kay called behind them, her voice already growing fainter as Shane led them down the main hallway. At the end of it he turned right and headed for the far corner, the very last door on the main floor. He stopped outside it for just a moment and took a breath, Christine's hand tightening inside his.

Shane looked at her once and nodded before releasing her grip and knocking on the door with the back of his hand, pushing it open as he stepped inside.

"Hey there, Mama."

The room was awash in half-light as they entered, all of it produced from the outdoor sun sifting through the blinds. The entire space was not more than fifteen feet square, a dresser and chair along the far side, a few paintings and pictures on the walls. In the center of the room was an oversized adjustable hospital bed and on it lay a shriveled woman, her size and age both indiscernible.

A mountain of blankets seemed to bury her body, cocooning her within them. Thick dark hair was streaked with swaths of silver, her skin splotched with age spots. A bevy of tubes and lines were connected to her, feeding oxygen into her nostrils and a series of fluids and narcotics into her veins.

Whereas the entire far side of the room was made to appear as homey as possible, the closer side was everything needed for a functioning care unit. A breathing apparatus rose and fell with each breath, a heart rate monitor beeping out an even pulse beside it. A silver tray used for medication and feeding was pulled alongside the machines, though at the moment was empty.

At the sight of her lying on the bed Molly wriggled herself free of Shane's grip, hitting the floor in two strides before bounding up. She walked right onto center mass and circled twice, curling herself into a tight ball.

Shane walked in behind Molly and leaned down to kiss his mother on the forehead, running a hand back over her hair. "How you doing today?"

Her eyes were open, her head angled to face out the window on the far side of the room. No indication of recognition crossed her face, not even the faintest flicker behind the eyes.

It had been years since the incident, but the mere sight of her still stabbed Shane in the heart. The slightest tinges of tears formed along the bottom of his eyes as he stood by her side, waiting until they passed before kissing her again and turning back to Christine.

"This never gets any easier, you know it?"

"No, I imagine it doesn't." Taking that as a cue to enter, Christine walked forward, grasped the withered hand lying atop the covers, and gave it a squeeze. "Hey Sandy, it's nice to see you again."

She held the hand for a long moment, looking down at Sandy's face before her eyes slid down to Molly curled up atop her chest.

"You know, I always wondered about that. You just never took me for a cat man."

Shane smirked and walked around to the opposite side of the bed, lowering himself in the chair and grasping his mother's opposite hand. "I'm not, at all. Funny thing is, she wasn't either, but for whatever reason these two always hit it off."

Aware that she was being discussed, Molly began to purr between them.

"When everything happened, I just couldn't bear to get rid of her. I know she won't last forever, and I know it sounds crazy, but as long as she's here, I feel like I still have a tangible connection to my mom."

A soft look crossed Christine's features, her gaze shifting from Molly to Shane. "You do still have a tangible connection to her though, she's right here."

Shane leaned forward and raised his mother's hand, running the back of it against his cheek. He remained that way for several seconds, his eyes closed.

"Do you remember the very first time we met?" Shane asked. "When you asked if I was afraid of you?"

A sound between a cough and a laugh slid out from Christine. "Yeah, and you looked at me like I was crazy."

Shane's eyes opened, the whites of them tinged with red, and he nodded towards his mother with the top of his head. "She was the meanest, most determined, dogged, intense, kind, loving, protective, caring woman I've ever known. I've seen her go into a courtroom and make tattooed gangbangers cry, then come home and make me grilled cheese for dinner."

Christine smiled, her dark eyes a bit glassy. "I remember. Did you know we even studied a couple of her cases in business school? Our professor referred to her as The Bulldog."

"Ha!" Shane said, the sound escaping him before he even realized it. "You serious?"

"Yeah," Christine replied, nodding her head, her own smile in place. "Don't think I wasn't big time that day, telling everybody I knew Sandy Laszlo."

"She would have liked that," Shane said, the side of his mouth turning up in a half smile. "So yeah, no disrespect, but I was never afraid of you. Just like I wasn't the least bit afraid of Connor Reed last week in that meeting. If I could survive losing her, I can survive anything."

Christine pressed her lips together in a half smile, regarding her friend. "How you doing with all that?"

Shane's gaze shifted to look at her, a long breath drawing in through his nose. "I'm okay. Tyler gets in on Thursday, opening statements start on Monday. I don't know that you ever feel ready, but I'm as prepared as I can be, so let's just get going already."

A small twist of the head from side to side was his response. "That's not what I meant."

A look of confusion passed over Shane's face, followed by a moment of clarity. His lips formed into a small circle as he stared at her, his eyes wandering up to his mother's face.

"I don't know yet. Like you said before, I know it's going to come out, it has to, but I still don't know how or when."

"Has the other side given any indication yet that they know?"

"No," Shane said, twisting his head, "but they know. Hell, she's my local attorney of record, her name is listed right on the complaint."

Christine's eyebrows shot up, the information surprising her. The two of them sat in silence for several moments, both staring at Sandy, lost in thought.

"So maybe that's your angle," Christine said, her voice drawing Shane's gaze towards her.

"What's that?" he asked, his voice thick and low.

"Well," Christine replied, her head making a non-committal gesture, "they know she's going to play into it somehow. Odds are, they'll try to do something to minimize her impact, maybe take her out of it altogether."

Christine fell silent, her gaze lingering on Shane. He matched the look for several seconds before nodding his understanding.

"I was setting a trap for them without even realizing it."

CHAPTER THIRTY-TWO

The plane touched down from Denver into Columbus at just after three in the afternoon. The journey had started in Worland nine hours before, featuring a drive to Cody, a connecting flight, a layover, and then the three hour trip back to Columbus.

Due to Tyler's special circumstances, Shane was allowed to pass through security without a boarding pass, sitting gate side as the passengers unloaded, an airport wheelchair by his side. He stood as Tyler approached, a knapsack over one shoulder, crutches propped up under both his armpits.

The time away had taken a toll, though he looked much better than their first video conference discussion six weeks before. He was still a lot lighter than the last time Shane had seen him, though there was some color in his cheeks, his spirits seemed better.

Shane left the wheelchair parked beside a row of interlocked airport seats and met Tyler just past the gate, his hand extended. Tyler stopped and returned the shake, his upper body supported by the metal crutches beneath him.

"Good trip?" Shane asked, the safest thing he could think of to open with. It was the first face to face encounter they'd had in over a year, and even then all interaction they had was confined to the teacher-student role.

"It was interesting," Tyler said, giving Shane a harried look and resuming the crutches. He wore a Wyoming football sweatshirt and gym shorts, the left leg of them swinging free around his thigh. Despite the crutches he moved well, motioning towards the wheelchair. "That for me?"

"If you want it," Shane said, hoping he hadn't made a faux pas in bringing it. "If not, the attendant there said we can just leave it, they'll have someone get it later."

"Hell, no," Tyler said, positioning himself beside it before hopping once over and dropping down onto the padded cushion. He remained motionless for a moment, his face upturned in relief, before opening his eyes and sliding the bag from his shoulder. "I tell you what, I don't mind hopping, and I'm almost used to the chair, but I hate those damn crutches."

Without waiting for Shane to move, he extended the crutches to him, motioning for him to take them. Once Shane did, he wheeled himself through the terminal, his arms propelling himself forward.

"Few more weeks and you won't need either of them," Shane said, falling in beside him.

"You know what's funny?" Tyler asked as they wheeled out past the food court and the ticket counters, a thin crowd parting for them as they went. "Used to be, I never even noticed the stares. Every once in a while someone would come up and ask for an autograph or something, but otherwise, they didn't even enter my mind. Now? I am very aware of it at all times."

Shane glanced down to see Tyler facing forward, his face locked in a matter-of-fact stare. "Got a lot of that today, huh?"

"Maybe I'm just hypersensitive to it, but it sure as hell felt like it."

They left the airport wheelchair by the curb and got into the Honda, Shane maneuvering them straight across town towards campus.

He knew Tyler must be exhausted and want nothing more than to lie down after his journey, but there wasn't the time to allow it. Every minute of the previous weeks had been spent in intense preparation, it was now time to lay out the full strategy for everybody, piece together all the roles they had been playing into a larger format.

Prescott, Heath, and Abby were waiting for them as they entered the same conference room Shane used his first day back just a month before. Despite all three of them ready and waiting, an avalanche of paper spread out before them, the place still looked vast and empty, only a fraction of its massive space in use. The room was silent as they arrived, each person poring over papers.

"Good afternoon, everyone," Shane said, walking to the head of the table and dropping his briefcase into his chair. He wouldn't be sitting much over the next few hours and didn't have a single thing in his bag that hadn't already been committed to memory many times over. With one hand he grasped the chair back and pushed it off to the side, pulling a rolling whiteboard over in its stead.

Behind him Tyler leaned his crutches against the side of the table and took up the last chair on the right, falling in beside Abby. She turned and offered him a small smile as he did so, nodding her head.

"First of all, I know we've met via video conference, but allow me to introduce you to Tyler Bentley, here and in the flesh," Shane said. On cue, all three transitioned from casting curious glances his way to outright staring. "Tyler, this is Professor Alfred Prescott, Heath Wilson, and Abby Hill, the people that have been working the last month on your behalf."

A bit of color rushed to Tyler's cheeks at the comment. Using the table for leverage, he pushed himself to a standing position and extended his hand across the table, shaking each of their hands in turn.

"It is very nice to meet you all. Again, and this goes for you too Shane, I can't begin to thank you enough for this."

Shane nodded his acknowledgement as the other three did the same, everyone retreating back to their seats. He waited a few moments to let them get settled and silence to fall over the room. He then clasped his hands in front of him and turned to the white board, taking up a blue pen and scrawling across it, starting in the top left corner.

"Alright," Shane said, "so here's how I envision this going. I apologize for the late start time, but this was the earliest we could get a flight in here for Tyler. This may not surprise some of you, but I was shocked to discover there isn't a direct 747 from Worland to Columbus."

All the faces around the table broke into smiles.

At the end of it, Tyler raised his hands by his side and said, "Who knew?"

That elicited chuckles from everyone as Shane jammed the cap on the bottom of the pen. "So even though it's a little later than we would all like, trial begins in three days, and time is of the essence. I wanted to get everybody in the same room and outline what we're planning to do in the next few weeks. This is the time to flesh things out, so if you see holes or have questions, don't be bashful."

He paused and looked at each of the faces before him, hoping to drive home the directive. There was no ego involved at this point, no concerns about appearance. If something seemed wrong or needed to be addressed, it should be, and fast.

"Alright, first and foremost," Shane said, whirling to the white board and writing the Roman numeral one. "Courtroom positioning. I've been thinking a lot about this, and sitting at the table will just be me and Tyler, for two reasons. First of all, Professor I know you can't always be there, and Heath, Abby, I wouldn't dream of trying to pick one over the other. That being said, I think it would be better to reserve the entire first row on our side of the courtroom and have you three lined up right there as much as possible."

Heath and Abby both nodded in agreement. Prescott extended a finger towards him and said, "You are the only one of us licensed to speak anyway, so that makes perfect sense."

"Which kind of leads me to the second part," Shane said, nodding. "My supervising attorney, for purposes of my *pro hac vice* forms anyway, will not be joining us."

Shane shifted his attention to the back of the room, his hands pressed together before him, making no attempt to elaborate further on the comment.

"Tyler, I don't know how comfortable you're going to be with this so please speak up now, but I'm thinking you leave the crutches at home for the duration of this. I know we talked about waiting until after trial to get your prosthetic, but seeing you getting off the plane today it occurred to me that the jury needs to see you either in a chair or hopping."

Tyler stared back at him, his lips drawn into a tight line, saying nothing.

"I know what you're thinking, and believe me, the idea here isn't to paint you as some sort of charity case. What we need to relay to the jury is how profound an impact this has had on your life. We need them to understand that SynTronic took you from a world-class running back to someone that requires great effort for basic mobility."

Three gazes turned to regard Tyler, who considered the notion in silence for several long moments. After he was done, he blinked himself alert and shifted his focus back to Shane.

"Makes sense. Besides, I already told you I hate those things anyway."

"Good," Shane said, nodding in appreciation, thankful that Tyler wasn't trying to challenge him on it. If he had, Shane would have backed down, but it would have made for a tougher sell in front of the jury.

"Second," Shane said, moving down the board, writing in all capital letters beside the Roman numeral two, "Monday will begin with jury selection. Professor, *voir dire* is something you've spent a great deal of time studying, would you care to outline what we're trying to do?"

"Certainly," Prescott said, his thick English accent rolling out over the room. "Every lawyer in the world states that the purpose of *voir dire* is to find a fair and impartial jury pool, but that is pure bollocks. What we're trying to do is find the fifteen most sympathetic individuals we can.

"In this instance we are at a distinct advantage because of the unique situation our client finds himself in. A young, handsome, local celebrity that had his livelihood and his physical well-being removed from him by a faulty device. There is very little a jury can't find favorable in that scenario.

"Still, it will be our goal to find women, mothers if we can. We will want to find anybody that might have been an athlete themselves, and any major sports supporter. Race doesn't much matter here, nor does gender beyond what I just mentioned. The only groups we may want to avoid will be the geriatric and the occasional blue collar worker, not because they wouldn't be on our side, but because they have a history of limiting the amount of damages awarded."

Shane stood with his arms folded in front of him as Prescott spoke, Heath and Abby both taking notes. When the explanation was complete, Shane turned back to the board and wrote down a third Roman numeral.

"Now, bear in mind I expect them to make a motion for change of venue at some point, but that might not be until after jury selection is complete and they see the hand they've been dealt. If that happens, I'll be shocked if the judge allows it, but we'll have to be prepared to argue it if he allows them to file."

"Who is the presiding judge?" Prescott asked.

"The Honorable Richard Lynch, appointed in '98 by Clinton. Liberal, but not over-the-top."

Prescott nodded his approval. "I agree. I have met Richard on a handful of occasions, seems a forthright man and if I'm not mistaken, a bit of a football fan."

A smile tugged at Shane's mouth. It was harder to find men in Columbus that weren't football fans than those that were. That alone was the chief reason he was suspecting a change of venue motion to be filed any moment, SynTronic reasoning that they could never receive a fair trial in football-crazed Ohio, not with a fallen demigod as the plaintiff.

It was a fact that Shane had been using as a basis for almost every move his case strategy had employed thus far.

He turned back to the board and wrote out numbers four and five, blue ink now scrawled over half the available white space. "Once we have a jury in place, we'll move into opening statements. After that, we'll begin calling witnesses."

Block letters A through F went up on the board, Shane narrating without turning around. "For obvious reasons, we'll open with Tyler. Tomorrow morning he and I are going to sit down and go through every question I intend to ask twice, followed by everything I think SynTronic will try to draw out of him on cross. Professor, thank you for looking over those lists and making additions, appreciate it."

Prescott nodded without replying.

"After Tyler will be his mother Margie, the basic reasoning being to corroborate Tyler's story and humanize it even more."

Shane continued writing names as he went down the list. "After that I'll be calling Dr. Manningham, the surgeon that performed the surgery, and William Curl, the trainer that was overseeing his rehab. We'll finish up with Dr. Ben Lomax and Martina Graham, both as subject matter experts. Dr. Lomax to discuss the faulty design of the KnightRunner, Martina to discuss Tyler's prospects as a future pro football player."

Heath and Abby both continued to write as Prescott looked on. In the back of the room, Tyler made a pained grimace at the mention of Graham and the testimony she would be providing, though he remained silent.

"I received SynTronic's list of witnesses two days ago, and was surprised to see it is a little thin. The best I can figure is they either plan to attack our witnesses under cross and try to minimize their testimony to the point of being moot, or they still have plans for forcing a settlement."

"How long do they have to try for a settlement?" Tyler asked, his voice snapping Abby's head to the side.

"They can offer a settlement clear up until the day of closing argument," Shane said, still writing on the board. "But if we get anywhere near that far, they'll just wait it out to see what happens with the jury."

Tyler nodded his understanding as Shane finished writing, turning back to face the room.

"They are going to call Dr. Leonard Pinkering, the supervising physician on Tyler's case, along with Marcellus Sarconi, the SynTronic rep that has been spearheading the entire KnightRunner project. He is serving as their material and product expert on this one, Pinkering as their medical guy.

"Last, they will be calling a Mel Hinderly, an NFL draft analyst from New Jersey."

A loud snort sounded out from the back of the room.

"Tyler and Mr. Hinderly have a bit of history together," Shane said, a half smile on his face.

"The guy's a hack," Tyler said. "Hates OTU, hates me, hates our entire conference. Thinks if it's not played in Texas or the Deep South it doesn't count as football."

"So he's there to refute any testimony about your draft position?" Heath asked, his first words of the entire meeting.

Another snort slid out from Tyler. "Odds are he'll try to convince the world I shouldn't have even started on my high school team and had no chance at being drafted."

The smile on Shane's face grew a touch wider. "Excellent, I look forward to seeing him try to make that one stick here in Columbus."

Heath and Prescott both nodded while Tyler scowled towards the table. Abby remained motionless, no reaction to the discussion of football around her.

"After that, we have closing arguments," Shane said, not bothering to turn and write anything down. "So that's the long and short of it, the next few weeks of our lives in six bullet points. Any high-arching questions before we get to work?"

All four heads were turned towards him, nobody saying a word. Shane shifted his eyes up to the clock on the far wall, the time just after five o'clock. They all had a long night ahead of them, the first of what was sure to be many in the coming weeks. He dropped the marker back into the white board tray and unbuttoned the cuffs of his sleeves, rolling them up almost to his elbows.

"Alright, let's get started. Heath, tell me anything new you've uncovered on product liability cases."

CHAPTER THIRTY-THREE

The request was very simple, a directive cloaked as a suggestion, the way most things were when they came to Ute. Nobody ever had the fortitude to come right out and tell him to do anything, but most everybody he dealt with needed something from him. What that might be varied a great deal, a nod both to his arrayed skill set and the aura of mystery that surrounded him.

Nobody knew what they could or couldn't ask of him because nobody knew what he could or couldn't do.

This request was very simple, so simple in fact that Ute had not yet decided whether or not he should be offended by it. Three days before, Reed had reached out to him. As there were only two people alive that knew his direct number, and he was certain his mother hadn't given it away, it meant that Reed had climbed the corporate ladder wishing to speak to him. The fact that he had put in such effort, and pushed aside the fear that he possessed, spoke volumes to the necessity of the call.

That was the only reason Ute had not taken offense to the request, he had already seen what was at stake. While the job at hand might seem trivial, the kind of thing any chapped ass monkey with two hands and a flashlight could perform, he knew where the case could and most likely would end up. He'd known it for some time, having started on the job even long before being asked to do so.

"Um, Mr. Carbone, this is Connor Reed," Reed stated into the phone, his voice bearing a hint of strain in it. "I am calling to ask that you look into something for us, should it become necessary later on."

Ute preferred meeting in person. It gave his imposition of will a much greater gravitas. As his legend had grown though, people had become too fearful of dealing with him in person and his act had been forced to grow as well.

"What?" Ute asked, a single word that he spit into the phone receiver, not a question of clarification but a demand to know what Reed wanted.

"I would like to revisit the question you asked last week at our strategy session," Reed said, pretending not to notice the venom in Ute's voice. "If you are available, we think it might be prudent for you to begin keeping tabs on Laszlo and his team."

"Why?" The malevolence was the same as the first question, the tone even sharper.

There was a long pause followed by a deep sigh, Reed contemplating his response, trying to avoid saying the words.

Ute was not about to let him do so.

"Through the discovery process, we have become increasingly aware that our position, however well thought out and intended, is just not coming together as we'd hoped."

Sitting alone in his car, Ute shook his head in disgust. Leave it to a lawyer to say fifty words to sidestep a question that could have been answered in two.

"You're fucked, and you need me to unfuck it."

"No no no," Reed responded a bit too fast, defensiveness in his voice. "I didn't say that, and I asked you to do no such thing. Right now we are just requesting that you start keeping tabs on them should a situation arise in the future. You will of course be paid your standard fee plus expenses for your services."

"You don't pay me anything," Ute shot back, the words clipped and harsh. "Don't act like you're doing me any favors, or I'll start keeping closer tabs on you. That pretty little wifey of yours still like to play tennis on Thursdays? Or how about that fat bastard Ramirez and those two little brown sausages he takes to the park every weekend? Or maybe my favorite, that luscious little blonde you've been jerking off to for the last three years?"

There was a sharp intake of breath on the other end of the line, though no words of any kind were said. Ute let the silence hang in the air long enough to make his point, a thin smile spreading across his face.

"I'll look into Laszlo and his crew, see what I can turn up. You let me know if you get the stones to act on it, otherwise don't ever call this number again."

Ute slammed the phone down before Reed could respond and hadn't heard a word in the three days since.

A light rain began to dot the windshield of his Toyota as he sat in the parking lot outside the Ohio Tech law school, a sack of Wendy's on the passenger seat beside him. This was his fourth different vantage spot of the afternoon, moving his car often to keep from arising suspicion. His neck ached from sitting behind the wheel for hours on end and the car stunk of fast food grease, but he kept a sharp lookout on the front door of the school, anxious for a sign of any of the five people he knew were within.

On the floorboard of the passenger seat was a file almost two inches thick he'd amassed in the previous two weeks. The four members of the legal team he had covered, ranging from Prescott's family back in Britain to Laszlo's visit to his mother the weekend before. This was the first sign of the man himself though, of Mr. Tyler Bentley, in Columbus since the operation.

The plan at first wasn't to spend the day following the team, the file on the floorboard sufficient to do everything he needed and then some. Ute took a great deal of pride in bringing new meaning to the phrase *painfully thorough*, a fact that any member of that team could fast learn if he was given the go ahead. While doing some light surveillance on Laszlo that morning he grew curious and decided to follow him.

When he'd seen him walk out the front door of the airport pushing Bentley, there had been no doubt what he would be doing the rest of the day.

Enough years spent in this line of work had made one thing very clear to Ute. If you want to stop a case dead in its tracks at any point, take out the one named in the suit. If there is no plaintiff, there can be no trial.

That was the thought that kept running through his head as he leaned low behind the steering wheel and watching Laszlo and Bentley both exit the building, Laszlo holding the door as Bentley walked through on crutches. The rain on the windshield and the steam from within masked his windows as they went by and climbed into a faded Honda two rows over, neither one even glancing in his direction.

After all, he'd been the one that put this entire thing in motion six months before when he called Sarconi to tell him to turn on the TV, the opportunity they'd all been waiting for was staring them right in the face. Of course, the only reason he was even watching the game that night was because in less than a week he was planning to do what the free safety from Virginia State did to Tyler Bentley's knee anyway.

The only difference was he wouldn't have used a helmet and Bentley would have suffered a lot more.

SynTronic decided long ago their new toy was going into Tyler Bentley. They just never imagined it would be coming back out of him quite so fast.

CHAPTER THIRTY-FOUR

An early lesson Shane learned from his mother was how to read opposing counsel. One of a very few women working as a full time litigator in the late nineties, she fast uncovered every trick she could in turning a courtroom in her favor. Part of that was choosing the opportune moments to remind everybody that she was in fact a woman, whether that was from showing a hint of leg or tearing up at the testimony of a grieving widow. Just as important though was being able to take the measure of the men sitting across from her, sizing them up in a matter of seconds and using that information to her advantage.

Sandy Laszlo's favorite way of doing that was by analyzing the way opposing counsel was dressed. Courtroom etiquette mandated that men wear suits, but there was still a lot that could be gleaned. If a man wore a black suit, he was aiming for reserved, stoic, almost unapproachable. Grey gave the appearance of neutrality, blue of loyalty.

Even more telling was the tie someone chose, where there was a lot more room for personal choice and interpretation. Red was the penultimate power color, the obvious go-to for a man wanting to assert his presence in a room. Blue was the yin to red's yang, a statement of being trustworthy and approachable. A man choosing brown was opting to convey a sense of down-to-earth, while someone that chose green had money on the brain.

On the first morning of trial, Shane found himself standing in front of the closet of his rented room, dressed only in his briefs and undershirt, remembering those extensive lessons of courtroom fashion. Whether they were a conscious choice on her part or the unavoidable spillover from her professional life into their personal life Shane could never be sure, though he hung on every word just the same.

"What do you think Molly?" Shane asked, shifting his gaze over to stare at the cat as she took her customary spot atop his pillow. The red digits of the bedside clock burned bright beside her, announcing that it was six minutes after six. A small smirk slid from Shane as he realized he had already been up for hours, his entire night's sleep consisting of fitful dozing and nothing more.

Molly didn't bother to even turn his way as she lay on the pillow, instead rolling onto her back and stretching, her light gray belly flashing up at him.

"Good call," Shane said, pulling down a gray two-button suit, a gray and blue design pattern tie to match. He moved fast in the half-light of the room and was gone fifteen minutes later, a mountain of folders tucked under his arm.

There was no traffic as he angled his way back to the law school, even beating rush hour onto the streets by well over an hour. He parked in the first spot in the lot and was at his customary spot in the library well before seven, reading and re-reading the notes from Prescott about the *voir dire* process.

Abby was the first of his team to show up, arriving two minutes past eight, dressed in a skirt suit and blouse. Just a couple of minutes later Heath arrived, wearing khakis and a blue blazer. Both looked pale and nervous, their first foray into a world they'd only been hearing about for the last eight months.

"Relax guys," Shane said, offering them a smile that relayed confidence he wasn't sure he possessed. "At this point, your heavy lifting is done. You get paid to sit and watch me sink or swim."

The remark had its effect on his assistants, color returning to their faces as they each took deep breaths and began to go through the notes in front of them. The words had the opposite effect on Shane, calling again to mind the harsh reality of his situation.

Tyler Bentley was short a leg because of something SynTronic had done to him. If he was ever going to be made whole, financially if not anatomically, it was going to come down to the as-yet-unknown quantity that was Shane's courtroom skills.

Twenty minutes before nine, Prescott joined them and all three people gathered up their papers and everybody headed outside. They made the short walk to the courthouse together in silence, all deep in thought, ignoring the glorious morning sunshine that painted the sidewalks or the handful of pedestrians that offered sideways glances at the four severe looking people in suits walking together.

A single man in wrinkled khakis and a plaid shirt was sitting on the front steps of the courthouse as they approached, a miniature microphone in one hand, a Steno pad in the other. Upon seeing them he jumped to his feet and descended the stairs, falling in step as they headed into the courthouse.

"Shane Laszlo? Hanson Byers, *Columbus Herald*. Is it true that you are the counsel of record for former Charging Knights running back Tyler Bentley in the case set to begin here this morning?"

Of all the things Shane had considered, from his opening remarks to the color of his tie, the press was one thing he had overlooked. The thought hit him hard in the pit of his stomach, bringing with it the undeniable fear of what else he might be forgetting.

"Yes, I am," Shane said, giving Byers a sideways glance as he ascended the stairs, his pace picking up.

"Shane, how do you like your chances here today, going up against the heavy hitters SynTronic has been known to trot out for cases like this in the past?"

The question gave Shane pause for a moment, a small smile tugging at the corner of his mouth. He paused at the top of the stairs and half turned to Byers, looking once at each of his companions, all of whom seemed a bit confused by his stopping.

"Lucky for us, we don't have to worry about that here today. This morning we're here to select a jury of Tyler's peers, starting tomorrow they'll be the ones deciding that. Good day, Mr. Byers."

Byers nodded a farewell, his face a bit disappointed, no doubt seeking something a little juicier for the afternoon run.

The enormous double doors of the courthouse opened wide as they entered, the polished oak smooth to the touch. Inside, the cavernous interior of the courthouse spread out in every direction, white marble comprising the floors and crawling halfway up the walls. Above it hung row after row of vintage photographs, former judges and magistrates stretching back over a hundred years. A pair of marble staircases rose and twisted up to the second floor on either side, a handful of employees going in various directions on them.

Right in front of them was a second set of doors, made of solid wood with a square black sign with gold letters inlaid on them.

United States District Court – Southern District of Ohio.

A buzz already hung in the air, a conglomeration of small talk and nervous energy that seemed to reverberate through the space. Clusters of people were gathered around the foyer, some standing with shoulders hunched, trying to avoid eye contact, others turning to stare at Shane and his team.

Two matching benches were pushed against the wall on either side of the door, both simple affairs of solid wood and straight backs. On the right sat a young man and woman, both shuffling through stacks of handwritten pages. On the left sat Margie Bentley, Tyler in his wheelchair parked beside her. Both looked sullen and subdued, staring at Shane.

"You guys go ahead and go in," Shane said, turning over his shoulder to speak to his team. "I'm going to talk to Tyler and Ms. Bentley for a moment, be right in behind you."

All three departed without a word, the sole reaction of any kind being a small nod from Heath. Shane waited until they passed through the heavy doors before approaching the Bentley's, hand outstretched in front of him.

"Ms. Bentley, I didn't realize you were coming in already. Nice to meet you in person."

She returned the shake with a surprising grip, squeezing Shane's hand as she regarded him with watery blue eyes. "I took leave until further notice. Decided I needed to be here for every minute of the trial."

"We appreciate it," Shane replied, "but today won't be trial. This morning we pick the jury that will be hearing the case, which some people say is eighty-five percent of the battle."

"No pressure," Tyler interjected, a half smile on his face.

"Thanks," Shane said, matching the face and motioning towards the courtroom. "We should head inside now." He leaned in and lowered his voice, casting a sideways glance to make sure nobody was listening. "Also, I know this is going to kill you Tyler, but it wouldn't be a bad idea to let your mom wheel you in and out every day."

Tyler's face broke into an immediate rejection of the idea, but Margie beat him to it.

"I agree, that sounds like a fine idea," she said, rising and grabbing the handles of his chair before he had a chance to react.

Shane stepped inside first and held open the door, standing off to the left as the Bentleys entered. He waited until they were through and on their way down the aisle towards the front of the room before letting the door close, taking in the scene around him.

The largest courtroom Shane had ever seen stretched out around him, line after line of benches spread in both directions from the aisle. A waist-high wooden barrier split the room in half, separating the benches from the actual proceedings. In front of it was a pair of counsel tables, Reed and Ramirez already present at the one on the right, Margie positioning Tyler on the left.

The front end of the room was a wooden stage, the judge's seat, witness chair, and court reporter's chair each allotted their own compartments. The left side was comprised of the jury box, over fifty polished wooden chairs that would soon be filled.

Shane's eyes slid closed for just a moment as he drew in a deep breath, his shoulders rising and falling with the effort. The words of Byers came back to mind, the question about how he, a country rube from Ohio Tech, felt to be going up against major judicial heavyweights.

A sense of calm seemed to settle in over Shane, the wide-eyed shock fading from his features, replaced instead by resolve. His entire legal career had been defined by being the scrappy underdog, the one that always gave worse than he got. It was the reason he had earned that position with Webster, Banks & Cohen, it was the reason Rex Hartman was still standing somewhere in Boston with his jaw hanging open.

These guys, Connor Reed, William Ramirez, whoever else they trotted out against him, were in for a fight.

Shane walked the length of the aisle and passed through the barrier, laying his briefcase down. He went straight over to the opposing table with hand extended, gaze unwavering.

"Gentlemen, good morning," he said, shaking first Reed's hand, followed by Ramirez. Both mumbled a good morning back to him, trying their best to stare him down, Ramirez even going as far as to try and crush his hand in his meaty paw.

Shane ignored all of it, focused only on trying not to laugh at the black pinstriped suits and red ties they both wore.

Ten quick minutes passed as Shane settled in, spreading his notes out on the table, a blank pad in front of him. Behind him Abby and Heath were both poised and ready to go, sitting in a row with Prescott and Margie.

Five minutes before the hour, a door beside the jury box opened and the bailiff, an aging black man with a ring of curly gray hair stepped into the room, his uniform neat and pressed. He shuffled forward to the jury box and held it open, extending a hand as a row of potential jurors filed in.

Shane kept his gaze averted as they entered the box, casting only occasional glances over. From what he could tell, it was just the kind of mixed bag the system was designed to bring in, with individuals ranging in age from their twenties to mid-sixties, clothing choices running the gamut from ties to flip-flops.

At nine o'clock, the bailiff closed the panel door to the jury box and turned to face the room. "All rise, the Honorable Judge Richard Lynch presiding."

The words still hung in the air as a walrus of a man waddled into the room, the effect accentuated by the billowing black robe and oversized mustache he wore. His thin brown hair was heavily oiled and combed straight to either side from the middle, a pair of wire-rimmed glasses rested on his nose. He shuffled over into his chair and swung his considerable bulk down into it, the springs on it wheezing for all to hear.

"Good morning everyone, please be seated," he announced, his voice a bit higher than expected, his tone a bit sharper. "We are here this morning to begin the jury selection process for *Bentley v. SynTronic*, docket number 000216. Would the respective counselors please rise and introduce themselves, those seated at their table."

His gaze shifted back to the papers in front of him as Shane stood, the slightest bit of moisture reaching his forehead and the small of his back. Beside him, Tyler lifted himself to his foot, using the table for leverage.

"Good morning Your Honor, my name is Shane Laszlo, counsel for the plaintiff, along with my client, Mr. Tyler Bentley."

"Good morning," Lynch said, still reading the document before him.

"Your Honor, I apologize for speaking out of turn, but I would like to ask that if it pleases the court my client be allowed to remain in his wheelchair from this point on in the proceedings?"

Lynch's mouth opened to respond as he turned to face Shane, though no words came out as his attention focused on Tyler and the single leg he stood on, the wheelchair behind him. "Yes, of course."

"Thank you, Your Honor," Shane said, he and Tyler both retaking their seats.

Across from them Reed rose, scowling at Shane already. "Good morning Your Honor, Connor Reed, my co-counsel William Ramirez, here on behalf of SynTronic Corporation."

"Good morning," Lynch said, shifting his attention to the jury box. "And good morning to each of you, all of whom have been summoned here as prospective jurors. This case concerns a medical malpractice claim of negligence against the defendant.

"I am now going to ask you a series of questions. If the answer to any of these questions is yes, I ask that you raise your hand and wait to be dismissed. Once I am done with this, respective counsel will begin individual questioning until we have fifteen chosen jurors, twelve permanent and three alternates. Is everyone clear? Please raise your hand."

All fifty hands went up at once, punctuated by a handful of nods.

"Okay," Lynch said, continuing to read from the documents before him. "Has anyone talked with you about this case, or discussed this case in your presence?"

Not a single hand went up. Lynch paused and swept his gaze twice over the box before pushing forward.

"Okay, are any of you familiar with the facts of this particular case?"

This time, a small number of hands went up, belonging to a few middle-aged men and one young woman. The proceedings paused as Lynch dismissed them, thanking them for their time as they went.

"Have any of you formed or expressed an opinion, whether from newspapers, televisions, or other source, on this case?"

A trio of hands went up around the table, all belonging to middle aged women. Shane let the slightest of grunts pass through his nose as the women were excused, taking with them a piece of the demographic he was hoping to capture.

The general questioning continued for almost an hour, Lynch covering everything from possible blood relations to past employment status. Most of the questions were met without a single hand raised, the cumulative effect of his effort taking the pool down from fifty to thirty-eight. When he reached the end of his script, he flipped the stapled pages back to the beginning.

"That concludes the questions for the entire panel. From this point forward, counselors will begin their *voir dire* process, asking you individual questions. Answer them full and honest, as they will have a direct bearing on the outcome of this case."

He paused another moment to add a bit of gravitas to his statement before shifting his attention back to the counsel tables.

"Counselors, you may each strike eight jurors without cause. If at the end of *voir dire* an excess of jurors remains, you may be awarded more to get the pool down to the required fifteen.

"Mr. Reed, you may proceed."

Shane cast a sideways glance to Reed, who sat with shoulders hunched forward as he stared down at a paper in front of him. He remained that way for several moments before turning his head towards Ramirez and whispering something, which was responded to with a curt nod of agreement.

After almost a full minute he rose, straightening his tie and fastening both buttons on his suit coat, the effect accentuating just the smallest beginning of a paunch. He walked from behind his table and over in front of the jury box, standing for several long moments with his fingers interlocked in front of him.

"How many of you are Ohio Tech football fans?"

.

CHAPTER THIRTY-FIVE

The hours for the Ohio Tech law library were posted as nine to nine six days a week, ten to six on Sundays. During those hours either one of the staff librarians or a student on work study was guaranteed to be around, unlocking the doors and retrieving reserve materials for overeager first year students. The hours never changed, save for a retraction the week of Christmas and expansions twice a year for finals. Otherwise, they were one of the few constant things that took place in the building.

Just two days into Shane commandeering his own corner of the library and making it his de facto office, the head librarian saw that those hours weren't going to cut it. Already familiar with the long and insomnia-riddled schedule of Shane after three years of staring at him in that same corner, she knew better than to even try suggesting he find someplace else to work or worse yet, just telling him to leave.

On a Thursday night, just over a month before, she waited until all the other students had left before approaching him, sitting in the corner alone, pretending not to know what time it was. There was no reprimand, no disapproving look, instead she just walked over and slid a single brass key onto the corner of the desk.

The move shocked Shane, pulling his head away from the notes and towards her already retreating towards the door, staring back at him through thick framed glasses. The two locked the pose for several long moments, her growing further away, until Shane smiled and offered a silent thank you, dipping his head in appreciation. She returned the gesture, neither of the two ever mentioning the incident again.

That same key now sat on the ring atop a stack of case files, sharing space with his car key, room key, and a Red Sox keychain he didn't care for but kept because it held everything together. Shane leaned back in his chair and stared down at it, the sole reason he and Abby were now still parked in the corner of the library, an hour after everybody else was gone.

"You can go home, Abby," Shane said, throwing his pen down on the stack of papers in front of him and lacing his fingers behind his head. His sleeves were rolled to the elbow, his hand chosen blue tie long since discarded. "It's getting late, there have to be things you'd rather be doing."

Abby looked up from the case she was reading, a yellow highlighter poised just an inch above the page. "No, but now that you mention it, it is getting late."

"We're not back on until Wednesday, and believe me, this will all still be here in the morning."

Abby nodded, capping the pen in her hand and leaning back in her chair. "I've been meaning to ask, how do you get to stay here so late?"

Shane gave a sharp jut of the chin motioned towards the keys sitting atop the desk. "Madge gave me my own key. I think she got sick of me waiting on her every morning, begging her to stay later every night."

"Just like that? After a few weeks?"

"Naw, it's been a problem dating back a few years now. Poor old girl must have wanted to cry when she saw me show up again."

Abby smiled, the same exhausted look on her face that Shane could feel spreading across his. She turned her head to check the time on the wall before conceding defeat and nodding.

"See you in the morning?"

"I'll be here," Shane said, raising one hand from behind his head to wave. He watched in silence as Abby gathered her things and departed, smiling again as she headed for the door.

After a moment Shane returned to the pages in front of him, row after row of handwritten notes. All of it was scrawled out in deep blue ink, the spacing somewhat uneven, large blots erasing words or entire sentences. Smudges of ink dotted the pads of his fingertips as he wrote, mumbling the words over and over again, searching for the perfect cadence.

"Big hot shot lawyers always talk to themselves in the dark?" a voice asked, lifting Shane from his chair. He spun around towards the sound of it, surprise on his face, a hand raised to his chest.

Standing in the place Abby had been just a few minutes before was Christine, still dressed from work, a paper sack in her hand, a mischievous smile on her face.

"I hope you don't scare that easy in court," she said, walking around the table and taking up the chair Abby had just vacated. "That could be very bad for the Bentleys."

"Do I even want to know how you got in here?" Shane asked, his pulse slowing in his ears, the color retreating from his face.

"Used my Spidey abilities to scale the outside wall and sneak in through a window, of course."

"Of course," Shane echoed, raising his eyebrows at her.

Christine held the gaze for a moment before angling the top of her head towards the door. "The wallflower held the door for me on her way out. Hope I wasn't interrupting any kind of late night tryst."

"Is that jealousy I hear? And Chipotle I smell?"

A corner of Christine's mouth creased upwards as she slid the bag across the table. "Just wondering if you'd decided to pursue some alternative stress relief before trial gets started. And yes, chicken burrito, heavy guac, light sour cream, just as you like it."

"Bless you sweet woman," Shane said, tearing into the food with reckless vigor. "How'd you know I'd be here?"

An arched eyebrow and disdainful look was the only response to the question.

"I hear you did well today."

Shane's brow furrowed a bit at the comment, a snort rolling out as he chewed. "I don't know about all that. Besides, jury selection is the easy part. The real show starts on Wednesday."

"You'll be ready for it."

Shane shrugged and glanced down at the pages of notes in front of him, wishing he had the same confidence in himself that she seemed to.

"Did you get what you were looking for?" Christine asked.

"Not too bad. A pair of single mothers, which should be good, couple of middle-aged guys that look like definite football fans. Kind of a mixed bag."

"Isn't that the point?" Christine asked.

"I suppose," Shane said, laying the back end of the burrito down onto its foil and wiping his hand clean with a napkin. "Bastard opposing counsel's first question was to see who were OTU fans and go right after them. I damn near died."

"I bet," Christine said, settling a cool gaze on him, "but that's not what I meant. Did you get what you were looking for?"

It took a moment for Shane to place what she was referring to before a small smile settled across his face. "You mean asking about Tyler standing?"

"Drawing first blood, as it were."

Shane pursed his lips and nodded, considering the words for a moment. "If nothing else, it got Reed's attention."

CHAPTER THIRTY-SIX

The ice clinked down in the bottom of the glass, making a distinctive sound across the space of the suite. Reed gave a long look at the fully-stocked Omni mini bar just a few feet away before pouring himself a glass of seltzer water and returning to his chair. He reclined himself back against the leather wingtip, extending his legs out in front of him and resting them on the matching ottoman.

"One of these days we're going to have to rethink this whole going-dry-for-the-duration-of-trial thing," Reed said, taking another long, unsatisfying pull from his drink.

Across from him Ramirez smirked, his bulbous body twisted to the side in a matching wingtip, his suit and tie traded in for a velour jogging suit. In his hand was a liter-sized bottle of cola, less than an inch remaining in the bottom.

"I think you said that last time."

"I say it *every* time," Reed countered, shaking his head. "Doesn't make it any less true."

Ramirez offered a non-committal shake of the head in response, unable to think of anything that could counter the simple logic of his colleague. Instead he said, "That was a damn good steak though."

The words seemed to find their mark, bringing to Reed's face into the first smile it had seen in days. "Yes, it was."

With the frost in the room cracked, if not thawed, Ramirez pushed forward. "So how did you see it playing out today?"

Reed's first response was an elongated sigh, followed by finishing the last of his water. He stared down at the glass for several seconds once it was empty, either contemplating the question or trying in vain to refill it with Scotch using only his mind.

Maybe a little of both.

"I think the jury turned out about as well as we could have hoped for, all things considered. I'm still not happy that a pair of single mothers made it on, but with only eight challenges there wasn't much we could do."

"Yeah," Ramirez said, smirking as he nodded his head, "if that's a fair and accurate portrayal of peers in this state, there must be a lot more unplanned pregnancy in Ohio than I realized."

Reed moved right past the comment without acknowledging it. "After that, I was glad to see a couple of folks even older than I make it through, a couple of blacks as well."

"Really? The angry minority card?" Ramirez asked, holding his hands out to his side.

"Scoff all you want, but there's a strong track record there and you know it. I still think those two rednecks in the back row were lying through their teeth about not being football fans, but again, only having eight challenges made it tough."

"You mean lying through their *tooth*," Ramirez corrected, staring off into space. He remained that way for several long moments before shaking himself awake and shifting his attention to Reed.

"Remind me again why we haven't filed for a change of venue?"

"We haven't and we will not," Reed said, his gaze aimed at the floor in front of him. His chin dug into his throat for several seconds before he pushed out a small burp and stood, helping himself to another glass of seltzer water, reusing the same ice.

"For the simple reason that we are going to keep as much back as possible for the appeal. You and I both know we're never going to get a fair trial in front of jurors anywhere in the country, not with a former All-American hopping around on one foot."

"So you're already planning on losing?" Ramirez asked, surprise evident in his voice.

The comment drew a sharp look from Reed, his gaze hard. "If you're trying to anger me, it's working. I am in no way preparing to lose, I am just putting in place a contingency should it happen. That includes accepting the fact that no jury is ever going to be sympathetic to our case. Our best bet, our only bet, may well be to wait until it goes to appeal and is heard by a panel of judges."

Ramirez nodded. "Apologies. I didn't mean to insult you."

Reed waved off the apology with a look of disgust.

"You think change of venue could be enough to get us up on appeal?

"I don't know," Reed said, settling back into his chair, his tone softening a bit. "But it doesn't hurt to have it in the back pocket, just in case."

Again Ramirez nodded at the statement, his eyes wandering to the far wall.

"What did you think of that little stunt Laszlo pulled this morning?"

The features on Reed's face again grew hard as he sat in silence, no doubt replaying the incident over in his head. He remained that way for two full minutes, his head rocking back and forth, exasperation and anger plain on his face.

"We knew going into this that they would play the fallen hero card, but I wasn't expecting it to be quite that overt."

"And that was just jury selection," Ramirez said, his voice far away. "Only going to get worse going forward."

The words floated in the air, Ramirez again shifting his attention to a vacant expanse of wall. Across from him, Reed seemed to seize on them and their meaning, the muscles in his jaw working in high speed as he clenched it.

"Not if we put a stop to it," Reed said, rising from his chair. He paced across the room to the mahogany desk pressed against the back wall and took up his cell phone, turning to face the room while leaning back against the desktop. He remained that way for several moments, his features drawn tight.

Ramirez watched him for several moments, his curiosity piqued. "What are you doing?"

"We have one distinct advantage in this case. It's time we used it."

The phone was pressed tight to his face for several seconds before Reed pulled it away and changed the output to speakerphone. It rang twice before a familiar voice answered, his tone as curt as ever.

"Speak."

From his chair, Ramirez's eyes grew wide, a bit of realization setting in.

"Ute, Connor Reed here."

Ramirez's eyes slid shut, his breath catching in his throat.

"I know who it is, the damn phone has caller ID. I told you not to call me again unless you changed your mind."

Reed paused for a moment, staring over at Ramirez. Across the room, his partner twisted his head from side to side, discomfort evident on his features. After a moment, Reed raised the phone up close to his mouth.

"We have changed our minds," Reed said, his voice a little stronger than usual, or even necessary. "Not Laszlo and not Bentley. Nobody gets killed either. Just enough of something to make sure a message is received."

There was a moment of silence on the other end, during which Reed could almost picture the look of sadistic pleasure that was spreading across Ute's face. Deep within him some small bit of his conscience tried to object to what he was doing, but just as fast it fell silent.

"And what message is that?"

The phone receded from Reed's face as he stared off, trying to articulate what he wanted to convey to Laszlo. When it came to him, the phone was back to his mouth in an instant, a flash of light behind his eyes.

"If he's not going to play by the rules, we're not either."

CHAPTER THIRTY-SEVEN

Cliché would have the world believe that three times is the charm, the ideal number of trial and error attempts before everything comes together. Under that thinking, by the sixth time Shane practiced his opening statement, alone and pacing in the conference room of the second floor of the law school, it should have been twice perfect. Still, as he walked over to the courthouse, the first real day of trial just minutes away from beginning, he sure as hell didn't feel like it.

"Mr. Laszlo," Hanson Byers asked as he approached, microphone extended before him, wearing the same exact uniform he'd been wearing two days before. Flanking him on either side was a pair of young ladies, both wearing vests and hipster glasses, iPads poised in the crook of their arms. "What do you expect to happen in there today?"

The question gave Shane pause for a moment, a look of consideration passing over his face, the nerves deep in his stomach still dancing.

"I honestly don't know. We're going to give our opening statement and road map the case as we intend to present it the best we know how. I'm sure the SynTronic team will do the same. From there, I'll put Tyler on the stand and see what happens."

Byers pulled the microphone back and spoke into it, his face making no attempt to mask his excitement. "So you're telling me Tyler Bentley *will* take the stand today?"

Shane kept moving for the front door, the young ladies circling around to follow him, Byers remaining on his hip. "I have no idea if we'll get that far today, it is Judge Lynch's courtroom and what he says goes. If he does open it for me to call my first witness though, Tyler will be taking the stand. Good day, Mr. Byers."

A wan smile crossed Byers face as he reached the threshold of the courthouse, pulling up short as if held there by some imaginary force field. He raised a hand in farewell to Shane's retreating blue suit and said, "Good day, Mr. Laszlo."

Several heads turned to stare at Shane as he walked through the foyer of the courthouse, the heels of his shoes clicking out a steady cadence as he went to the double doors and stepped inside. A healthy crowd had gathered by the time he entered, the rows of benches well over half full, already more than had been there two days before.

Seated in the front row was Prescott and Abby, Margie by their side. Parked at the counsel table was Tyler, turned to face the others behind him. He was the first to notice Tyler as he approached, gesturing towards him with his chin, sending the others to turn and look as well.

"Good morning, everyone," Tyler said, setting down the box of materials in his hands and straightening his blue and brown patterned tie. "No Heath this morning?"

"Haven't seen him," Abby said, raising her hands by her side.

"Huh," Shane said, considering and dismissing the information in just a matter of moments. "Abby that means you'll be on for note taking, pay special attention during the defense's opening. They're going to outline what they intend to prove, so it's vital we get it all. I'll be taking notes at the table, but I want you to take down everything too. We can compare later."

"Got it," Abby said, drawing her mouth tight and nodding once.

"Professor, if at all possible, I'd like for you to be watching the jury today. See how they're reacting to me and the defense both, if they give away any physical cues, if particular points seem to be sticking with them, anything. Is that doable?"

"Certainly, sir," Prescott said, a pad and paper of his own out and ready.

Shane shifted his eyes down the bench, his gaze alighting on Margie. "And Ms. Bentley?"

"Yes?" Margie asked, her face pulled tight, her attention focused on him.

A smile creased Shane's face, his first sign of mirth in days. "How are you today?"

Margie stared back at him for several moments as if something was growing from his forehead before her own visage shifted to a smile as well. "I'm fine Shane, how are you?"

"We're about to find out," Shane said, raising his eyebrows a fraction and taking his seat at the table. Beside him Tyler turned to face forward as well, his fingers interlaced atop the table, his right leg bouncing up and down in a frenetic pace.

In the back of the room the bailiff entered, his uniform an exact replica of the one he wore two days before. Again he opened the jury box and motioned for them to enter, the procession much smaller than the first time. Once they were in place, he closed the box door and turned to face the court.

"All rise!"

"You might be taking the stand today," Shane whispered to Tyler, sliding his chair back from the table. "Your leg can't be going a mile a minute like that, makes you look nervous."

"I *am* nervous."

"Yeah, but you can't let them see it, makes it look like you have something to hide."

Tyler nodded as Shane rose, doing his best to keep his face and his foot motionless.

At the head of the room Judge Lynch walked in, the robes ballooning out around him. Under his arm he carried a thick sheaf of papers, dropping them onto his desk with a thud and swinging himself down into the chair.

"Please be seated," he mumbled into the microphone, a bevy of shuffling and low murmuring rising from the crowd as they retook their chairs. Lynch didn't bother to look up as the room settled in, his attention on the pages before him as he rifled through them, getting everything in order.

"Good morning, everyone. We are back here today to hear the opening statements in the case of *Bentley v. SynTronic,* docket number 000216. Counsel for the plaintiff, are you ready to proceed?"

On cue, Shane stood, calm confidence and rampant fear fighting for the upper hand in his stomach. Again he could feel a trickle of moisture run down the small of his back, his lungs constricting just a bit.

"We are, Your Honor."

"You may proceed," Lynch said, peering down at Shane over the rim of his glasses.

Shane paused for a moment at the table, glancing down at his handwritten notes, the same ones he'd rehearsed a half dozen times that morning, the same ones he'd practiced twice that much the day before. He used the moment to draw in one last deep breath before stepping away from the table and his safety, out onto the biggest stage he'd ever known.

"Ladies and gentlemen of the jury, good morning. My name is Shane Laszlo and I here before you today on behalf of my client Tyler Bentley."

As the words began to flow from him, his feet started to move, a steady gait back and forth across the floor, one that allowed him to look each of the jurors in the eye as he spoke.

"The reason Mr. Bentley and I am here before you is to seek justice from the defendant, SynTronic Corporation, a medical device manufacturer. The testimony you will hear is going to be complicated at times and the job you will be tasked with doing is quite difficult, but allow me to start this morning by telling you that all you need to know, all you need to keep in mind while this plays out, is that in the end you are going to be asked to apply one very simple rule: Did the SynTronic Corporation build a faulty device that led directly to the loss of Tyler Bentley's leg?"

Shane paused for a moment and scanned the faces before him, all of them listening close, staring back.

"Six months ago, Tyler Bentley was a football hero, the pride of Worland, Wyoming, the star player on the top ranked Ohio Tech Charging Knights. A finalist for the Heisman Trophy, awarded each year to the best player in the country, the MVP of the Centennial Bowl, despite playing in just the first half.

"It was during the Centennial Bowl that Mr. Bentley suffered a very serious knee injury, through the fault of no one. An injury that was so severe that he was flown straight back to Columbus for treatment, not even waiting for the game to end.

"The next morning he awoke in a hospital bed in the OTU Hospital to find his leg in ruins, all three bones of his leg broken, his kneecap shattered, the ligaments and tendons holding it together shredded. Conventional wisdom would dictate that such an injury takes a minimum, *minimum*, of eighteen months to recover from, but it would recover. The combined efforts of staff physician Dr. Leonard Pinkering and SynTronic representative Marcellus Sarconi convinced him that his leg was beyond repair and the only way he could ever hope to walk unaided again would be through the use of their new toy, the *KnightRunner*.

"Now, what is a *KnightRunner* you might ask? The *KnightRunner* is a hot-off-the-presses artificial knee replacement that promised to get Tyler back on the field in time for this season, stronger and faster than he was before the injury. Despite his initial uncertainty, Dr. Pinkering and Mr. Sarconi convinced Tyler that this was the sole possible avenue for his recovery.

"Faced with the possibility that he may never walk, let alone play football again, Tyler did the only thing he could do, what any of us would do. He allowed them to use the *KnightRunner* implant on him.

"Just three months later, the damage done by the *KnightRunner* was so severe, doctors had no choice but to remove his leg."

Shane paused there, letting the words hang over the courtroom, shifting his head to glance at Tyler, Margie sniffling behind him on the front row.

"Over the next couple of weeks, you are going to hear from a lot of very intelligent people speaking about engineering designs, about standard medical procedure, about informed consent. You might even hear the defense assert that all this was somehow the fault of Mr. Bentley, that somehow in the course of normal athletic training, *he* caused the implant to become faulty.

"All of that information should be taken quite seriously and I urge you to consider it as you make deliberations, but at the end of the day I ask you to keep in mind that one simple question: Did SynTronic build and implant a device into Tyler Bentley that culminated in the loss of his leg?"

Once more Shane paused for effect, panning each of the faces before him with a slow and even gaze. When all fifteen of the people before him had met his eye, Shane nodded once and retreated towards his chair.

Prescott gave him a tiny, imperceptible nod as he did so, Tyler offering one that was a little more pronounced.

"Thank you."

At the front of the room, Judge Lynch shifted in his seat and turned a page before him, his attention moving to the opposite side of the room. "Would the defense like to make an opening statement?"

The sound of a chair scraping across the floor sounded out as Reed pushed back from the table. He rose to full height and straightened his solid red tie, buttoned his textured black suit coat across his midsection, and strode into the center of the room.

Shane watched with a mix of nerves and curiosity as Reed stood ramrod straight, rotating on the balls of his feet, his fingers interlocked before him.

"It is already quite clear to me that what you are about to hear in the coming weeks are two very different stories," Reed began, his voice deep, almost operatic in its delivery. "One is the story Mr. Laszlo just shared with you, the story of a small town boy making good, of going out into the world and by the sweat of his brow managing to better his lot in life, only to have it stolen from him. Taken away by some nameless, faceless corporation, some greedy empire bent on turning a profit and conquering the world.

"What Mr. Laszlo's story fails to incorporate are a couple of key facts. Facts such as the one that SynTronic was not just some unthinking, unfeeling corporate behemoth trying to make a buck on the back of a promising young athlete. It was represented by men, medical professionals who were there with him every day, who saw and felt the same anguish he did, that acted in the way they saw fit to do right by him, both as an athlete and as a human being.

"It also fails to take into consideration things such as the role that his client, Mr. Bentley, played in his own injury, wantonly disregarding product limitations in an attempt to get back on the field and regain his glorious past."

Reed paused there for a moment, his feet still planted in the same spot as he when began, turning just a small swivel from side to side to see all fifteen faces before him.

"Before I forget, I want to thank you all for being here today. Your presence, your active participation, is the cornerstone by which our entire judicial system works and I urge you to take that responsibility seriously. I know that being here presents at the very least an extreme inconvenience to you, and at the very most lost wages and time away from loved ones.

"Despite that though, I want you to give this case the time and attention it deserves. I want you to consider that maybe this isn't as simple as Mr. Laszlo's one catchphrase would have you believe, that maybe there was no second gunman, that perhaps what happened to Mr. Bentley was nothing more than a series of unfortunate occurrences."

He paused, as if there was more he wanted to add, but opted against it. He pressed his lips together and nodded once.

"Thank you."

Spinning on his heel, Reed turned and headed for his seat, his face impassive, his fingers still laced in front of him. Shane watched as he headed towards the defense table, a small but persistent feeling of loathing starting to grow in the pit of his stomach. Before he could let that feeling fester and grow, use it to fuel him as he prepared to call his first witness, a small tug at the bottom of his jacket pulled his attention away.

Once, twice, the tug gnawed at his coat, forcing him to turn towards the bench behind him. A look of surprise and confusion passed over his face to see Abby leaning forward, strain visible on her face, the bottom inch of his coat between her thumb and forefinger.

"Counselor, is the plaintiff ready to call its first witness?" Judge Lynch asked, his voice still with a trace of boredom.

"What?" Shane mouthed back at Abby, his face a mask of agitation, waving a hand towards the judge to indicate he was being called.

Abby raised her other hand to reveal a pink cell phone, twisting it back and forth.

"Counselor?" Judge Lynch said again, his voice rising.

"Um, one moment Your Honor," Shane asked, sliding back so his face was just inches from Abby's and lowering his voice to a whisper. "What the hell is going on? I'm about to call my first witness."

"A friend of mine at Columbus General texted and said Heath was just brought in. His car exploded this morning, and he's in bad shape."

Shane's face fell flat as he stared at Abby, her eyes already rimmed with moisture, puffiness just a moment away. His tongue felt like it had swollen several times too large for his mouth, every bit of moisture within him evaporating.

"Counselor!" Judge Lynch said, his tone unmistakable.

"Permission to approach the bench," Shane spat out, spinning and rising to full height in one movement.

Judge Lynch stared down at him over the rims of his glasses for several long seconds, malevolence splashed across his face. At last he relented, motioning him forward with a flick of his hand.

Reed fell in beside Shane as they walked forward, Shane's legs feeling like they were made of lead, every bit of the confidence he felt just a short time before gone. He continued trying to work some saliva back into his mouth as they walked, the Judge's glare burning into his chest.

"What is this all about?" Judge Lynch asked, his voice just able to be contained in a whisper.

"Your Honor, I apologize, but we were just given some very distressing news," Shane said. "A member of my legal team was in a serious accident this morning on his way to court and is in bad condition. If it pleases the court, I would like to request a recess so we may see to our colleague."

Judge Lynch continued to stare at Shane, his face softening just a tiny bit. He shifted his attention over to Reed and asked, "Objection, Counselor?"

Reed flicked his gaze from the judge to Shane and back again, his hands shoved deep into his pockets. "None."

The sound of the gavel pounding against the desk shot through Shane's head, leaving a dull, persistent buzz in his ear.

"The court will now stand in recess until nine o'clock tomorrow morning, at which point the plaintiff will call its first witness."

"I hope your man is alright," Reed said, reaching out to pat Shane on the shoulder.

The hand never got there, as Shane was already back to his desk, gathering up his belongings.

"Abby, text your friend back and tell them we're on our way."

CHAPTER THIRTY-EIGHT

Thunderstruck by AC/DC pouring out of the speakers, the steely voice of Brian Johnson filling the tiny space of the Honda, reverberating off the windows. Abby winced as the music burst to life, hunching her shoulders in the passenger seat, the combined things of both her and Shane balanced on her lap.

"Sorry," Shane mumbled, reaching out and snapping the music off as he exited the parking lot, heading straight for the hospital. The silence seemed just as startling in the small space, coming right on the heels of the pounding music.

"Little something to get you going this morning?" Abby asked, her voice distracted, her gaze watching the streets outside.

"Everybody has their own pregame routine," Shane said, his voice just as distracted. "General's on Rivers, right?"

"Yeah," Abby said, shooting a finger out to the left, pointing across Shane's field of vision. "Take Henderson and come in the back way, it's quicker."

Shane turned a hard left onto Henderson without question, nosing the speed on the Honda up over forty and passing through two consecutive yellow lights. Both sat in complete silence as they went, their faces drawn and tight.

Under normal conditions it would have taken ten minutes to make the drive from campus to the hospital, fifteen if traffic was heavy. Shane made it in just under five, swinging up alongside the curb and reaching over to take the materials from Abby.

"Go on in and see where he's at. I'll park the car and be right behind you."

Nodding her understanding, Abby climbed out of the car and headed inside, Shane dropping the box in place behind her and heading for the parking lot. The midday crowd was heavy and he had to park near the back of the lot, leaving everything but his phone and wallet in the car and jogging back to the front door, sliding between rows of parked cars as he went.

Shane burst into the front lobby of the Columbus General Hospital and slid to a stop in an open-air foyer, a pair of fountains spaced equidistant apart in front of him. A bevy of foot traffic moved in various directions, ranging from aged individuals in hospital gowns to young children visiting relatives. He slowed his pace to a walk and stepped forward through the space, twisting his gaze from side to side in search of Abby. Not until he was almost to the reception desk against the back wall did he notice her tucked off to the side, deep in conversation with a pair of officers in matching black uniforms.

Shane waved off the woman sitting behind the reception desk staring at him and walked over to Abby and the officers, concern on his face. Abby turned towards him as he approached, motioning a hand in his direction, her words inaudible. Both officers turned as well, one holding a pencil and notebook in hand, the other with his thumbs looped into the waist of his pants.

"Hi, sorry to interrupt," Shane said, extending his hand, "Shane Laszlo."

The closer of the two returned the shake, a middle-aged man standing a few inches shorter than Shane, his hair gelled into place, a dimple on the end of his chin. "Mr. Laszlo, I am Officer Murphy, this is Officer Ryan, CPD."

Behind him Officer Ryan, a light skinned black man with a thin mustache that looked to be somewhere between twenty-five and thirty nodded, the pencil and paper still poised before him.

"Ms. Hill here was just telling us that you worked with Heath Wilson?"

"Yes, that's right," Shane said, glancing between Murphy and Ryan. "I'm sorry, I know I'm a little late, but is he okay?"

"Mr. Wilson is in surgery now to repair his arm and some minor burns," Ryan said. "The injury is serious, but not fatal."

"My God," Shane whispered, his gaze drifting towards the floor. After a moment, he returned to Murphy and asked, "What happened?"

"From what we can tell, Mr. Wilson came out to get into his truck this morning, based on his attire when we found him, we assume it was to head to court," Murphy said, his tone matter-of-fact as he rattled off the information.

Shane nodded. "Yes, we were scheduled for nine o'clock this morning."

Murphy looked over his shoulder to Ryan, who nodded. "That fits the timeline."

"The crime scene techs are going over it now, but from what we can tell, Mr. Wilson was approaching his truck from the driver's side and used his keyless entry to unlock the vehicle. The moment he did so, the entire truck exploded. Mr. Wilson was hit with some bits of shrapnel but managed to call 911 before passing out. Uniformed patrol found him unconscious in the parking lot of his apartment building, EMTs brought him straight here."

Shane's eyes bulged as he heard the recount, glancing over to see Abby with a hand raised to her nose, tears streaming down her face. He stood slack-jawed for several seconds, forcing his body to process what he was told.

"Wait, you mentioned the words *crime scene*, does this mean you're suspecting foul play? That this wasn't some kind of electrical malfunction?"

"Our guy that specializes in these kinds of things told us earlier that there was no way an electrical short could cause that kind of explosion," Ryan said, waving the pencil and paper around as he spoke. "No chance that would stem from unlocking the doors. At most there would have been a fire."

Dazed, Shane shook his head and tried to comprehend what he was being told. Twelve hours before, he had been discussing the narrative portion of his opening statement with Heath, an hour before he'd been delivering that opening statement. Now, he was standing in the lobby of a hospital talking to two officers about a situation that could have easily taken a life.

"Mr. Laszlo, what is the nature of the case you're working on with Mr. Wilson?"

Shane pushed his lips out a bit. "Simple negligence claim, medical malpractice. You don't think the two are connected do you?"

Murphy ignored the question, his tone not quite firm, but not conversational either. "Is that the only case you and Mr. Wilson are working on?"

"Yes," Shane said, nodding for emphasis, turning to extend a hand towards Abby. "I hired Heath and Abby both about a month ago to help me with it, which I'm handling for a friend. I had never met either one of them before, in fact I was working at a firm in Boston up until two days before they agreed to come on board."

Murphy regarded Shane as Ryan scribbled into his pad, the look on Murphy's face making it clear he was debating what to make of Shane. After a moment he nodded and extended a hand towards him.

"Mr. Wilson is in the surgery ward in the basement. There's a waiting room on the first floor where you can stay until he's out. His family has been notified and should be here within the hour."

"Thank you, Officer," Shane said, returning the handshake.

"Do you have a number we can contact you at if we need anything further?" Ryan asked, closing the pad and stowing it in his front shirt pocket.

"Absolutely," Shane replied, pulling an old card from his wallet and passing it to Ryan. "The address and law firm are both in Boston, but the number on it is my cell."

"Thank you," Ryan said, holding up the card in acknowledgement before putting it in his shirt pocket as well. Both officers nodded to Shane and Abby before excusing themselves, heading towards the door.

"What was that all about?" Shane asked, standing beside Abby and watching them go.

"They happened to be standing by the front desk when I came in and asked what room Heath was in. That guy Murphy came right over and asked if I was an associate of his, then they both pulled me to the side and started asking questions."

Shane shoved his hands down into his front pockets and rose up onto his toes, his mind still trying to piece together everything they'd just been told. It seemed ludicrous that any sort of foul play could be associated with a medical device case, but the timing of it seemed too much to ignore.

"You think somebody was out to get him?" Abby asked, her hand sliding through the crook in Shane's elbow, resting on his forearm.

Shane gave the move just a slight glance before shaking his head from side to side. "I don't know." He paused, still rolling around the possibility, before sighing and motioning down the hall with the top of his head. "Come on, let's make sure somebody's there when he gets out of surgery."

CHAPTER THIRTY-NINE

From the moment Shane Laszlo first asked to approach the bench, Connor Reed knew what had happened, the same way a parent knows when a child is sick without having to be there to see it. It was a sort of ingrained intuition, the kind of thing that develops over years of working in similar situations, just one of many skills Reed was beginning to wish he'd never picked up along the way.

Tapping into a second skill he'd honed working in courtrooms across the country, he kept his face neutral as it was happening, even feigned surprise while walking to the judge to see what could be wrong. Deep down he knew though, he knew why Laszlo was suddenly scared to death, almost begging to adjourn for the day. He didn't know who the victim was, or how extensive the damage, but he knew who had caused it.

Not Carbone, though that would have been the obvious choice to lob blame at. The man was a ruthless thug, but that was all he ever held himself out to be, a ruffian that used fear and physical force to acquire whatever he needed in the world.

Reed knew the real blame in the situation rested on his shoulders, the man with the perfect hair and three thousand dollar suit, the man that stood in front of juries and lauded them for keeping the justice system running smooth right after making phone calls telling Carbone to send a message. The look on Ramirez's face as Reed walked back to his table, both of them trying not to look at Laszlo as he gathered his things and rushed outside, told him his partner knew it too.

The years weren't the only thing beginning to pile up. The tiny hits his conscience, his soul, had taken had left him wrapped in a layer of scar tissue that was almost impenetrable. A decade before he never would have let a little stunt like Lazlo pulled two days earlier get to him, now he was sending out a monster to make sure it didn't happen again.

Shoulder to shoulder he and Ramirez walked back to the Omni, their entire team already far ahead of them, cutting a trail for the conference room to prepare for the following day. Only Lauren lingered with the two lead counselors, falling in line a step behind, sensing her services would soon be needed.

The trio walked the entire way back in silence, each of them lost in their own thoughts. Every so often, one or the other would pass a glance between them, but no words were ever exchanged, even as they walked through the front door of the Omni and bypassed the conference room, heading for the elevator. Together they rode up to the top floor and waited for Reed to unlock the door to his executive suite, a somber tone hanging about them.

Reed and Ramirez passed through first, ignoring their own rule and going straight for the mini bar. Reed upturned three glass tumblers and filled them with ice while Ramirez surveyed the fare, selecting a bottle of Knob Creek. He carried it over and filled all three glasses most of the way full, well past what would be considered normal working lunch levels.

Lauren watched the proceeding with her back pressed against the door, the same position she'd been in since they arrived.

"Boys, what have we done?"

Reed turned and looked at her through heavy lidded eyes and blinked twice before gesturing to the glasses on the table. "Drink."

The two held the look for several moments before Lauren pushed herself away from the door and walked over, taking up her glass while Reed and Ramirez did the same.

"Dare I ask what we're drinking to?" she asked.

"To Hell," Ramirez said, holding up his glass and examining the light as it filtered through the dark brown liquid in his glass, "may it not be as hot as I've always feared."

Reed didn't respond to the comment in any way, his eyes on the glass before him. He stared in stony silence for so long that Lauren and Ramirez both fixed their gaze on him, wondering what he was thinking. When at last he spoke, his voice sounded much older, graveled, weary.

"That it just ends quickly, while I still have some shred of humanity left to hang on to."

He raised his glass into the center of the impromptu ring, the other two both touching theirs to his before all three drank in long swallows. Reed was the only one to finish everything in his glass, keeping his arm tilted towards the ceiling long after the others had placed theirs aside. Gulp by gulp he imbibed the whiskey, until there was nothing left but ice in the bottom of his glass. Even then, he continued tilting it upward, on and on until the ice cubes dislodged themselves and fell down against his lips.

With a heavy sigh he lowered the glass and wiped a hand across his face. Lauren and Ramirez both watched as he placed the glass down and took his cell-phone from his pocket, scrolling through his call log until he found the number he'd dialed just twelve hours before.

Only a single ring sounded out through the speakerphone before the same grating, malevolent voice filled their ears.

"*What?*"

Just hearing one word caused Lauren to shiver, taking several steps back away from the phone. Across from her a deep frown settled in on Ramirez's face, his gaze fixed on Reed.

"I thought we requested that nobody be hurt?" Reed said, no prelude, no introductions.

"No, you said nobody gets killed. The little bastard will be laid up for a while, but he will survive. Word is he'll even keep his arm."

The last sentence was added as an assertion of dominance, an unnecessary hat tip to make sure everybody in the room recognized he did whatever he wanted, whenever he wanted. Reed knew the leer was there in his voice because he was a sadistic bastard and couldn't hide it, not to further drive home a point.

"You don't think a car bomb was a bit over the top?" Reed asked, turning and pacing between the wingtip chairs, his colleagues both watching him.

"Hey, you're the one that told me we weren't playing by the rules anymore."

"Yes," Reed spat into the phone, his voice rising, "but I meant you grab one of them on the street, throw a few punches, tell them to back off."

"Well, what you got was even better, so quit your bitching," Carbone retorted, an obvious challenge rising in his voice, the message clear that he did not appreciate the tone Reed was taking with him.

"We asked that a message be sent," Reed asked, his voice evening out a bit.

"Trust me, that message was sent," Carbone replied, biting finality in his voice.

Reed shook his head, trying to keep the disdain within him from spilling out. "But you blew up a truck! How will Laszlo ever know that was a message intended for him?"

A deep chuckle rolled out through the line, making Lauren again cringe. "I left a note."

"You did what?" Reed asked, his eyes open wide, his head leaned forward to speak right into the phone receiver.

The line was silent for several moments before Carbone replied, his voice dripping with rage. "Are you telling me how to do my job?"

Reed opened his mouth to respond, but paused and exhaled, stopping himself before he took the bait. He looked Lauren and Ramirez both in the face, his expression somber. "No, we wouldn't deign to know how to best accomplish your objectives. We were just calling to say that you have completed your task, we will no longer be needing your services."

The line fell silent for several moments, the only sound the loud breathing on the opposite end. Reed's face fell blank as he tried to determine what was happening, his eyes focused on nothing in particular as he listened.

"Let me tell you something you arrogant prick, and this goes for the fat ass and the bitch cause I know they're standing right there too, *nobody* tells me when I'm done.

"Just remember, *you're* the one that said we weren't playing by the rules anymore."

CHAPTER FORTY

Tyler stared down at the tip of the blue and grey diagonal striped tie held between his fingertips, a gift from Shane before the trial started. Growing up in Worland there had been no occasion to ever wear a tie. While playing ball in college, every tie he owned featured the Crimson and black color scheme of OTU. Apparently there was an entire chart somewhere dedicated to tie colors and what they said about the person wearing them.

To Tyler, all he ever thought about when seeing someone in a tie was how uncomfortable they must be.

The tip of the tie was dotted with perspiration as he sat in the witness chair, the stares of over two hundred people in the courtroom burning hot against his chest. For the previous three years he'd played football in front of a hundred thousand people every Saturday, millions more watching from home, and never thought twice about it. Tucked away behind his facemask, attention locked on the field around him, not once did he think of how many people might be scrutinizing him.

Now, sitting there in front of the room, knowing they were all hanging on his words, he was acutely aware of every last one of them.

Just a few feet away, Shane walked back and forth, serving him up easy questions, letting Tyler tell his story. He asked just enough to keep Tyler on point, never once pushing him one direction or another. His voice even and conversational, he was doing everything he could to make Tyler feel comfortable on the stand.

Still, Tyler couldn't help but feel his shirt sticking to his back, perspiration bleeding through. Every few seconds he reminded himself to take a deep breath, just hoping to keep the jury, or the other side, from seeing him sweat. Still, after over an hour in the chair and the most important part of his testimony fast approaching, Tyler was starting to feel the wear.

"So walk me through this," Shane said, stopping and turning to face both Tyler and the jury. "You were in the indoor practice facility, just you and Coach Curl. Correct?"

"Yes," Tyler said, nodding for emphasis.

"And then what happened?"

Tyler continued to finger the end of his tie, his hands held too low for the jury to see. "Things started the same as they have for years. Coach Curl put me through a basic warm-up before stretching me out. After that we spent about an hour doing conditioning exercises. Speed ladders, shuttles, sprints, sled work."

"Anything you haven't done before?" Shane asked.

"Oh, no," Tyler said. "It's the same program we've been on since I got here."

"I see," Shane said. "Did you ever have any trouble performing these exercises before the injury?"

Tyler paused and looked down at his fingers a moment, more dots of perspiration evident on the tie. "Never. They were hard for sure, always left me gasping for air, my muscles burning, but not once did I ever have any joint pain."

Shane paused and looked at Tyler a moment, shifting his gaze to the jury for effect.

"During the course of this workout, did Coach Curl ever comment on the state of your knee? How you seemed to be moving?"

"No," Tyler said, shaking his head, his focus on Shane. "But while we were stretching, he did comment that my leg seemed to have an awful lot of bruising, more than he'd seen in the past."

"Objection, calls for speculation," Reed called out, his chair scraping against the floor as he sprung to his feet.

"Your Honor, my client is relaying a conversation that was had on the day of his injury," Shane countered. "Mr. Curl is on our witness list should opposing counsel wish to question him about the intent behind those remarks in the coming days."

Judge Lynch worked his mouth up and down several times, his walrus mustache moving in a flapping motion across his face. "Overruled."

"Thank you, Your Honor," Shane said, turning his attention back to Tyler. "Did Coach Curl have any opinions on what might have caused the bruising in your leg?"

"No, not really. He and I discussed it and I told him that Dr. Pinkering and Mr. Sarconi had assured me this sort of thing was normal. We both figured we weren't doctors, so we'd give them the benefit of the doubt."

Complete silence fell over the courtroom for a moment, the statement hanging in the air. Tyler glanced up to see his mother sniffling in the first row, wringing her hands over and over again in her lap.

"So you were working out," Shane said, "almost done for the day. What happened next?"

"One new wrinkle we'd added this winter to help strengthen my leg was lateral band work, where we'd put these big rubber bands around my ankles and shuffle from side to side. It was how we finished every workout.

"That particular day I was doing my shuffles to finish up, moving from right to left, when I started to feel a little pain in the knee."

"And just to be clear," Shane interjected, "moving right to left would put the bulk of the stress on the right knee, correct?"

"Yes," Tyler said. "The right knee would push out first, the left one would drag along behind."

"Okay, so then what happened?"

"Like I said, I started to feel a little bit of pain in my left knee while shuffling, but didn't think anything of it."

Shane held up a hand, motioning for him to pause. "And I'm sorry to interrupt, but why not?"

Tyler raised his hands by his side, let them drop back against his thighs. "To be honest, I'd had pain in the knee since they put the *KnightRunner* in. They insisted it was normal and it didn't seem any worse than usual, so I kept going."

"What happened next?" Shane said, his voice low, setting the tone for what everyone already knew was coming.

"I started back the other direction. I made it about four steps when I heard a snapping sound, felt a searing pain rip through my entire leg. Still, I thought it must be part of the recovery process, so I gritted my teeth and took another step."

His voice low and cracking, Tyler stopped there. He shifted his eyes back towards the tip of his tie, willing himself not to cry.

"After that, everything cut straight to black. Coach Curl told me after the fact what happened, but I don't remember any of it. I just remember waking up in a hospital bed, most of my left leg gone."

Shane stood rooted in place, staring back at Tyler, the entire room silent. Tyler matched the gaze as long as he could before looking away, shifting his attention to the jury box. About half of the people were looking back at him, a few with tears in their eyes. The others were doing anything they could to avert their attention, supreme discomfort evident.

Shane turned and walked back to the counsel table, pretending to consult his notes, letting the moment linger as long as he could. He had told Tyler beforehand he was going to do this, but Tyler had no idea it would seem to last so long. Several moments passed, people fidgeting in their seats, but still Shane did nothing.

After an eternity, he raised his gaze from his notes and returned to the middle of the floor, skipping ahead in the narrative.

"Tyler, when you were a college student-athlete, what would an average day consist of? We don't need a perfect itinerary, just give us the general gist."

Tyler pushed a heavy breath out from his cheeks, thankful the uneasy silence was past. "Pretty much the same thing, day after day. Get up early and come in for a morning workout, flexibility and conditioning work followed by some weights. After that hit the training room, sit in the whirlpool, get treatment, that sort of thing.

"Get out of there around nine, head back over to campus for classes, lunch, be back by two for film study and to get taped. Practice all afternoon, more training room afterwards. Dinner and homework in the evening, rinse and repeat the next day."

"And now," Shane asked, "back home in Worland? What do those days look like?"

Tyler's lips parted, the reality of what he was about to admit setting in. He pressed them tight and looked down at his lap before raising his gaze back to Shane. "Get up, do some chores around the house, wheel myself down to the hospital for rehab, stop by the library on the way home for some reading materials, help mom make dinner every night."

The words rolled out just like he and Shane had practiced, minimizing every activity into as few words as possible, emphasizing how little he was able to accomplish day to day.

"Forgive me," Shane said, "but compared to the first schedule you gave, that seems pretty light."

Tyler gave an oversized nod to the question, the frustration with his situation on full display. "Light is an understatement. Simple tasks that I once did without thinking now take me a half hour or more to perform. Every day I find myself looking around, wondering where my time has gone, asking if this is the schedule I'm bound to keep for the rest of my life."

"Tyler, I have just two more questions for you," Shane asked, walking over and standing right in front him, but a few feet away, one hand deep in his pocket, the other with his thumb and forefinger pinched together, poised in front of him. "If given the choice between never playing football again and keeping your leg, or having the possibility of playing again and going through what you are now, which would you choose?"

Tyler shifted his attention from Shane to the jury box, his face beseeching them to listen to what he was about to say.

"I would hang up my cleats without thinking twice. I would never wish this on anybody as long as I live."

Shane walked up even closer to the stand, resting his hand on the rail right in front of Tyler. "And were you ever given that choice?"

"No," Tyler said, no pause of any kind before responding, no elaborating on his response.

Several moments passed before Shane patted the rail and retreated from the stand. "No further questions, Your Honor."

Over his left shoulder, Tyler could hear papers shuffling as the judge looked through them, taking notes and checking something before proceeding. Tyler remained still in the chair for several long seconds before looking up at the judge, wondering when his time would be up, praying for these endless stretches of silence to end.

"Defense counselor, your witness," the judge said, his voice thick, bordering on sleepy.

Tyler shifted his attention back to the front and watched as Connor Reed rose from his seat, staring down at handwritten notes on the desk before him. Shane had spent the last several days prepping him for this, pushing even harder on this aspect of his testimony than his own.

"Good afternoon, Mr. Bentley," Reed said, his face still turned downward.

"Good afternoon."

The man paused again, still staring down at his notes, before finding whatever he was searching for and walking out into the middle of the floor. Just as he had done in his opening statement, he found a spot in the exact center of the room and stood rooted in place, twisting at the waist to speak to Tyler or the jury.

"Mr. Bentley, I have only a few quick questions for you. First of all, I would like to congratulate you on a very successful athletic career. The numbers and accolades that you and Mr.

Laszlo went through earlier are nothing short of incredible. Tell me something though, in all that time, did you ever miss a single game?"

Tyler paused for a moment, the question taking him by surprise, he made no effort to hide that fact from his face as he rifled back through the years in his head, trying to recall if he'd ever sat out.

"No."

A look of surprise washed over Reed's face. "Never? Not once?"

"Not that comes to mind," Shane said, shaking his head back and forth.

"Okay," Reed said, nodding pursing his lips in front of him, "how about practices?"

"Objection," Shane called, rising from his seat. "Relevance, Your Honor?"

Judge Lynch paused for several long moments, debating the merits of the claim, glancing from Shane to Tyler and then to Reed.

"Overruled."

Shane lowered himself back into his chair as Reed bowed the top of his head in appreciation. "Thank you, Your Honor. Mr. Bentley?"

Tyler shook his head from side to side. "Sure, everybody in college football has missed one or two practices over the years."

"But on the whole, you would say it was very rare for you to miss one?"

Far in the back of his mind Tyler could sense this was going somewhere he didn't want it to, he just couldn't quite put it together.

"Yes."

"So," Reed said, shifting his shoulders to face the jury, "for someone like yourself, a very durable player that never missed a game, rarely missed a practice, the prospect of missing an entire season must have been very difficult, right?"

There was another lengthy pause as Tyler considered the question, feeling a bit of sweat rise to his forehead. "To be honest, I didn't get a chance to think of it like that. Everything happened pretty fast."

A small smile crossed Reed's face as he opened his mouth to

respond, but he closed it just as fast. "We'll get back to that in a moment."

Reed turned on his heel and walked back to his table, taking up a thin stack of papers. He walked over to Shane and handed him one of the stapled sets of pages before walking up to the judge and extending him a set as well.

"Your Honor, these are official copies of the surgical consent form signed by Mr. Bentley prior to the surgery. I'd like to enter them into the record as Exhibit A."

Judge Lynch accepted the forms and looked up to Shane. "Counselor?"

"Agreed," Shane said, leaning forward in his seat to study the document.

"So entered."

"Thank you, Your Honor," Reed said, accepting the form back from the judge and handing it to Tyler. "Mr. Bentley, could you please read the heading at the top of this page aloud for the court."

Confusion crossed Tyler's face as he glanced down at the form and back up at Shane sitting across from him, who met his gaze and gave the tiniest of affirmative nods. "Patient Consent to Surgery Form."

"Thank you," Reed said, having resumed his position in the middle of the floor, his hands now clasped behind his back. "And could you please flip to the last page of the document?"

Tyler did so, a sense of dread welling within him. He could feel blood rushing to his face, pounding in his temples, starting to form sweat on his upper lip.

"Mr. Bentley, could you please tell the court whose signature is on the bottom of this consent form?"

The feeling exploded across Tyler's core, feeling like it would start to seep from his pores at any moment. His tongue felt rough and dry against the top of his mouth as he stared down at his own signature, a mark he didn't even remembered making.

"Mine."

"Thank you," Reed said, nodding his agreement with Tyler's statement. He shifted again to face the jury and said, "Mr. Bentley, based on the consent form that you now hold in your hand, and the testimony you just provided about your durability as a player, isn't it possible that you were fully apprised of the risks that came with implanting the *KnightRunner*, but in your haste to return to action you ignored them?"

A full-on sweat broke out across Tyler's brow, beads of moisture that shined beneath the overhead lights. He willed himself to stay still in the chair, to refrain from squirming, to not let the jury think that Reed was right. A dozen different answers went through his mind as he tried to remember what Shane had coached him on, but in the end, they all seemed to fade away, leaving room for the one simple truth that he'd been battling with for almost six months now.

"To be honest, sir, I don't remember."

A low murmur passed through the crowd as Reed stood in the center of the room, his mouth half open, head cocked towards the witness chair.

"I'm sorry Mr. Bentley, but you don't remember?"

"No sir, I don't. Like I said, the entire thing happened very fast."

A look of incredulity spread over Reed as he took two sharp steps towards Tyler before catching himself and coming to a complete stop. He gave a disbelieving look to Tyler and the jury before offering a disdainful smile and turning back towards his table. "No further questions, Your Honor."

Tyler's heart continued to pound in his chest as he took a deep breath, looking down to see his hands trembling against his legs.

"Mr. Laszlo, redirect?" Judge Lynch asked.

"Yes, thank you," Shane said, rising from his chair and walking straight out into the floor to stand in front of Tyler.

"Mr. Bentley, do you drink?"

"No."

"Smoke?"

"Never."

"Do drugs of any kind?"

"Absolutely not."

Tyler rattled off his answers in rapid fire fashion, his mind racing to figure out where the line of questioning might be going.

Shane paused and shifted just a bit, looking out over the jury. "Please tell us, when you first injured your knee, what were you given for the pain?"

"Morphine."

"Morphine," Shane repeated, pausing again for effect. "And how much time elapsed between the time of your injury and the surgery to implant the *KnightRunner* in your leg?"

"Uh, the injury happened on New Year's Day, the surgery was first thing on the morning of the fourth, so about two and a half days."

"About two and a half days, and tell me, in that entire two and a half days, how much of that time were you *not* under the effects of morphine?"

"Just a few hours leading up the surgery itself. They told me it was so they could get the anesthesia right during the procedure."

"Huh," Shane said, taking a step forward and again placing his hand on the rail of the witness stand. "Just one last question, when did they have you sign the consent form for surgery?"

It was all Tyler could do to keep from smiling, the pieces of what Shane was getting at clicking into place. "The afternoon before."

CHAPTER FORTY-ONE

During midday recess, the entire team retired back to the conference room on the second floor of the law school. Shane and Tyler stripped off their jackets, Prescott went to check on some affairs in his office, Abby ran out with Shane's credit card to purchase lunch. For a few moments while Margie excused herself to the restroom, it was just Shane and Tyler, two guys sitting around and talking about the morning's events as if it were the locker room after a big game.

"So, how'd I do?" Tyler asked, rolling his sleeves to the elbow, tugging his shirt away from his chest to let in a little air.

"Very solid," Shane said, a half smile on his face, an arm propped up on the table beside him. "I almost yelled out loud when you told Reed you couldn't remember. I looked straight down and started scribbling gibberish as fast as I could to keep the jury from seeing me smile."

"It was true though!" Tyler said, his arms spread wide. "I couldn't remember you and I going over that, and I honestly can't remember anything from back then, so I just went with it."

"It was beautiful," Shane said, shaking his head. "I'm certain Reed had way more he wanted to ask you, but you threw him so far off his game, he just gave up and ran away. Decided to wait and try again on the next go-round."

The smile faded a bit from Tyler's face as he stared off into the distance, recalling the incident in his head. In the moment he was just glad his time in front of Reed was over, but in retrospect he could see how Shane was right, the cross examination *had* ended on an odd note.

"Speaking of which, how did you know to come right back up and start firing all those questions at me? Drinking and drugs and stuff?"

A laugh slid out of Shane as he extended his index finger towards the stack of papers piled high on the table nearby. "Totally off the cuff. A month's worth of preparation over there and sometimes the best things are the ones that just sort of happen."

Tyler nodded his head, raising his eyebrows, deep in his own thoughts. "Sometimes busted plays are the best kind," he mumbled, drumming his fingers on the table. After a moment he shifted his attention back to Shane, his face serious. "You're pretty damn good in there, you know it?"

"Oh, I don't know about all that. We've still got a long way to go yet," Shane said, waving aside the compliment.

"Well yeah, I get that, I'm just saying, you're good on your feet, you're good in front of a crowd. I was a wreck in there, all those people staring at me. Put me in a helmet and shoulder pads, I don't care how many people are there, but set me on the stand and make me talk about my leg, my feelings? Terrible."

Before Shane could respond, Margie returned from the restroom, shifting the conversation over into prep work for her turn on the stand.

Three hours later, standing out in the middle of the courtroom, Margie on the stand before him explaining how Dr. Pinkering and Sarconi had presented the *KnightRunner* as the only possible answer, Shane realized Tyler had been right and wrong.

Shane was comfortable in a courtroom, had sort of grown up in them, watching one of the best in the business peddle her craft across half the country. For some people it might have instilled a feeling of inferiority, set them up for a lifetime of trying to chase some unattainable standard. For him, it had served to provide him with the ultimate blueprint, an outline for how things were to be done.

At the same, Shane knew that if he did his job, *truly* did his job, the most important thing he could do was deflect most of the attention away from himself. He wasn't there to be a court jester and make people laugh nor a snake charmer to keep people mesmerized, he was there as a facilitator, meant to coax the story out of the people he put on the stand.

Right now that person was Margie, her hands twisted into a knot in her lap, her face pink with the tears that were never more than a second or two away.

"Ms. Bentley," Shane asked, one hand thrust in his pocket, moving back and forth in his methodical slow gait between her and the jury box. "At any point while Dr. Pinkering and Mr. Sarconi were hyping the *KnightRunner* to you, did you think to seek a second opinion?"

Margie nodded at the response, a crown of curls visible atop her head. "I did. I even asked Dr. Pinkering about it at one point while Tyler was sleeping."

"And what did he say to you?"

Silence fell as Margie looked down at her hands, her fingers twisting atop each other like a tangle of snakes, writhing in her lap. "He told me that the only way Tyler's scholarship would cover the procedure was if it was done there at OTU."

Shane stopped moving, a look of shock splayed across his features. He fixed his attention on the jury and panned the length of the box, speaking as he did so. "He *told* you that unless it was done at OTU, you were on your own for the costs?"

"Yes," Margie said, her voice dropping to just above a whisper. "He also said that he was the best in the hospital at dealing with knee injuries and that nobody would ever dare go against him."

"Ms. Bentley, did Dr. Pinkering ever put a price tag on this procedure? Tell you down to the penny how much it would cost?"

Margie ran her tongue out over her lips. "At one point he asked if I had one hundred thousand dollars to spend on a second opinion."

Again Shane stopped and looked at the jury, his jaw hanging open. "If you don't mind my asking Ms. Bentley, do you? Have a hundred thousand dollars for a second opinion?"

"No," Margie whispered, her gaze falling to the floor.

"Of course not," Shane said, waving a hand by his side for effect. "None of us do. So let me get this straight. The attending orthopedist at a major university hospital told you that you either do the surgery where and how he says, or somehow find an incredible amount of money to do it somewhere else?"

Margie lifted her head back to Shane, a tiny bit of understanding on her face. "Yes."

"Tell me, how did that make you feel?" Shane asked, stepping up to the stand and taking the same place he had beside Tyler just hours before.

Her gaze focused on him, Margie said, "At first I was just shocked. Whenever Tyler was awake and they wanted him to be their poster boy, Dr. Pinkering was nothing but nice. The second I started asking questions though, things got ugly fast.

"I guess it worked though, because after the initial shock and even a little anger wore off, I just got scared. I was worried about my son, about his health, about his career, so I let it go. I knew I couldn't pay for the surgery he needed, so I kept my mouth shut to make sure he was taken care of."

The last words from her were almost inaudible as Margie's chin dipped to her chest, shoulders heaving up and down as she cried. Shane stayed by her side for several long moments, a sympathetic look on his face, before stepping away from the stand.

"No more questions, Your Honor."

Shane pushed away from the stand, watching Margie the entire way as he headed back to the table. Not until she raised her face towards the courtroom did he offer a tiny nod and turn to take his seat.

Across from him William Ramirez rose and circled out from behind the counsel table, leaving Reed reclined in his chair, legs crossed, a frown on his face. Mimicking the style of his partner, Ramirez walked to the middle of the floor and chose a spot between Margie and the jury, his hands folded behind his back, orange tie resting atop his protruded stomach.

"Good afternoon, Ms. Bentley."

"Hello," Margie said, her voice still thick with tears, offering a forced nod.

"Again, we would like to offer our deepest condolences on Tyler's injury and the impact it has no doubt had on your family."

"Thank you."

Ramirez paused, his head cocked to the side, debating how to phrase his first question. He remained in that position several moments before asking, "Ms. Bentley, do you have a copy of Tyler's scholarship?"

A look of surprise came over Margie's features, causing her to lean back in her chair. "No, I do not."

"You don't?" Ramirez said, cocking his head even more for effect.

"No. I've never seen a copy of it, just the letter of intent he signed when he committed."

"I see," Ramirez said, nodding his head up and down. He turned and retreated to his counsel table, taking up two documents, holding one in either hand, just as Reed had done that morning. The first he passed over to Shane, the other he brought forth to Judge Lynch.

"Your Honor, I have in my hand a copy of Tyler Bentley's scholarship. Mr. Laszlo, do we agree on this?"

"We do," Shane agreed.

"I would like to enter this into the record as Exhibit C."

"So entered," Judge Lynch said, boredom evident in his tone.

Ramirez walked to the witness stand and handed the document to Margie before returning to his spot in the middle of the floor. "Ms. Bentley, could you please turn to page six of the scholarship agreement and read the highlighted portion found there?"

Shane rifled through the document before him to page six, his gaze scanning the length of it for what Ramirez was referring to. His copy wasn't highlighted, but he knew without a doubt what they were going for. In front of him Margie cleared her throat to read, but he was already tuned out, scribbling notes in the margins.

"Section D," Margie said aloud, "Physical Injury. Should the student-athlete become injured while participating in athletic competition, or in a school sanctioned function relating to the sport for which this scholarship is awarded, all related medical expenses will be covered."

Margie stopped reading there and flipped the paper closed, dropping it onto the rail in front of her, a look bordering on disgust across her face.

"Thank you," Ramirez said, hands clasped behind his back, attention turned to the jury. "Now, Ms. Bentley, you were by your son's side the entire time he was in the hospital for his injury, were you not?"

"I was. The entire town had thrown a party to watch the game together, but once the injury happened, I caught a ride to Cody and jumped a plane here."

"Impressive," Ramirez said, nodding. "No doubt the kind of thing most mothers would do in your situation. Tell me, during that time, were you under any sort of medication? Anything at all that might have impaired your judgment?"

"Um, no?" Margie said, her face contorted with confusion.

"So, during this time while Tyler might have been feeling the effects of the injury, of morphine, of being in the hospital, you, his mother, were there and cognizant the entire time?"

Shane's head popped up from the document in front of him, the question resonating in his ears. Already he could see where this was going, a tiny bit of dread swelling in the recesses of his mind. Without thinking, he scratched out the notes he'd been making and started anew, the new goal for redirect to be damage control.

"I was," Margie said.

"Yet, during all that time, you never questioned what was going on beyond one brief conversation with Dr. Pinkering? And even after that, never thought to check the veracity of his statements?"

Ideas continued to spread out on the legal pad in front of Shane, his hands almost flying across the page. If the defense was so willing to offer Pinkering as a sacrificial lamb, their approach was already taking a far different course than what he had anticipated, almost as if they were trying to minimize blame as opposed to full exoneration.

Margie stared back at him for several seconds, her bottom lip quivering. After a moment her eyes slid shut, two heavy tears sliding down her cheeks. She again lowered her face towards her chin. "No."

"How much money do you make, Ms. Bentley?" Ramirez asked, twisting his neck in a faux attempt to look up at her lowered face.

A heavy sigh passed from Margie as she continued to keep her eyes aimed downward. "Thirty-two thousand dollars a year."

"And tell me, how much money does a NFL running back make?"

"Objection!" Shane roared, springing to his feet.

"Withdrawn," Ramirez said, raising his hands by his side and falling back to the defense table, not even waiting for Shane to get out his reason for objecting or for the judge to make a ruling on it.

An open scowl crossed Shane's face as he lowered himself back into his chair, looking up to notice the same expression on Judge Lynch's face. In the witness chair Margie sat with her mouth agape, looking between Shane and Ramirez, trying to make sense of what just took place.

"Redirect, Mr. Laszlo?"

"Of course," Shane said, rising and glaring at Reed and Ramirez, both avoiding his gaze. He walked out into the middle of the floor and fixed his attention on the jury.

"Ms. Bentley," he said, his voice masking a roiling anger just beneath the surface, "you mentioned a moment ago what your salary is each year. Would you mind telling the court what you do for a living?"

Her voice came out from off to the right, but Shane didn't turn to look at her. "I am a crane operator at the Washakie County Sawmill."

"And I imagine you underwent a great deal of training to learn to operate those cranes right?"

"I had to attend a school and serve as an apprentice for six months before becoming a full-time operator."

Shane still kept looking at the jury box, making sure they were following him.

"And I imagine if someone like, say, myself were to show up and start trying to operate one of them, bad things would happen, right?"

Shane glanced over just long enough to see Margie's eyes open wide, a look of shock on her face. "Moving around logs that weigh thousands of pounds? Yes, bad things would happen. Somebody would get hurt or worse."

"Get hurt or worse," Shane said, nodding his head, looking at the jurors. He turned and walked up to the witness stand, his focus now on Margie.

"Ms. Bentley, are you a doctor?"

"No."

"Are you a lawyer?"

"No."

"So a moment ago, you seemed shocked at the mere notion of me attempting to jump in and operate your crane, is that correct?"

Margie nodded. "Very surprised, for sure."

Shane paused and looked over at the jury, his head angled towards Margie. "So is there any situation in which you would try to do a doctor's job and diagnose a knee injury?"

"No."

"How about a lawyer's job, and decipher a college football scholarship?"

Another twist of the head from Margie. "No."

"No further questions, Your Honor."

CHAPTER FORTY-TWO

Shane nodded to the girl working the front desk, not bothering to stop and let her interrogate him about where he was going. The sun was already dropping beneath the cityscape outside, the ambient glow of Columbus just starting to rise above the horizon. Within an hour it would be dark, another day fast drawing to a close. Where he was going, he didn't want to appear like he was in a hurry, but he didn't have all night to spend in banal chitchat either.

The heels of his dress shoes clicked against the tile floor as he stepped out of the stairwell and walked the length of the hall. At this late hour the mood in the ward was subdued, a third of the overhead lights already cut for the night. The sound of televisions playing could be heard emanating from some of the rooms as he passed, half-asleep individuals in various states of repair staring at the screen with listless disregard. A handful of orderlies moved between some of the rooms, collecting dinner pans and tending to patient needs, none of them even glancing Shane's way as he passed.

His journey ended at the last room in the hallway, a tiny space with a single bed, a couple of chairs, and a television mounted high on the wall above. Shane stopped just outside it as he approached, wrapping on the door with the back of his knuckles before entering.

"Yeah?" a familiar voice called, pulling Shane into the room.

In front of him, Heath sat upright in bed, a hospital gown covering the top half of his body, a stack of thin blankets doing the job for the lower half. His entire right arm was bound in a thick white cast, enveloping everything from his fingertips to his shoulder. A diagonal support disappeared under the gown near his ribs, holding the monstrosity up in the air.

Seated beside the cast was a woman in her mid-fifties with thin blonde hair pulled back and clear blue eyes, not a trace of makeup to be seen. Her head turned as Shane entered, a look of disdain appearing on her features, her eyes drawing narrow.

On the left side of the bed sat Abby, Heath's hand encased in hers, embarrassment on her face, though she made no attempt to release the hold.

"Hey there," Shane said, walking in and standing at the end of the bed. He had shed his jacket and tie, rolled his sleeves to the elbows. Weeks of insomnia were starting to wear on him too, his eyes feelings puffy and heavy.

"Hey," Heath said, a pained smile on his face. "Abby here was just telling me about how you put it on them today."

"Oh, I don't know about that," Shane said, a half smile in place. He shifted his attention from Heath to the woman beside him and extended a hand across the end of the bed. "Mrs. Wilson, I presume? Shane Laszlo, I've been working with Heath this summer."

Her hand was thin and cold, the grip firm as she returned the gesture. "Charmed, I'm sure," she said, her eyes boring into his. She held the pose for a full moment before rising, releasing the shake and drawing her purse up from the ground beside her chair. "I'm going to run down to the cafeteria for some coffee, anybody need anything?"

Shane retreated back to the end of the bed and stared down at it, waiting as Abby and Heath both said they were good and Mrs. Wilson departed. Once she was gone, he looked up at Heath, a questioning look on his face.

"Don't worry about her," Heath said, waving a hand. "She's a farmer's wife, her bark is way worse than her bite."

"Still, that's a pretty vicious bark," Shane said, twisting at the waist to glance out into the hall. "Did I do something to offend her?"

"Naw, right now she just needs something to lash out at. My folks wanted me to come back and run the farm the minute I was done with undergrad. I told them why I decided to go to law school, but they thought it was foolish, my time was better spent there.

"This is pretty much their worst fear come true. My very first case, the truck explodes and I end up in the hospital, neither of which comes cheap. She's angry, and right now all she has to be angry at is this Shane Laszlo she keeps hearing about."

Shane slid a low, shrilled whistle between his teeth. "So I could have come in here like Oprah singing songs and handing out gifts and it wouldn't have mattered, huh?"

Heath snorted, his head tilting to the side to look at Abby. "I don't know if I'd go that far. Everybody loves Oprah, right?"

Abby's face turned a deep shade of red as she looked up at Shane and shrugged. "I'm a fan. Sorry."

A deep laugh rolled out of Shane, his body tilting backwards. "Don't be, that's fantastic." He rocked forward onto the balls of his feet and extended a finger towards them, wagging it at their interlocked hands. "So tell me, was I the matchmaker or the idiot that hired lovebirds and never once realized it?"

Heath's head rolled back towards Shane, the smile still on his face. "Yes. You're the idiot that played matchmaker and never once realized it."

"Ah," Shane said, raising his eyebrows and nodding. "Well, at the very least, it looks like you're doing well. A lot better than when they wheeled you out yesterday."

"Yeah," Heath said, twisting his head at the neck to glance down at his arm. "Feeling a lot better than yesterday too. They said I should be able to go home the day after tomorrow, be healed up in six weeks or so."

"Good," Shane said, nodding for emphasis, "that's great news, it really is. Any word from the police? Why this happened?"

Heath turned to Abby and motioned with chin towards a small nightstand in the corner. "Not since this morning."

Beside him, Abby released her grip on his hands and rolled her chair over, taking up a thin manila folder and passing it to Shane. He accepted it and glanced at each of them in turn before opening it, turning it sideways to look at the photos inside.

"I guess once they got the truck up and moved yesterday afternoon, they found that spray painted on the ground beneath it," Heath said.

Shane raised the photo so it was just a few inches from his nose. It was a glossy color print of charred asphalt, bits of metal and oil stains visible. Sprawled across it in neon green spray paint was the words *stay away*.

"Stay away?" Shane said aloud, his face relaying how perplexed he felt. "From who? Or what?"

"No idea," Heath said, shaking his head. "I tried every way possible to think about how it could relate to us, but I can't make it fit. No way a case like ours causes someone to climb under my truck and spray paint that on the ground."

The photos came back up to Shane's face, his features squinted tight as he tried to pick out any little detail that might shed some light on the culprit. After several long seconds he lowered them and extended the folder back to Abby.

"I'm sorry, but I've got nothing. Like you said, doesn't seem to fit."

Abby replaced the folder on the table and wheeled herself back over to the bedside, her hands finding Heath's again. Shane smiled at the interaction and shook his head, still wondering how his focus in the case had made him that blind for the past few weeks.

"Alright guys, I hate to cut and run like this, but we've got the good doctor and Marty both on the stand tomorrow. I've got some more legwork to do tonight."

"Do you need me to go with you?" Abby asked, her voice sounding sincere, but the look on her face relaying she had no intention of leaving.

Shane smiled at the offer and stepped back from the bed, peeking his head out into the hallway. "No, thank you, but unless I'm mistaken, you guys still have a few minutes left before Mrs. Wilson gets back. Consider them a gift from your boss."

Heath and Abby both put on matching smiles as Shane excused himself, pulling the door shut behind him. For a moment he stood with his back pressed against it, smiling at the first bit of normality he'd witnessed in weeks, before pushing himself down the hallway and extracting the cell phone from his pocket.

Christine answered on the first ring.

"Hey, you got an hour? I need to step away for a bit."

CHAPTER FORTY-THREE

For the first time in the entire course of the trial, the roles were reversed. No longer was the person on the stand a sweating, nervous wreck, an individual unaccustomed to having a hundred faces turned their way, withering under their combined stares. No longer was their counselor a calming presence, a guiding hand to help them navigate the situation.

Today, the steady hand was Manningham, a veritable rock, nothing short of an oak tree as he sat on the stand fielding Reed's questions. One by one they came flying in, each a bit more outrageous in the direction they were going, a bit more salacious in the insinuations they were laden with.

Sitting on the outside, watching the scene unfold with a growing sense of rage, an underlying current of indignation, was Shane.

The direct examination had gone as expected, beginning with Manningham discussing how he was approached to perform the surgery because of his expertise in knee replacements. The discussion went on to include that he had never used the *KnightRunner* implant before, had no prior experience with its successes or failures. Shane concluded his questioning with both of the surgeries to Tyler Bentley, how well the first one had gone, and how the leg was beyond saving in the second.

Despite everything that Manningham said, damning the SynTronic product and being quite upset at having to remove Tyler's leg, Reed came out firing. It only took a matter of seconds for Shane to ascertain that part of the defense was to attribute the fault to Manningham, blaming the outcome on poor surgical work and not on a cut-rate product.

The moment Shane put together in his mind where Reed meant to take the line of questioning, a white flame started to grow within him. Years of watching his mother had taught him to keep his face impassive, a blank canvas that only looked up to watch the proceedings, back down to take notes. Every other part of him seethed with anger, a coiling and recoiling of tension and rage that ebbed and flowed to the surface, dying for the chance to spring forward and save his witness.

Despite his inclination to do just that, by every appearance Manningham needed no saving. Prior to trial he told Shane that he had testified in over a dozen cases before, always as an expert and never a material witness, but that sitting in the chair did not bother him. He was a man used to performing eighteen hour surgeries under intense lights and heavy lead gowns, answering questions from an old man in a suit was not a concern.

For his part, Reed did his best to contradict that statement, coming after Manningham with an aggression he had not yet employed over the first week of trial. Abandoning his statuesque position in the middle of the courtroom, he opted for a back and forth approach, retreating to the jury whenever Manningham spoke, rushing towards him whenever he asked a question.

To Shane, the movement was recognized as an attempt to add emphasis to his question, to make them more memorable by overdramatizing. What he surmised, what he hoped, everybody else in the courtroom took from it was a man realizing the case was getting away from him.

"Dr. Manningham," Reed said, pacing in the middle of the room, his fingers laced in front of another in his unending collection of red ties, "how long have you been performing knee replacement surgeries?"

Manningham looked back at him, his eyes unblinking, his face void of sweat or even the slightest wrinkle of apprehension. "I performed my first full replacement in my fourth year of residency, so three years as a resident, ten years as a staff physician, and the last four as an attending. Seventeen years in all."

"I didn't ask for the resume," Reed said, pacing back and forth, "impressive though it may be. Tell me doctor, in those seventeen years, how many knee replacements, ballpark, would you say you've done?"

"Three hundred and forty-three."

The number spun Reed back to face him, a look of shock on his features. "Three hundred and forty-three? Exactly?"

"Yes, that is correct," Manningham said, shifting his head to stare back.

Reed nodded twice, collecting himself, before beginning yet another slow march on the stand. "And of those three hundred and forty-three, how many of those dealt with a shattered kneecap?"

"A fair many, maybe a quarter or so."

"Maybe a quarter or so? So, eight-five?"

Manningham nodded. "I don't have that particular figure right on hand, but it sounds about right. I'll be more than happy to look it up and get back to you if you'd like."

Reed raised a hand, twisting it at the wrist. "That won't be necessary doctor. You say eighty-five, that is a number we can work with.

"Now, of those eight-five, how many had a broken tibia also?"

A twist of the head as Manningham debated a number in his mind. "The tibia is one of the easier bones in the body to break, narrow, with a long surface area. Probably two-thirds, if not a few more."

"So, perhaps fifty-five or so?" Reed asked, creeping up on the stand, his fingers pulling back so just the tips touched together in front of him.

"Objection, Your Honor," Shane said, pushing his seat back and rising to his feet, stopping Reed in his march on the stand. "Permission to approach?"

"You may," Judge Lynch said, waving Shane forward with his index finger.

Reed remained rooted in place, a look of incredulity on his face that he was being challenged, waiting until Shane was almost to the bench before shifting himself forward and approaching as well. The look remained on his face as he moved, his gaze boring into Shane.

Shane ignored him.

"Your Honor, Dr. Manningham is not on trial here. He can't possibly be asked to remember the exact statistics of all three hundred and forty-three knee replacements he has performed over a seventeen year period."

Judge Lynch nodded his understanding, shifting his eyes to Reed, the glasses still perched on the end of his nose beneath them.

"Your Honor, Dr. Manningham has been called to the stand as a material witness and an active participant whose actions may have had a direct impact on how this situation played out. I am trying to ascertain the severity of this case in particular and if that may have had some bearing on the outcome."

The judge exhaled, pushing a mighty gust of air out through his nostrils. He looked from Shane to Reed and back again, his moustache twitching as he considered the objection.

"I'm going to overrule this one, but your objection is noted. Mr. Reed, I would suggest you bring this line of questioning back to the matter at hand, and fast."

"Yes, Your Honor," Reed said, bowing his head in acknowledgment. He cast a sideways glance at Shane as they departed, resuming his stance in the middle of the floor.

Once more Shane ignored him, his gaze on the front row as he returned to his seat. There, Margie and Abby both stared back, faces drawn, not quite blank. Beside them Prescott sat with a look that relayed approval, a touch of pride mixed in around the edges.

Tyler leaned over as Shane took his seat, lowering his voice to just a whisper, twisting his body so as to speak over his shoulder. "What was that about?"

"Interrupting his flow," Shane said, his voice just as quiet. "Protecting our witness."

"So, Dr. Manningham," Reed began anew in the middle of the floor, resuming his previous stance before the jury. "We were down to the number fifty-five. Fifty-five of an original three hundred and forty three that had both a shattered kneecap and a broken tibia.

"Might I ask, how many of those also had a broken fibula?"

"Perhaps half? Maybe a few less?"

"So, twenty-five?" Reed said, circling forward once more. "Would that be a fair number to use?"

"Yes, that sounds fair," Manningham conceded, nodding.

"Okay. Please, tell me, of those twenty-five, how many also had a broken femur?"

"All three bones broken?" Manningham asked, his eyebrows raised a bit. "That would take quite an extreme amount of trauma. No more than a handful."

Reed turned on a heel, headed for the jury, a look of small victory on his face. "So what you're telling me is that this particular case, Tyler Bentley's knee, presenting with all three major bones broken and the kneecap shattered, was one of a very, very small number of cases you've ever seen?"

"Yes."

"No more than, what, one or two percent of the cases that you've ever seen in your career as an orthopedic surgeon?"

"The math adds up. Yes, I would say that."

Reed turned again and walked away from the stand, pausing just long enough to look up at Shane, a half smirk visible in the corner of his mouth. "So then, isn't it possible Dr. Manningham, that the combined effects of the rare and violent injury sustained by Tyler Bentley along with your own admitted inexperience with these kinds of cases, might have been what caused the failure of Tyler Bentley's left leg, and not a faulty product from my client, SynTronic?"

"Objection!" Shane yelled, snapping to his feet so fast his chair toppled over behind him, the sudden noise sending a ripple through the crowd.

"Withdraw the question, Your Honor," Reed responded, just like Ramirez not even waiting for Shane to state the grounds of his objection. He raised his hands by his side as if conceding defeat, turning and heading for his chair while giving a sideways smile to Shane, a tiny hitch in his step for effect.

Shane remained on his feet glaring back at his opponent, everything in him fighting to keep his vehemence from becoming visible to the room. His entire body felt as if it were trembling with fury, his fists resting atop the hardwood desk to make sure he remained still.

"Counselor, your witness," Judge Lynch said.

Shane remained where he was for several long moments, glaring over at Reed, before dropping his gaze to his notes in front of him. He already knew what he wanted to ask, but needed the extra time to make sure his voice was clear and even when he spoke.

"Dr. Manningham, you mentioned that you have performed three hundred and forty-three knee replacements over the years. Of those, have you ever operated on a single person that didn't need it?"

A hint of smirk moved Manningham's head backwards, followed by a sharp twist of the head. "Never. Not only would that be unethical, no insurance company would ever sign off on it."

"So, the issues that Mr. Reed already outlined notwithstanding, what types of things would normally necessitate this sort of operation?"

Manningham pursed his lips, his head moving from side to side as he thought. "Most knee replacements are for people fifty years and above, the decades of pounding on the joint causing it to break down or wear out."

"Meaning it would be fair to say that no knee replacement is ever performed without major damage to the joint?"

"It wouldn't just be fair, it would be accurate," Manningham said.

"And that trying to differentiate the severity of one versus another is kind of a moot point?" Shane asked, turning so he could see Manningham, the jury right before him.

"The procedure is the same, regardless of the state of the joint when it arrives, because the entire thing is being replaced anyway."

"Because the entire thing is being replaced anyway," Shane said, nodding his head and pacing away from the jury a few steps before turning and retracing his steps. "Dr. Manningham, just a couple more questions for you. Of those three hundred and forty-three, how many had to have their leg amputated three months post-operation?"

Manningham drew himself up straighter in the chair, his face pinched, a mask of indignation. "No others. Not three months post-op, not ever."

"And of those three hundred and forty-three, all those people still walking around, still with the full use of both legs, how many used the *KnightRunner?*"

The air grew heavier, tense, as the entire room seemed to lean forward, a collective group waiting for Manningham's response. He was sure not to disappoint, looking at Shane for a moment before focusing on the jury.

"Only Tyler Bentley."

Shane stopped his movement, glancing at Manningham, at the jury, and at last to Tyler before turning and walking back to his chair. "No further questions, Your Honor."

CHAPTER FORTY-FOUR

There was no sound beneath Lauren Egan's shoes as she walked around the polished floor of the Omni's foyer, her usual stiletto heels traded in for a basic pair of Nike running shoes. The well-shaped calves she preferred to keep on display for the world to see were hidden beneath a pair of blue jeans, a zip up pullover extended past the wrist, almost touching the cups of coffee she held in either hand. Her hair was swept back in a simple pony tail, accentuating the lines that were beginning to form around her eyes.

She could still pass for twenty-five, but her actual age was starting to peek out from around the next corner.

After a night of less than three hours sleep, Lauren was back on the clock, despite it being a Saturday. She walked through the lobby without a word to anyone and stepped inside the executive conference center, most of the chairs in the space already full, nobody saying anything.

Everybody in the room was dressed as she was, a vast step down from their usual courtroom attire. The Twins had traded in their Brooks Brothers gear for polo's of the same color scheme, their shirttails tucked in tight, a hint of Axe body spray rolling off them. The two paralegals were both in hooded sweatshirts, looking like they'd either been up all night scouring case law or each other's bodies, most likely both.

Across from them sat Dr. Pinkering and Sarconi, each trying to pull off the dressed down look, each looking very uncomfortable doing it. The two of them appeared to be aging in dog years, each passing day bringing more folds around the mouth, more bags under the eyes.

Sarconi watched Lauren as she entered, his face perking up as he smelled coffee, pushing himself a little higher in his chair as she walked past him and placed them on the end of the table. He stared at the cups sitting alone for a moment before looking back up at her, a scowl on his face as she returned to her chair.

"Piss on the rest of us, huh?"

"She doesn't work for the rest of you," Reed said as he swept into the room, Ramirez on his heels. Dressed in jeans and a dress shirt he walked to the front of the room and picked up his coffee, taking a long pull from the cup, smacking his lips for effect. "Damn, that's good. Thank you, Lauren."

Beside him, Ramirez walked to the front and took up his as well, lifting it in thanks to the corner. Lauren nodded to both of them, shutting the door behind her.

Reed took another hit from the coffee before lowering it to the table and lacing his fingers across his stomach, assuming his standard pose while looking around the room. After a moment he sighed and raised his eyebrows, twisting his head to one side.

"Well then, that was an eventful first week, wasn't it?"

The left side of the room plus Lauren had worked with Reed long enough to know that was not the opening they wanted to hear. They were aware that the case was not going their way, but this was something else entirely. This was their boss, their fearless leader, showing his hand and letting them know how dire their position was. All five squirmed a bit in their chair, knowing this was not the start to the weekend they were hoping for.

In the years she'd worked for him, Lauren had seen it twice before, both cases of accidental death where the blame was squarely on SynTronic. Her eyes slid shut and her head lowered a bit, knowing that only a few realistic options were on the table, none of them good.

"Eventful?" Sarconi asked, one nostril raised in a faux snarl. He said just the one word, but the open accusation on his face filled in the rest for him.

Reed shifted his attention over to Sarconi, his head leading his entire body in a change of direction to face the right side of the room. His face changed from tired to hard in a matter of seconds, the transformation plain to see for everybody in the room.

"Is eventful not a good enough word for you? How about calling it a losing battle? A lost cause? Or, I know, how about a shit show, because that's what you handed us when you stuck your cockamamie contraption in that kid's leg!"

Sarconi's face flushed red, his chin digging deeper into the folds of skin around his neck. "You think this is our fault? You stood up here a week ago and said yourself this was the kid's fault for misuse, it was the surgeon's fault for putting the damn thing in wrong."

"Jesus Christ, you *believed* that?" Reed asked, surprise across his face as he shook his head from side to side. He maintained the pose for several seconds before taking up his coffee and pulling away, turning his back on the room. "Willie, help this idiot see the big picture here, will you?"

Ramirez stepped forward, shaking his head, a look of disgust in place to match the one Reed wore. "Perhaps you weren't listening last week when we went through all this. What we said was we were going to try and toss some of the blame on the doc and we were going to try to throw a little at the kid. Problem is, no opportunity presented itself on either front. The only two times we've managed to get any jabs in we've had to withdraw the questions, making ourselves look like dicks just to try and make a point."

"But you're the attorney, it's your job to create those opportunities," Dr. Pinkering said, leaning in on the backside, trying to aid his colleague.

"And you're a doctor," Ramirez countered, "it's your job not to maim your patients, yet here we are."

"Don't blame us because the Laszlo *kid* is kicking your ass in there," Sarconi replied, emphasizing the word kid to mock the term they had used just days before.

The comment spun Reed back around to the table, his face twisted with rage, the coffee cup in his hand threatening to explode from the pressure on it. "The Laszlo kid is kicking our ass in there?"

He kept his gaze locked, resting his coffee on the table and leaning forward across it, pushing forward until his face was just a foot away from Sarconi's.

"No, what the Laszlo kid is doing is following the paint-by-numbers case you two idiots handed to him. What he's doing in there, a damn trained monkey could do."

"So what does that make you?" Sarconi asked, leaning in so just six inches separated them.

Reed held the pose for several seconds before smirking, twisting his head at the neck to face the end of the table. "Ute, get him out of here."

The look of resolve faded from Sarconi's face, sheer terror flooding in. He swung his gaze to the back of the room where Ute stood, a sick smile on his face, thumbs hooked in the front pockets of his pants.

"No, this was just a misunderstanding," Sarconi said, pressing himself low in the seat, leaning back as far as he could. "There's no need for any of this."

"Take his friend with him," Reed said. "They don't need to be here."

"With pleasure," Ute said, fixing a wild-eyed stare on the pair, almost salivating at the sight of them both cowering from him.

"They might have to take the stand next week, so no broken bones, no facial markings," Reed said. "Otherwise, I don't care."

The Twins stared down at their tablets as the scene unfolded, both pretending they weren't witnessing what was going on. At the end of the table, the paralegals both looked on in horror before averting their gaze as well, careful not to see anything they could be asked about later.

In the corner Lauren sat upright and stiff, her eyes closed, forcing bits of air in through her nose, otherwise not moving.

Reed watched as Ute went across the table in a flash, not around, but over it, standing between Pinkering and Sarconi before either one even knew what happened. He grabbed each of them by an ear, yanking them to their feet, gasps of pain sliding out.

"Come on, boys," he said in a breathy tone, looking back and forth between them. "If either one of you makes a sound, I promise I'll mail these ears back to your families in an envelope."

Reed glanced to Ramirez, both of them watching as Pinkering and Sarconi were escorted out, the grip on their ears so tight their heads were twisted towards the ground in an attempt to ease the pressure. Once they were gone, the entire room sat in silence for almost a full minute, nobody making eye contact.

"So what's the plan?" Grey Polo asked, his voice low, his gaze on the pad between his hands.

"The plan," Ramirez answered, "is to call Laszlo and set up a meeting, ask to discuss another settlement."

"How high are we prepared to go?" Blue Polo asked.

"No higher than usual," Reed said. "But we intend to exert a little extra pressure this time around."

"Do we have the leverage for that?" Blue Polo said.

Reed paused a moment, flicking his gaze to the door and the enormous presence in denim that just left them. "We will."

More uncomfortable silence fell over the room, the paralegals continuing to squirm, the Twins not moving at all.

"What if he still doesn't take it?" Grey Polo asked.

Another glance passed between Reed and Ramirez, Reed's eyebrows raised in a questioning look, as if the thought had never occurred to them.

"Then we put those two idiots on the stand and see what happens."

CHAPTER FORTY-FIVE

The overheard security light to the garage kicked on at nine o'clock, the timer set to the time of day and not the amount of light left outside. The first time Ute noticed this a sadistic smile spread across his face as he sat tucked away behind the wheel in the dark, casing one of a half dozen different places. He had no idea if he would need the information he'd just obtained, even less how he might use it if the moment arose, but the simple thought brought a smile to his face anyway.

By his estimation, the sun went down for good somewhere just shy of eight-thirty, leaving him a full twenty minutes to operate in near darkness. The closest house on the cul-de-sac was a hundred yards away, close enough to hear a scream, but nowhere near close enough to hear the muffled sound of a bat or fist slamming into flesh. So long as he kept his victim from crying out, he could be in and out long before anybody noticed.

The first time he uncovered the secret of the security light was two weeks before, parked in the same exact spot he now sat. Everything about the last month was nothing more than one long, unending bore, a blur of sitting in the car watching things happen, taking notes, compiling habits and tendencies, schedules and circumstances.

For as much as everybody feared his physical imposition and the sheer pleasure he derived from imparting it, they overlooked his dedication to the craft. The hours spent in cramped spaces, the lengths gone to to ensure a message was received, the research that went into every move he made. In total it should have been enough to make even the most seasoned academic envious, but if anybody knew they would overlook it as the deranged obsessions of a madman.

Ute had long since let it go, prescribing to a Machiavellian maxim of eschewing any form of public acceptance for its total and widespread fear of him. It was an ideal he had taken up years before, and it had served him well in the time since.

Tonight, in a rare moment since arriving in Columbus, there was no underlying current of angst running through Ute, no feeling of disrespect, no wondering when his talents might be appreciated. Instead he felt a calm that bordered on the serene, a deep-rooted feeling that came with operating well within one's comfort zone and emanated into every action.

The feeling had started that morning, when the sanctimonious prick Reed at last recognized him for what he was — a game changer, a force to be reckoned with. Instead of trying to argue with the two worthless bastards from the hospital, he turned them over to Ute, letting him do what he did best.

The most rewarding part of the encounter was that Ute didn't even realize Reed knew he was there, his presence folded into the far corner, his entire being coiled against the wall like a snake ready to attack. The moment Reed gave him the green light he was up and across the table, on the two men in a matter of seconds, carrying them away as if they weighed nothing at all.

It was a glorious morning, from the time he marched them out of the room to the moment he took them up the back stairwell and into the guest room he had booked in SynTronic's name for just such an occasion. Despite having him outnumbered two to one, neither one tried to escape, neither one making so much as a sound in protest.

Not when he drug them into the rented room just beyond the scope of security cameras, not when he put the doc in a chair and battered his ribs with a bar of soap wrapped in a pillowcase. He was careful not to break any bones, but made sure the bastard remembered him with every breath he took for the next three days.

After he was done with the skinny ginger, he went to work on the fat man, employing some old school tactics he'd picked up in places he couldn't name if he wanted to. He tied the Italian's hands to the chair and tilted him backwards, the chair leaning against the edge of the bed, his knee in the man's chest to weight him down. With one hand he held a wet towel over the man's face, with the other he poured a pitcher of water onto it, watching as his prey reacted the same way everybody does to water boarding. Deep gurgling sounds rolled out of his throat, followed by thrashing, his hands straining against the ropes, his feet flailing at air.

Ute could have stopped after only a single round, but went back for seconds anyway, scratching an itch that had started when he first called Sarconi months before. By the time he was done both men were in the fetal position on the floor, whimpering with their eyes closed. Neither one even saw him leave, their backs to the door, their bodies pleading for it to be over.

When the call came in from Reed an hour later, Ute assumed he was about to be chastised for his efforts, that both men had run downstairs and cried their eyes out, telling on him for being too rough. To his surprise, Reed never said a single word about the encounter, the first positive sign he'd seen from the old man since things got started.

It had taken longer than Ute would have liked, but the team was starting to embrace the unique role he could play in the trial moving forward.

Rather than call to talk about the encounter, Reed had said that a second stab at a settlement was going to be attempted the next day. As it stood, they didn't have enough leverage to entice Laszlo to settle, but thought that Ute could provide them with something that would do just that.

A demented laugh rolled out of Ute at the directive, filling the airspace for almost a full minute. By the time he was done, Reed's voice was no more than a whisper as he again asked that the target not be Laszlo or Bentley and that there be no bodies.

Anything else was fair game.

Given that Wilson was already out of the picture and Laszlo and Bentley were both off limits, the choice was an easy one to make. Ute never touched a woman if at all possible, not in accordance to some sort of chivalrous code, but because of their penchant for screaming at the slightest brush. There was no way one of his victims could ever overpower him, but alerting everybody within shouting distance was something he had to at least give a passing consideration to.

That left the old man, a task that was so simple it bordered on not even being a challenge. Fortunately for Ute, he was still riding high from his morning spent in the hotel room, his body just starting to come down from the effects of the adrenaline surge he'd received.

Right on schedule, the sun overhead disappeared from sight at eight-thirty, cloaking the world in darkness. From where he was parked Ute could see the old man's house around the corner, a one story Mediterranean with stucco walls and ceramic tile ceilings, as out of place in central Ohio as it was being owned by a British man.

Pulling gloves on, Ute grabbed one item in each hand, exited his car and crossed over the street, remaining in the shadows as he stepped through the intersection and up the driveway of the house. His head swiveled from side to side as he went, checking for any signs of life in the neighborhood. With the exception of a few lights on several hundred yards away, the street was deserted, void of any late night joggers, no young couples taking a dog for a stroll.

The wide concrete driveway wrapped around the side of the house, feeding into a two-car garage. Beside it was an outdoor patio, framed by floor-to-ceiling screens, a rocking swing and bevy of deck furniture visible within.

Free from having to worry about any elaborate set up, or even an escape path, Ute walked up to the door on the patio and banged on it with the side of his fist, beating against the wood in a steady, persistent manner until a light went on inside. He knew from days of observation that there was no dog inside to start barking, no wife that would come to the door and ask who it was. There was just the old man, who would walk straight out, stepping right into a trap he had no idea was waiting for him.

Once the light went on, Ute stepped to the side and waited, his body hidden from sight, the shadows swallowing him up as he crouched next to the garage door. Muffled movements could be heard coming from inside, the sound of a lock turning, of the door wrenching open.

"Yes? Is someone there?" the old man asked, his thick cockney accent revolting to Ute's ears. Still he waited until his prey stepped outside, a profile visible in the porch light behind him.

Ute waited until the old man was about a foot outside the door before slicing a knife hand chop across his throat, bending him at the waist, his hands clawing for air, breaths coming in ragged gasps. His momentum carried him forward several steps out onto the driveway, his internal functions shutting down as his body tried to force air back into his lungs.

The same sadistic smile spread Ute's face as he watched the man stagger, waiting until he was positioned where he wanted him. Only then did he raise the object in his right hand, a two foot piece of lead pipe, and smash it across his victim's knee, folding it backwards in half.

The slightest hint of a wail escaped from the man before he fell unconscious, the pain receptors in his brain so overwhelmed they short-circuited, sending everything straight to black. Unable to control his fall, the old man twisted into a heap on the ground, his leg twisted at a grotesque angle.

Ute waited for him to hit the concrete before switching out the lead pipe for the can of spray paint in his left hand and scrawling a quick message out just inches from the old man's shattered knee. The moment he was done he stepped into the man's house and crossed over into the living room, grabbing up a cell-phone from an end table beside a still playing television. He walked back out onto the driveway and dialed 911, hitting send and dropping it down on the old man's chest.

From there he returned to the shadows, down the driveway and across the street, tossing the pipe and the paint in the car and sliding in behind the wheel. He sat there for almost two full minutes before the overhead security light overlooking the man's driveway kicked on, bathing the entire area in harsh fluorescent light.

Only then did he start the car and swing up around the corner, driving slowly to admire his handiwork, the old man's body framed just right in the middle of the drive. At the end of the street he risked turning around in a neighbor's drive and made one more pass through before the sound of sirens in the distance precipitated his exit into the night, the vindictive smile in place the entire time.

CHAPTER FORTY-SIX

It was the third hospital Shane had been to in the past two weeks, all about as different from each other as three entities serving the same general purpose could be. The Ohio Tech University Hospital was a teaching hospital through and through, the floor layout open, every nurse and doctor in the place followed around by a gaggle of aspiring young medical professionals. Columbus General was a working facility, manned by grim faced health providers that spent their days seeing things that most people never would, what none ever should.

Capital City Care, the 3C as locals called it, where Shane now found himself sitting, was set apart from the other two in one key way. It was private. Funded through a trust fund set up decades before by a widowed billionaire, everything in the place was sparkling new and state of the art. The rumor was that half of the supplies found in other facilities around town were hand-me-down's from 3C, which replaced all equipment every three years.

While excessive, and even wasteful, such an adherence to innovation showed in everything they did. Every surface in the building sparkled, whether it be cast from marble or stainless steel, every employee wore a smile, every room was singular and private.

None of that mattered a bit to Shane as he sat in an armchair beside Prescott's bed, leaning forward with his elbows on his knees, staring down at the cuffs of his jeans, the laces on his sneakers. In the bed, Prescott sat with his left leg suspended in the air, a silver stirrup hanging from the ceiling, supporting it. The entire limb was wrapped from hip to toe in thick gauze, doubling its size and adding stability.

Only two sounds filled the space as Shane sat thinking, the steady din of the heart rate monitor and the uneven push and pull of the breathing machine, rising and falling with each breath.

A hundred thoughts filled Shane's head as he stared at the ground, trying to make sense of everything that was happening. It was suspicious when a member of his team was almost blown up on the day he gave his opening statement, but the fact that a second member was now in the hospital, an old man that may never walk unassisted again, was too much to overlook. The fact that it appeared to be an attempt to recreate the injury they were now litigating made it all the more alarming.

A menagerie of emotions floated to the surface as Shane sat and tried to make sense of it. Anger at the senselessness of attacking a gentle old man, guilt at getting him involved in the first place.

"It's not your fault you know."

The voice sounded close, but very far away, like the person saying it was on the other side of a wall, the sound muffled. Shane's head snapped up to see Prescott's eyes flutter open, his face turned to look at Shane.

"It's not your fault."

Shane jumped to his feet and pushed close to the side of the bed, starting to reach out and take his friend's hand, but thinking better of it and pulling back. "Hey, how you feeling?"

Prescott forced his eyebrows up a bit and rolled his eyes, the faintest trace of a smile on his face. "Not the first Sunday morning I've woken up in a world of pain."

The comment brought a smile to Shane's face. "Somehow I find that hard to believe."

"No, it's true I assure you," Prescott said, "but at least those times the blokes had the decency to get me good and liquored up first."

Another chuckle slid from Shane before he could stop it, an immediate feeling of guilt riding in right after.

"How bad?" Prescott asked.

"Pretty bad," Shane said. "You've got a broken leg, but luckily the blow came in above your knee, no structural damage at all. The bone gave way before it could tear anything in the knee."

"Hmm," Prescott said, nodding his head. "I always told my mum that drinking milk was a load of bollocks."

Shane nodded his head, unable to force another smile at his friend's attempt for levity.

"Professor, I am so, so sorry, for all of this."

"You have nothing to be sorry for, Shane. You had no way of knowing, no reason to believe that any of us were going to be in danger. You don't even know that's what all this is about."

"I..." Shane said, extending a hand from his side, a blank expression on his face. "How can you say that? Heath's truck blows up just days before you, the nicest man I've ever met in my life, get attacked on your driveway?"

"You need to meet more people."

Shane stopped, an involuntary half smile crossing his lips.

"Shane, every day in this country thousands of cases are litigated, the vast majority of which never see anything resembling what's happening here."

"I know," Shane said, shaking his head from side to side, a bitter look on his face. "And I drug you all into it with me."

"But most of those cases aren't as important as what you're doing here either Shane."

"What am I doing?" Shane asked, forcing himself to keep his voice low, to match the slow and methodical tone of Prescott, to remind himself that the old man was on morphine and in a tremendous amount of pain. "Besides getting a lot of my friends hurt, what am I doing here?"

"What you've always been doing," Prescott said. "You are protecting your friends. At first, that was just Tyler. Now it has grown to encompass Heath and myself."

Shane continued to shake his head, staring at the patch of plain white wall across from him. "I can't keep going. Not like this, not knowing that people are getting hurt because of me."

"But you must," Prescott said, his voice clear, his tone non-negotiable. "Otherwise, everything you've done, everything we've all been through, is for naught. Then Shane, only then, would any of this be your fault."

The small squeak of tennis shoes on tile spun Shane around, a diminutive nurse with dark hair and eyes standing in the doorway, a smile on her face. "Sorry to interrupt, but now that Mr. Prescott's awake the doctor would like to speak with him."

Shane's mouth dropped open as he attempted to respond, but Prescott beat him to it, his accent a touch thicker for emphasis.

"That's alright dear, Mr. Laszlo here was just leaving. He has quite a lot of work ahead of him today, don't you Shane?"

Shane turned back to regard his friend, who pressed his lips together and nodded. Without thinking, Shane reached down and took up Prescott's hand, wrapping it in both of his.

"I'll see you soon."

"I know," Prescott said, nodding as Shane released his hand and departed.

Another swirl of thoughts spun to Shane's mind as he stepped outside, all of them interrupted as *The Good, The Bad, and The Ugly* erupted on his hip. He pulled the phone out and looked down at it, an unknown area code appearing on the caller ID.

"Shane Laszlo."

"Mr. Laszlo, this is Connor Reed. Sorry to call you on a Sunday but we were wondering if you might be willing to revisit the idea of a settlement. Are you busy? Could we perhaps meet later today?"

Shane pulled the phone away from his face and stared down at, incredulity and realization spreading across his face. He turned and stared back at the 3C behind him, thought about Prescott in his bed, of Heath in his across town. The plastic casing of the phone groaned as he squeezed it tight in his hand, pressing it back against his ear. A hundred responses sprang to mind, but he held them in, careful not to overplay his position.

"I'm sorry Mr. Reed, but we're not interested in a settlement."

"Mr. Laszlo, I would urge you not to be hasty and consider our proposition, for the good of your client."

Shane turned away from the hospital, hatred burning on his face. Every part of him knew he should keep his mouth shut, but something deep within just wouldn't let it happen.

"Mr. Reed, the reason I refuse to even listen to your offer for a settlement is because you guys made this about a lot more than just my client."

Several seconds of silence passed, Reed's breathing the only thing to let Shane know he was still there.

"So you're saying you don't want to even listen to our offer?"

"I'm saying take your blood money and shove it up your ass."

CHAPTER FORTY-SEVEN

The scent of caramelized sugar and ripened bananas hung in a heavy cloud over the table, a transparent veil that filled the senses, so thick it almost needed to be brushed back by hand. Shane was never one for the spectacle of tableside flambé, but the payoff of Bananas Foster always made it worth the effort, tonight being no exception.

Across from him Christine sat looking down at her plate, a wedge of banana speared on the end of her fork, a look of concentration on her face as she used the fruit to sop up melted ice cream and caramel. When she amassed just the bite she wanted, she lifted it to her mouth and used her lips to pull it away, a look of supreme satisfaction on her face.

As she chewed, her face raised to meet his, eyes closed, jaw working at the tasty morsel in her mouth. Once it was chewed and swallowed she opened her eyes, head propped up on a wrist and stared over at him.

"Alright, out with it."

"Enjoy your dessert?" Shane asked, trying in vain to keep his amusement from showing.

"Immensely. Now, out with it."

Shane lifted his eyebrows and leaned back in his seat, turned his head towards the television screen above the bar, an NBA playoff game on it. "What makes you think I want anything?"

"Three things," Christine said, sliding the wrist out from beneath her chin and holding three fingers up for him to see. "First, bone-in rib eyes and Bananas Foster. Come on, you know that's my kryptonite. For you to be bringing out the big guns means you must want something major.

"Two, this place," she said, waving a hand around the small restaurant, made entirely from wood, holding no more than ten booths and a handful of tables. "It's a great gem, I'll give you that, but it feels a bit like hiding out.

"Third, and most important, every time that door opens you either turn and stare or pretend to check the game, which I'm guessing is just a front to use the glass behind the bar to see who's coming and going."

The faint smile remained on Shane's face, his head turning as an older couple stepped outside. He opened his mouth to respond, to pick apart her argument one at a time, but the truth was there was nothing he could say to refute her. Just as she had done for the better part of a decade, she had nailed him while appearing to not even be trying.

"I need a favor," Shane said, watching Christine's face for any sign of a reaction.

"Since when do you need to butter me up or hide out to ask me for a favor?" Christine asked, the wrist back beneath her chin, the aroma of burnt caramel still in the air.

"It's not that kind of favor," Shane said, resting his forearms on the table and leaning in close. "I need you to go away for a while."

The statement raised Christine's eyebrows a half inch, but otherwise she gave no reaction at all. "Are we planning another outing? Been a long time since we hit the road together."

"Not we, you," Shane said, a frown tugging at the corners of his mouth. "I have to be here to finish the trial."

Christine pursed her lips, scrutinizing her friend, trying to figure out what Shane wasn't telling her. She held the pose for the better part of a minute before asking whatever it was she was trying to work out in her head.

"Why just me? And where do you think I should go?"

"Anywhere," Shane said. "Go find a warm beach somewhere, put your toes in the sand, find a cabana boy to rub oil on you."

"You know I don't use tanning oil."

"So find a cabana boy and rub oil on him," Shane said, exasperation creeping into his voice. "I don't care. Just go somewhere safe, somewhere with lots of people around, please."

Christine maintained her pose for several moments, letting the words hang in the air, her gaze fixed on him. She raised her chin from her wrist and folded her arms in front of her, matching Shane's pose.

"You ever gone on a trip by yourself? It sucks. Not what I would call a vacation."

"Okay, so you go now, I'll join you when I can," Shane offered.

The offer brought a small snort. "What's this really about?"

A heavy sigh rolled from Shane as he eased back, circling his gaze around the room once more, not-so-subtly checking out each of the other patrons in the bar.

Across from him Christine rolled her eyes, making no effort to hide doing so. "Is all that necessary?"

"Prescott was attacked outside his home last night," Shane said without preamble, dropping the statement on the table as an answer to every question she'd already asked. It had the intended response, concern clouding her face as she leaned back an inch.

"Attacked? How? Is he okay?"

"Okay in that he's alive, but he has a snapped femur and a ton of tissue damage. He's lucky it didn't tear his whole knee out."

Christine's jaw sagged open, her expression blank. "My God, that's terrible. Do they have any leads yet?"

Shane leaned in a little closer, his voice dropping just a bit. "Officer Ryan from CPD called me this morning and told me what happened, said they wanted to speak to me later in the afternoon about the incident, they had reason to believe it was connected to Heath's truck blowing up."

No change of expression at all, Christine's complete attention focused on Shane. "Is it?"

Shane paused a moment, considering where to jump into the story. The details he was about to share had not be released to the public, and while he wasn't worried about telling Christine everything he knew, he still wanted to be careful as to how he approached it.

"Earlier this week, after they moved Heath's truck, they found the words *stay away* spray painted on the ground beneath the truck in neon green. They took pictures of it, included it in the incident report, but nobody thought a whole lot of it. Heck, I saw the pictures in Heath's hospital room and didn't put much stock in it.

"Last night, the assailant spray painted the word *stop* beside Prescott's body. Same neon green color, same handwriting, lab tests even proved it to be the same can of paint."

Christine nodded her head, taking in the information. "And I'm willing to guess the only thing that tied those two together, besides being around the law school, was working on your case."

"Yeah," Shane said, another rush of guilt rising to the surface.

"So they figure out what the enormous interest is in your case, they should be able to figure out who the attacker is."

"Doesn't even take that much detective work," Shane said, turning his head from side to side. "They left us a note, something I should have noticed the first time and didn't."

"*Stay away?* Come on, how were you supposed to have picked up anything from that?"

Shane looked at her, his expression dour. "The ST in stay was capitalized. Same with the ST in stop last night."

He watched as Christine's gaze moved back and forth, focusing on nothing, putting the pieces together. After a moment the information clicked, her face registering clear understanding.

"Son of a bitch. They wrote it in paint on their crime scenes, daring somebody to come get them."

"Ballsy, huh?" Shane asked, nodding in agreement.

"And then some," Christine agreed, a perplexed look on her face, shaking her head in dismay.

Shane watched as her face worked through the various emotions, running the gamut from surprised to repulsed and on into dejected. He remembered earlier in the day going through the same sequence of thoughts, his own interlaced with a heavy dose of guilt.

"See why I'm asking you to go?" Shane asked, his head turned to the side, watching as a middle-aged man in a trucker's cap and jean jacket departed, the bell above the front door announcing it for all to hear.

A soft chuckle slid out of Christine, a hand snaking across the table and resting on his forearm. "Those weren't your fault you know. Someone called and asked you to take a case, you did it, the defendants happened to be a large organization used to throwing their weight around.

"It's unfortunate, in the case of Wilson and Prescott even tragic, but it isn't your fault, and there was no way to see it coming." She shook his arm, lowering her face so she could look up into his. "You hear me?"

"I'm listening to you," Shane responded, lowering his face so it was even with hers, "it's the same thing I've been telling myself all day, but that doesn't mean I hear you. Not yet anyway."

"And that's why you think it's time I took a vacation," Christine said, a flat statement, no inflection of a question at all in her voice.

A half-smile creased Shane's face. "No, that was more out of concern for your tan. Been a long winter, you're looking rather pasty."

Christine squeezed his arm and used it to push herself back away from the table, a snort rolling out of her. "That's crap and we both know it. I've got an olive complexion, ten minutes in front of a strong lamp and I'm tan."

The smile on Shane's face grew wider, a mix of mirth and knowing she was right. "Just tell me you'll think about it. There are only two people that I really care about, and I've already made arrangements to make sure Mom is covered."

The statement brought faux flattery to Christine's face, her hands pressed to her chest. "Aw, you think of me in the same category as your mom."

Shane dropped his gaze to the table and shook his head, drawing in a long breath and releasing it. He raised his gaze up to see Christine smiling above him, hands still pressed to her chest, body twisting back and forth at the waist.

"Don't make me beg. Please."

One last chuckle shook Christine's upper body as she leaned forward, her forearms resting on the table, each hand gripping an opposite elbow. "I tell you what, you agree I'm not going anywhere, and I'll agree to be more careful until this thing's over."

Shane continued to shake his head, the half-smile returning. After eight years, he knew it was the best he was going to get.

CHAPTER FORTY-EIGHT

"Dr. Pinkering, what is your relationship with SynTronic Corporation?" Shane asked, not even making it out of the counsel chair before launching into his cross-examination. The front row had thinned even more, the only people sitting there being Abby and Margie, both pressed tight against one another, their faces solemn. At the counsel table sat Tyler, weathering the storm of trial, knowing that his part was over, just wanting the rest to be done so he could return home.

Shane had called a meeting with all three of them at eight o'clock that morning to tell them in person what happened to Prescott and the connection between each of the crime scenes. He explained to them that he understood if any of them wanted to back off, to go away until everything was done, but that after speaking with Prescott he was going to continue on. It was uncharacteristic for a plaintiff not be in the courtroom during trial, but not impossible. If the Bentley's wanted to go into hiding, they could do so until it was time for a verdict to be read.

He would go it alone until the end.

All three had just as much reason as he did to keep going, each acting like they were offended that he even suggest such a thing.

Unable to shake them from their stance, he insisted that the Bentleys stay together and take extra precautions at every turn, that Abby be with him or some male she trusted at all times until things quieted down.

They had agreed to the terms, but only after Shane explained to them that he had put both his mother and Christine under extra precaution as well.

"My relationship?" Dr. Pinkering asked, adjusting his glasses and squinting out at Shane, acting as if the question was coming from left field. Unlike Manningham, he had chosen to wear his white physician's coat into court, a move that was no doubt suggested by Reed and Ramirez.

Shane smirked when he saw the attire upon arriving, driving home the fact that his opponents had no idea where they were or the crowd they were working with.

"Yes, the terms of your arrangement, how Ohio Tech and SynTronic came to be in business together," Shane asked. "You spoke at length under direct examination about the products that were offered by SynTronic and the exemplary record they have, but you seemed to have skipped right over how the two sides came together."

Pinkering shifted in his seat, his forehead revealing a sweaty film under the overhead lights. "Every procedure that requires implants of any kind, whether they are simple screws or an entire joint replacement, must have them supplied from somewhere. No hospital manufactures those things themselves."

"I'm not questioning why there was a partnership Dr. Pinkering, I'm asking how this one came to be. I must not be making myself clear, so allow me to back up and come at this again. You are the head of the orthopedics department here at OTU hospital, are you not?"

"I am."

"And as the head of the department, it is under your authority to select a medical equipment provider, correct?"

Pinkering nodded, his demeanor stiff. "Yes, that is correct."

"Now, prior to you taking over, the department had a long standing tradition with EquipMed, didn't they?"

"They did."

"So what made you decide to switch providers?"

Pinkering reached up and adjusted his glasses, running his thumb across his forehead in an attempt to wipe away a bit of perspiration. "Our existing contract with EquipMed had expired."

Shane continued moving back and forth in an even pace across the floor, one hand in his pocket, the other out in front of him, controlling the cadence of his words like a conductor leading an orchestra. "Okay, so your existing contract expired, and you decided to open the floor up to all bidders for the next one, that kind of thing?"

"Yes, exactly."

The walk came to a halt, Shane just feet away from the jury, his body facing towards the box, his head shifted to look at Pinkering on the stand. "So what made SynTronic the winner? What set them apart from all the others?"

Pinkering slid his tongue out over his lips, wetting them as he drew in a deep breath. Shane could tell by the look on his face that he didn't appreciate where the questioning was going, a fact that made it all the more imperative he continue.

"Mr. Sarconi and SynTronic were by far the most innovative of the equipment manufacturers we spoke with. The new product designs they were looking to introduce would put us at the cutting edge of orthopedic medicine."

"And no doubt turn a tidy profit for the hospital," Shane added, picking up right where the doctor left off.

"Objection, Your Honor," Ramirez said, rising from his stand and adjusting his solid orange tie against his midsection. "Prejudice."

Judge Lynch swung his attention to Shane, asking with a wave of the hand if he would like to respond.

"Your Honor, I am just trying to ascertain the exact relationship of SynTronic with OTU Hospital, since the very device in question here was an innovative design that sprang from it."

Judge Lynch nodded a bit, his eyes closing as he lowered his head toward Shane. "Overruled."

"Thank you, Your Honor," Shane said, shifting back to Pinkering, no reaction to winning the objection on his face. "Doctor, if you'd please."

Pinkering's jaw dropped open for a moment, followed by a flush of color rising to his cheeks. He opened and closed his mouth several times before any sound escaped.

"I'm not sure I understand what you're insinuating."

Shane took two quick steps forward before stopping again, drawing the jury's focus tighter on Pinkering. "I'm not insinuating anything Doctor, I'm just saying, it bears to reason that if you were going to partner with SynTronic in designing new devices and serve as a training ground for them, there must be some compensation, right?"

Two loud huffs were pushed out from Pinkering, his chest swelling with defensiveness. "OTU is a non-profit teaching facility. We do not accept kickbacks of any kind."

"Really?" Shane asked, a crooked grin spreading across his face. "You expect us to believe that you offered up your hospital as a testing center, gave up the university mascot for naming rights, extending the school's star player to serve as a poster child for the new product, and there wasn't a single cent of remuneration involved?"

Pinkering stared hard at Shane for several moments, his lower lip quivering, though out of rage or indignity Shane wasn't sure. "Again I say Mr. Laszlo, OTU is a non-profit teaching hospital."

Shane paused a full moment, staring at the jury, toying with the words in his head. He knew full well they would bring Ramirez to his feet, would draw a bit of ire from Judge Lynch, might even be the first real strike against him with the jury. Still, for all those thoughts telling him not to, the images of Heath and Prescott in their hospital beds, of Tyler hopping on one leg, of his mother with a guard outside her door trumped them.

"So maybe OTU isn't the one getting the kickback, are they Dr. Pinkering?"

"Objection!" Ramirez shouted, on his feet with remarkable speed for a man his size.

Shane ignored the objection, pressing in tight on Pinkering, watching the doctor squirm in his seat, his face quivering as he looked around for help from his counsel.

"Maybe you made a deal with a company offering what you knew to be an inferior product because they offered you a sweeter retirement package?"

"Objection, Your Honor! Please!" Ramirez said.

"That is enough, Mr. Laszlo," Judge Lynch said, dropping his gavel hard on the bench. In the background a ripple of energy went through the crowd, murmurs and glances exchanged.

Shane could hear them back there, could feel their emotion swell, but it didn't serve to deter him, only emboldening him more.

"And maybe that deal is why Tyler Bentley is now missing his left leg?" Shane said, his voice loud enough so everyone in the courtroom could hear, even over the combined noises of all the commotion.

As the last words left his mouth, Shane grasped the rail of the witness stand with both hands, peering straight in at Pinkering. In front of him, the doctor kept his gaze turned down, his entire body shifted to the side, cowering as if Shane might lash out at him at any moment.

Above, the hammer continued to pound on the bench.

"Counselor, one more word out of you and I will hold you in contempt of court," Judge Lynch said, slamming his gavel down two more times for effect.

Shane remained fixed in position a full moment before pressing himself back and straightening his cornflower blue tie atop his belt buckle.

"Apologies Your Honor, withdraw the questions."

Spinning on a heel, Shane returned to his table, making a point of staring at his opponents as he went. On one side sat Reed, shaking his head, his jaw set, his gaze shifted down at the table before him. On the other stood Ramirez, still on his feet from the objection, complete surprise engulfing his features.

In the crowd, people shifted in their seats to get a better look at him, extending their necks out to see where this side of Shane had come from. Abby and Margie both sat with their hands balled into fists, tense as they waited for his next move.

Shane's face gave away nothing as he walked. "No further questions, Your Honor."

CHAPTER FORTY-NINE

Three hours had passed, but Shane could still feel the adrenaline pulsing through his veins, setting his skin on fire, making his muscles tingle. The first signs of it had settled in as he was talking to Prescott the day before, fighting its way to the surface once he released the guilt that he knew would consume him if he let it.

"There are things you can control and there things you can't," his mother had always said when in the middle of a case. "The other guy is trying to win just as hard as you are, and they might not be willing to play by the rules the way you are. The key is to always react quicker and adapt better, that's where victory lies."

It wasn't a mantra per se, some recited line that preceded a movie montage style rise to the front, but a deep rooted belief, in herself and in the system. Shane had heard the words over a hundred times throughout his childhood, the words sometimes a bit different, the meaning always the same.

There will be times when you question your case, your abilities, even why you went to law school. Don't fight against them, don't try to win those internal battles. Just let them go, push them aside to another day if you must, and focus on the task at hand.

Those very words came to his mind as he stood outside the 3C, right after listening to Reed try and convince him that settling for pennies on the dollar was his only recourse. The guilt of the morning was gone, the burning rage at Reed was receding, all that was left was an adrenaline drip that ebbed and flowed as needed, pulling back to near nothing as he ate with Christine, coursing through his body as he fired away at Pinkering.

Sitting in his chair, watching Reed examine Sarconi, he could feel an internal dilemma begin to build. Whatever latitude he had with the court had been used that morning, well spent to crucify the doctor for crawling into bed with a corporate giant at the expense of his patients. The point was an important one and Shane was not the least bit sorry he'd made it, but he couldn't afford such strong arm tactics again. The jury had spent two weeks watching him in his carefully selected attire delivering hand crafted statements, holding himself out as the antithesis of his opponents in every way.

Two outbursts though, against the first two defense witnesses called no less, would go a long in destroying that image. He could not allow his temper to do that, to forget for a moment that this was about Tyler, and Heath, and Prescott, not himself.

Shane sat leaning forward over his desk, taking notes he didn't need, his pencil scratching across the yellow paper in even loops. Every few seconds he would look up at Sarconi, his face impassive, before going back to his legal pad. As he did so, he became aware that Reed was sneaking glances his way throughout his examination, the look a mixture of curiosity and revulsion.

"Mr. Laszlo, your witness," Judge Lynch said, Shane looking up in surprise at the abrupt ending of Reed's direct. He was aware that Sarconi had far less to offer than Pinkering did, but didn't expect Reed to corral his questioning to just a half hour.

Must be waiting for redirect, to try and extinguish any flames Shane ignited, was all he could figure.

"Thank you, Your Honor," Shane said, noting the judge's lingering stare, the unspoken warning not to have another outburst like the one that morning. With a tiny nod, Shane rose and straightened the front of his suit, stepping out from behind the table.

"Mr. Sarconi, you have been working with SynTronic for fourteen years now, is that correct?"

Sarconi leveled a malevolent glare onto Shane. Thick jowls outlined his face as he stared, giving him the appearance of an oversized bullfrog. He seemed to sit upright and stiff in his chair, a position mirroring the one used by Pinkering that morning, a pose that reflected they both seemed to be in a great deal of pain.

Shane made a mental note of it, wondering if SynTronic had turned their goons after their own trial team as well.

"Yes, that is correct," Sarconi said.

"And how much of that time has been spent here at Ohio Tech?" Shane asked, his voice normal, his demeanor back to the one he'd employed every day before, not even a trace of the episode from that morning visible.

"The last five years," Sarconi said, his voice low, his tone mistrusting. He was dressed in a well cut Italian suit with a solid black tie, the somber attire giving his entire appearance a very dark hue.

"Five years," Shane said, nodding his head, back to moving in even steps across the floor. "And in that five years, how many new devices have you introduced to Ohio Tech?"

Confusion crossed Sarconi's features, causing him to shake his head, a small wince tugging at his eyes. "I'm sorry?"

Shane paused, one hand in his pocket, the other in front of him, and looked at Sarconi. "How often are new products, designs, etc. introduced?"

"Well, it depends on the product," Sarconi said, his gaze shifting to Reed and back.

"Okay, that's understandable," Shane said, resuming his pace. "Let's say for a knee replacement product, how many of those have you introduced since coming to Ohio Tech?"

"Two."

Shane glanced back towards the court behind him, Abby with her pad and pen out on her lap, Margie beside her, staring down at a tangle of fingers in her lap. In front of them sat Tyler, watching close, the same as he had since the trial started.

"So, the *KnightRunner* and one other?"

Sarconi's eyes narrowed a bit as he processed the question, his bulbous head nodding in agreement. "Yes, that is correct."

"And could you tell us, when was the last model introduced, before the *KnightRunner*?"

Silence hung for a few moments, Sarconi staring back at Shane, trying to determine where the questions were going, how much he should divulge.

"Not quite two years ago."

A small light bulb went off in the recesses of Shane's mind, the realization that the impending payoff was what he wanted, that Sarconi had stumbled upon it without realizing it. He forced himself to remain stoic as he walked, allowing his prey to walk into a trap it didn't know existed.

"Mr. Sarconi, you were present for Dr. Lomax's testimony a couple of days ago, correct?"

"I was," Sarconi said, nodding his head.

"Realizing of course that there are small differences with the way SynTronic does business, would you agree with the general process that he described? From idea inception to product design to testing, back to design and then more testing?"

Sarconi gave a wary glance to Reed before offering a nod. "Like you said, there are some differences with the way we do things, but that's the general process, yes."

Shane nodded. "Okay, so let me get this straight. The previous knee replacement model was released two years ago, and you said it was the first to come out during your time at Ohio Tech, meaning that none were released during your first three years here, correct?"

"I suppose."

"Which would mean that there was at bare minimum three years of study and design that went into making that model, yes?"

Again Sarconi looked over at Reed before nodding. "Yes."

"And what was that model?"

"It was an upgrade over a previous model, using a different alloy to allow for smoother movement in the joint."

It was all Shane could do to keep from smiling. Not only had Sarconi walked into the setup without realizing it, but now he had also used the exact word Shane was hoping he would.

"Okay," Shane said, holding his hand up to his mouth, pursing his lips as if deep in thought. "All that being said then Mr. Sarconi, I can't help but wonder then why an *upgrade*, as you called it, warranted three years of production work, whereas a whole new and innovative model like the *KnightRunner* was able to be rolled out just one year and change later?"

Sarconi stared back at Shane, the blank, venomous glare of someone just realizing they've been tricked. He somehow managed to smash his head even lower into his shoulders, giving him the appearance of a cranky, Italian, Jabba the Hutt.

"That's not how it went," Sarconi muttered. "We often have many products under development at the same time. The timing of their releases can't be taken as a statement of the legwork that went into their development."

"But at the same time, wouldn't it be in the best interest of SynTronic to spread out those release dates? To maximize product success? It doesn't seem to make much sense to have multiple products competing with each other."

Sarconi stared back at Shane in anger for several moments, his eyes narrowing until they were two small black slits. "They won't be competing with each other."

"And why is that?" Shane asked, taking a step closer to the stand.

"Because the *KnightRunner* won't be available to the public for some time yet."

For the first time, Shane let a smile come to his face. Not one of self-satisfaction, or even of cockiness, but of realization. He turned towards the jury, letting them experience the profound impact of what Sarconi said along with him.

"It won't be available to the public for some time? Yet you still felt it safe to put into Tyler Bentley?"

Sarconi leaned forward in his seat, the blood draining from his face, his jowls twitching as he glanced between Reed and Shane. "Yes, of course. Of course! When I said it won't be available, I didn't mean that it wasn't safe or fully vetted."

"So why the lag time?" Shane asked, taking another step forward, keeping his body angled between Sarconi and the jury. "Was it completed ahead of schedule?"

"No, it was tracking as we expected it to."

"Was the redesign phase shorter than in past models?"

Sarconi shook his head, his posture relaying a bit of panic. "No, like I said, it was tracking just as expected."

"Hmm," Shane said, taking one more step forward, "or is it possible that perhaps the *KnightRunner* was rushed ahead a little bit premature to coincide with the injury to Tyler Bentley? To provide you with a poster boy for your new product design?"

Sarconi paused before answering, turning his attention to Reed, almost begging him with his eyes to stand and object, to save his witness from having to answer. He stared so long that Shane swiveled at the hip, acting as if he was looking for whatever Sarconi had fixed his gaze on.

Despite the movement, Shane knew what he was looking for. More than that though, he knew there would be none coming, the question constructed to avoid giving Reed any chance at having it struck from the record.

"Mr. Sarconi?"

Sarconi held his gaze on Reed for several more seconds, the silence in the courtroom growing in magnitude, every person seeming to lean in as one. It lasted so long that Shane knew his point was made, regardless of what Sarconi said next.

"Preposterous. Tyler Bentley's injury was an unfortunate occurrence for which we had a product we thought could speed along his recovery. Had it been placed and maintained properly, it would have done just that."

Shane raised his eyebrows, glancing to the jury. "So you're saying the entire fault lies with the surgeon and the patient?"

Sarconi raised his chin, the folds around his neck unfurling like an accordion, so he could stare down his nose at Shane. "Yes, that is what I am saying. There are examples of others receiving the transplant that have done just fine, we even brought one in to speak with Tyler. He will be here tomorrow, I'm sure he will be happy to tell you the same thing."

A faint half smile rested on Shane's face, every bit of his body language making Sarconi and the jury aware that he knew he was being lied to. He held the pose for several moments, mirroring Sarconi's stare.

"Yes, I'm sure he will. No further questions, Your Honor."

Shane walked back to the table, every eye in the court room on him, his gait even, his face drawn into thought, his eyes on the back wall. He didn't hear Judge Lynch ask for a redirect, didn't notice Reed turn down the invitation or even hear Lynch excuse Sarconi from the stand.

All he focused on was Officer Murphy in the back of the room, staring right at him, making a small beckoning gesture with his index finger.

CHAPTER FIFTY

It took six minutes for Judge Lynch to call the court into recess until the next morning and the jurors to file out, every last second of it ticking by in Shane's head. He tried his best to maintain that the visit was just preliminary, even better that they had a suspect in custody. There was just no way to shake the overwhelming dread in the back of his mind that the officer was there to deliver more bad news though, his mind running through the short list of people that consisted of Christine and his mother.

Everybody else was sitting within arm's reach.

The moment Judge Lynch slammed his gavel on the bench declaring the court done for the day, Shane leaned down, a hand resting on the edge of the table. "Tyler, Officer Murphy back there is asking for me. He's the guy that's been looking into Heath and Prescott's attacks. I'm going to go talk to him and circle back with you later tonight."

"Yeah, for sure," Tyler said, wheeling his chair around to look for the officer. Already the crowd was spilling into the aisle way, blocking him from view.

"Abby, can you grab my stuff?" Shane asked as he walked by,

motioning with his chin towards the rear wall. "I need to talk with Murphy back there."

"Is it about Heath?" Abby asked, rising to her toes and trying to peer over the crowd, her face shrouded in concern.

"I don't know," Shane said, "but I'll come get you if it is."

Abby nodded and went for the counsel table as Shane continued moving, ducking and weaving his way through the crowd. Around him people stared as he went, some even offering comments as he passed, ranging from advice to telling him to fornicate with himself. He let them all go without reaction.

The spot Officer Murphy had been standing in was empty by the time Shane got there, his head twisting in both directions to try and find him. He stepped out into the foyer to see Murphy standing alongside Officer Ryan, both with hands on their hips, tucked away along the side of the room.

Shane waited for a break in the torrent of people spilling from the court room before sliding across the space, coming to a stop just a few feet away from them.

"What's happened? Is somebody else hurt?"

Officer Murphy held his hands up by his side, his face neutral. "No, nothing like that. We've come to talk to you about that message you left at the station last night."

Holding up a finger, Shane looked around and motioned with his chin towards the corner, further removed from the crowd still drifting by.

"Can we step over there to continue this? There are a lot of people walking by right now that might be listening."

"Is that a problem?" Murphy asked, his eyebrows raised.

"Seeing as how my team keeps getting picked off? Yeah," Shane said, "I'd rather keep this conversation private."

Murphy made a show of rolling his eyes and motioned back towards the corner, Ryan and Shane both following him. The three walked the few paces in silence, Murphy putting his back close to the wall and staring out, a bored expression on his face. "This good enough for you?"

"Thank you," Shane murmured. "So what about my phone call?"

"First of all, we don't need you doing our job for us," Murphy said. "We were aware, or would have soon been aware, of everything you mentioned."

Shane ignored the statement, chalking it up to residual anger from his overstepping boundaries. All things considered, he may have felt the same way in a similar situation.

"Did it help at all?"

Sliding the notepad back from his shirt pocket, Ryan held it out and flipped through the pages, coming to a stop about halfway through. His lips moved slightly as he read through his notes before finding what he was looking for.

"Forensics was able to determine that the paint used was the same exact stuff, basic spray paint, green apple color, RustOleum, available at any of a hundred places in the greater Columbus area.

"The bigger find was on your clue regarding the words. A handwriting expert was able to determine that the S and the T in both words were capitalized, which led us to believe your statement that the attacker was somebody affiliated with SynTronic."

"And boy you know how to pick your enemies," Murphy said, opening a manila folder matching the one they had left in Heath's hospital suite, extracting a photo from it and handing it to Shane.

Shane looked at Murphy while accepting the photo, his gaze shifting down onto to it. Looking back at him was a man with brown hair buzzed short and a couple days of facial hair growth, a placard with the name U. Carbone and an inmate number written on it in block letters.

"Carbone?" Shane asked, making a face. "Never heard of the guy."

"You sure?" Ryan asked. "How about the face? Maybe you've seen him around?"

Shane shifted his attention from the name to the face, studying every detail. For the most part it was a very unremarkable face, the kind of mug that most middle-aged men were walking around with. The only thing that jumped out at him were the eyes, jade green, a deviant stare in them as he looked back at the camera.

There was no way he had ever seen them before, he would remember if he had.

"No, I'm sorry," Shane said, handing it back. "Who is he?"

"One bad hombre," Murphy said, putting the photo back in the folder and closing it tight. "Did two years for assault with a deadly weapon in ninety-nine, a nickel a few years later for armed robbery. He's been out now for six years and laying low, employed the entire time by none other than the SynTronic Corporation."

"After your tip, we did a background check on everybody in the company. Most of them came back clean, but this guy jumped off the page. We did some digging to try and figure out what he does for the company, but nobody seems to know. His only listed job title is as a Special Consultant, and even that was almost impossible to track down. If not for the fact that he was listed on the payroll, we wouldn't even know he existed."

Shane nodded, a deep frown on his face, turning to check the hall around them. Most of the foot traffic for the day had moved on, leaving a couple small pockets of people still milling about. Among them were the Bentleys and Abby, all glancing over every few seconds, concern on their faces.

"What makes you think this is the guy?" Shane asked, nodding towards the folder in Murphy's hands.

Ryan turned another page in his notebook and said, "Just this morning a plane ticket was booked from Columbus to Kalispell, Montana in Carbone's name." He lowered the notebook. "We checked, Kalispell is two hours south of Canada by car."

The frown on Shane's face grew even deeper, the fact that he now had a name and a picture to assign to whoever was assailing his team making it that much more harrowing. Again the images of Christine and his mother played through his mind, interspersed with Heath and Prescott lying in their respective beds.

"When is the ticket scheduled for?"

"First thing Sunday morning," Murphy said, a knowing look on his face.

"Closing arguments will likely be set for Monday," Shane whispered, his head turned to the side, his gaze staring off into the distance.

"Yep," Murphy agreed. "Either he figures if he hasn't scared you by then, he's not going to..."

"Or he's planning something between now and then," Shane finished, glancing back to the officers in front of him. "Why can't you guys just go after SynTronic right now?"

"On what?" Murphy asked. "You're a lawyer, you know how probable cause works. Right now we've got a couple of letters spray painted on the ground, nothing that ties them to anything."

"We believe Carbone to be our guy, but it's circumstantial at best," Ryan added. "His parole ended years ago, booking a flight out of Columbus means nothing."

"Yeah," Shane conceded, nodding. "Half the SynTronic legal department is here, they could claim he's just on hand consulting."

All three fell silent, the reality of the situation sitting heavy. There was little doubt in Shane's mind that this was the guy they were looking for, but without some way of tying him to the scenes, there was nothing they could get to stick.

Assuming they could even find him to begin with.

"We'll continue pounding the pavement on this one, but we wanted you to be aware," Ryan said. He fished a business card from his pocket and extended it to Shane, embossed with the CPD logo and a direct line to both him and Murphy scrawled across it in ink.

"If you see anything at all, give us a call," Murphy said. "Seriously, no cowboy shit. Give us a call, get somewhere safe."

Shane looked down at the card, back up to each of them. "Thanks for the heads up."

Murphy and Ryan stood before him for several long moments of silence, all three faces grim. The officers both nodded and slid past, leaving Shane standing in the corner, his stomach twisted in knots. He remained rooted in place, his mind running over everything he'd just learned.

After a moment, he forced his legs to start moving again, back to where the Bentleys and Abby stood waiting, all three watching him. Before he got there, Hanson Byers crossed his path long enough to hold up a business card between his index and middle finger, his arm bent at the elbow so the card rested below Shane's nose. He didn't say a single word, or even look at Shane as he went, just another curious member of the public there to watch the proceedings, not a journalist trying hard to uncover a story.

Shane accepted the card without acknowledgement, his momentum still carrying him forward as he looked down at it in his hands. On one side was the *Columbus Herald* logo, with Byers' personal and office contact information. On the back were four words written in blue ink.

Sherman's Bar, 7 o'clock.

CHAPTER FIFTY-ONE

There were three things that always came to mind when Shane thought of home, three things that no matter how hard Boston tried, it just couldn't replace. The first, without fail, was his mother. The sad fact was though that his mother had been gone for a long time, a shell of her former self. He missed her every day, as any son would, but even more so in moments such as these when he could use her guidance. It had been painful for him to even list her as his supervising attorney on the case, a reminder of what was and never would be, but he'd had no choice. She was still a licensed attorney in the state, and while he knew plenty of law school classmates that he could have asked to ride shotgun, he didn't feel right doing so.

What had happened to Heath and Prescott only served to confirm the decision.

The second thing he missed was Ohio Tech football. Leaves changing, crisp air pouring in after a humid summer, thousands of people filling the streets on game day, tailgates that started at sunrise and continued well after midnight, depending on the opponent. During undergrad he never missed a home game, only a small handful throughout law school. Sometimes Christine would join him, sometimes random people from class or the dorm, once in a great while he'd even go alone, it didn't matter.

The third thing he missed about being gone, the one thing he tried the hardest to replace in Boston, but just never could, was the Shermanator.

Tucked away on a side street three blocks from campus, Sherman's was a local legend that had become a national phenomenon. The place had started two decades before when brothers from Tennessee hung up their cleats for the last time with OTU, but decided they loved Columbus so much they weren't going to leave. Instead, they called in some favors and scraped together enough money to open a corner pub, serving beer on tap and burgers off the grill, nothing more.

Over time, the bar and its menu expanded, becoming a hidden gem that people spoke about in hushed whispers. The transformation began with the expansion of the bar, offering over one hundred different ales on tap. It took on a life of its own though when the oldest brother handed over kitchen duties to an up-and-coming chef and a new menu was born.

People began flocking in from miles around for the burgers, ranging from the mushroom Swiss to the foie gras burger served between two doughnuts, drawing the attention of national audiences on the Food Network and Travel Channel. The single item that drew in the most though, that stood out above the others, was the Shermanator.

Stacked high, the burger entailed two twelve-ounce hand formed patties, bacon, sautéed mushrooms and onions, ham, a fried egg, hot peppers, cheddar, provolone, and American cheeses. It was a heart attack on a bun, a monolith to all that people loved and hated about America.

Shane made it a point to eat at least one a week for seven years.

The moment Byers handed him the card, the first thing that entered Shane's mind, ahead of what Byers could be wanting or what he was about to say to Abby and the Bentleys, was the Shermanator. For two solid hours it jockeyed for the prime position in his head, popping up as Shane tried to prepare his cross-examination questions for Kenny Walker the following morning, a fact that made him both hungry and ashamed.

At a quarter to seven, Shane left the library and went to Sherman's, arriving a few minutes early to find Byers already sitting at the bar, a half-drunk beer in front of him, watching a Celtics game on television. The smell of charred meat and fried food hung heavy in the air, bringing with it a swirl of memories.

The walls were covered in OTU memorabilia, covering the expanse from autographed football jerseys to discarded pom-poms. Almost every other square inch of the place was decorated in either faded Polaroid's or graffiti, added by patrons with whatever writing implement they had available.

Shane nodded to the hostess as he walked in, he the only one in the place wearing a tie, and took a seat next to Byers at the bar. Byers was leaning forward with his elbows resting on the polished wood, his beer halfway to his mouth. He lowered his glass a few inches away from his face and glanced over at Shane, nodding once.

"Thank you for meeting me."

Shane nodded in response, motioning for the bartender, a young girl in her mid-twenties with hair pulled back into a ponytail. She walked over with an expectant look on her face, sliding her gaze the length of Shane before offering a smile. "What can I get for you?"

"I'll have whatever he's having," Shane said, motioning to Byers, "and a Shermanator."

The girl gave a look of approval, nodded, and moved away as Shane settled in, leaning forward to match Byers's pose. "So what's this all about?"

Byers paused a moment before lowering his beer, looking at Shane through the glass behind the bar. "Maybe nothing, I don't know. Just doing a little fishing here."

Shane paused a moment, regarding Byers reflection, before shifting his attention up to the game where the Celtics were leading the Heat late in the third. In the background he could hear the bartender shouting out his order, the sound of beef sizzling on a grill. "Why me?"

"You've been pretty fair with me so far," Byers said. "I know working the federal court beat isn't the most glamorous thing on the planet, most attorneys treat us like scum. You're pretty tight lipped, which I can respect, but you seem like a decent guy."

"Still doesn't answer why me," Shane said, nodding at the bartender as she sat the beer in front of him and retreated. He picked up the glass and took down a heavy pull, a summer ale with a hint of orange.

"Because I'm sick of working the court beat, and I think there's a story to what's going on with your team."

Shane's hand stopped mid-drink, lowering itself to the bar as he swallowed the half sip in his mouth, tasting nothing. He put the beer back down on an old Jose Cuervo cardboard coaster and stared at Byers in the mirror, the older man doing the same.

"What do you know about that?"

"I know Heath Wilson's truck blew up earlier this week and almost killed him and I know a few days later Alfred Prescott, by all accounts one of the nicest men that ever lived, was found in his driveway, his leg shattered. I also know that in both instances, some sort of message was spray painted on the ground, but CPD covered it before anybody outside the force could see it."

Shane's face betrayed nothing, the lawyer in him pointing out every warning sign that this situation presented, telling him to proceed with caution. "That's still not a whole lot."

"I also know that both Wilson and Prescott were working with you when this case started, and now they're both lying in hospital beds."

"Hmm," Shane said, forcing himself to take another drink of his beer, to look up and check the score of the game. "And what is it you're looking for from me?"

"Something, anything, that can help me here. This could be the story that gets me on the front page, away from staking out the courthouse every damn day."

Several moments passed as Shane mulled the statement before shifting his shoulders towards Byers, leaning in and dropping his voice low. "You realize that I'm in the middle of trial right now, and anything you print could get the entire thing thrown out, right?"

Byers kept his shoulders facing forward, leaning to the side, dropping his head and voice to match Shane's. "So there *is* something going on."

"Of course there's something going on," Shane snapped. "You just laid it out yourself, doesn't take a rocket scientist to connect the dots."

A small grunt slid out of Byers in response, nodding his head. "If it helps, I won't print a word until after closing on Monday."

Shane pushed a long exhale out through his nose, turning back to face front. He wasn't just trying to scare Byers with what he said, there was a strong chance, even likelihood, that an article could get the case thrown out, or at least give Reed grounds for an appeal.

At the same time, his opponents had already proven themselves to be well south of ethical.

"How about we meet back here Monday night?" Shane said, looking at Byers through the glass. "I'll tell you everything I know then."

"Monday night means nothing goes to print until Tuesday morning," Byers countered.

"That a problem?" Shane asked. "Is somebody else looking into this?"

"Not that I'm aware of, doesn't mean it's not happening though."

On the screen above, the Celtics hit a three pointer, putting them up seven going into the fourth quarter. Shane watched the shot fall and took another drink from his beer, fighting to keep his demeanor even.

"Like I said, as much as I want these bastards to go down, I can't risk spilling my guts right now. It could kill my case and Tyler Bentley's future."

Byers nodded, his gaze drifting up to the screen as well. "So it is SynTronic."

The words were not a question, a deduction from Shane's prior statement. Shane's eyes narrowed a bit as he watched the screen, his mind spinning, trying to piece together how to use this situation to his advantage.

"I tell you what, how about I give you a piece now, something I myself just found out about, and let you spend the weekend digging. That should give you enough of a jump that once we're done on Monday, I'll be able to fill you in pretty quick. You can break it that night."

Byers remained motionless for several long moments before his head started to move up and down, a barely perceptible movement. "I can do that. You give me something now, you have my word I'll stay mum until Monday."

Without looking over at him, Shane pulled Byers own card out of his shirt pocket and reached across the bar for a pencil. He pulled it up and scrawled two words across the bottom, right beneath Byers's instructions on where to meet.

Ute Carbone.

Shane put the pencil back with his right hand and extended the card to Byers with his left, the logo for the *Columbus Herald* on top.

Byers accepted the card and flipped it over, turning it long ways to read what Shane wrote. He made a face as he stared at the words. "What the heck is a..."

A quick hand shot to his arm, resting across his wrist, warning him to stop. "Not out loud," Shane whispered, "and it's not a what, it's a who."

Slow dawning crossed over Byers face, his head rocking back in a nod. "That's who's been..."

"That's what CPD is checking into, but he looks like the prime candidate at this point."

Byers tapped the card against the palm of his hand and nodded his thanks to Shane. He downed the last inch of his beer and placed it back onto its coaster, rising from his chair. "Forgive me for my abrupt exit, but I have some research to get to."

Down the bar, the bartender appeared carrying Shane's Shermanator, tendrils of steam rising up from it. His gaze caught the sandwich right as it exited the kitchen, coming for him like something straight out of a dream he'd had many times over the previous twelve months.

"Not a problem."

Byers glanced over at the sandwich coming towards them and coughed out a laugh. He waited for the bartender to slide it over in front of Shane and raised a hand to her.

"Greta, put that and anything else he has on my tab, please."

Shane nodded his thanks to both of them as Byers departed. He pulled the burger over in front of him, for the first time in weeks letting his face relay to the world just how excited he was.

CHAPTER FIFTY-TWO

For parents trying to teach their children about right and wrong, the golden rule was always to treat others as they would like to be treated. For businessmen looking to amass an empire, the golden rule was he who has the gold makes the rules.

For lawyers cross-examining a witness, the golden rule was never *ever* ask a question you don't already know the answer to.

Despite that simple maxim that he'd heard in law school a dozen times and from his mother a hundred more, the thought kept creeping into the back of Shane's mind. A single idea that, if it failed, would be a blow for sure, though not fatal. If it worked, the case was all but over. His every experience, every bit of training told him not to go for it, to go through his paces, ask the basic litany of questions he'd already planned on, but that little something in the back of his mind wouldn't let it go.

On the stand sat Kenny Walker, a former basketball player that Shane had never heard of, despite numerous efforts to try and research him. The story he offered under direct examination was that his entire career had lasted about an hour in the NBA before injuries derailed him, but even at that information should have been available online about his college career, or even his high school recruiting numbers.

The dates he gave would have put him as coming out of high school in the early nineties, though based on his shaved head and smooth skin, Shane had no idea of gauging whether or not that was true.

"Mr. Walker," Shane said, walking into the middle of the court room in his gray suit, light blue shirt, and matching striped tie of the same two colors. "I would like to concentrate on the presentation you made to Tyler Bentley back in January."

Kenny bowed the top of his head a bit, the light reflecting from his shiny scalp. "I wouldn't call it a presentation, more like a friend asking me to stop by and talk to someone."

"Yes," Shane said, coming to a stop with one hand in his pocket, the other poised in front of him, "let's start there. You say you met Mr. Sarconi at a conference in Columbus about a year before, correct?"

"That's right."

"This was a conference for?" Shane asked, motioning with his free hand.

"It was a medical device conference," Kenny replied. "As I told Tyler, at that point I'd had ten different operations on my knee, none of which worked. I was in my thirties and already walking with a cane, I was desperate for any kind of help."

Shane seized on the word, forcing himself not to smile. "So desperation brought you and Mr. Sarconi together?"

A bright smile expanded across Kenny's face, his head swiveling towards the jury. "Now, I didn't say that, I said desperation took me to the conference. Pure dumb luck is what brought Mr. Sarconi and I together."

Shane glanced over at the jury, watching for their reaction. As expected, a few offered half smiles back, a couple more nodded.

"Pure dumb luck? You were willing to try anything to get back on your feet, Mr. Sarconi had a new product he was looking to begin testing. That right?"

"Yes," Kenny said, nodding.

Shane fell silent a moment and walked a few paces, his mind racing, registering that something was off-kilter. There was nothing wrong with what Kenny was saying, the answers were what he was expecting, the problem was in the way they were being delivered. The smooth responses, the clear diction, the animated interplay with the jury.

None of those things were a condemnation on Kenny. Shane had never met the man, knew nothing of his personality. All of them though flew in the face of what he knew from a lifetime of seeing witnesses on the stand. They almost always resembled Tyler and Margie, nervous balls of nerves, raw, exposed for all to see. Or they were like Pinkering and Sarconi, uncomfortable, surly, counting seconds for it to end.

Never were they like Kenny, a material witness that seemed to be enjoying his time on the stand, almost as if he was *acting*.

The word settled into Shane's mind, bringing along with it the golden rule of cross examination. He knew deep down, in his core, that there was no way he should ask the question that was almost daring itself to be heard. At the same time, as he watched Kenny again smile for the jury, there was no way he could ignore it.

"Five months after meeting Mr. Sarconi, seven months prior to meeting Tyler, you got the *KnightRunner* implant, is that correct?"

"Yes," Kenny said, "almost a year ago to this day."

Shane bit his lip to keep from smiling. The additional information that came with memorizing a script, no need for a pause to check his memory. It was now so obvious, he couldn't believe he hadn't seen it at first.

"And that would be the...eleventh surgery on your knee, correct, Mr. Walker?"

"Yes, eleven in total."

"Mhmm," Shane said, raising his off hand to his lips, appearing to be deep in thought. "And which knee would that be?"

"My right one," Kenny said without a moment's pause, another polite smile on his face.

Shane turned his back to the jury and continued to pace, his fist held to his lips, deep in contemplation. He looked up at Tyler sitting at the table, the same post he'd been at for two weeks, as intent as a sentry on guard duty. Behind him were Abby and Margie, both still hanging in for every last word of the trial, their gazes fixed on him.

The courtroom beyond them seemed dull and quiet, a malaise two weeks in the making, the coming down off one emotional high after another. Again Shane bit his lip to keep from smiling, knowing he was about to throw the entire place into pandemonium again.

The last place he looked was behind the opposing counsel's table, to Sarconi sitting on the front row, sunken and sullen. Shane fixed his gaze on him, his eyes shining with defiance.

Golden rule be damned, he was going for it.

"I wonder then Mr. Walker, if you wouldn't mind showing us?"

A murmur passed through the room as Sarconi's jaw dropped open, a film of sweat covering his mortified features. Shane smirked at him and turned around to see a similar expression on Walker's face, the cocksure smile of just a moment before long gone. His jaw worked itself up and down a time or two, his face panic-stricken.

"I'm sorry?"

"Mr. Walker," Shane said, "it bears to reason that if you have had eleven knee operations, the evidence of them should be pretty evident."

"Objection, Your Honor!" Reed announced, shooting upright out of his chair, his face growing a shade of crimson to match his tie. "This is absurd, this man isn't on trial. The question is out of line and prejudicial."

"Your Honor," Shane fired back without waiting for Lynch's acknowledgment, "the defendant held out this man as a past recipient of the *KnightRunner* to my client and his family. I don't think asking to see the scar from that operation qualifies as prejudicial."

A palpable buzz seemed to fill the airspace of the courtroom, replacing what was just moments before complete disinterest. Every person in the room, Shane included, seemed to inch their way closer to the bench, waiting for the judge's determination.

The anticipation was not lost on Judge Lynch, who sat on his perch, chewing his mustache, looking back and forth between Shane and Reed. "Overruled," he breathed out, turning his attention to the witness stand. "Mr. Walker, please do as the counselor asked."

Any trace of the confident witness was now gone from Kenny, his face masked with fear. He looked at the defense table long and hard for several moments before propping his leg up on the edge of the witness stand and pulling back the leg of his tan slacks, his hands trembling as they went. He kept his head turned to the side as he did so, his eyes pressed closed, a deep set frown on his features.

There was an audible gasp as the crowd moved forward, trying to catch a glimpse of what Kenny's body language was already telling them. Shane stayed where he was for a moment, praying that what he suspected was right, that he hadn't just violated the golden rule and dealt a terrible blow to his own case. He inched his way forward and looked at Kenny's knee, his breath catching in his chest at what he saw.

"Let the record reflect," Judge Lynch said, peering down from the bench at Kenny's knee, looking over the rim of his glasses, "that there isn't a mark of any kind on this man's knee."

Shane stood right where he was, hands thrust down into his pockets, as voices broke out behind him, every person in the courtroom sounding their surprise. On the bench, Lynch pounded his gavel demanding order. On the stand, Kenny pulled his pant leg down and returned his foot to the ground.

Shane stood rooted, his face impassive, making a point not to look at his team for fear that they might draw the triumph he was feeling out for the world to see. Instead, he just stood there, waiting almost two full minutes as the judge regained control of the courtroom, silence falling back into place.

Once it did, Shane looked at the jury, his face serene. "The *Knight-Runner* was a product of such poor design, so ill-conceived, that the only person they could get to vouch for it has never had a knee operation in his life. Wow.

"No further questions, Your Honor."

CHAPTER FIFTY-THREE

The mini-bar was littered with bottles, some smashed, leaving shards of glass everywhere, others toppled on their side, all of them empty. If anybody counted they would notice almost two dozen in total, featuring every major label from Grey Goose to Jack Daniels, an equal opportunity display of gluttony that would have made an eighties hair band proud.

There was a call to the front desk for a fresh infusion of spirits, but until they got there the three people in the room were on their own, left to nurse what they had left in their glasses, awaiting reinforcements like an army pinned down by enemy fire.

The only sound in the room was the background soundtrack of The Best of Billie Holiday, the volume turned low, just enough to be present without being overwhelming. Ramirez hummed along to "Good Morning Heartache," a rather fitting tune for the situation they were now in. He had dressed down for the evening, in sweatpants and a long sleeved t-shirt, his bulk spread sideways across the wingtip chair.

Opposite him was Reed, his eyes closed and his head reclined back, his legs extended in front of him, crossed at the ankles. He had removed his jacket and tie, but otherwise was still dressed from court, the drink moving every so often from the arm of his chair to his mouth the only sign of life.

The third point in the triangle was Lauren, barefoot, in jeans and a sweater, her eyes glassy as she stared at the floor between them, a half-empty scotch in her hand.

"What did Laszlo say when you said you wanted to talk about a settlement?" Lauren asked, her gaze still fixed on the floor, her voice empty, but not slurred.

A heavy snort pushed Reed's head up a half-inch off the seatback. "More or less the same as what he told me the other day. To stick it up my ass."

Ramirez shook his head in his seat, the bottom of his glass raised to his temple, his opposite thumb and forefinger pinching the bridge of his nose. "Can't say that I blame him. I'd do the same if I'd had the day he did."

Nobody said anything for several moments, the unspoken consensus being that Ramirez was right. Not only had Laszlo gotten their material witness to reveal he'd never had even a single knee operation, he then skewered their subject matter expert, getting him to admit on the stand that he didn't consider anything played in the Midwest to be considered real football.

Not only had their client been revealed to be lying to a patient, but any hope they had of mitigating damages was long gone as well.

"We can't let this be our last case," Ramirez said. "A mess so one-sided we were beat before we even started. Throw in all this other unforeseen stuff, talk about a no-win scenario."

The statement sat on the air for a moment, Lauren looking over at Ramirez before shifting her attention to Reed, looking for any kind of response. There was no visible reaction from him as he sat, his ankles crossed, his eyes closed.

"You'd think," he said after a long pause, not bothering to open his eyes, "that at some point in the last month, in the last six months, that

that son of a bitch would have thought to mention he brought in an actor."

"Yeah, no shit," Ramirez agreed. "Did he really think the guy was smooth enough to fool everybody and get away with it? To pull off having had eleven knee surgeries with an easy smile and a few winks to the jury?"

Reed shook his head across the seat, emitting a sigh that made no attempt to hide his disgust. "We should have just let Carbone kill him."

Ramirez and Lauren both winced at the mention of Carbone, turning their attention to face Reed.

"Where is that guy now?" Ramirez asked, his face cringing a bit, almost as if fearing what the response might be.

"Awaiting our call," Reed replied.

"What are we going to tell him?" Lauren asked, a hint of caution in her voice.

At that, Reed opened his eyes and sat up in his chair, placing his hands on either arm and raising himself to an upright position. He blinked several times to clear the fog from his vision and ran a hand over his face.

"The only thing we can."

Using his right hand, Reed reached down to the floor and retrieved his cell-phone, thumbing it on and scrolling through his call log. After a moment he pressed send, turning the volume to speakerphone and holding it out in front of him, a despondent look on his face.

Ramirez cast a quick glance over to Lauren and shifted his bulk to face forward in the chair, his feet hitting the floor. He leaned forward to match Reed's pose, the underside of his stomach spilling out from beneath his t-shirt, a sick look on his face.

Across from him, Lauren seemed to shrink away from the scene, her natural reaction to anything involving Carbone.

The phone rang twice, the shrill sound of it covering up Billie singing "No Regrets" in the background. It was snapped up mid-ring, no response coming back for several long moments.

"What do you want?" Carbone asked, his voice thick, his breath heavy in the mouthpiece.

"Laszlo," Reed said. There was no other word, no further explanation. One word and he hung up the phone, not waiting for Carbone to do the same thing to him.

Lauren's eyes grew to the size of saucers as she stared at Reed while Ramirez's narrowed until they were nothing more than slits. Reed looked at both of them in turn before shaking his head and dropping it towards the floor, running a hand back through his hair.

"I know, I'm not happy about it either, but we're in too deep now, and that's the only way this thing ends the way we want it to."

"Is *that* the way we want it to?" Ramirez asked, leaning forward, disbelief on his face.

"No," Reed agreed, shaking his head, "but the word has been passed down from on high. If we couldn't get him to agree to our settlement, we were to set that pit bull loose. I hope you realize, both of you, that these weren't my decisions to make."

Ramirez nodded, saying nothing. Opposite him, Lauren's mouth dropped open, the drink shaking in her hand.

"What's that supposed to mean?" she asked.

"It means they know where we live and where our families live," Reed said, his face ashen, his voice gravel. "If they have no qualms sending that maniacal prick after Laszlo and his team, you think for a second they'd hesitate to come after one of us?"

Tears formed at the underside of Lauren's eyes, collecting at the bottom, threatening to spill down her cheeks at any moment.

"So that's what this has been about all this time?"

"It damn sure wasn't our idea," Reed said, raising his eyebrows in resignation. Across from him Ramirez shook his head, his own eyes growing misty.

"And just like that, we tossed Laszlo and those poor people to the wolves? Let him do as he pleases with them?"

"Better them than my daughters," Ramirez said. "Or Connor's wife."

"Or your brother in Baltimore," Reed added, staring over at her. "Trust me my dear, they know everything, about all of us."

Lauren raised a hand to her mouth, the tears now cutting twin tracks down her cheeks. She dropped her drink to the floor and pushed herself back away from them, the legs of her chair sliding over the short loop carpet.

"How...how long has this been going on?"

"On and off for several years now," Reed said. "But most of the time, almost all of the time, it isn't necessary. One of those situations where we know he's around, but have no idea what he's doing."

"Which is all the better," Ramirez said, looking over at Lauren.

"This time though," Reed said, spreading his hands wide before dropping them with a smack against his legs. "This time, the climb was just too steep. There was nothing we could do, which I suspect they've known all along."

Silence fell among them as Lauren stared at the floor, tears spilling down her face, her features twisted into an angry mask. "So that's it then? He'll take care of Laszlo, we'll all go home and pretend this never happened, SynTronic gets to keep doing business as usual?"

Ramirez gave a doleful look to Reed, who shook his head.

"Not quite this time," Reed whispered. "This time I've taken a couple of precautions, left a few breadcrumbs around that should be sufficient to get him thrown back in jail for a very long time."

Ramirez and Lauren's mouths both dropped open, glancing between each other before looking at Reed.

"Will it be enough to save Laszlo?" Lauren asked. "To make sure nobody else gets hurt by that monster?"

"No," Reed said. "As you just heard from the call, Mr. Laszlo's time is up. On the flip side though, it will be his demise that rids us of Carbone."

Reed shifted his attention to Ramirez, his face morose. "But to answer your question Willie, while this shouldn't be the last case we ever work, there's no way we can ever set foot back inside a courtroom or collect a paycheck from SynTronic again. Not after what we've done."

Ramirez and Lauren both regarded Reed for a long moment, saying nothing. Before either one could offer a response, a sharp knock sounded at the door.

Room service, back to restock the bar.

CHAPTER FIFTY-FOUR

Shane glanced up at the clock on the wall behind the librarian's desk, the hands on it making a perfect ninety degree angle across its face. He leaned back in his chair and tossed his pencil down on the desk, running his fingers back through his hair.

"It's nine o'clock on a Saturday..." he said aloud, a bit of melody in his voice.

Across from him Abby looked up and smiled, her own visage appearing just as exhausted as he felt. She leaned back in her chair and jammed a pen behind her ear. "The regular crowd shuffles in..."

An instant smile came to Shane's face, followed by a look of approval as he bobbed his head up and down.

"Very impressive, nailing Billy Joel after only a single line."

"You know that song, considered his signature hit by most, never got higher than twenty-five on the charts?" Abby said, the comment evoking a bulged-eye look of surprise from Shane. She offered a shy smile and said, "My dad was a huge fan. I must have heard it a thousand times growing up."

A smile fell across Shane's face, looking up at the darkened ceiling.

"My mom liked Otis Redding, on vinyl. '"These Arms of Mine" and a glass of wine' she used to say."

Abby smiled for a moment. "Can I ask you something?"

The question pulled Shane from his memory, his head turning to look at her. "Shoot."

"I've went back and read her case, but there wasn't a lot to it."

"No, there wouldn't be," Shane said, any trace of a smile fading from his face. "The lawyer that handled it was scared to death to go up against SynTronic, so he jumped at the first settlement offer they made. Ended up taking pennies on the dollar for what it was worth."

"Oh," Abby said, her gaze drifting down to the stack of papers on the table before her. "Can I ask what happened?"

A sharp knocking on the front door to the library rang out, the sound causing both of them to turn towards it with a start. For a moment Shane's heart leapt up into his throat, pounding hard, but faded just as fast, reason pushing its way in. There was no way Carbone would track them to the library, even less chance he would stop to knock.

"Hold that thought," Shane said, rising from the table and extending a finger towards Abby. His sneakers padded across the floor as he went to the front door, checking to peer through the vertical glass windows on either side to see who it was. The hours were posted right beneath them, not another soul using the library the entire afternoon or evening.

A small wave of apprehension surged through him as he stopped and peered through, soon replaced with relief as he pushed the door open, a familiar face passing through.

"Evening, Stranger," Christine said, a brown paper sack in one hand, her purse in the other. She was dressed in heels and jeans, meaning she could either be on her way in or out for the evening.

Shane had long since quit trying to tell the difference.

"Why, hello there," Shane said, holding the door open until she was through before pulling it closed in her wake. "To what do I owe the pleasure of a visit this fine evening?"

Christine ignored the question, walking right on through towards the table in the back, spying Abby seated behind a stack of papers. "This guy has you working in here, in the dark, on a Saturday night? That's just not right."

"It hasn't been so bad," Abby said, offering a shrug and a half smile. "Sure beats sitting at the hospital. Besides, Shane was just serenading me with some Billy Joel."

"Oh, I am so sorry," Christine said, setting her paper bag down on the table and pulling out a chair on the corner. "I've heard this guy sing before, it sounds like a wounded duck."

Abby laughed out loud as Shane raised his hands by his side, ready to defend himself. Before a word could pass his lips, the front window of the library door exploded behind them, a menagerie of sound and glass shards that sprayed into the room. Smiles faded from all three faces, each of them spinning to stare at the door, fear and dread welling within them.

For several moments everything seemed to stand still until an arm dressed in black leather snaked its way through the busted window and reached down, pushing the release on the door.

Shane stood rooted in place as the door swung back and a roughneck man with short hair and a beard stepped through. He stood with his hands open by his sides, clenching every few seconds, a deviant smile on his face. The feeling of dread grew in Shane as he stared at the man, knowing in an instant that it was Ute Carbone.

Carbone paused, silhouetted against the door for several moments, before beginning to walk towards them, his entire body moving with a stalking gait. It wasn't until he was several steps into the room that Shane snapped himself into action, retreating to the table.

"Get behind the table, now!" Shane said to Christine, waiting a beat as she ran behind it and settled herself in tight against Abby. Gripping the edge of it with both hands, Shane flipped it up on edge, the broad top serving to block them from view.

"That's not going to help them one bit," Carbone glowered as he continued moving forward, malice in his voice.

Shane spun his gaze around for any sign of a weapon, his eyes instead spotting his bag on the ground beside his chair. In one step he snatched it up and dumped it over the table, right into Christine's lap. "There's a business card in my wallet for Officer Ryan. Get on the phone and get him here now!"

"He's not going to help you either," Carbone said, covering the last few feet between them with remarkable speed and grabbing Shane by the collar, jerking him backwards into the center of the library.

The motion threw Shane off balance, his arms and legs flailing as he tried to stay upright. His body careened several steps until slamming into the side of another table, a sharp pain rising in his hip.

It was nothing compared to the explosion of agony that erupted as a fist slammed into his kidney.

The shot caught him just beneath the rib cage, lifting his feet from the ground, pitching his body forward onto the table. The synapses in his brain told him to move, to push himself forward and out of harm's reach, but his body was unable to respond. Every muscle fiber in his core tightened up, seizing around his injured organ, pain coursing through him in waves.

"What...what the hell do you want?" Shane gasped, sliding his body forward along the table until he reached the end of it, depositing himself into a heap on the ground. In the background he could just make out Christine's voice screaming into the telephone as she called for help.

"I want you to go away," Carbone hissed, shoving chairs aside as he came around towards Shane, "but since you don't seem to be getting the message..."

The sharp point of a boot connected with Shane's ribs, again lifting his body off the ground. Every bit of air was forced from his lungs as he landed on his side, wheezing for precious oxygen.

"I will say I'm a little disappointed though," Carbone said, circling Shane, lining him up for another kick. "After seeing so much fight in the courtroom, I expected more out of you in a tussle."

Bit by bit Shane forced air back into his body, the bright lights before his eyes receding. He rolled over onto his knees and began to crawl forward, pushing his way towards the door, out into the hall, away from the ladies. Ahead of him a steel trash can was tucked against the base of a pillar, shrouded in shadow, out of sight from his attacker.

"Don't know where you think you're going," Carbone taunted, still circling behind Shane. "Nothing over there that can help you."

Shane kept his head lowered towards the ground, inching his way towards the can, keeping his body between it and Carbone. He forced his mind not to focus on the pain, instead honing in on the sound of Carbone's footsteps, of his heavy breathing.

Raising himself up onto his feet, Shane staggered forward a step, bracing himself against the pillar while listening to Carbone close in behind him.

"Now that's a little more like it," his opponent hissed, his voice strained as he bore down. In one quick movement Shane snatched the trash can up and swung it around, Carbone's fist connecting with it just inches away from Shane's nose. The contact rang out with a resounding clang, spilling through the closed space of the library.

The momentum of the shot tore the trash can out of Shane's hand, the polished steel hurtling end over end into the darkness. It also drew a guttural grunt from Carbone, clenching his fist and drawing it into his stomach. He bent at the waist for just a moment, folded over the hand, before rising tall, a new look of determination on his face.

"That's going to cost you," he muttered, making a direct line for Shane.

In three quick steps Shane retreated behind the pillar, using it to put space between them. He held it out at arm's length, peering out from either side.

Carbone humored him for just a moment or two, leaning one way and then the other before circling hard to the right, Shane staying just beyond his reach. Instead of continuing to follow him, Carbone abandoned the chase, making a quick movement for the overturned table in the corner.

Abby let out a high pitched squeal that reverberated from the walls as Carbone strode for them, a vindictive look in his eye. It took Shane a full moment to realize what has happening before circling around the pillar, charging hard for the back of Carbone, forgetting the pain in his body or the severe disadvantage he was under. He lowered his shoulder and ran hard for the outline of the man's black jacket, slamming his shoulder into him, tossing them both forward.

They rolled onto the floor in a tangle of bodies, knees and elbows flying between them, each fighting for the upper hand. Shane's knee connected with the soft tissue of Carbone's groin, a burst of air pushing forth, releasing foul breath between them. Carbone's elbow cracked against Shane's temple, an array of stars dancing before his eyes, a warm trickle of blood running down his face.

For a moment time stood still as the blow passed through Shane, his body falling slack, helpless against the floor. That was all it took for Carbone to seize his opportunity, rising and raising a fist to his ear, preparing to deliver the knockout blow to Shane.

Shane braced for it, but the sound of a dull thud rang out above him instead, followed by the smell of beer, the feeling of cold liquid dripping down on him.

"You little *bitch*," Carbone seethed, the unmistakable sound of flesh hitting flesh, followed by the pained cry of Christine. With a shake of his head, Shane pushed the cobwebs aside and rose to a crouch, firing a palm strike into the inside of Carbone's knee. The blow forced the joint out, locking his leg in place as Shane drew back, balling his fist and driving it into Carbone's groin.

A horrific moan slid from the man as he braced himself against the table, one hand on it for support, the other hand on his genitals. He stared in pure hatred at Shane for several moments before sliding his hand into the seat of jeans, emerging with a switchblade. He triggered the blade release and wagged it in front of Shane, the polished steel flashing beneath the overhead lights.

Rational thought fled from Shane's body as he took two steps back, his entire being focused on the blade in front of him. He watched as

Carbone slashed it from side to side in long swipes, each one coming a little closer to Shane's chest.

"Drop it! Now!" a voice barked from the entrance to the library, the front doors bursting open, Murphy and Ryan spilling inside. Both were dressed in civilian clothes with guns poised in front of them.

The warning didn't even register with Carbone as he stalked forward at Shane, brandishing the knife, coming ever closer to his abdomen, his chest, with the blade.

"Right now, I'm warning you!" Murphy barked, but Carbone ignored him, drawing the blade back for one more mighty swipe, moving his body to within striking distance of Shane.

His arm started its arc back towards Shane when the first shot rang out, jerking Carbone's upper body to the side, a spray of blood and tissue disappearing into the darkness. A second one followed right after, slamming into him center mass, forcing his arms to flail out on either side, the knife flying from his hands.

His entire body hung in the air, his face awash in surprise, his limbs beyond his control. He remained there, motionless, for several seconds before falling backwards, his body coming to rest flat on its back, limbs spread in four directions. Red bubbles foamed from the corners of his mouth, his eyes blinking, trying to focus. He remained that way for several moments as Shane stood rooted in place, Murphy and Ryan descending on him in measured steps, guns outstretched.

All three stood in silence as Carbone gasped his last breath, his focus on Shane, his head drifting back to the floor.

Abby and Christine rose from behind the table, Christine with a hand raised to her cheek, a red welt already covering half her face. Ryan and Murphy both snapped their attention to the girls, just as fast lowering their weapons and looking back to Shane.

"Was he alone?" Murphy asked.

Shane nodded. "As far as we know."

"Is everyone alright?"

Shane looked over at Abby and Christine, one a little banged up, both still standing. He raised one hand to his ribs, the other to his temple, and nodded.

"Yeah, we're okay."

CHAPTER FIFTY-FIVE

If you've done your job, closing argument is the easiest part of the entire trial.

The words sounded in Shane's head over and over again, starting when he gave up on sleeping sometime just after four. They stayed there as he stood under the shower head, wincing as the beads of hot water hit his temple, his ribs, his kidneys. Time after time the sentence replayed in his head, the same melodic voice his mother always saved for him, just a hint of the underlying hardened attorney she was.

The last two weeks had gone well, as well as Shane could hope for, inside the courtroom. Every moment spent outside was a complete mess, with half his team in the hospital, his best friend nursing a black eye, he himself feeling beat to hell. Within the confines of the courthouse though, things were going well. Shane had been able to coax what he wanted from his witnesses, found at least one damaging point to make on all of the defenses. Tyler and Margie had performed well in front of the jury, mixing sympathetic with determined, never once making it appear they were seeking a handout.

Most of the work was done, all that was left was for Shane to put a bow on it.

There was a subdued feeling in the courtroom as Shane arrived. Gone was the entire team he had first walked up the steps with two weeks before, Abby electing to stay with Heath, far from the possibility of any further danger. Byers was again posted up in his traditional spot, but gave Shane only a small wave and a knowing grin, their meeting already set for later in the day.

The crowd inside was much smaller than the previous weeks, many of the expectant gawkers having moved on now that there were no more witnesses to be called, no more bombshells to be dropped. By this point in the proceedings most everyone had already formed their opinion on what the outcome would be, the closing statements little more than a formality.

"Good morning," Shane said to Tyler as he walked in and set down his bag, drawing a double take from his client.

"Good Lord, what happened to you?" Tyler asked, his jaw hanging open, Margie making the same face on the front row.

Shane opened his shoulder towards the defense table, his head cocked to the side, voice loud enough to be heard. "*They* happened to me."

The extra day between the incident and arriving at court had given the defense team time to get past any initial shock. Shane watched from the corner of his eye as they busied themselves at their table, not once looking over or even acknowledging that they had heard him.

"Is everyone else alright?" Tyler asked. "Where's Abby?"

"Abby's fine," Shane said, nodding his head. "And thanks to a helping hand from CPD, their goon got far and away the worst of it."

"How much worse?"

The rear door into the court opened up and the bailiff stepped out, his uniform pressed, the top of his head polished to a mirrored shine. He waited as the jury made their way in and took their seats, all looking tired, some even annoyed. "All rise."

The sound of people raising themselves from their seats filled the air, Shane leaning over to whisper to Tyler. "Let's just say he won't be putting anybody in the hospital ever again."

Tyler's eyebrows shot up as he glanced to Shane, pointing a finger at him as if to ask if he did it. Shane shook his head in the negative and rose to full height as Judge Lynch entered, his robe appearing even larger than usual as he came into the room, swirling around his tremendous bulk. He swung himself down into his chair and went straight to the documents before him, mumbling a perfunctory, "Please be seated."

The room lowered itself back into place while the judge prepared his things, getting everything in order before raising his gaze to the counselors before him.

"Today we are here to receive the closing arguments in the case of *Bentley v. SynTronic*. The plaintiff will be given the floor first, followed by the defendant. Should the plaintiff wish to add a rebuttal closing, he may do so thereafter."

Judge Lynch shifted in his chair, aiming his gaze towards the jury, his bushy moustache bobbing up and down on his face. "Jurors, I would like to remind you that before you hear the closing argument, the burden of proof in this case lies with the plaintiff. Please keep that in mind both now as you hear his closing, and later as you deliberate.

"Mr. Laszlo, the floor is yours."

Shane nodded to the judge and stood, his attention turned down onto his notes, the words of his mother running through his head one last time. He did his best not to wince as he stood, not to show the stabbing pain that was shooting through his torso. Instead he walked out into the floor and turned to face the jury, one hand in his pocket, the other out in front of him.

"Good morning, ladies and gentlemen of the jury. I know you have all been put upon by being asked to take part in this case, and I sincerely thank you for doing so. I respect that many of you have been away from your families and jobs for quite some time, so I promise to be brief here this morning.

"As you just heard Judge Lynch state, the burden of proof in this case is on the plaintiff, and I am positive that after hearing all of the evidence over the last two weeks you would agree we have met that burden."

Shane paused for a moment, turning to walk back along the front of the jury box, his hand extended towards Tyler. "Last week you heard from the Bentleys, about how they were cajoled into a procedure they weren't certain of, how they were told by university employees that they must take part in the procedure or risk having to pay for the surgery out of pocket. You heard from the surgeon performing the surgery, about how he has performed *three hundred and forty-three* such procedures, but the only person to ever lose a limb was the one that received a *KnightRunner*.

"After that, you heard from Dr. Lomax, who described to you what the design and implementation process for a new prosthetic should entail, and you heard from Ms. Graham about the future that Tyler was robbed of as a direct result of the corners SynTronic cut."

Shane turned back, walking the length of the jury, the pain of his body fading into the background as he focused in on them one by one, making eye contact, weaving his tale.

"Taken together, those facts alone would be more than enough to mean that we have met the burden of proof. However, I think it important to look at what the defense was able, or rather not able, to muster as a response. The overseeing physician on the case more or less admitted that he signed with SynTronic through the encouragement of significant gain. The company itself confessed to rushing along the product to such a degree that the only person they could get to endorse it was a paid actor that has never had a knee operation in his life."

Shane stopped there, letting the words hang in the air, willing the jury to accept their importance. "Sometimes, being a juror in a case like this is a tough job, but I don't believe this is one of those instances. I truly feel that the evidence in this situation is so overwhelming, so damning, that there is only one way to look at it.

"Tyler Bentley was a star, bound for the fairy tale life of a professional football player. At the very least, he was a young man that was going to be blessed with a long and healthy life, replete with a lot of good stories to tell his friends. Now he is a young man, just entering his twenties, facing life minus a limb.

"Knowing Tyler, the kind of man he is and the way he was raised, I have no doubt he'll find a way to persevere and live a full and fruitful life. But he needs your help to do so."

Shane paused a moment, wondering how much more to say. There was still a well of emotions that had found their way into the pit of his stomach, reactions to everything that had happened the last few weeks, things he had kept bottled up for years. Deep within he could feel them all wanting to come out, to rise to the surface and be heard by the world, but he wrestled them down. He kept his face straight and nodded to the jury, already moving back to his seat.

"Thank you."

Halfway back to his chair Shane paused, his attention focused on the front row. At one end of it was Margie, in her traditional seat sitting and staring back at him, her fingers twisted into knots on her lap. On the other end of it sat Christine in an indigo blue sleeveless dress, her hair pulled back into a ponytail to reveal a bruise that stretched the length of her face. Shaped like the state of California, it started just past her temple and swung down in a sloping crescent, black with tendrils of purple and blue throughout.

Shane's lips parted in surprised as he stared at her, fixed in place until Judge Lynch told Reed the floor was his. With conscious effort Shane moved back to his table, nodding at Christine, a sad smile tugging at the side of his face. He had spent the night on her couch, as much to help ease his guilt as her jumpiness, but had left before she awoke. A small bruise had been present the night before, but nothing like what was on display now.

A folded piece of white paper sat on his chair as Shane approached. He slid it off with one hand and dropped down into his seat, pulling up the flap on it and reading the handwritten note once before closing it and raising his gaze to Reed.

What he saw brought a smirk to his face.

After two weeks, Reed had taken a small step in realizing where he was and what he was up against, trading in his assortment of blood red ties for one with a golden hue. His suit was downgraded to a dark charcoal, though still his posture was to stand in one place, his fingers laced in front of him.

"Ladies and gentlemen of the jury, good morning," Reed began, his voice deep, his tone somewhere between grandfatherly and condescending. "I am glad that Judge Lynch and Mr. Laszlo both spoke to you this morning about burden of proof, because that is the same topic I wanted to speak to all of you about.

"Ladies and gentlemen, I do not fault Mr. Laszlo for the way he presented that burden to you, but to say that he was entirely forthright would be misleading. The burden of proof in a civil case does lie with the plaintiff, that much is true, however that burden is not just to establish that a charge should be brought, but that the defendant's action alone were the direct cause of it."

Reed swiveled a bit at the waist, extending a hand towards Shane. "Mr. Laszlo makes a very compelling case that charges should be brought. His client, Tyler Bentley was a great athlete, a talented individual, and a very hard worker. You hate for what befell him to happen to anybody, but even more so to someone in his position, with so much to look forward to. In a span of just six short months he went from starring for his team to only having the use of one limb. This is a travesty, and someone should be held accountable.

"My client is not that someone though. It had nothing to do with the shoddy surgical work that contributed to the systemic failure of the implanted device, just like it had nothing to do with the blatant disregard for product warnings that also contributed to its demise.

"My client is just the one unfortunate enough to have the deepest pockets of those connected to this case."

Once more Reed turned towards the plaintiff's table, his face grave, almost accusatory. "There is no doubt many people responsible for what happened here, but SynTronic Corporation is not one of them. It just had the misfortune of being in the proverbial wrong place at the wrong time, of being on the receiving end of several coincidences that when taken together could be mistaken for guilt.

"I trust you will not make that mistake. Thank you."

Shane pushed an angry breath out through his nose as Reed returned to his seat, forcing himself not to flex his hands into fists and slam them against the desk in front of him. Grasping at straws, Reed had decided to go with smear tactics, to questions his ability as a lawyer and Tyler's integrity in hopes of gaining exoneration.

"Mr. Laszlo, would you care for rebuttal?" Judge Lynch asked, peering down over the rim of his spectacles. Shane met his gaze for a moment before lowering his eyes and rereading the note that had been waiting for him on his chair just a few moments before. He flipped the page open to see Christine's perfect script, the words echoing what she had said to him the very first night he returned to town.

It all has to come out, otherwise there is no closure.

Shane closed the note and turned his head, his chin just above his shoulder, Christine visible on the periphery of his vision. He nodded once and stood, straightening his tie against his stomach. "Yes, thank you, Your Honor."

Every one of the thoughts and feelings that he had tucked away for the past six weeks, for the past eight years, pushed their way to the front of his mind. If he was going to do this, was going to open the floodgates and let everything spill out, he had to do it right. It had to be orderly, it had to be comprehensive, it had to have finality to it.

"Ladies and gentlemen," Shane said, his voice low, almost inaudible in the recesses of the courtroom, "I won't continue to belabor the points of this case. We have all done that to you for two weeks now. I'm willing to bet that most of you have already made your decision at this point, and there is very little I can say right now that will shape how you feel about Tyler Bentley or his lost limb.

"What I would like to talk to you about though is something that seems to have gotten lost throughout this trial, a fact I blame myself for, and that is the character of those people involved. Now, on one side of the aisle you have the Bentley family, a mother and son from a town of three hundred and fifty people on a little windswept patch of asphalt in Wyoming.

"You have a young man whose coaches swore was always the first one to show up and the last to leave, that gave tirelessly of himself to local charities, that last Christmas delayed his trip home by a day to visit sick children in the hospital. You have his mother, who worked two jobs to provide for her family, that flew back as often as she could to see her son play, that has been here through every second of this trial, spending time and money she doesn't have to be by her son's side."

Shane paused to look at each of them, Tyler staring back, the slightest bit of a crack in his features, Margie behind him, tears spilling down her face.

"And on the other side you have SynTronic. A global corporation that makes business dealings by promising kickbacks to those that partner with them, that hires thespians to portray former patients, that keeps attorneys on staff who will stand in front of a courtroom and tell you that the reason a young man lost his leg was because he didn't read the rulebook they gave him, not because they designed a faulty product."

Shane paused and turned again, this time to face the defense table. Reed and Ramirez sat at it, neither one meeting his eye, both motionless.

"A few moments ago, Mr. Reed used the word coincidence. Good, let's talk about coincidences.

"Is it a coincidence that two weeks ago, the front row behind my counsel table featured a law professor and two young law students, all here to help me, and today none of them are here? Is it coincidence that one of them was almost killed when his three year old pickup exploded? Is it coincidence that another was savagely beaten outside his home just a few a nights later? That the third, after almost being assaulted herself, felt afraid to be present here today?"

Shane turned and stared at Christine, her dark eyes peering back into his. "Is it coincidence that the only person sitting there today is my best friend, her face mangled, her only crime being coming to visit me?

Or that I stand before you with three stitches in my forehead and two broken ribs?

"Is it a coincidence that not one of us had ever so much as been in a fight three weeks ago, but after going to trial with SynTronic, we are all the walking wounded?"

Shane paused again, allowing his voice to even out, to push back the anger that was threatening to burst through his every word. He had waited eight years to say what he was about to, there was no chance he was going to mess up the delivery, to let the gravity of their meaning be lost on anyone in the room.

"Perhaps the biggest question though, the one that Mr. Reed should be asking himself, or maybe even my client Tyler Bentley should be asking himself, is it a coincidence that I stand before you today? That six weeks ago I was quite content practicing environmental law in Boston, and now I am here, working a civil case in front of you?"

Shane turned away from the counsel table, his back to the defense. He made sure the judge was beyond his scope of vision, narrowing his entire focus to the fifteen people sitting in front of him.

"If you were to look at the original complaint I filed with this court, or the waiver I put in with the state to be allowed to practice this case, you will see that my attorney of record here in Ohio is Alixandra Laszlo. She hasn't practiced in quite some time, but her license is still active.

"You might not recognize the name because to her friends, she was always Sandy. I sometimes don't recognize the name because to me, she was always Mom."

A few eyebrows went up on the jury, a pair of women exchanged glances.

"My mother was one of the all-time great trial lawyers in this state, in this country, and that's not just the opinion of a proud son. A simple Google search will confirm this, as will any person involved in advocacy while she was active. She is the entire reason I went into law, the person whose voice gives me advice every step of the way, whose approval I try to seek each day.

"For all her many great attributes, my mother had only one flaw, one weakness, and that was chronic rhinitis, more commonly known as hay fever. For most people it would be an inconvenience, but for a trial lawyer, it was a real concern, a potential threat to her livelihood. She was always on the lookout for some remedy for it, some new product that would alleviate her of the ailment, allow her to perform her craft without worrying about sneezing in front of a jury.

"Just the same way SynTronic went after Tyler Bentley, wanting him to be the face of their new toy, rushing it out before it was ready, they came after my mother with a new antihistamine spray, told her it would cure her of rhinitis forever.

"Sadly, just like Tyler, my mother agreed. Even more sad than Tyler though, when that particular SynTronic product proved to be faulty, it wasn't a leg she lost, it was her mind. It only took a single spray for the chemical cocktail they used to pass up her nasal cavity and into her brain, frying the synapses right where they were.

"One day, she was a high powered attorney. The next, she couldn't even form a sentence or recognize who I was."

Shane's voice broke as the last words tumbled out, moisture clinging to the corners of his eyes. He raised his hand to his nose and held it there for several seconds, watching as the women before him did the same, even a couple of the men.

"I was only eighteen years old at the time, had just lost any real semblance of my mother without even the chance to say goodbye. I didn't know any better when SynTronic came around and offered a settlement. To my eternal shame, I accepted the money, using every last bit of it to put her into long-term care."

Shane paused again, sniffling, running a hand across his face. For the first time he turned his head to see Tyler and Margie both crying, to see Christine smiling at him, tears dripping from the bottom of her chin.

"So, was it a coincidence that I came back here eight years later to seize the second chance that I had been given? Not at all. I am not here for pride or for vanity, I am not here to get my name in a newspaper or to bring home some major windfall.

"I'm here to make sure that the *coincidence* that happened to my mother doesn't happen to Tyler Bentley, or anybody else, ever again."

CHAPTER FIFTY-SIX

The foot traffic at Port Columbus airport was thin, exceedingly so even, for midday on a Thursday. There were no holidays on the horizon, no long weekend travelers trying to beat the rush, no reason for most people to be anywhere near an airport.

Of course, at the moment, Shane didn't have reason to be anywhere else in particular either.

Shane sat in front of a floor-to-ceiling window at the far end of the airport, his feet propped up on a sill, mind void of a single care in the world. He sat with his arms folded across his chest, his bare calves exposed beneath cargo shorts, sandals on his feet, watching as one plane after another departed, lifting itself from the runway and rising into a pristine powder blue sky.

He had been at the airport for almost six hours now, arriving at seven that morning to drop off Tyler and Margie to fly back to Worland together, both springing for first class for the first times in their lives. Both had cried as Shane left them at the curb, Margie squeezing him tight, thanking him for everything he had done. She held the pose for almost three full minutes, long enough that Shane began to feel uncomfortable, not quite long enough to make him start squirming. When she at last pulled back, her face was bright pink and wet with tears, her mouth whispering thank you over and over again.

Shane assured her it was okay, that she was more than welcome, that they always knew where to find him if they needed anything.

Tyler was a bit more conservative, starting with a handshake before going in for the hug, squeezing Shane with the strength of a former college football player. Balanced on his new prosthetic leg, he pulled back, his eyes wet, and thanked him for all he had done.

"Really, it was my pleasure," Shane said, nodding his head in earnest. "That was as gratifying for me as it was for you, a win eight years in the making."

Tyler nodded, swallowing hard, wiping his face dry. "You'll stay in touch? Let me know when you get settled somewhere?"

"I will," Shane promised. "I'm going to be moving around a little for the next month or two, but you'll be able to reach me. Keep me posted on your rehab, how the new leg treats you."

"I'll do that," Tyler said, catching the stare of an onlooker passing by. He avoided the man's stare but noticed his OTU t-shirt, shaking his head in disgust.

"I take it you won't be coming back in the fall?" Shane asked, watching the man as he departed inside.

"No offense, but I may never be back in Ohio," Tyler said, his voice firm, not a trace of doubt within it. "I'm looking into transferring over to UW in Laramie for the fall, but it might be winter before I get there."

Shane nodded. "That's understandable. Take your time, don't in be such a rush to jump back in, you've got a little flexibility now."

The comment drew a smile from Tyler, who shook his head and hefted a duffel bag to his shoulder, again extending his hand. "We can't thank you enough, for everything."

"You're more than welcome," Shane said, taking the hand in both of his.

"If any of those travels include Yellowstone, you be sure to let me know. It's quite a place to behold."

Shane nodded, releasing Tyler's grip, his gaze far away as he thought about the offer. "I just might do that, thank you."

"Take care," Tyler said, nodding one final time and departing to join his mother.

Shane waved and climbed back into his car, driving it out to the long term lot and parking it. He took his time getting back to the terminal, stopping in Bob Evans for breakfast, waiting until the Bentleys departed before walking up to the first departure counter he came to and buying a ticket.

For the first time in years he felt as free as the planes rising into the afternoon sun, without a care in the world. He had nowhere to be, no agenda once he got there, no reason to look over his shoulder at all.

"So is this the GQ look for young, freshly minted millionaires?" a familiar voice asked, bringing a smile to Shane's face. One at a time he lowered his feet to the floor and leaned forward in his seat, turning to see Christine standing behind him, nobody else within fifty yards of them.

"Of all the gates in all the airports in all the world..." Shane said, letting his voice trail off.

"You were lucky enough for me to walk into yours," Christine said, circling around and falling into the seat beside him. Shane glanced over to her face, the bruise faded a great deal, the remaining portion of it extending only half as far as it once did, almost entirely concealed with makeup.

"At the risk of asking, I seem to remember your face being a bit more colorful just a few days ago."

"Is that a question" Christine asked, "or are we just going to both pretend that we know I might have embellished a bit for the courtroom and leave it at that?"

Without waiting for Shane to respond, she extracted a rolled up newspaper from a shoulder bag and slapped it against his chest, the paper making a loud smack of pages. "You see this?"

Shane unfurled the paper to the front page of the *Columbus*

Herald, a single headline in bold letters stretching the entire width of the page.

SynTronic set to pay much more than just $31M.

"Catchy," Shane said, his gaze wandering down to see the name Hanson Byers on the first line. He smiled, recalling the excitement of Byers during their conversation on Monday, hearing every last detail Shane had. Some he attributed as being from the counsel for the plaintiff, others were quoted from an anonymous source.

Nothing was left out.

Shane ran his gaze over the article, taking up the full top half of the page, before rolling it closed and handing it back to Christine. He reclined himself back in the chair and stretched his legs out, his heels falling into place at the base of the windows.

"Not even going to read it?" Christine asked, sliding low in her chair to assume the same position.

"No need," Shane said, shaking his head. "I gave him ninety percent of the material in the article. No reason to relive it."

Rotating her head at the neck, Christine regarded his profile for a long moment. He could feel her eyes on him, but said nothing, not even letting himself smile.

"So remind me, how much is the contingency fee on thirty-one million?" she asked, an eyebrow arched.

"Too much," Shane said without pause.

"Almost ten and a half?" she pressed, ignoring his comment.

"Again, too much," Shane said.

"Whatcha going to do with all that scratch?"

A small smile passed across Shane's face, the result of years of back-and-forth. There was no use trying to hide anything from her, in trying to steer a conversation anywhere but where she wanted it to go. He sighed, twisting his head to the side.

"The first two payments went to 3C and Columbus General, squaring all medical bills for Prescott and Heath. The next two went to him and Abby, paying them for their time, a nice bonus included for their troubles."

Christine rolled her head back to face forward, a bemused smile on her face.

"You're such a softy. You'd never survive a day in business."

"The next check went to Shady Lane, offering them a nice little incentive to take Molly off my hands."

Christine pursed her lips out, nodding in approval. "Nice move. I'm guessing that works out well for the both of you?"

"I'm not sad about it, if that's what you're asking," Shane said, his voice monotone, his eyes watching as a luxury liner's front wheels rose from the ground, dragging its back end into the sky at a thirty degree angle. He fell silent as he watched it climb, his gaze tracking it until it disappeared above the window.

"Well Mr. Big Spender, dare I ask if you spent a cent on yourself?"

"I bought a plane ticket," Shane said. He rolled his head to the side and stared over at Christine, for the first time noticing the shoulder bag on the seat beside her. He ran his eyes the length of her body, taking in the t-shirt, jeans, flip flops she was wearing.

"Speaking of which, how did you get back here? Shouldn't you be at work right now?"

A loud snort rolled from Christine, pushing so much breath out that it rocked her head back against the seat. "Weren't you the one that just a few days ago told me I needed to take a vacation?"

A smile rose to Shane's face, his eyes locked on hers. "I do seem to remember someone telling me that traveling alone is terrible."

"Sounds like a smart lady," Christine said, raising her eyebrows. "You should grab her, go get into an adventure together."

Shane rolled his head back to face forward, his gaze focusing on the next jet rolling down the runway.

"Sounds like a plan. Any idea where to?"

Christine turned and focused on the jet as well, picking up speed as it moved forward over the asphalt, its fuselage rising up into the air.

"Does it even matter?"

Turn the page for a sneak peek of one of my new standalone novels, *Just A Game*.

SNEAK PEEK
JUST A GAME

Prologue

The Dirty Half Dozen.

That's the name the Huntsville Herald bestowed upon the Senior Class of 2012. Six boys that made it through several long years of football and were ready to take their place at the head of the table. Ready to be the face of the Huntsville Hornets.

For all intents and purposes, the face of Huntsville itself.

The group started as fourteen seventh graders just six years earlier. Barely enough in numbers to field a team, more than enough in talent to challenge for the league crown each year.

The exodus started the summer before eighth grade, when the Monroe brothers moved to Michigan.

Twelve.

Two months into freshman year, Hank Rogers was in a car accident and injured his neck. He would be fine to live a full and productive life, but he would never be able to wear the blue and yellow again.

Eleven.

The next summer Jake Hill and Brent Hobarth were both told they were needed to help on the family farm. In Huntsville, such a thing was never questioned.

Nine.

After their sophomore season, Kevin Snyder was the next to go. He told everybody that while he loved football, he wanted to spend all his time concentrating on baseball.

Everybody saw right through the lie, but nobody cared enough about his absence to press it. Huntsville wasn't the kind of school where kids concentrated on a single sport. If a kid was good enough to play a sport, he played.

Truth was, Kevin was never really good enough. And he shied away from contact, a mortal sin on the football field.

Eight.

The last two casualties were the toughest to take. First was Danny Bernard, who tore his ACL at the county track meet in May. A full replacement surgery was performed, bringing with it a minimum recovery time of ten months.

Seven.

The final man to fall by the wayside was Shaun Brandt, who fervently believed his status as a football player would be enough for the school to overlook his 1.2 GPA for the final grading period of the year. He was wrong.

Six.

Six senior football players, the smallest class the school had fielded in over four decades. Since back when teams still played six- or eight-man football.

Six young men to represent the hopes and goals of Huntsville. Six individuals to serve as the personification of a town's pride.

The Dirty Half Dozen.

Chapter One

The wooden stairs sagged just slightly under the weight of Clay Hendricks's feet as he trudged up the visitor bleachers. A dull throbbing poked at the bottom of his right foot with each step and the cold night air nipped at the open cuts on his hands.

The other five seniors were already there, strewn haphazardly across the top few rows of bleachers.

"Did you kiss her once for me?" Jason Golden asked by way of introduction.

Clay snorted and said, "Sure did, Goldie. Your mom said thanks and to tell you not to be home too late tonight."

A few chuckles went up as Goldie countered, "Well if you were with my mom, guess that means little old Chelsie needs someone to keep her warm, huh?"

Clay threw a glance at Goldie and said, "Wasn't with Chelsie, smartass. Wanted to talk to Pop before he took off for the fields."

"Taking beans off?" Rich Little asked.

"Yup."

Clay reached the top row of the bleachers and sat down, propping his feet on the row in front of him and leaning back against the metal rail that encircled the structure. He pulled a bottle of Gatorade and a hot dog wrapped in foil from the front pocket of his hooded sweatshirt and set them on the seat beside him.

From the top row he could see each of the other five and slowly surveyed them.

Down two rows and off to his right was Jon Marks.

Marksy stood an inch or two over six feet tall and weighed just north of two hundred pounds. He played tight end and defensive end for the Hornets and came from a corn family on the edge of the county.

Down a few more rows and off further to the right was Matt Richmond. Matt was the newest of the group, meaning he had moved to Huntsville in the fourth grade. To say he was five and a half feet tall and weighed a hundred and a half pounds would be quite generous, though his reckless abandon and fiery will often made up for it.

In the middle of the bleachers sat Rich and Lyle Little, twins that bore an exact semblance of one another everywhere but their faces. Together the Littles made up the starting guards and defensive tackles for the Hornets, two boys that compensated for a lack of God-given ability with a willingness to put in long hours of work.

Below them and just on the other side of the aisle from Clay was Jason Golden. He and Clay had known each other since birth and had been playing together since the first grade. Jason was a running back for the Hornets, Clay the quarterback. Together they comprised the linebacking corps on defense.

Never had two people that were so different been such good friends, but somehow the two just clicked. Always had.

Clay unwrapped the hot dog beside him and took a bite, chewing slowly as his gaze panned the field in front of him from one side to the other.

The tradition had started nearly twenty years before, a gift from the school to the local farmers. Huntsville County was so flat that the lights from the stadium could be seen by every farm in the area. The only valid excuse for missing a game in Huntsville was tending to the fields, and even then, only once or twice a season. In the rare instance that such a thing happened, the town would leave the lights on after games. If the Hornets won, the lights would blaze forth all night long, burning like a beacon into the night sky.

If they lost, the lights went out one hour after the game.

The field before them was lit up brightly. A plain blue and yellow H could be seen straddling mid-field and the word Hornets was stenciled in block letters across each end zone.

The stadium was completely void of life, save the six players sprawled on the bleachers and a single maintenance man. Clay watched as he slowly worked his way up the sidelines on a riding mower, pulling behind it a flatbed cart. Every ten yards he would stop and pick up a padded sideline marker or end zone pylon and toss it on the flatbed before moving on to the next one.

"Old George better hurry," Goldie said, "he's only got twenty more minutes before it gets mighty dark in here."

CATASTROPHIC

Clay sniffed sourly and bobbed his head, crumpled the tin foil wrapper and stuffed it in the front of his sweatshirt. "How the hell did we blow that one tonight?"

Marksy looked back and raised his palms upward, shaking his head in disbelief. Richmond stared off into the distance, saying nothing.

"Ran out of gas," Lyle said. "Only thing I can figure."

Goldie snorted and said, "How? How the hell could we ever run out of gas? Murph has ran our asses off this year. I could run a marathon tomorrow and then go for a jog afterwards."

Lyle spun on the bleacher below them and raised his feet onto the plank. He draped his wrists across the top of his knees and said, "I don't mean, we literally ran out of gas. I mean, the numbers game eventually caught up with us."

Clay cracked open the Gatorade and took a long pull.

Lyle was at least partially right. Huntsville was far and away the smallest school in the Hill Valley Conference. It boasted a total population of just over five hundred students, less than half of them males.

The conference had been brought together many years before, created solely on the basis of geographic proximity. Outward growth from Dayton and Cincinnati had started to ebb into their tiny corner of Ohio and the surrounding schools were growing by leaps and bounds. These days, it wasn't uncommon to match up with an opponent that had almost a thousand students to draw from.

That was the case tonight. Culver High rolled into Huntsville with a team of seventy-four players and barely escaped with a 34-33 victory. When the two teams lined up after the game to shake hands, the forty-two Hornets were dwarfed in comparison.

"Six and three," Goldie spat out into the night air. "You believe that? Six and three."

"We kick the shit out of Sentinel next week, we finish seven and three," Rich said.

"Win the conference," Richmond added.

"Tie for the conference, you mean," Goldie said.

"Does it matter?" Richmond said. "We still go out as champions."

"'Yeah, it matters," Goldie said. "Co-champions is like kissing your sister."

"True, but your sister's hot," Richmond said.

Goldie rose to his feet and shouted, "My sister's fourteen!"

The other three started to laugh as Clay reached out a hand and motioned for Goldie to sit down.

"What do you think, superstar?" Goldie asked as he slowly lowered himself back to his seat. "Co-champions the same as champions?"

Clay finished the Gatorade, screwed the cap back on and said quietly, "I don't really care either way."

In unison, everyone slowly turned to him and Marksy said, "Why's that?"

"League champions or not, seven and three doesn't get us into the playoffs."

The words hung for a minute in the air as each person weighed the words.

"You wanted another state title or nothing, huh?" Goldie asked.

"Not necessarily," Clay responded. "I just wasn't expecting it all to be over so soon."

Marksy let out a low shrill whistle as the other boys' heads bobbed slowly up and down.

"Hadn't really thought about that," Rich admitted.

"I hadn't either, until Pop pointed it out a little bit ago," Clay said. "One last go-round. Seven days and that's it."

Darkness fell over the field as the boys sat in silence, thinking about what Clay had said.

Continue reading *Just A Game* now:
dustinstevens.com/JAGwb

ACKNOWLEDGMENTS

There are two quick points that should be made about *Catastrophic*. First, Ohio Tech is in no way a stand-in for Ohio State in this story. I wanted the story to be set in the football-crazed rust belt I grew up in to add gravitas to the tale, so I invented a college and put it in the most football crazy place I've ever known. A compliment, all things considered.

Second, I am aware that I cut a few small corners on the legal/courtroom aspects of this novel (namely the timeline). This was deliberate. For as entertaining as the legal field can be at times, it can also be a bit slow and monotonous. I just chose to cut those aspects out.

Thank you for reading,

THANK YOU

Thank you so much for taking the time to read my work. I know you have literally millions of options available when it comes to making Kindle purchases, and I truly appreciate you taking the time to select this novel. I hope you enjoyed it.

If you would be so inclined, I would greatly appreciate a review letting me know your thoughts on the work. Going against traditional writer protocol I look at all reviews, not in some form of misguided vanity but in hopes of producing a better product. I assure you I do take what is said to heart and am constantly trying to incorporate your suggestions.

In addition, as a token of my appreciation, please enjoy a free download of my novel *21 Hours*, available **HERE.**

Best,
    Dustin Stevens

WELCOME GIFT

Join my newsletter list, and receive a copy of 21 Hours—my original bestseller and still one of my personal favorites—as a welcome gift!

dustinstevens.com/free-book

BOOKSHELF

Works Written by Dustin Stevens:

Reed & Billie Novels:
The Boat Man
The Good Son
The Kid
The Partnership
Justice
The Scorekeeper
The Bear
The Driver

Hawk Tate Novels:
Cold Fire
Cover Fire
Fire and Ice
Hellfire
Home Fire
Wild Fire

Zoo Crew Novels:
The Zoo Crew
Dead Peasants
Tracer
The Glue Guy
Moonblink
The Shuffle
Smoked
(Coming 2021)

Ham Novels:
HAM
EVEN
RULES
(Coming 2021)

My Mira Saga
Spare Change
Office Visit
Fair Trade
Ships Passing
Warning Shot
Battle Cry
Steel Trap
(Coming 2021)
Iron Men
(Coming 2021)
Until Death
(Coming 2021)

Standalone Thrillers:
Four
Ohana
Liberation Day

BOOKSHELF

Twelve
21 Hours
Catastrophic
Scars and Stars
Motive
Going Viral
The Debt
One Last Day
The Subway
The Exchange
Shoot to Wound
Peeping Thoms
The Ring
Decisions

Standalone Dramas:
Just A Game
Be My Eyes
Quarterback

Children's Books w/ Maddie Stevens:
Danny the Daydreamer...Goes to the Grammy's
Danny the Daydreamer...Visits the Old West
Danny the Daydreamer...Goes to the Moon
(Coming Soon)

Works Written by T.R. Kohler:
The Hunter

ABOUT THE AUTHOR

Dustin Stevens is the author of more than 50 novels, the vast majority having become #1 Amazon bestsellers, including the Reed & Billie and Hawk Tate series. *The Boat Man*, the first release in the best-selling Reed & Billie series, was named the 2016 Indie Award winner for E-Book fiction. The freestanding work *The Debt* was named an Independent Author Network action/adventure novel of the year for 2017 and *The Exchange* was recognized for independent E-Book fiction in 2018.

He also writes thrillers and assorted other stories under the pseudonym T.R. Kohler.

A member of the Mystery Writers of America and Thriller Writers International, he resides in Honolulu, Hawaii.

Let's Keep in Touch:
Website: dustinstevens.com
Facebook: dustinstevens.com/fcbk
Twitter: dustinstevens.com/tw
Instagram: dustinstevens.com/DSinsta

Made in the USA
Coppell, TX
05 November 2021